Praise for
A Pinch of Ooh La La

"Renee Swindle writes about the complications of love with great humor, compassion, and sass. *A Pinch of Ooh La La* is pure delight!"
—Ellen Sussman, *New York Times* ...
French Lessons a...

"I dare you to read Renee Swindl... *A Pinch of Ooh La La*, without pulling o... scanning your music collection for the perfect ... companiment. Swindle hits all the right notes with t... ...que and satisfying tale of love, friendship, and family."
—Julie Kibler, bestselling author of *Calling Me Home*

"Touching and honest, with humor and romance in just the right measures. Swindle's novel confirms the healing power of family, and her writing sparkles with endearing characters. A fully satisfying read, *A Pinch of Ooh La La* left me with heaping spoonfuls of hope."
—Amy Sue Nathan, author of *The Glass Wives*

"You might think you know where *A Pinch of Ooh La La* is going when you begin reading it, but you are in for a surprising and outrageous journey. I laughed, I nodded, I shook my head and said, 'Girl. . . .' I could not put this book down, and when I finished, I felt like I was saying good-bye to now-dear friends. I'm still missing the likable lead and her colorful family. So worth a read."
—Ernessa T. Carter, author of *32 Candles* and *The Awesome Girl's Guide to Dating Extraordinary Men*

continued . . .

Praise for
Shake Down the Stars

"Yes, I know you hear it all the time, but get ready for an absorbing story told with a unique and compelling voice. *Shake Down the Stars* is a treat. Renee Swindle's writing is funny, sharp, heartbreaking, and quirky, and her non–stock characters wonderfully memorable. . . . Enjoy the ride."
—Lalita Tademy, *New York Times* bestselling author
of *Cane River* and *Red River*

"Renee Swindle's *Shake Down the Stars* is a rich, savvy exploration of the many kinds of love, loss, and dysfunction that can unearth us or save us, bedevil us or deliver us . . . as complex and hilarious as it is surprising and lovely. *Shake Down the Stars* holds a mirror up to our best and worst selves, and Swindle writes with unflagging compassion and irresistible humor."
—ZZ Packer, author of *Drinking Coffee Elsewhere*

"This novel is a true gem. Beautifully written, it's full of emotional impact that touches the heart without weighing the reader down. Themes of love, loss, and addiction will reach into the soul."
—*RT Book Reviews* (Top Pick)

"I love, love, love Renee Swindle's *Shake Down the Stars*! It's fresh and unfamiliar—which is quite the trick these days! I love the protagonist and the very unlikely yet charming love interest. The novel manages to be both light and heavy all at the same time. I cannot tell you how much I liked it. Well, I can . . . *I loved it*. Seriously. One of my favorite reads of the past couple years."
—Nichelle D. Tramble, author of *The Dying Ground* and
The Last King

"You are about to get a big treat. . . . Renee Swindle's novel *Shake Down the Stars* is funny, bitter as coffee, sweet as sugar, and as moving as an earthquake. Enjoy!"

—Farai Chideya, author of *Kiss the Sky*

"I love this story of a woman trying to pull herself together after a tragic incident. Renee Swindle is a great writer and storyteller. Her characters are smart and witty and will stay with readers long after the novel ends. I hope you love *Shake Down the Stars* as much as I do!"

—Jacqueline E. Luckett, author of *Searching for Tina Turner* and *Passing Love*

"Renee Swindle's novel *Shake Down the Stars* has lyrical, poignant prose that promises to resonate with readers. The characters are emotionally and culturally charged, and their lives remind me of my own. While reading, I was transported inside an unbelievable world of crazy, wonderful folks."

—Deborah Santana, author of *Space Between the Stars: My Journey to an Open Heart*

ALSO BY RENEE SWINDLE

Please Please Please
Shake Down the Stars

a Pinch of Ooh La La

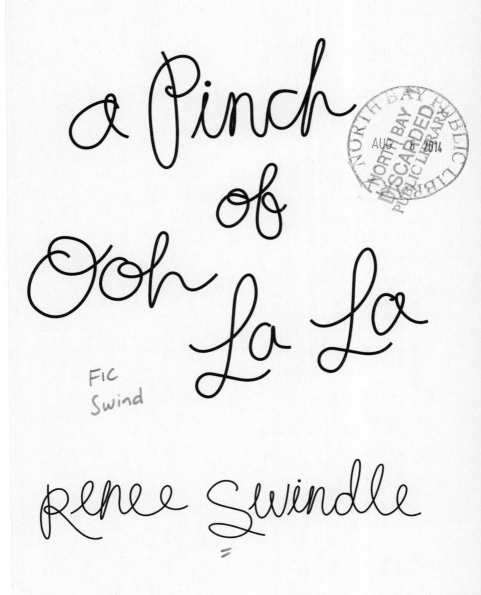

FIC
Swind

Renee Swindle

 NEW AMERICAN LIBRARY

New American Library
Published by the Penguin Group
Penguin Group (USA) LLC, 375 Hudson Street,
New York, New York 10014

USA | Canada | UK | Ireland | Australia | New Zealand | India | South Africa | China
penguin.com
A Penguin Random House Company

First published by New American Library,
a division of Penguin Group (USA) LLC

First Printing, August 2014

 REGISTERED TRADEMARK—MARCA REGISTRADA

LIBRARY OF CONGRESS CATALOGING-IN-PUBLICATION DATA:

Swindle, Renee.
    A pinch of ooh la la/Renee Swindle.
      p. cm
    ISBN 978-0-451-41665-0 (paperback)
1. Divorced women—Fiction.   2. Female friendship—Fiction.   3. Man-woman relationships—Fiction.   I. Title.
PS3569.W537P53 2014
813'.54—dc23   2014004118

Printed in the United States of America
10 9 8 7 6 5 4 3 2 1

Set in Bell MT
Designed by Spring Hoteling

For my father

Acknowledgments

I'm a lucky writer because I get to work with Ellen Edwards. I'm humbled by and grateful for her eye to detail and the magic pixie dust she tosses on my sentences. Thanks as well to everyone at New American Library, including Elizabeth Bistrow and Courtney Landi.

Hugs and smiles to my agent, BJ Robbins.

Thank you to the Finish Party—Alyss, Deborah, Farai, Jackie, Lalita, Nichelle, and ZZ.

For generous feedback on the early pages of this novel, I'd like to thank Kelly Allgaier, Kelly Damian, Toni Martin, Emily Morganti, Eric Pfeiffer, Molly Thomas, and Sean Whiteman. It has been an honor and pleasure to work with "the group" over the years. Each of you inspires me. Emily was kind enough to help me with my Web site. Thanks, Emily!

Thanks to Bryce Giddens for years of friendship and fun times. I'd also like to thank Tim, Sari, Taya, and Ziggy Henry; Donald Weise; Jerry Thompson; Melody Fuller (hugs and love, mademoiselle); Deborah Stalford; Valari Thomas; Amy Nathan; Bonnie Azab Powell; Linda Lenhoff; Ayize Jama-Everett; Tim Milot; Linda Childers; Nick Allen; Margaret Johnson-Hodge; and Chris and Claudia. For her friendship and support, a very special thanks to Liz Gonzalez.

Thanks to friends and family in Vallejo, Kentucky, and Texas. I appreciate you and love you.

Thanks to John, Alison, and everyone at Diesel Bookstore, Oakland; Kathleen Caldwell of A Great Good Place for Books; and thanks to Blanche Richardson of Marcus Books. Each of you proves that local bookstores really do support local authors and I can't thank you enough.

Mom and Pops, you make every book possible. Thank you.

a Pinch
of
Ooh La La

1

~~~

Intro

Whenever I was at my lowest about what happened between Avery and me, I'd conjure a list of other women who, like me, had been publicly humiliated by a man. My list was usually made up of a handful of women who'd married politicians—a particular breed of woman who'd inevitably stand by her man while he looked into the TV camera and apologized for lying to his constituents, and, oh, by the way, *I'm sorry, honey, for cheating on you with the hot young intern,* or the twenty-year-old house aide, the thousand-dollar call girl, or whomever. The only difference between women like this and myself is that they at least received some form of apology. Avery had disappeared on me altogether.

When it comes to love, there's nothing worse than public betrayal. I was thirty-three when my heart was drop-kicked and sent flying through the air. Months later, when one of my stepmothers suggested I *"get back out there and start dating again,"* I looked at her as if she'd asked me to pour hot oil over my body

and roll in dirt. *You want me to date? After what I've been through?*
Are you insane?

Three years later, though, and you wouldn't have known I
was that same sad sack of a woman who didn't want to do much
more than sleep on her couch. Thanks to hard work and deter-
mination, I became the living, breathing embodiment of Gloria
Gaynor's "I Will Survive." A mere three years later and I'd
opened my own bakery and bought a home. I had arrived. I was
woman—hear me roar! I needed a man like a bicycle needed a
fish! Or however that feminist saying went.

There was just one teensy-weensy problem. Years of living
alone, and as chaste as Mother Teresa, and I was beginning to
wish for—actually started to crave—the attention of those hairy,
non-emotive creatures that often left the toilet seat up. What do
you call 'em? Men. Yeah. That's it.

My heart, bruised and beat-up, began holding sit-ins with lit
candles and music playing in the background to the tune of John
Lennon's "Give Peace a Chance." *All we are saying,* my heart sang,
is give men a chance.

But a part of me was scared of men. One particular man. Not
that any of this is about him, Avery, but he turned out to be a
catalyst, if you will, the goad, the hot prod that convinced me I
needed to make changes in my life. I saw his face in the *New York
Times* and felt all my I-am-woman bravado diminish. My best
friend, Bendrix, had a point, after all. My vagina was aging and
my eggs were shriveling and I needed to move boldly from behind the wall I'd created, my comfy, safe wall of work, work,
work, and cable on Sunday night.

By now, though, I suppose I should start from the beginning.
Enough with the preamble, my stepmom Bailey would say. *If you're
gonna tell it, tell it.*

To that end, imagine the interior of a bakery with wood

floors and a menu written on a large blackboard in chalky pastels, high ceilings dotted with low-hanging silver retro lamps (which cost the owner a fortune), an exposed brick wall behind the counter, and, near the entrance, a mahogany bar where the regulars like to sit. The smell of freshly baked croissants hangs in the air, and the sound of bass, piano, and drums pipes through the stereo system.

Actually, since I'm the daughter of a jazz musician, I'd like to start things off like my dad might, right before playing a gig with my uncles: his fingers poised above the keys of his piano, and just under his breath, a quiet *A one . . . a two . . .*

2

~

Pick Yourself Up

*B*rad Mehldau's song "Intro" blared through the stereo system the morning I finally decided to make a few changes in my life. His drummer, Jorge Rossy, moved into a six-four beat that forced the trio to amp their groove. It was seven a.m. and my bakery, Scratch, was empty except for a handful of early-morning regulars. While Dad had a more soulful sound and was an honest-to-goodness jazz legend, Brad was a technical powerhouse and one of the best of his generation, and his takes on "Intro" and Nick Drake's "River Man" were just two of my favorites.

Jazz—not that *smooth* jazz Muzak crap that literally made me want to puke anytime I heard it, but rather *authentic* jazz— was almost always playing at my bakery. Some days we tossed in singers like Otis Redding or Sam Cooke, Etta James or Frank Sinatra—singers who, as Daddy would say, *saaang*, but more times than not, patrons stepped inside Scratch and heard Louis Armstrong's trumpet over the hiss of the espresso machine, or Bill Evans playing a melodic solo just when they needed to hear Evans most.

Dad taught us that we should listen to every genre of music out there and shun nothing, but I always returned to jazz. Coltrane. Bird. Billie. Ella's version of . . . *anything.* Jazz was pretty much all I listened to. Even the menu at Scratch paid homage. There was the Chet Baker cupcake, made with Madagascar vanilla; the Sarah Vaughan, a bittersweet chocolate truffle tart; and the Miles Davis, a dark chocolate cupcake with chocolate chips, topped with chocolate icing. Other items on the menu included the doughnut of the day, old-time favorites such as cobblers and sweet potato pie, and seasonal items like plum tarts and strawberry shortcake.

I hummed along to Mehldau as I helped Beth, second-in-command pastry chef, roll out the last of the sourdough loaves for the lunch crowd. Bendrix was there by then, drinking espresso at his favorite booth in the back and reading the paper on his tablet. He'd been on twenty-four-hour call at the hospital and, as was his habit, had stopped by for coffee before going home.

After making a cappuccino for myself, I took out two pains aux raisins and joined him. He continued reading while I began returning e-mail on my laptop. After a moment, I heard him mention something about the People's Republic of China and mumbled a noncommittal reply. I wasn't in the mood for world events so early in the morning but didn't want to flat-out ignore him either.

"Not China, silly," I heard him say. *"Va-gina."*

I looked up from my laptop, knowing I'd missed something. *What is going on with the Chinese and their vaginas?*

Bendrix shook his head ever so slightly and continued to peruse his tablet. "I was at the hospital and trying to remember the last time you went on a date. I went as far back as the eighteenth century."

I played along. "Ah, right, that dreaded Count Vladimir. Hated that guy."

"It's been too long, Abbey. If you don't have sex soon, that vagina of yours is going to forget what it's there for. If you don't have sex soon, that vagina of yours is going to dry up and wither away."

"Thanks for thinking of my—*vagina*," I whispered, "while you were at the hospital, supposedly saving lives."

"Call it multitasking. It's been close to three years."

"Almost four, but who's counting?" I made a show of glancing around the bakery before going back to my e-mail. "Unlike you, I'm not good at multitasking. I've been busy creating a business. Besides, my"—I whispered—"*vagina* is perfectly fine."

"Your vagina is as dry as the Sahara. Your vagina is so dry it crunches. Your vagina is so—"

"Okay, okay. I get the point. What's with you this morning? Why are we talking about my *you know what*? It's too early. Go back to your paper or whatever you're doing. I don't need sex right now, okay? I'm in my celibate phase. Besides, whatever is going on with my . . . private body parts is none of your business."

"*Private body parts?* You sound like you're five years old. It's a *vagina* and you have one for a reason."

I shushed him, thinking of my customers trying to enjoy their muffins, not that anyone was nearby. I also wouldn't dare say the word *muffin* aloud. I knew Bendrix would run with it: *You need someone enjoying your muffin. Your muffin needs attention.* And whatever else he'd say.

He swung his tablet around and I stared at a series of cupids fluttering alongside four couples who kissed and smiled. *LoveMatch.com* floated at the top of the screen in a swirly font.

I shifted my gaze from the dating site and looked at him directly. "Uh . . . you need to go home and get some sleep; you're obviously delirious."

"It's time you got out there again. Your dream of Prince

Charming walking in here and sweeping you off those clogs you're wearing isn't gonna happen."

"And neither is online dating."

"'Meet your perfect match,'" he read. "'Find love by browsing our top singles, all at your convenience.'"

"It's not going to happen, Bendrix."

"It's time, Abbey."

"Is not."

"It is."

Thankfully, Noel, one of my baristas, walked over to tell me my eight o'clock appointment would be late. A definite hipster, Noel had good looks and a superior talent for chitchat and remembering names, all essential to our early success. He had the required tattoos and his hair was perfectly coiffed to look messily neat. His interruption gave Bendrix and me a momentary break from sounding like children.

I didn't understand why Bendrix was being so pushy, frankly. There was a time, years ago, when he'd tried to convince me to start dating again, but those conversations had petered out once I became fully committed to opening Scratch. Besides, he was one to talk. If I feared getting hurt again, so did he, and he was as shut down as I was.

The year prior, the love of his life, one Anthony Wilson, had confessed to making out with another man at a party. Bendrix was so upset after hearing Anthony's confession, he broke up with him. Mind you, these two had been dating for more than two years by that point and were planning on buying a house together. I, for one, stood on the side of common sense and told Bendrix that he should give Anthony a second chance. At least hear him out, I'd said. It was a kiss, after all, not a full-blown affair, or anything close; and Anthony had confessed, which was a clear indication that the kiss was a cry for help. But Bendrix, stubborn and prideful, wanted nothing more to do with Anthony. I was so upset after their breakup, you would've thought I'd been dumped. I never knew anyone who was a better fit for Bendrix, who could make him do that rare thing he so disdained—smile— as often as Anthony could. They were good together. Then again, if Bendrix knew me better than anyone, I knew him just as well, and my guess was that after two years with Anthony, he'd been falling hard, and loving a person so deeply scared him, and that kiss had given him a way out. Bendrix waved away my take on the situation, calling it psychobabble, and after the split he rarely wanted to talk about Anthony, or, God help him, dis- cuss his feelings. When it came to love, I was the Cowardly Lion and Bendrix the Tin Man. If I dealt with the Avery debacle by baking, Bendrix dealt with his heartbreak by working longer hours at the hospital, volunteering at a free clinic in East Oak- land, and watching esoteric foreign films from the sixties.

Anthony's name worked like kryptonite against Bendrix's cool exterior, and he had a way of recoiling whenever he heard it. Even so, I thought, if he kept bugging me about dating, I was going to pull out the name and throw it at him.

He waited for Noel to leave the table before starting up again. "You have to think about egg production."

"You have to think about leaving me alone. You're getting on my nerves."

"I'm concerned. From what I learned in medical school, eggs get old, and when they do, they don't lay as well, making it harder to create the necessary zygote that eventually leads to diaper changes and midnight feedings."

It wasn't fair that he mentioned kids, but he had a point and he knew it. Forty loomed: a six-foot-high billboard lit up on a dark highway and drawing closer and closer and closer. What's more, if my heart was holding sit-ins and quietly requesting that I find romance, my uterus was holding protests with a megaphone and placards: *What do we want? Sperm! When do we want it? Now!*

I looked at him from across the table. "Why are you putting all of this in my face? Why are you being a jerk?"

He leaned in, his voice low. "If you want a family as much as I know you do, now is the time to start trying. The older you get, the higher the risks of ectopic pregnancy, high blood pressure, diabetes—"

"You've made your point."

He reached over and took my hand. "I worry about you."

"I know. Stop it. It's annoying."

I wasn't a believer in reincarnation, but if past lives existed, I had to believe that Bendrix and I had lived together through several. I imagined us bumbling along through one lifetime after another as brother and sister, husband and wife, mother and son—we'd experienced it all together, only to reach this point now, best friends. We had met the first day of our freshman year of high school. When I saw him in the cafeteria in his oversized T-shirt with a picture of the Cure, it was love at first sight. His Afro had been straightened to within a short breath of its life, dyed lime green, and styled so that several oiled strands fell perfectly over his left eye. His pants were held together in spots by safety pins. I was in my black phase—black jumper, black stockings, black shoes—and my own hair was shaped like a block of cotton candy. Frankenstein's bride had nothing on me.

He was reading Baudelaire and eating an elaborate sandwich on a toasted baguette with various kinds of sprouts and vegetables sticking out. He didn't look up from his book until I made a show of clearing my throat and opening my Plath. When he saw what I was reading he smiled. "Child, I cannot believe we have another four years of this shit. I feel like Oliver Twist trapped in that damn orphanage."

"More like *Carrie*," I rejoined.

"Yes," he said, widening his eyes. "Pig's blood and all. Bendrix Henderson."

"Abbey Lincoln Ross."

J took a bite of my pain aux raisins and Bendrix sipped his espresso while staring at me. In the momentary silence that followed, I felt a sense of anxiety coming from him that I hadn't noticed before. I could feel my heart quickening because I just knew that something was up. Something was wrong.

"What happened?"

He stared down at his tablet longer than necessary. Waffling, I believe it is called.

"Bendrix."

He sighed and swiped, then pushed his tablet in front of me. I picked it up and stared directly into Avery Brooks's caramel peepers and shockingly white teeth. Avery stared back at me from the photo as if no time had passed at all. I read the headline—AVERY BROOKS MAKING QUIET COMEBACK IN AMSTERDAM— then let my gaze wander back down to the photo. He stood in front of a large abstract painting flanked by potted plants and an oversized red chair; a staircase peeked out from behind. Sunlight shone through the windowpanes to his left, and at his feet there was a small stuffed rabbit, a kid's toy. His home, presumably, in Amsterdam.

"I guess Mexico didn't work out," I heard Bendrix say.

I remained quiet, until—"How long have you known?"

"I found out a few hours ago while I was at the hospital."

I skimmed the text long enough to catch familiar phrases like *impassioned artist, fraud, Oscar-nominated documentary*, and the more unfamiliar *phoenix rises, sales doubling*, and *second life*. I clicked to the next page and saw Avery with his arm around a ruddy, freckled girl whose blond pigtails flipped upward as though pulled by strings. She wore clogs and lederhosen.

I exaggerate, but only slightly. She was in her twenties and pretty in a pale, freckled, Scandinavian way.

"They have a son," Bendrix said.

"That explains the pink rabbit. Good for them. Pippi Long-stocking and Basquiat's love child." I pushed the tablet toward him and covered my eyes with my fingers as if I'd been reading for hours. "What else?"

"Apparently he's working on a series of paintings."

"*Original* this time?"

"So he says. He's been selling. The price for his work is up. They love him in Europe. His show hasn't opened and most of the work has already sold."

Bendrix gave me the necessary time to pout before speaking. "He's putting his life back together—all of his life, not just work. That's what I've been trying to tell you, Abbey. I love what you've done with Scratch as much as you do, but you need to get on with living."

"But you don't understand. I need time. Yes, you were there, but you don't know what it's like to be humiliated in movie the-aters and on Blu-ray and DVD and live streaming."

I always fell back on my humiliation when I was pushed too hard. And why shouldn't I? Who else could say they had dis-covered their fiancé was cheating while watching a documentary about his life? Show of hands? *Anyone? Anyone at all?*

Avery B: His Rise and Fall was a Sundance Audience Award winner and went on to be nominated for an Academy Award for best documentary. I mean, how does something like that happen?!

"That movie was years ago, Abbey."

"Feels like yesterday." I glanced around the bakery. By now the tables were filling up and a line was snaking to the screen door in the front. My bakery was a success, but the article made me feel like a complete failure. He had a baby—a son. During all those years with Avery, I had dreamed of starting a family with him. Avery was making a comeback and had a kid and a girl-friend, while I was spending my life making cupcakes. Where was my child? Where was my family?

"You of all people know how much that man hurt me," I said.

"I also know that you're letting your fear take over. I also know you're so afraid, you've stopped trying." He looked up from his tablet. "What are you going to do? Spend the rest of your life hanging out with your best friend?"

"*Yes?*" I said weakly.

"Abbey, you're not getting younger. Life is short. There are no guarantees. You're the star of your own show." He was on a roll now and enjoying himself. "The driver of your own car. Only *you* can make it happen."

I rolled my eyes.

Thankfully, Noel called over that one of my suppliers was on the line, saving me from breaking out into tears on the spot. My life sucked!

I told Noel I'd take the call in my office and rose from the table. "Thanks for the morning pep talk and news about my ex. I feel much better about life. You are a fine friend, Dr. Hender-son. Thanks. Heading home yet? You must be exhausted."

He eyed me from over his espresso cup before holding up his tablet with a grin, and the online dating site flashed before my eyes.

Jerk.

3

Let's Face the
Music and Dance

A quote from *New Yorker* art critic Charles Rappaport: "Avery Brooks's artwork speaks on a level outside the realm of abstraction and encapsulates the vitality of the mean streets where he grew up and the irony of his generation. Even at his young age, his work stands with that of the great artists he once studied."

I was twenty-eight when I met Avery and working at *Contemporary Art Now* as a staff writer. I'd been following his career since grad school and lucked out when I was assigned to interview him at his opening at Kerr Gallery in San Francisco.

I'd recently earned my master's degree in art history, my thesis on Kyrah Hegl, an artist who'd worked with mixed media before her suicide in the early 1980s. I was never an artist myself and not nearly as talented as my musically and artistically inclined siblings, but Bendrix and I had earned a name for ourselves back in high school as graffiti artists. We were serious enough that we were getting commissioned gigs by the time we were seniors. (Oh, how I was tempted at times to tell people that the one and only Dr. Bendrix Henderson was once known as Benz to the graffiti world.)

Bendrix had felt even more trapped in high school than I had and was always coming up with oddball ideas: "Let's go to a hockey game!" "Hockey? Who goes to hockey? We live in Oakland." Or, "Let's go see Pearl Jam!" "They're in town? Where are they playing?" "Oregon! We could take the train!"

He'd been going through some of my art books one night (I was obsessed with graffiti art back then, especially that of Barry McGee and Shepard Fairey), and he looked up from one of the books and suggested that we find an abandoned building and make graffiti art just as easily as you might say, *We should take a walk*. I was hardly paying attention because I was struggling through my algebra homework. Bendrix had been whisked off to gifted and Advanced Placement classes two weeks into freshman year and was already taking trig, but math remained my nemesis. "What do you think?" he asked.

"Uh-huh."

"Are you listening?"

I tried the formula I was working on for the millionth time. X *minus* Y . . . "Yeah. Graffiti. God, I hate algebra. Who cares about Y? I hate Y. I hate Z. I hate all these stupid formulas. And why are we using letters with math?"

At this point Bendrix sighed, climbed down from my bed, and grabbed my book. "Here, child." He took my pencil and began marking up my page like Zorro signing his signature with masked flair. "There."

I stared at the answer.

"Now will you pay attention?"

Neither Bendrix nor I could really draw, per se, so we made abstract portraits of our favorite artists instead. Van Gogh riding a skateboard. Paul Klee bungee jumping. Or we'd spray-paint a poem or haiku.

Daddy was big on three rules: Be honest, be yourself, and stay out of jail. So when I told him I wanted to try my hand at graffiti art, he made me promise to make my mark only on abandoned buildings and freight trains—as if we knew where to find a freight train. Our odd creations caught on, and at the height of our "fame" an indie rock band took a picture of one of our designs and used it on the cover of their CD. Later, the owner of a skateboard shop in Alameda asked us to come out and paint the side of his building. Thanks to those early years in high school, I hadn't merely *studied* art like my colleagues in grad school; I'd also created it. I'd learned in some small way what it was like to feel a creative spark, to experience the aliveness and elation that come from creativity.

All this is to say, while I wasn't model gorgeous like the women Avery usually dated, I was able to meet him in a place other women couldn't—that place where we could spend hours on end at MOMA gazing at a piece of art or sitting at a café discussing favorite artists and evaluating their work. I also introduced him to artists he'd never heard of, mostly female, who were ignored in academe and the art world. I knew a bit more about art criticism and history than he did, only because he was mostly self-taught. He once told me he thought one of the sexiest things about me was my love and knowledge of art. He proposed a year after we met while we were traveling together in Italy.

*L*ike Pollock and his alcoholism, Frida and that pole (!), van Gogh and that ear (!), Avery also came with the requisite Artist's Story, his involving a drug-addicted mother and a series of foster parents. It also didn't hurt that he was *fine*, as my stepmother Bailey noted more than once. Years of climbing the art

world's ladder led to a two-page spread in *Vanity Fair* that cata-
pulted him into the national spotlight. Even readers not interested in art stopped short when they saw Avery standing next to
one of his drawings, barefoot and wearing a clean white T-shirt
and jeans. Oh, those light brown eyes and that caramel-like skin;
those muscles, and that grin starting at the corner of his mouth.
Ladies on Park Avenue sitting in gold-plated chairs turned the
page of *Vanity Fair*, saw Avery Brooks, and sucked in a breath
of air.

Hollywood came next. Larsen, a documentary filmmaker,
asked if he could make a movie about Avery's creative process
and life. Avery and I were three years into our relationship and
had already formed an impenetrable bubble around us against
the ever-mounting requests for his time and attention. Larsen
seemed trustworthy, though, and the opportunity of a rising
documentarian filming Avery's life was too good to pass up. We
said yes, and the camera crew began following Avery around.

Sometime during the filming of *Avery B*, it was discovered
that Avery had forged his last series of paintings off a former
assistant. Admittedly, he was already heading into territory
where artists begin to copy old ideas. Think Factory Warhol and
those tired stills, or late Keith Bosworth and those dreaded cartoons. When Avery's assistant took him to court, he eventually
admitted that he'd copied "a few ideas." He was sentenced to pay
damages and was sued on all fronts by people who'd bought
paintings from his last series of work and by other patrons and
gallery owners who feared they'd been scammed. He put the loft
in San Francisco on the market, as well as his New York City
studio. Everything had to go. Larsen changed the title of his
documentary from *Avery B: His Rise and Genius* to *Avery B: His
Rise and Fall*.

I watched movers come in and take everything from our loft.

I watched Avery try to work his smile on his manager, curator, patrons, and press as he did his best to explain his way out of the shithole of lies into which he'd dug himself. I'd had to defend myself as well. *Did you know about the forgery, Ms. Ross?* No, I hadn't. I hadn't known a thing. I could have added that there'd been a time when Avery had told me everything and asked my opinion on whatever project he was working on, but that had ended months before—as had the sex and most of his attention.

So, yes, I was as surprised as anyone. I mean, forgery? Cheating is no surprise in places like Wall Street or the government, but in the art world—where creativity, *your* creativity, your insight, is your absolute treasure—to forge, to cheat another artist . . . it was unthinkable. Naturally his crime was the talk among critics, reviewers, and other artists. Charlie Rose dedicated a segment to the scandal, and when the movie premiered, Larsen was invited to speak about his movie and Avery on *Fresh Air.*

About a week after the scandal broke, I told Avery off and moved in with Bendrix for a while. Avery knocked on the door a few days later and asked if we could talk. He told me he was going to Mexico because he needed time to think. The documentary was showing at Sundance that month and he didn't want to have to "deal" when it opened. When I said I'd think about going to Mexico with him, he told me not to bother because he was going alone. That's when I knew we were finished and tugged off my engagement ring. He refused to take it back, though. He loved me, he said, and he was "deeply sorry." I deserved the ring and should keep it. He told me he'd be in touch, and then he turned and walked away.

Since I had tickets to the festival, I went with Bendrix to see *Avery B.* We pointed out actors and directors and acted like kids. We sat in the back of the theater during the showing, and I gripped his hand, humiliated every time I appeared on camera;

my nose alone looked six feet tall. All in all, though, I had to say, it was an excellent documentary, just as much about the creative process and the importance of art as a story about Avery's life. I started to relax and enjoy myself. Until the nymphs appeared: one blond, one brunette, both thin boned and wide-eyed and full lipped.

The brunette, Charlotte, looked like she belonged in a silent picture, a modern-day Mary Pickford with her coiled hair and pencil-thin eyebrows that exaggerated her perfectly oval face. She stared directly into the camera as Larsen asked when her affair with Avery began. "Like, maybe, like, a year after he and Abbey got engaged. I know this is supposed to make me the bad guy in all of this, but I believe when there's true love between two people, no one can come between them. I mean, like, if I could so easily come between those two, it wasn't love."

Larsen (offscreen): So what happened?

Charlotte (shrugging): We're both Scorpios, so it was crazy! We were all, like, *so* hot for each other; then things played out. It's like those—what do you call 'em?—those meteors in the sky. We burnt out. He didn't want to hurt Abbey either, so we stopped. I know he must seem like a player or what-ever, but he's just very passionate.

I turned to Bendrix, my mouth agape. Even in the darkened theater I could see that his eyes were as big and wide as mine.

"Do you know her?" he whispered.

"Of course not! I've never seen her before in my life!"

Someone from behind shushed us.

The blonde appeared next. Already she looked like she had more of a brain than the first bimbo. She wore glasses; her long braid was an accessory that draped over one shoulder. Her name appeared at the bottom of the screen: Josie.

Larsen: When did your relationship with Avery start?

Josie: We met at a party. He said he wanted to draw my hands. I know that sounds corny, but that's exactly what he did. He was very respectful and drew my hands all night while we talked. I'm an artist myself. I design jewelry.

Close-up shot: Josie fingering her necklace, made of what looks like icicles held dangling from a thin silver chain.

Larsen: And how did the relationship end?

Josie: Well, to be honest, it hasn't. I'm not proud of how we started, but we're very much in love. Avery Brooks is the love of my life.

Larsen: You know he's engaged.

Josie: Abbey is more like his business partner at this point. What Avery had for Abbey died a long time ago. He loves her more like a sister.

Cut to: Josie and Avery strolling through Golden Gate Park. He picks Josie up and throws her over one shoulder like a sack of flour, then twirls her around. Cue cheesy-sounding classical music.

Cut to: **Larsen** (offscreen): Do you ever worry about infidelity?

Cut to: *Me* (smiling into the camera—*like a gullible idiot!*): Oh, no. Never. Avery and I have our ups and downs like any couple, but I know Avery is as faithful to me as I am to him.

Besides, I wouldn't know where he'd get the time to sneak around behind my back. His art and his career are all consuming.

The word *idiot* flashes on and off at the bottom of the screen.

Okay, it didn't, but it may as well have.

"Let's get out of here," Bendrix said.

"No, I need to see this."

"You'll have to fight me off, then. There's no way I'm letting you torture yourself."

He grabbed my hand and dragged me out of the theater.

I considered suing Larsen but let the idea go since it was Avery who'd hurt me. Or was I to blame? How had I missed not one but two women? And when exactly had his love for me "died"?

I was devastated. Hurt enough that I wanted nothing more to do with men—in particular artists and musicians and anyone in the performing arts industry. And Scorpios.

*I*n the meantime, however, I still had Bendrix to deal with and that dreaded article in the *New York Times*, dredging up old memories. After Noel mentioned I had a call, I went to my office and spoke about fruit with my apple supplier. When I hung up, I remained in my chair and took in the pictures of my nieces and nephews covering my desk. My brother Theo was the first in the family to have a child, and I'd fallen instantly in love with my nephew and wanted to be the best aunt ever. As our family grew (and grew), I couldn't keep up with all the recitals and baseball games, but I always sent a gift every birthday and over the holidays, and I attended their school plays and activities whenever I could.

Yes, Daddy had babies by women he never married, but he made sure to remain in all his children's lives. He hated the words *step* and *half* and wanted us to treat one another as brothers and sisters. Period. As the oldest female, I'd learned to potty train, diaper, and entertain toddlers and babies as well as a professional nanny could. I was a kid who liked to please, and I never grew tired of all the snot and dribble and phlegm that came with looking after my younger siblings. My long way of saying I always knew I wanted to be a mother. I always knew it was something I wanted to do.

So yes (*okay, okay, okay!*), Bendrix was right about my fear, and the clock inside my uterus ticked and tocked all the louder as I stared at the pictures on my desk.

With a heavy sigh, I walked back to the front of the bakery, feeling envious of Avery and alone and lonely. A rain cloud formed above my head as I walked past Beth, rolling out piecrust; when I stepped into the bakery itself, the storm cloud burst and dumped pellets of hard rain. I donned a black scarf and continued to drag myself around tables as thunder boomed and lightning flashed. I was woman—watch me mope.

Bendrix was working on a second cup of espresso by then. He didn't bother looking up from what he was reading, even after I stood in front of him and thanked him for ruining my day with his news.

"Hey, I'm just trying to help. Just doing my part to wake you up."

He swiped and turned his tablet toward me. I stared at a picture of Avery and the Danish Pippi Longstocking holding their son.

"Wow, you really are a jerk."

He snickered.

Noel came over. "Your eight thirty is here." He jutted his chin toward a couple near the front of the bakery, holding hands and grinning at each other.

"Thanks, Noel. Will you tell Beth to bring out the cakes?"

"Sure thing."

I said to Bendrix, "I wouldn't mind if you were gone by the time I'm finished."

"Love you, too."

For obvious reasons I had to let go of my foul mood before talking weddings and wedding cakes with the couple I was meeting with. By chance, Rosemary Clooney sang "Pick Yourself Up" on the stereo. I listened for a few bars while willing the rain cloud over my head to go away.

The couple, twentysomething Google employees, pointed at the taster cakes Beth was setting out.

My bakery was popular, but my reputation and expertise lay in so-called wedding cake artistry. The couple I was about to meet had discovered me after seeing one of my cakes at their coworkers' wedding. Their coworkers Adhitya and Minu were more artsy than techie and had wanted an eye-popping cake with a contemporary design. They'd been to Scratch a few times, and after trying several bakeries in the Silicon Valley, they thought they'd see if I could come up with anything. I knew that having the opportunity to make a wedding cake for a pair of Google techies could be a boon if I played it right, and thanks to my background in art I felt ready for the challenge.

My first Google cake, as Bendrix and I called it, was an abstract creation based on Henry Lair's *Flamingo*. I knew Minu would be wearing a red-and-gold sari, so I'd covered the cake in a deep red fondant that matched her dress. On the top tier I created gold leaves and abstract shapes that also harkened back to Lair's work. The cake was a success and generated enough buzz that my name was taking hold not only throughout the Internet behemoth but in other tech giants in Silicon Valley as well.

Hence the Google couple sitting across from me. "So, are

you ready to discuss your wedding cake?" I could only hope that my smile and overly bright tone hid my sense of hopelessness: *My vagina is drying up! I'm the wedding cake designer who's never had a wedding of her own!*

"We're very excited!" said the future bride. She kissed the future groom in a burst of youthful happiness and Google money and optimism. "We're so in love!" she exclaimed.

"We just had sex in the car!" said the future groom.

"We have sex four times a week!"

"And we make a shitload of money!"

"In exactly one year we're going to start making a baby!" admitted the future bride.

The future groom to me: "If you want a baby, I suggest you start soon. You look *old*!"

"Yes," agreed the future bride with added concern, "you look *very* old!"

They turned to each other and burst into laughter: *"We're so rich!"*

Actually, I'm not sure what they said. Their mouths moved, but I was somewhere else. Rosemary Clooney droned on while I stared into one of the mini-cakes I'd made, a delicate yellow cake, iced in lemon rolled fondant, as if I were gazing into my future. I saw myself making wedding cakes until I was old and gray; Avery, meanwhile, would be surrounded by his grandchildren and latest girlfriend.

I mentioned something to the couple about the first cake but my head remained elsewhere. Bendrix was right. I'd given up. I'd given up on finding love because I was afraid of getting hurt. The future bride took a bite of the cake. "Oh my gosh, honey, this is delicious!"

I thanked her while thinking that they were a concrete re-minder that love was possible, and even though we failed at it at least fifty percent of the time, it was worth the effort, right? Yes! Yes, it was!

I stood abruptly. "I'm so sorry, but would you give me one second, please?" I was already backing away. "I'll be right back. Forgot something."

I marched over to Bendrix. "Okay. I'll do it."

"Do what?"

"Online dating! I'll give it a try."

"Good, because I've already created your profile."

"You what?"

He clicked a few times and turned his tablet. I stared at a picture he'd taken of me last year at my sister's birthday party. At the top of the picture I saw my profile name.

"Abbey Lincoln Ross, say hello to JazzyGirlinOakland."

4

Pent-up House

I hugged my nieces and nephew in the foyer of my dad's house. It was about a month since Bendrix had signed me up for online dating, and I was there along with family and friends to celebrate Daddy's sixty-fifth birthday.

My nephew Duncan was seven and his sister Bessie, five. Hope was three. When I picked up Hope, Bessie jumped up and down and begged that I pick her up, too. My older brother Dizzy, their father, watched from a few feet away, then told them to give their aunt Abbey some space. "It's fine," I replied.

"Where's the cake?" Duncan asked. He thought I had cookies or cake on me at all times.

"Don't worry, Duncan, it's being delivered. It should be here within the hour."

"Is there chocolate?" Bessie asked.

"Yep. I've got everyone covered. I made cookies, too."

They both threw their hands in the air and kicked their feet like shadow puppets on speed. *Yay! Our sugar dealer has arrived! We want sugar!*

Dizzy waved the bright red chicken leg in his hand, and the spicy scent of tandoori wafted in the air. "Hey, hey, you two, calm down. No cookies if you keep acting like you have no sense." He bit into the chicken and planted a kiss on my cheek. "Welcome. The house is packed."

I wiped the wet spot with my hand. "Really, Diz?"

He licked his tandoori-stained fingers. "Aw, a little grease'll do you good. Works like moisturizer." He took another bite and rubbed his shiny lips together as proof.

I gave Hope a bounce and she threw her head back as if taking an Olympic dive off a high board, arms splayed. I supported her back until she touched water, then drew her back in for a hug. "Again!" she said.

Dizzy pointed toward the ceiling. Over the din of party noise, I heard a loud succession of chords on top of the thump of bass. The piano picked up speed and cymbals tinged and clanged. Dizzy nodded to the beat. "Dad is on fire tonight. Phin and Miles were foolin' around, and Dad sat down at the piano and started schoolin' 'em. I stood to the side and watched—I'm no dummy. They've been at it for the last five minutes. Listen to Pops go, man." He closed his eyes briefly.

Dizzy played in a jazz quartet with my two older brothers Miles and Theo and my younger brother Phin. Dad called my three older brothers and me the full-bloods because our mothers were African American, while all of our younger siblings were biracial—a veritable "We Are the World" of races and colors. There were thirteen of us in all, and we were all named after jazz musicians and singers. Dizzy's full name, for example, was Dizzy Gillespie Ross and Theo's full name, Thelonious Monk Ross. I was named after the jazz singer Abbey Lincoln. All my adult siblings were musicians or artists of some kind, with many living beyond the Bay Area and even out of state. Everyone had made a point of coming to Daddy's party, though. Even when it meant canceling gigs and changing schedules.

Dizzy and I listened to Phineas strum the bass as he did his best to save his solo, but his counter was behind and he was threatening to throw the song. Dizzy laughed and shook his head. "Man, Dad is all over Phin. He sounds like an ox. He sounds like an ox pulling a cart. An ox pulling a cart uphill." He listened for another bar. "And backward!" He laughed and bit into the chicken.

"Don't give him too much *s-h-i-t* about it," I said.

"Oh, you know I will." He grinned.

My brothers were so used to perfection, any sign of weakness gave them an excuse to tease one another. Phin's solo may not have been his best, but he was one of the top bassists in the country, and even when his playing was "off" he was damn good, and Dizzy and I knew it.

Bessie took my hand and asked for a glass of water. Dizzy told me he'd take care of it and that I should enjoy the party. I sent Hope for another free-falling dive before handing her over to her father. When she reached for Dizzy's chicken, he gave her the leg so she could help herself. Dad had trained my brothers that when they were home from the road they needed to spend as much time with their families as possible. *"Don't make the same mistakes I once made,"* he liked to say.

I watched Dizzy trot off with his family, my heart sinking a little. I was officially dating again, but so far the dates had been disastrous. I'd had a drink with Ronald Reagan at a bar in SOMA and listened while he espoused the glories of the Republican Party. Marcel Marceau had showed up for my second date in a striped red-and-white shirt and red beret. He hadn't talked much, just grinned at me. Finally, there had been Mr. Throwback— relatively good-looking but instead of using my name, he preferred to call me *dollface* and *babe*. And when other women passed our table, his head craned to follow.

Dating sucked.

I started to make my way through the living room. Since Dad loved Indian food, we'd decided on an Indian-themed party. Caterers roamed the room dressed in saris and tunics while serving the crowd platters of *chaat* and curry. Every inch of the high ceiling was covered with Indian fabric, and an ornate oriental lamp hung from the center, all of it giving me the feeling that I had accidently stepped into a massive tent owned by a nomadic tribe of artsy partiers.

I greeted, kissed, and hugged my way through the crowd. Even though many of my siblings had arrived a week before and we'd already spent time together, we still hugged and said hello like it had been months.

I noticed Bailey making her way around a server and marching toward me, her mouth contorted in its usual frown. Bailey was Dad's first wife and mother to Thelonious, Miles, and Dizzy. She'd been making the circuit as a jazz singer when she met Dad. Later, she became a backup singer; now, thanks to her early, hard-core fan base, she was having a resurgence and sang in different clubs throughout the country. She had never learned the difference between dressing for a gig and dressing for regular life. For Bailey, all the world was a stage. She liked to dye her hair one bright color or another, and that night it was the same magenta as her dress, which looked a size too small and was currently giving up the struggle to cover her thick thighs. She'd tug at the sides of the dress, but sooner or later it would inch back up.

She gave me a hug and helped me with my coat. She then motioned toward the corner of the room where I saw two of Dad's ex-girlfriends, Leslie and Dahlia, talking with each other.

Bailey started in right away. She was one who didn't avoid gossip, especially when it involved Dad's ex-girlfriends. "Leslie had the nerve to ask your father for a bigger allowance so she can switch Louis to a better school. He already goes to one of the best private high schools in Oakland. Gold diggers, every last one. And that Dahlia *Whore*deen! Don't even get me started on her." Dahlia's last name was Wardeen, fuel for Bailey's fire.

There were four ex-girlfriends or baby mommas in the family. Dad had other ex-girlfriends, but we considered only the baby mommas part of the family. I often imagined the wives, as we called them, and the ex-girlfriends in a musical in which Dad's four ex-wives danced on one side of the stage and his four ex-girlfriends danced on the other in a Sharks-versus-Jets fashion. I didn't include his fifth (and final?) wife, Aiko, in my musical because she was busy raising my three-week-old brother, Ornette, and nineteen-month-old brother, Bud.

Who knew if the wives would have remained as close as they were if Bailey hadn't suffered from colon cancer while I was in high school. She had no family to speak of, so the wives had pitched in, transporting her to chemotherapy appointments and taking turns looking after her when she was sick in bed. Their bond became stronger than ever during the ordeal.

The wives resented the ex-girlfriends, or exes, because while they'd married Dad, for however long, and had committed themselves to him, the exes basically got knocked up and were then able to take advantage of Dad's blind devotion to his children and cash in on his money. But Dad insisted that we all get along, and for his sake, and presumably for the sake of the children, the wives and ex-girlfriends smiled and were polite—if only on the surface.

"Dahlia lost yet another job. That's right. Another job. How many is that? I lost track. I keep telling your father he needs to cut her loose; otherwise, she's never moving out of the guesthouse. Why should she? At this rate she's gonna get free room and board till she dies."

Dahlia turned when she felt us staring. Bailey raised her glass and smiled gaily and waved. "Hussies," she muttered under her breath.

I stifled a laugh. I wanted to honor my father's wishes, but I had to agree with Bailey: The exes had a way of taking advantage— especially Dahlia.

Bailey turned and stared at me. "Four years, Abbey?"

"Four years what?"

"If I had known you were going without that long, I would have forced you to start dating years ago. Who goes that long without sex? I could see if you were my age, but you're still young!"

Crap, I thought. "You spoke with Bendrix."

"Yeah," she mocked. "I spoke with Bendrix. He's upstairs. You are young and beautiful and it's not right to go that long without sex."

A man I didn't recognize brushed past. "Will you lower your voice?"

"Are you sick?"

"No, I'm not sick. I just haven't met anyone I like."

"Like? Like? What does liking a person have to do with any-thing? You see somebody who looks like he can handle you, and after you make sure he's not married, you climb into bed and do what comes natural. It's easy, baby. Liking has nothing to do with it. It's a crime and a sin to be as young as you are and go without for *four long years!*"

"Bendrix has a really big mouth."

"He cares about you. Anyway, he was just showing us that

computer dating Web site, and wait until you see who he found for you."

"Wait a second . . . *What?*"

"Yeah, he found somebody for you. A very good-looking somebody."

Visiting the LoveMatch site made me feel like I was shopping for a man, which I found completely unromantic and nauseating, so I let Bendrix vet profiles for me and forward any possibilities my way. I certainly hadn't wanted him to tell one of the wives—or anyone. "This is embarrassing."

"He's upstairs waiting to show you."

"Well, let him wait. Dad's cakes should be here soon."

"Don't try to get out of it. Someone will let you know when the cakes are here."

I sighed.

"You won't be making that ugly face when you see the man Bendrix picked out."

We continued to make our way through the house. Dad had finished playing and I could hear my younger sisters, Ella on the violin and Billie on guitar. Their bandmate, Sam, played clarinet. They made a sweet trio and were enjoying a growing popularity after a recent appearance on a late-night TV show.

Rita, an ex-wife, walked up and grabbed my hand just as I snatched a flute of champagne from a passing waiter. She kissed me on each cheek, European style. She was stunning in a deep purple sari with gold trim. Her hair was short and coiffed and she wore long dangling earrings. Where Bailey liked short, tight skirts and low-cut blouses, Rita was all glamour and high style. "Did Bailey tell you Bendrix found someone for you?"

"Yeah. Whoopee."

"Oh, don't be like that. Wait until you see him. He's wonderful. Reminds me of a young Marquis Jones, a man I danced *Firebird* with years and years ago. He was so gifted. Anyway, let's all go up so you can see. And I love the Web site. Makes looking for a man as easy as shopping for a dress."

"Hardly."

Rita's grandparents were Afro-Cuban, but Rita was born and raised in the States. She'd danced with Alvin Ailey for several years and met Dad when he was commissioned to write a piece for the troupe. Rita was Dad's third wife and together he and Rita had Dinah. Rita was a stickler for rules and propriety. While others prayed for world peace, Rita prayed for a world that had better fashion sense and etiquette.

We joined Bendrix upstairs in the library, which was one of the best rooms in the house, with floor-to-ceiling windows and a view of the bay. It wasn't a library, per se, but had taken on the genteel moniker after Dad started sending us there to read when we were being punished or making too much noise. Over time it became the wives' hangout, and the ex-girlfriends knew to keep out.

"Perfect timing," Bendrix said. "Now, I will admit that the first three men didn't work out—"

"Didn't work out?" I turned to Bailey and Rita. "Did he tell you about the guy who showed up dressed like a mime?"

Rita crossed her long legs, and a jeweled gold sandal peeked out from beneath her sari. "Never mind all that. Show her, Bendrix."

"I found him last night," he said. "I thought I'd wait to show you."

"Yeah, me and everyone else. Thanks for keeping my dating life private, Bendrix. Did you have to show them the guy before you showed me?"

"Child, hush up with all that whining," Bailey snapped. "Bendrix is grown and he can do whatever he wants. Now, show her the damn picture."

I sat next to Bendrix and he turned his tablet toward me. "JazzyGirlinOakland, let me introduce you to RelaxinbytheBay."

I stared at a man walking away from the camera while laughing over his shoulder as if someone had said something funny and caught him off guard. He wore a leather jacket with a wool scarf and had nice eyes and an actual cleft chin, as deeply pronounced as Cary Grant's.

I heard Bailey: "Yeah, who's whinin' now? He's fine, isn't he? Hell, if you don't want him, I'll take him!"

Rita said, "Bailey, would you hush, please?"

The guy was *fine*. Truly. But I was skeptical. The other three guys had all looked fine in their pictures, too, but they'd turned out to be freaks.

Bendrix read from his profile. "Six feet one. No kids. Enjoys long walks, cycling, and dining out. Stanford grad. Corporate law."

Rita noticed the horror in my expression: "There's nothing wrong with law, Abbey. Doug studied law." Rita and Doug had married years ago, after her divorce from Dad.

"Yeah, but corporate law? I bet he's a bore."

"Oh, and you're just a thrill a minute," said Bendrix.

I ignored him and went back to reading. Under the topic *Why You Should Get to Know Me*, he replied that he'd lived abroad for a year and knew how to make the best marinara sauce this side of Italy. In response to *What I'm Looking For*: "I'd like to meet a woman with a kind heart, sharp mind, and deep soul. A best friend I can share my life with."

"Doesn't he sound fabulous?" Rita sang. "Abbey, if this works out like I think it will, I'd love for you to have your engagement party at Doug's club. You could have the top floor. The views of San Francisco are spectacular."

"Engagement?" Bailey said. "Now who's talking nonsense? They haven't been out on a *date* yet."

"I'm optimistic. I have a *very* good feeling."

"I'd like to meet him first, at least," I said.

Bailey replied, "Of course you want to meet him. I don't care how all this ends except that I want you to get what's yours. And if this guy can give it to you, I'm all for it."

"All for what?" Enter Joan, wife number four. Joan was the only wife who'd already known about my dry spell with men and told me not to worry; I'd start dating again when I felt like it. Born in Sussex, England, Joan had moved to the States when she'd turned twenty-one. She was now a sculptor who exhibited internationally. Straightforward and laconic, she was the only wife who'd never had kids; maybe that was why we had struck a bond. When I was young she'd toss books my way and ask me what I thought. *The Bluest Eye, Their Eyes Were Watching God, The Lord of the Rings, The Catcher in the Rye.* I'd sit in her studio and read, or she'd listen to me ramble about my teenage woes. She wore women's suits and leather gloves and hats as though there were a 1940s motorcade waiting.

Bendrix gave her a tour of the dating site while she looked on. "Love and romance as algorithm. Interesting." When he showed her Relaxin's photo she said, "A photo doesn't mean much until you meet a person and can look him in the eye."

"She's not looking for a conversation," cracked Bailey.

"Joan's right," said Rita. "But if you're going to look him in the eye, Abbey, you need to contact him. Right, Bendrix?"

"Yes," said Bendrix. "We need to make contact and send him a note. See what he says."

I looked around the room. "Do I get a say in any of this?"

"Not really," Bendrix said.

"Write and tell him Abbey hasn't had a good lay in four years," said Bailey. "That should get his attention."

I leaned back against the couch. "I don't know," I moaned. "He's cute, but—"

"Buuuuut . . ." Bailey dragged her mouth for all it was worth. "This is exactly what happens when you stop having sex. You become a whiner, bringing everybody down."

"You only live once," offered Rita.

"And your life is passing you by," said Bendrix. "I have no idea who you're looking for if not someone like this. As far as I can tell, the only thing wrong with him is that he's straight."

"I guess." I looked at Joan.

"Do what you want." She shrugged. "Doesn't matter what anyone else thinks. This is your life, not ours."

I gazed around the room until Bailey sat up and sighed. "Goodness, child, you're not marrying the guy. Just send him a damn note."

"Okay, okay! Forgive me for wanting to think this through." I wiggled my fingers at Bendrix and he handed me the tablet. "What should I say?"

Bailey laughed. "Tell him he's fine as hell and you want to fuck his brains out."

Rita clicked her tongue. "Even after all these years . . ." She crossed her legs, looking peeved. Bailey's loud mouth, in other words, still riled her at times.

I took a moment to gather my thoughts. "Let's see . . . 'Dear RelaxinbytheBay, in the world of online dating, you seem like a find. I hope you like my profile and I hear from you soon. Sincerely, Abbey.'"

"I love it," said Rita.

"Short, sweet, and to the point," said Bendrix. He moved my hand aside and clicked "send" before I had a chance to reread the note, edit the note, or otherwise chicken out. "That's that. Now, what do you say we join the party?" He rose from the couch and extended his hand to Rita.

"We need to work on you next, Benny," she said. "We can't let your good looks go to waste. It's time you started thinking about settling down."

"Yeah, Bendrix," I said sarcastically. "How long has it been since Anthony?"

He stood erect as soon as I dropped the A-bomb. He pulled his shoulders back and tilted his chin upward like an aristocrat speaking to his servants; sometimes Bendrix could be so haughty he seemed best suited for coat, tails, and a monocle over one eye. "This isn't about me," he said, going for his tablet.

"It should be," I said. "Word on the street is that you only live once."

"Well, I . . . at least I—"

Bailey shot up from the couch, saving him from having to finish with the bull. "Dinah is ruining my song," Bailey shot out. "You all hear that?"

My sister's voice seeped up through the floor. She sang "Trouble Is a Man" in a slow, breathy voice. "Why is she singing it like she's at a funeral? She needs to speed that shit up. She should know better." Dinah was Rita's daughter, but Bailey had taught her everything she knew about music.

"Go easy on her," Rita said lightheartedly.

"I'm gonna show her what's what; that's what I'm going to do. Messin' with my song like that."

We followed Bailey downstairs to Dad's large practice room. Dinah stood at the mike singing while my dad, Uncle Walter, and Uncle Dex backed her.

Guests sat in chairs or stood against the walls or in any space they could find, with more guests flowing out into the hallway. Dad had knocked out two walls to enlarge his practice room. Albums lined the shelves and there were photos everywhere of artists he'd played with. Growing up, I'd spent hours and hours in Dad's practice room. Sometimes I'd surround the piano with stacks of his LPs, then crawl in through a tiny opening and tell him I was hiding out in my fort, where I would occasionally watch Daddy's feet pressing the pedals as he worked on a song.

Dad gave a nod and Uncle Dex went into his solo. They were brothers in spirit, and in all their thirty-plus years together, they'd never once talked about disbanding.

The room erupted into applause when everyone saw Bailey make her way up to Dinah. She grabbed a second mike, and— "Baby, I love you like you were my own, but it's time I schooled you on how to sing my song!" Everyone laughed and applauded, including Dinah. She took an exaggerated bow. "Give it up for Momma Bailey, everybody."

Bailey snapped her fingers high in the air, faster and faster. Dad and my uncles doubled, then tripled their speed until "Trouble Is a Man" was no longer a torch song but a snappy tune that had us all tapping our feet and clapping our hands. "Aw right. Y'all feel that?"

Bailey sang "Trouble" as only she could. Dad closed his eyes and sent his fingers crisscrossing over the keyboard in a race of snazzy agility. Uncle Dex let out a shout and slammed the cymbals.

I felt Bendrix give my shoulder a bump. "It's too bad your family throws such boring parties."

"It is, isn't it? We're a sad bunch when you get down to it."

"Yes, and don't get me started on the lack of talent."

I said, "You're not forgiven, by the way, for showing everyone my online profile."

He continued staring at the stage. "And you're not for-given for bringing up a certain someone I'd prefer not to hear about."

At that, we smirked at each other and went back to clapping along with the rest of the crowd of friends and family.

5

Say It Isn't So

One of my employees, Nico, who helped with deliveries and assisted in pretty much everything, sent a text during Bailey and Dinah's second number: He'd arrived with the cakes and was waiting in the kitchen. I'd made three cakes for the night: almond, finished with almond dacquoise; chocolate cake with rum-laced buttercream; and a spice cake made with freshly shaved ginger. The cakes were covered with a marbleized background softened by a burst of lilies and hibiscus made from gum paste. I'd decorated the bottom cake with Dad's initials, each letter made to look like embroidered silver.

The few people in the kitchen oohed and aahed as Nico and I finished assembling the cakes. Once we were done, I asked Nico if he wanted to stay, but he opted for a plate of food to go. He was taking classes at Laney Community College and said he had a paper due on Monday.

After watching him drive off, I caught sight of my sister Carmen sitting on the wide wraparound porch of the guesthouse next door, smoking a cigarette as though it were part of her everyday routine.

I marched over. What the hell was she doing, smoking? And so brazenly.

I stood over her with my hands on my hips. *"What* are you doing?"

"What does it look like?" She put the cigarette between her lips and inhaled like a TV actress—hardly inhaling at all but making a show of blowing a long stream of smoke from between her lips.

Carmen was Dahlia's daughter (Dahlia *Whoredeen* as Bailey liked to call her). After Carmen started junior high school, Dahlia had convinced Dad to let them move into the guesthouse until she was on her feet. Dahlia was still there now, even though Carmen was in college and living in the dorms.

I bent over and snatched the cigarette before Carmen could take a second puff. "You look ridiculous."

"I have a pack, you know." She held up the carton and cut her eyes.

I sat next to her and we listened to the music coming from next door and the steady sounds of laughter and merriment. I asked Carmen what was going on and was met with a flat "Nothing."

"Why aren't you at Dad's?"

"Don't feel like it." She snatched the cigarette I was holding and took a hit. When she coughed, I grabbed it again, broke it in half, and tossed it into the yard. "You shouldn't smoke, Carmen. What's wrong with you?"

She clicked her tongue and leaned back on her elbows. "Whatever. I'll have one when you leave."

I stared at her briefly in disbelief. I was closer to Carmen than to any of my other siblings because we were the only two in the Ross clan who didn't show a natural ability toward music or art. Sure, I'd had my days as a graffiti artist, but they were long gone, and regardless, I never had the talent to seek out a full-blown career in the arts. Carmen, too, had seemed adrift amid all the family talent, and after disastrous attempts to study the French horn, and later drama, she had settled on majoring in business with the goal of going to law school, two decisions that were as odd to the family as if she'd announced she planned to walk through the Ozarks while reading Greek philosophy. I always kept a special eye out for her because I could tell early on that she wasn't getting the support she needed. Dahlia was only twenty-two when she had Carmen and never seemed all that interested in being a mother. Since the wives had long since moved on by the time Carmen was born, she seemed to flounder more than the rest of us.

My relationship with my own mother helped me relate to Carmen's situation. Karen, wife number two, taught musicology with an emphasis in ethnomusicology. She and Dad had divorced soon after she'd earned her doctorate, and when I was ten, she was hired to teach at a private arts college in Connecticut, where she and I relocated. I hated Connecticut, though, and was beyond miserable—the snow, the boredom, the shock of leaving behind a loud, messy household with people coming and going in order to live with Mom in her small apartment, were too much. (Just thinking about those days put me in a mood.) I missed seeing my older brothers every day, and I missed roughhousing and looking after my younger siblings; I missed hearing my dad's music and seeing his face. I missed Bailey's cooking and Joan and Rita. I begged Mom to let me move back home. She agreed when I started showing signs of depression—for instance, sleeping all weekend and losing most of my appetite. She finally let me return only after discussing the situation with the wives, who promised to look after me as though I were their own flesh and blood. It was agreed I'd live with Mom in the summers and visit for Christmas—which was too bad, since Christmas at the Ross house was crazy fun.

My bookish, academic mom was in no way, shape, or form as wacky or loose as Dahlia, but she had a way of ignoring me that was similar to the way Carmen's mother treated her. Mom did her best, but she had a passion for her work and her students that sometimes left me feeling envious. We managed—or I grew up and expected less, I wasn't sure which—and maybe I was projecting my stuff onto Carmen, because truly, her situation was much worse. But I did feel the need to look after her, let her know, as the wives had let me know, that she was loved and that I was there for her whenever she needed anyone to talk to.

My way of saying, I did not understand what was up with all the attitude, or what the hell was going on.

I touched my shoulder to hers. She had Dahlia's large round eyes, dark brown instead of green. A trail of faint freckles trekked across the bridge of her nose, and she had Dad's full mouth and lips. She was nineteen and hadn't a clue she was beautiful. She was always ten to fifteen pounds overweight, and even when Carmen was a child, Dahlia had harped on her size . . . and everything else about her daughter she thought needed improvement.

"What's going on?" I asked.

Carmen flung herself forward and buried her head in her arms. "You'll hate me."

"If you say so."

She sat up and started bouncing her leg rapidly; her body began to shake as though she had a chill.

"What is it?"

She looked toward Dad's house, then drew her hands over her face. She kept hidden when she spoke: "I think I'm pregnant."

My first reaction was to scream. *Pregnant?! You cannot be pregnant!* I was prepared for anything except pregnancy. Give me an STD over pregnancy! I'd take syphilis or gonorrhea, but not pregnancy! No!

I had to bite my tongue to stop from yelling. I was her go-to adult and I needed to stay calm or risk losing her confidence. One breath. Two. *Okay, take it slow, Abbey.*

"Are you sure?"

"As sure as an over-the-counter pregnancy test."

"But those aren't always accurate. Maybe you're late."

"I took four tests, Abbey. I'm pregnant."

Shit!

She picked up the cigarettes and matches. "I am positively with child," she said. "I'm preggers. I'm carrying a bun in the oven. A pea in the pod. I'm knocked up."

"Okay, Carmen, I get it."

"I'm a walking incubator." I watched her light up and take one of her pseudo puffs.

"You shouldn't be smoking."

"Why not? It's not like I'm gonna keep it."

I snatched the cigarette before she could take another drag and placed it between my lips. There was a time when Bendrix and I would sneak a cigarette after finishing one of our pieces, and for the time it took for me to show my little sister what a real drag looked like, the time it took the smoke to trickle down my throat and fill my lungs, I left my pregnant sister and relived those moments as a graffiti artist.

Carmen stared wide-eyed while I took one more drag. Fate was a bitch: I didn't want Carmen to be pregnant; *I* wanted to be pregnant.

I took one last drag from the (delicious) poison stick before burying it underfoot. "How did this happen? I mean, I know how it happened, but who? Do you have a boyfriend I don't know about?"

She took out her phone and scrolled until she found what she was looking for—a picture of herself and a few friends. In the center of the photo stood a clean-cut guy wearing a jacket and loose-fitting tie.

"He looks decent enough. Does he know?"

"Not him," she said, "the guy on the right." I shifted my gaze and stared at the guy wearing his glasses upside down with a paper hat on his head. He had raised a gallon of generic whiskey in the air and was pretending to slug it back. "Oh boy."

"I know. My baby daddy is a goofball."

"I thought we discussed using protection."

"Yeah, we did."

"So why didn't you use it?"

"No lectures, please. It's too late. I'm already being punished as it is."

"We should make an appointment and find out for sure if you are or not. Have you told your mother?"

She looked at me like I was crazy.

She had a point, although I knew what I was supposed to say: "Car, she should know so she can be there for you."

"Yeah, right. You're the only one I've told. Will you go to the clinic with me?"

I leaned over and forced a hug on her. I wouldn't say it aloud, of course, it was too early, but I already thought that I could help her by looking after the baby while she finished school. Maybe RelaxinbytheBay would be as great as his profile made him out to be and *we* would raise my sister's baby. "It's going to be okay, Carmen. I can—"

"Abbey?"

"Yeah?"

"I'm not going to have it. I'm just not. I want to go to law school. I've got things I want to do, and having a baby isn't one of them. But I'm afraid if I get rid of it, I'll regret it. Like, I'll never be able to forgive myself."

"Well, it's for you to decide. You have to make the decision that's best for you. It's a very private, personal decision, and whatever happens, we're here for you. You have to believe that."

My thoughts shifted from taking care of Carmen's baby to protecting her from pro-life zealots. I saw myself holding her close as I pushed her through a mob of hatemongers protesting in front of a nondescript women's clinic. If she wanted to terminate the pregnancy, it was no one's business. Not even mine.

"Let's find out if you're pregnant first. Maybe you're late."

"Please. We both know I am." She leaned back again. "Just what this family needs—another kid."

I started to respond—to defend our big, bustling family— but the front door of the guesthouse slammed, and then someone's foot appeared: a man's foot, clad in shiny black. No, wait, a deep, dark blue shoe, landing right between Carmen and me as if we weren't sitting together at all. He took his time striding down each step like a Broadway performer making his entrance. I half expected him to snap his fingers to a show tune running through his head. He wore a blue suit and carried a garment bag over his shoulder. I guessed he was in his thirties, and when he hoisted his bag up, I saw he had the body of a man who spent hours in the gym, and I imagined jumping up and down on his taut stomach while he smiled up at me, not feeling a thing.

He paused and snapped his fingers as though he remembered something. When he grinned at us, the gold on his left incisor caught the light of the moon and gleamed. Okay, there was no gold tooth, but I could tell that's the kind of man he was: Every time he looked in the mirror, he pointed and said, *You look good.*

"Who's that?" I asked.

Carmen remained indifferent. "Lamar? Shamar?" She leaned further back on her elbows. "Barbar?"

Still grinning, the man took a step toward Carmen. "You tell your mother I want my money back. Every cent. Six hundred dollars."

"I'm not her go-between."

He gave a huckster chuckle as he looked at Carmen. He reached down next to her and picked up the packet of cigarettes. "May I?" Before she could say anything, he gave the carton a couple of taps against his palm, then tilted the box. A cigarette slid out. "Haven't had one of these in years." He lit up and took a long pull. On his exhale he looked over at the main house. "You know," he said, blowing a stream of smoke, "I heard your father play live once back in 'ninety-two. Newport Jazz Festival. Good show."

"Of course it was," Carmen quipped.

"Yeah." He kept his eye on the house and took a long, hard pull. "I don't know how he deals with all those women, though. Man must have some serious skills." He laughed to himself and hoisted his garment bag farther up his shoulder. "Thanks for the cig, ladies. You all have a good night."

We watched Lamar or Shamar walk to his maroon sedan.

"My mother sure knows how to pick 'em," Carmen muttered.

We heard the door open behind us. "Is he gone?"

"Yes," Carmen sighed.

"Who was he?" I asked.

"Nobody." Dahlia stepped out. "Absolutely nobody." She began fussing with her bushel of chestnut hair.

"Yeah," Carmen said, "a nobody who says you owe him six hundred dollars."

Dahlia snorted at the idea. She thumbed the gold chain

resting high atop her milky boobies and held it out for us to see. "He bought me this necklace and now he wants me to pay him for it. But he's nuts if he thinks I'm paying him back for a gift. Whoever heard of that?"

After I'd first met Dahlia, I immediately concluded that she and Dad, without talking much, had gone straight from making out in the corner of the club where they met to Dad's hotel room. I had to assume that if they'd had an actual *conversation*, an actual dialogue about anything in life, before he slept with her, her lack of brains would have made him change his mind. Dahlia hadn't even known anything about jazz! A friend had dragged her to Dad's concert. But his potent sperm went to work on her free-falling egg and—*bam!*—two months later, guess who's knocking on the door? A paternity test confirmed another baby momma had entered our lives, and soon I had another sister.

The box of cigarettes caught her attention and she picked it up. "Smoking, Carmen? Really? These things will give you wrinkles before you're thirty. And do you want yellow teeth? There are other ways to lose weight. Diet pills are better than smoking, although if you get to the gym now and then, that would be even better. And why aren't you at the party?"

Carmen grabbed the carton. "I'm not in the mood."

"You're not in the mood for anything lately except moping around." She kicked the edge of Carmen's foot. "Sit up, Car. Why aren't you at the party? You look like a slug, you know that? What were we discussing last night? You have to think of yourself as a brand. You want attention in life, you have to draw upon positivity. You behave positively and positive things will come to you. It's physics!"

"Physics," Carmen scoffed.

"Yes, physics. Don't give me that attitude. I don't appreciate it. Just because you're in college doesn't mean I am not your mother. Whatever you believe comes back to you. It's been proven."

"So some thirteen-year-old girl sold into prostitution in some poor remote country, chained to a bed, and forced to have sex all day—all she has to do is *believe* someone will save her?"

Dahlia frowned. "Yes, Miss Smarty-pants. If she believed hard enough, it would happen."

Carmen and I exchanged looks.

"Regardless, Carmen, your dad is celebrating his birthday and you need to get over there and smile and have a good time. Help me out, Abbey."

I saw she had a point for once. "Maybe she's right. You should eat. Plus the cake's here."

"She could do without the cake."

Carmen shot daggers her way. Heck, I threw in a few myself. God, she was annoying.

"I think I'm going to go back to the dorms."

"No, you're not; you're going to stay and celebrate your father's birthday. I refuse to let you leave. What's wrong with you? Are you okay?"

I waited, wondering if Carmen would tell her.

"I'm fine."

Dahlia frowned. "Let's go, then. It would kill your father if you didn't at least give him a hug and wish him happy birthday. I don't understand why you wouldn't want to do that. All his other kids are there, and if—"

"Okay, okay! Jesus. Let's go."

Carmen and I followed while Dahlia clicked and clacked her way across the pathway and to the main house. When Carmen looked at me, I put my arm around her and smiled. I did my best to tell her with my eyes that keeping the baby or not was her decision, but if she kept it, I promised to help her take care of it. She could even move in with me. Or I could raise the baby for her and we'd never let the child know that Carmen was the actual mother and then she'd grow up and find out that we'd lied and she'd hate me and hate Carmen and have to go into years and years of therapy, but at least we'd have our memories, right?

I had to wait through most of the night to talk to Dad. I knew I wouldn't have much time, but I wanted to plant a seed in his ear about Carmen, something along the lines of—*Could you spend a little more time with your daughter? She's having unprotected sex and might be pregnant.* Sometime after eleven, Dad rose from the piano and announced they were taking a break but the show wasn't over. He thanked everyone for coming and said they'd start playing again in fifteen minutes. (We'd tried to convince him not to play on his birthday, by the way, but he said he wanted to do what made him happy. He'd promised not to play the entire night.)

I knew it was now or never and pushed my way through the crowd. Dad was standing in the corner of the room and talking to a couple of people I didn't recognize when I rudely butted in and gave him a hug. I smiled and said hello to his admirers, then pulled him—not too forcefully, I hoped—back toward his piano.

Asking Dad for a minute of his time was like asking him for a day. He was spread bare among family, friends, business associates, other musicians who wanted his time, fans, and, let's not forget, his music, the one constant in his life that got his attention at least four hours a day plus any gigs.

Dad was tall, with a high forehead. Except for around the eyes and mouth, his skin was taut and wrinkle free. He'd been practicing tai chi since I could remember, and his soul patch and the shades he wore whenever he left the house were also permanent markers. As Bendrix liked to say, in the Mount Rushmore of cool, Lincoln T. Ross was up there with the best of them.

He followed my lead when I sat on his piano bench. I decided to jump right in. "I'm worried about Carmen, Daddy. When you get a chance, would you check in on her? Take her out for breakfast or something?"

"What's got you so worried?"

"Nothing in particular." *Except that she might be pregnant.* "It's just that . . . well . . . she's . . ." I kept tripping on my words because what I really wanted to tell him was the unfiltered truth for once. As much as he wanted to believe otherwise, not every child was meant to grow up in a large family with a father who was kind and loving, yes, but who was on tour as much as he was home and who kept marrying and impregnating women—*no offense. And Dahlia? Really, Daddy? What the hell did you see in her? Well, I get what you* saw *in her, but did you have to knock her up? I'm glad we have Carmen, but I wish you'd at least kick Dahlia out of the guesthouse.*

A man walked up and shook Dad's hand. "Nice set, man. I can't believe I'm here."

"Enjoy yourself. This is my daughter. She made the birthday cakes."

The guy shook my hand. "Nice to meet you." He turned back to Dad. "I've always wanted to ask about your duet with Chick—"

I put on a wide fake smile. "Would you mind giving us one second, please?"

"Yeah, sure. Good set, man. Happy birthday."

"Yeah, thank you." Dad watched the man leave, a grin inching across his face. "I don't know half the people here tonight. Damn good party, though." He held up his wrist and showed me a thick silver cuff. "You see this? It's from Louis and Charlie.

Nice, huh?" My brothers Louis and Charlie were still in high
school.

I complimented the bracelet and tried again to bring up Carmen. "Thing is, I think Carmen could really use some one-on-one
time with you. Can you take her to lunch or something?"

"Yeah, baby. Of course."

But Dad's *"Yeah, baby, of course"* didn't amount to much unless
he made a note to himself or you made the appointment with his
manager or with Aiko.

"Seriously, Daddy. Don't forget, okay?"

"Something I need to know about?"

I hesitated when I saw the concern in his eyes. Oddly enough,
I often felt I should protect *him* when it came to family problems.
We all did. We were so busy clamoring for his time, we didn't
dare ask for more than the little he could give. We knew he loved
us, would do anything for us, and who would dare ask for more?
His head was filled with music as it was. "I just wish Dahlia had
better parenting skills."

"Dahlia means well," he said. "You need to remember, not
everyone grew up with people who loved them."

That was the other thing. If there was a positive side to a
situation or person, Dad was going to mine it out and focus on it,
which made it difficult to—

"Pops!"

My brother Theo walked in wearing his long coat and carrying his trumpet case. He'd had a gig and told us he'd be late.

Dad stood up from the bench and they embraced as though
they hadn't just seen each other the day before.

"Happy birthday, man."

"We were gonna start a second set soon. How you feelin'?
You bring that trumpet of yours?" Total rhetorical question.

Theo looked at him in mock astonishment. "Did I bring

my trumpet? *Did I bring my trumpet?* Does a bird bring his wing? Does a chicken bring hot sauce?" He held up the trumpet case.

Dad laughed and kissed the side of his face. He then held Theo's chin between his fingers and gave it a shake. "Yeah, you brought that trumpet, but are you up for playin' or are you tired already? You gettin' old yourself, son, and I don't want you to pass out from fatigue."

"I'm ready when you are, old man. I'm ready to teach the old dog a few tricks. You better focus, 'cause I might have to leave you in the dust. I don't care that it's your birthday."

"You just try, son. My skills may intimidate you. Get that trumpet squawkin' like a dyin' bird."

They laughed and embraced again.

"We have to get everybody together and jam before the night is over," Dad said. He smiled at me, then kissed my cheek and gave my hand a squeeze. "I got all my kids together under the same roof. Can't ask for a better birthday present."

His eyes lit up as he looked from me to Theo. That was Dad. You couldn't stay mad at him if you wanted. Despite any faults, despite all the women, we knew we were loved, and that made all the difference. He grinned at me. "What can I play for you to-night, baby? Next set, first song is yours."

I ran through the hundreds of songs I could choose from. I settled on "How Deep Is the Ocean," one of my favorites.

He took his pencil and a piece of paper from his pocket and wrote it down. "You got it, baby."

I gave him a long, hard hug. It was not lost on me that I could ask the one and only Lincoln T. Ross to play me a tune.

"Abbey."

"What?"

"Abbey."

I opened my eyes just as Bendrix pushed my head off his shoulder. It took a second to find my bearings. Joan sat on my left, Bendrix on my right. I traded in Bendrix's shoulder for Joan's and leaned against her and closed my eyes. "What time is it?"

"Ten minutes until midnight," I heard Bendrix say. "Wake up."

I snuggled against Joan. Working as a baker meant I often had to be at Scratch by four a.m., sometimes three, so I was usually asleep by ten.

Bendrix again: "Abbey. Wake up. You can do this. We believe in you." He sounded distracted and like he had no faith in me at all.

I opened my eyes. I didn't want to miss out and could already feel that the quick nap had given me a boost.

The living room was packed wall to wall with people. I saw my brothers Dizzy and Miles laughing with my sister Billie. Theo was making a fool of himself trying to play someone's saxophone: Every few seconds a whale died. Rita and her husband, Doug, and my sister Dinah and her husband sat on the opposite couch talking.

Joan handed me a cup of steaming chai. "Have some of this. It'll help wake you up."

"Thanks." I recalled the evening's events while taking a couple of sips: I had danced with my niece and later Rita; my older brothers had killed it with their rendition of "Pent-up House"; I'd eaten too much of my own cake. And, oh yeah . . . *Damn*, my nineteen-year-old sister might be pregnant.

"You awake now?" Bendrix asked.

I closed my eyes. "Yep. I'm ready to roll. Ready to boogie."

"Good. I want to show you something." He held up his tablet.

"*He* responded," Joan said, as though maybe God himself had made contact while I'd napped. She laughed lightly.

"*He* who?" I mimicked.

Bendrix swiped to a new page and I saw RelaxinbytheBay's picture. I suppose I'd remembered everything that had happened thus far except that I'd sent a note to a complete stranger on an online dating site.

Bendrix gave me the tablet.

```
Abbey,

So glad you wrote. You seem intelligent
and honest and the qualities you mention
in your tagline. Can I give you a call
sometime? I'd enjoy meeting if we find
there's a connection. (You have a beautiful
smile, by the way.)

                              —Samuel
```

"See," Bendrix said. "You had him at hello."

"Goody," Joan blurted.

Bendrix and I exchanged looks. Joan never said words like *goody*.

She laughed and I wondered if the brandy had gone to her head.

I reread the message and thumbed through Relaxin's pictures. "He *is* cute; I'll give him that." I hit "reply" and typed a quick note, telling him I'd like to talk.

"Let the games begin," Joan said, raising her brows high and taking a gulp of her brandy.

Bendrix put his arm around me. "Good girl."

6

Stay as Sweet as You Are

$\mathcal{I}$ was brushing my teeth when I heard the doorbell. My date with RelaxinbytheBay, or rather Samuel, was within the hour, and I was taking my time getting dressed, including a nice leisurely bath. Samuel and I had talked on the phone the night after Dad's birthday party and made a date for the following Sunday. I had no expectations. (Well, except I thought it would be great if we hit it off and he turned out to be the love of my life, but I sure wasn't counting on it.)

I checked the peephole and saw Rita's face, as round as the moon. *Huh.* Out of all the wives, Rita rarely stopped by without a heads-up.

"Hey. This is a surprise."

She watched me brushing my teeth. "I'm sorry? *What did you say?*"

"I said, 'This is a surprise.'" I continued working on my upper canines with my toothbrush. For the record, there was barely any paste on the brush by then, and she could understand every word I was saying; she just didn't like the fact that I dared to open the door with a toothbrush in my mouth.

"Would it be too much to ask that you not greet guests while brushing your teeth?"

"You're family."

"That may be true, but you look like a rabid dog foaming at the mouth."

"You're exaggerating." I used my finger to wipe away a tiny dot of toothpaste on the side of my mouth. "Better?"

She stood on the porch as though waiting for something else. It took me a second to figure out exactly what, and when I did, I bowed down low like a court jester before a princess. "Would you like to come inside, Rita?"

"Yes, thank you." She kissed me near the cheek and stepped inside. She wore a soft pink coat and soft pink leather gloves and carried a soft pink handbag large enough for a small animal to climb into and live comfortably for years. She gazed absently around my living room as though, if she could, she'd quickly repaint the walls and rearrange the furniture. She meant no harm by her internal judgments; she simply thought her decorative and fashion skills were a benefit to all humankind.

Rita's husband, Doug, stepped inside next, grumbling about the lack of parking. He was a hulking six-four, and his height and girth immediately shrank my living room down in size.

"This is a surprise," I said. "What gives?"

He gave me a quick peck on the cheek. "Don't mind me. I'm playing chauffeur." He brushed his thinning blond hair from his forehead and began checking his phone. He had a ruddy round face and gave the impression that somewhere behind his small blue eyes he was remembering a naughty joke.

"Mind if I turn on your TV?"

"Not at all."

He found the remote and settled in with his arm stretched across the back of the couch. A sports commentator highlighted plays as whistles blew and men in tight pants and helmets chased a ball across a field.

"What's that?" I asked.

"That right there," Doug said, playing along, "is called football. Those men in the red and white are trying to take the ball from the men in silver and black."

It was a running joke with Doug and the family that most of us knew absolutely nothing about sports.

"Grown men chasing a ball," I teased. "Very exciting."

"That it is. I love my wife like nobody's business, but football is more exciting than watching a bunch of men in tights leap across a stage; I don't care what she says."

"Douglas," Rita said halfheartedly. They both knew going into their marriage that Rita would never like football. Once a year, however, she dressed in her finest silver and black and went to a Raiders game, and Doug, who would never like the ballet, would put on a tux and attend the annual gala for the Oakland ballet, which he and Rita helped fund.

He shot up and held his hand toward the TV. "Catch it! Catch it! *Yeah!* Curtis Randolph is killin' 'em tonight."

Rita and I exchanged looks: *Silly game. Very silly.*

Doug was an investment banker with a gift for making money but no real interest in keeping it. He handed most of it over to his wife while using what was left for his favorite hobby, making his own beer with the original marque Doug's Beer. Mostly he liked food, and he prided himself on his ability to put away three servings of Bailey's gumbo and eat a cream puff from Scratch in two bites. *Speaking of which . . .*

"Say, Abbey, you have anything I can snack on?" Doug asked.

"One of your chocolate chip cookies or something like that from the bakery?"

"Sure, help yourself."

He hoisted himself up and started toward the kitchen. I, meanwhile, excused myself to wipe my face and put away my toothbrush.

When I returned, Rita was still standing in the living room. I explained that I was happy they had stopped by but I had to leave within the hour.

"Yes, that's why I'm here. We were in the neighborhood and I remembered you had your date."

Doug bellowed from the kitchen: "In the neighborhood by a long shot. My wife is just putting her two cents in when no one asked, nothing new. She's as cute as she can be, but try not to pay her any mind."

Rita looked at me and shook her head. "I'm only curious about what you're going to wear." She pitched her voice toward the kitchen, adding, "And we *were* in the neighborhood. We had drinks with friends."

Doug walked past with a small plate loaded with cookies from Scratch and chips from the grocery store. He paused when he reached Rita. "If you call Lafayette 'in the neighborhood,' I'd like to stop by LA before we head home." He continued to the TV with a chuckle.

Rita gave me a look: *My silly husband.* She loved him, though. After all, she liked to be looked after and he liked to look after her: perfect match.

"You came all the way here to see what I was wearing on my date? I'm not some thirteen-year-old schoolgirl going to her first boy-girl dance."

"I realize that. I was there for your first dance, and you should be grateful I talked you out of those bell-bottoms, and you should be grateful I'm here now. So, what are we planning to wear?"

"We? I don't know about you, but I know what I'm wearing and it has nothing to do with you. Believe it or not, I've been on a few dates before and I've managed just fine."

"Oh, really? You, who's been single for how long? Sweetheart, that's exactly why I'm here. Something isn't working. You want a man? You have to attract a man. I haven't seen you in a dress since Dinah's wedding." She glanced over her shoulder at Doug. "Isn't that right, honey? When was the last time you saw Abbey in a dress?"

"Yeah, a long time ago. Fumble. . . . Fumble! *Fumble!*"

"You remember how pretty she looked in her bridesmaid's dress?"

"Yeah, real pretty. Get it! Get it! Interception! Run! Run!"

Rita held me by the shoulders. "Let me help you. You need male energy in your life, and I don't mean Bendrix or your brothers." She chucked her head toward Doug. "You need *that* kind of male energy, and I can help you get it. We'll do something with that hair of yours and find a nice dress. There must be one dress in that closet of yours." She held my chin between her fingers and examined my face. "And we'll put on a little lipstick and eye shadow. It'll be fun."

Doug shouted from his seat, "You idiot! What kind of stupid call is that?"

After Rita and Doug left, I stared at my reflection in my full-length bedroom mirror; Rita's version of me stared back. I had on heels that I'd unearthed from my closet and a dress I'd worn to a friend's engagement party. Rita had curled my eyelashes and added enough mascara to make my eyes look wide and awake. Blush brought out my cheekbones, and my wild tumble bush—sometimes known as hair—had been curled and was held back from my face by two stealth bobby pins. The dress paired with the shoes made my legs look longer and gave my hips some curve. I turned slightly to the left so I could see the ass I'd forgotten I had.

Avery had never cared about things like high heels and straight hair, and we'd both liked dressing funky and making a statement with our clothes. After I bought the bakery I'd made my fashion statement with the assortment of clogs I wore in every color. My hair was rarely out of a ponytail.

The woman in the mirror stared back at me. She would turn heads. She was sexy and confident. The woman in the mirror knew what she wanted and went after it. She didn't care if she found love or had babies, because she needed no one; no, the woman in the mirror knew it was only a matter of time before she met the perfect guy, and she would give birth to her child while wearing full makeup and heels.

I liked the woman in the mirror, appreciated how put together she was, that she was the type who'd get her nails and toes done every two weeks and visit the beauty parlor weekly to keep up her hair. But no, the woman in the mirror was not me.

I was a woman who wanted to wear jeans and a vintage top. I was a woman who heeded her parents' advice and knew it was best to be myself. I was a woman who was savvy enough not to overly romanticize a single date with a stranger. In fact, I was a woman who was prepared for the date to go poorly and who knew she'd go home afterward and call her best friend and give him details while changing back into her sweats; then she'd curl up with a glass of wine and watch a movie. Besides, I was a woman who wanted someone who loved me for me.

I checked the time. I had roughly fifteen minutes to change into a different outfit and get to the restaurant. I took off my high heels, tossed them back in the closet, and unzipped my dress. If the date didn't go well and Samuel turned out to be a bore or a jerk or an ass, I'd at least be comfortable. Sorry, Rita.

*D*uring our chat on the phone, Samuel and I had agreed to meet at Bucciolio's, an Italian restaurant we both liked. The dating site recommended that people meeting for the first time should stick with coffee or lunch, but our phone chat had been pleasant enough that we'd decided to go for dinner; we'd even joked that if there wasn't any chemistry we'd at least get a good meal out of the evening. Now it was a matter of seeing if he came close to looking like his picture and if he knew better than to pick his nose or do any number of other things that could make the date go wrong.

I'd told Samuel I owned a bakery but hadn't told him it was within walking distance of the restaurant where we were meeting. I paused in front of Scratch's dark windows, then walked up to the sign hanging from a blue ribbon on the inside of the door. I'd made the sign with my niece, Mykaila, who was ten at the time. On black construction paper I'd drawn two silhouettes of a woman in an apron. Mykaila had cut the silhouettes and pasted them on either side of heavy paper, then painted *fermé* (French for closed) on one side and *ouvert* (open) on the other. It was a happy time. I was only a day from opening and everything was in place. Mykaila and I had the bakery to ourselves and took our time working on the sign while eating chocolate chip cookies.

I thought about how far I'd come since that afternoon as I continued walking. I had a lot to be proud of. My business was booming and I could bake the hell out of a cake, a cookie, a pie— you name it. I was fine. I was woman—hear me roar! Did I really need to date? Except for sex (oh, how I missed it at times!), did I really need to bother? I mean, cupcakes and wedding designs I understood, but men? Men were an entirely different species when you got down to it. And if Samuel was as normal as he sounded on the phone and as good-looking as he appeared in his photos, and I liked him, he might not like me, and then I'd have to deal with the awkward *I'll call you* as his parting shot. Blech. Dating: Who needed it? My comfort zone was my comfort zone for a reason, and if I wanted to spend my life growing my career and not worrying about having a family and all the rest, that was my prerogative. I caught my reflection in a store window and played with my hair before checking the time on my phone. Prerogative or no, I was running late, and I told myself to clam it and deal. *Get over yourself, Abbey. Let's do this.*

The host greeted me while I searched the restaurant (wood tables, open kitchen, a full bar lit up like Christmas) for Samuel. I was saying a little prayer that he'd at least somewhat resemble the photo he'd posted on the Web si—

There.

A table near the left wall.

His skin was the same dark brown as Dad's, and it glowed warm and soft under the dim lights. Skin you could lose yourself in, I immediately thought. He sat up straight as he read the menu; his shirt was crisp and his jacket was draped neatly behind him on his chair. And there, right below his perfectly kissable lips, was the Cary Grant cleft in his chin as promised in his photos. He was so gorgeous, so fiiiiine, as Bailey would say, my first impulse was to crawl into his lap and say, *Marry me?* My second impulse was to run home as quickly as possible and change back into the dress. I could hear Rita in my ear then: *I told you! I told you!*

I started to take a step backward, but as soon as our eyes locked, I knew it was too late to turn and run.

It was when he began to stand from the table that I saw Ella

Fitzgerald, enshrouded in a golden light and magical pixie dust, floating down from jazz heaven. Not the skinny Ella but the Ella who'd dwarfed Louis Armstrong in size. She wore a yellow dress that flowed around her feet as she drifted to and fro behind an unknowing Samuel. When music began to play, she beckoned me forward and said in her surprisingly girlish soprano, *He's so handsome! You are so lucky! Don't be afraid. Come say hello!* She then began singing "Someone to Watch Over Me."

When we were kids, Dad would tell us that all musicians went to jazz heaven after they left the earth, and sometimes they liked to come back to pay a visit. Bendrix often said he'd heard gunshots before he went to bed as a kid, while I was being tucked in with stories about jazz heaven. What could I say? That's how we grew up. And while I didn't really see visions (no, I wasn't that wacky), I did like to imagine the greats looking out for me.

On the night I'd first met Avery, for instance, I'd imagined Miles Davis paying me a visit. He leaned next to one of Avery's paintings at the gallery, playing "My Funny Valentine" on his trumpet. I stared at Avery and then at Miles and knew I was done for. When I stepped closer, Miles said in his gravelly, throaty voice: *This Avery Brooks motherfucker is the fuckin' real deal; he's a fuckin' cool cat.* (Sorry to drop the f-bombs, but that was Miles—*F this, F that.*) He continued: *If I was alive right now instead of in this fucking fantasy of yours, I'd buy all these motherfucking paintings.* I should've known that seeing an image of Miles when I'd met Avery was a bad sign, though. *Miles and that fusion period.* What was that about? Dad, and everyone, said he needed to expand—that's what a genius does, but I still thought his foray into that period opened the road to all the pseudo-contemporary mess we have to put up—

"Abbey? I'm Samuel."

"Yes, you are. I'm Abbey." I'd been so lost in thought I hadn't realized he had approached me.

"Yes, nice to meet you."

"I should have worn a dress."

"Excuse me?"

I felt myself grow hot. Had I said that out loud? Shit. "Nothing." I reached for a save: "I just said I feel—slightly underdressed."

"You look fine." I caught him looking me over as he pulled out my chair.

I hadn't realized I'd been holding my breath until he smiled full on, a razzle-dazzle, top-hat-and-tails, kick-up-your-heels smile. "It's very nice to meet you in person."

Ella peeked out from behind him with a big grin and pinched both of his cheeks. *He likes you! Isn't he cute?* She sang a few bars of "Stay As Sweet As You Are" before floating back from whence she came.

Samuel sat down across from me and stared as if he'd just received good news from a friend.

"What?" I asked.

"Nothing," he said.

"Tell me." Now I was smiling, too.

"It's nothing. I just . . . I'm happy you look like your picture—better, even. I've been looking forward to this, but you know, you just never know if a person, if, well—"

He started to stumble over himself. But knowing that he was relieved that I looked like my picture meant that he'd been nervous about meeting me, which helped me relax a little. "You don't have to explain," I told him. "I feel the same. You never know with online dating, right?"

"Right."

He smiled his smile and I felt myself grow warm around my

neck and chest. I watched as he evened out his knife and fork so that the ends were aligned. It struck me that he hadn't a clue about how handsome he was. Erase that. Surely he knew; how could he not? But at least he didn't carry himself with an *I am the man; I am all that and then some* vibe, which, as we all know, can be a total turnoff. I wondered how it came to be that he still had some self-conscious humility intact, if he was raised not to focus on looks, or if maybe he'd been hurt in a relationship, or both. I knew I couldn't ask about either after we'd barely said hello, but I was determined to say something about the hot, sexy elephant in the room: Why did a man like him need to meet people through online dating?

I waited as we discussed the weather and asked, "How was your day?" We'd chatted on the phone, after all, so it wasn't like we were complete strangers. I folded my hands on the table. "So I'm curious," I said. "Why does someone like you need online dating? Seems to me all you have to do is walk out the door."

He chuckled. "I could ask the same about you."

"Thanks. But you're avoiding the question."

"It's nothing you haven't heard before. I don't like the bar scene, stopped going to clubs years ago, and I put in long hours at the office. It's as simple as that. Why are you doing the online thing?"

"My best friend sabotaged me. Although right about now, I'm really glad he did."

"Same. In my opinion, it's not how a couple meets; it's whether they stay together or not. I have to tell you, Abbey, I'm looking for something that lasts, and if I have to find her through online dating, that's fine with me. I just want to find her. Dating gets old." Embarrassed, he smiled and centered his already centered plate between his aligned knife and fork. "I'm sorry. Way too much information."

I imagined little hearts fluttering from my chest and floating toward him.

"No need to apologize. I feel the same."

He took out his phone and laid it on the edge of the table. "Sorry about this, but my father is out of town and I'm looking after my mother. She tends to worry if I don't pick up. Do you mind?"

"Not at all."

The waitress came with the wine list and they began talking Wine. I couldn't speak that language so let them have at it. When he saw a wine he liked listed on the menu, Samuel asked if I would mind if he ordered a bottle for the table. I realized how much I was starting to like him. Not because he knew wines, but from the way he spoke with the waitress and carried himself. He reminded me of Bendrix in that he was smart and handsome and had a smattering of pretention around the edges. Although, goodness knew, with Bendrix there could be much more than a smattering.

The waitress returned with the wine and poured a touch in Samuel's glass to see if it was to his liking. It was. After pouring, she clasped her hands in front of her long white apron and described the specials. "Tonight's special is Samuel Sterling Howard. Thirty-seven. Six feet tall with a sexy, toned body. He's been a partner with Gibson Davis McCarthy for several years. Unlike other men you've dated in the past, he does not come with the requisite artist's baggage, which, let's face it, once appealed to you. He follows politics, reads *The Economist*, and listens to NPR. He's not a fan of Brussels sprouts or broccoli. If you notice the phone on his left, he's obviously a man who loves his mother."

"I'll let you look over the menu and decide?" She bowed slightly and left the table.

. . .

e chatted about anything and everything, letting the conversation fall on whatever topic it wanted to land on.
Something about the way Samuel ate his food—with exact movements, his long fingers like a praying mantis over his knife and
fork, which he used at the same time—completely charmed me.
He chewed thoroughly between bites and sat up properly. He ate,
in short, like a man who'd grown up in a series of boarding
schools. But I knew he'd gone to public schools in Alameda and
later El Cerrito: nothing fancy. He was shy in telling me he'd
earned a 4.0 and was valedictorian of his class.

Halfway through the meal and the bottle of wine, we were
flirting heavily, tasting each other's food, and laughing and talking
in overlapping sentences. The men in the restaurant shook their
heads and thought, *Looks like* he's *getting laid tonight,* while the
women sighed with envy: *I remember when my husband/boyfriend/
partner looked at me like that. She's so lucky.*

When his phone dinged, he held up his finger and apologized. "It's my mother. Mind if I take it?"

"Of course not."

"Mother? Yes. Hello. No, I told you that wouldn't be possible.
No, Mother. I told you I didn't have time." I wasn't sure if I
thought it was odd or endearing that he addressed his mother as
Mother. He shot me a look, then turned slightly. "I can't right
now," he said in a muted voice. "No, I'm not." He glanced my way
and mouthed, *One second.*

I decided to stop staring and check my messages so that I
wouldn't appear to be eavesdropping, even though that's exactly
what I was doing.

A text from Bendrix: *????????!!!!*

I texted back: *Hot smart nice!*

My second message was from Carmen. Her appointment for

the pregnancy test was tomorrow, and, as promised, I was taking her. She wanted to know if she could sleep over tonight. I texted back a yes. Carmen spending the night was a win-win, actually. The old Abbey had a habit of sleeping with a man before she knew his middle name or how he liked his coffee. I was determined to date responsibly, and I liked that I was now locked into my decision: No matter how attractive I found Samuel, he would not be coming home with me.

"No, Mother. Saturday. Yes. Father told you he would pick them up directly. How was your doctor's appointment? What did she tell you? Good. Glad to hear it."

Okay, yes, he might have sounded like he belonged in an era when men wore black tie to dinner, but it was obvious that he cared about his mother and looked out for her.

"I'll call later tonight to see how you're doing. Because. *Because*," he said, lowering his voice further. "I'm out. It doesn't matter where. If I have time, but I'm not sure right now. Yes. I'll call you later. Yes, I *promise*. Bye." He hung up. "Sorry about that."

"Didn't want to tell her you were on a date?" I teased.

"*Date* is a dangerous word as far as I'm concerned. I use it around my mother and she'll immediately jump to marriage."

"It's nice that you look after her."

"I feel it's my duty. I have a lot of respect for my parents. Dad is originally from Trinidad. Mom is from Atlanta. They met in college and have been married for over thirty years. I know marriage is passé in many respects, but I grew up seeing two people work damn hard to raise their kids and stay together no matter what. My parents are old-fashioned, and I appreciate their values. I'm just old-school when it comes to certain things. Like marriage. I think we as a nation, and especially we as a people, have completely lost sight of the value of the institution. Nowadays people marry and divorce like a vow means absolutely nothing in the world. Anyway, don't get me started. How about you? Your folks married?"

"Uh . . ." I thought for a second. How to explain that my family was anything but old-fashioned? As for the institution of marriage . . . *ha!* I took a sip of wine. "Uh . . ." Then another. Wait. One more. "Well, let's see. . . . My mom and dad divorced when I was ten. She lives in Connecticut. My dad? My dad . . ." *Has been married so many times it'll make your head spin.* "My dad is married to a woman he loves very much and they recently gave birth to a baby boy." I felt something closing off inside. Sure, I'd told him the truth, but that I'd omitted the rest of the story made me feel guilty. I'd never been ashamed of my family and I didn't want to start now. So I told him everything. I told him about the wives, the exes, and my twelve siblings. So much for the value of the institution or whatever he was ranting about. I had a feeling I'd reached the breaking point. Which was fine. It wasn't as if I didn't value marriage. I loved the idea of two parents—together forever. I wanted to know what that would be like more than anything, but I didn't want someone judging my family either.

I watched Samuel whirl the wine in his glass, his eyebrows knitted. *"Thirteen of you."* He let out a hollow-sounding whistle. "And you said your dad has been married *four* times?"

"Five. But who's counting?"

He didn't smile as I'd hoped. He looked at me, his tone earnest. "Do you see yourself ever getting married, or are you one of those free spirits?"

"I love my dad and my mom, but I would like to spend my life with one person. As much as I love my stepmothers, I'd like for my own kids to have *one* mother."

"So you do want kids?"

Yes!

"Yes, I do. And I know my family sounds strange, but they're very important to me." I felt my cheeks grow warm. "Now I'm giving too much information."

"Don't worry about it. We're being honest with each other." He reached across the table and gave my finger a shake. "It's been nice getting to know you. I feel very relaxed around you. You're a relaxing person." He looked down and saw that our fingers were still touching, then took his time to hook his finger around mine and pull it toward him. When I tried to take my finger back, he grinned and pulled harder. It was silly, our game of tug-of-war across our table, but it was a way to finally address all that sexual energy going on between us. I liked him. I also thought I got him. I even gathered what he was like as a child and could so easily picture him at the age of five, dressed neatly in a long-sleeve shirt tucked into crisply ironed pants, making sand castles in the school yard, every detail of his castle painstakingly neat and perfect. And then my five-year-old self would come along, my hair in two huge Afro puffs, and I'd laugh and start to destroy his sand castle, thinking that was the point of a sand castle, the destruction! And later we'd color together and he'd tell me I was doing it all wrong because I'd colored the people on my page purple and green. I'd ruined everything because I'd colored outside the lines. That's when I'd laugh and take my crayon and color all over his page, too. I saw us so clearly as kids.

After letting go of my finger, he cleared his throat and straightened his fork on his plate.

At this point there was only one last hurdle. I swallowed. "So. I have a question."

"Shoot away."

"Do you like jazz?"

"Is that the kind of music your dad plays?"

"It is. He's actually well-known. Lincoln T. Ross?"

His face remained blank.

People either freaked out when I told them who my father was or they responded like Samuel, clueless to the jazz world. (I will confess that I was disappointed, however, because if he didn't know Dad's name, that meant he didn't know jazz.)

"Can't say that I know the name," he said. "I'm not a big fan of jazz. I don't like it."

"How can you not like jazz? That's like saying you don't like happiness."

He grinned. "I don't know. All that tootin' and blaring." He wiggled his fingers in the air and made loud noises like a player high on acid. "It's too much."

I sucked in a breath. "I'm trying my best not to judge you right now."

He laughed. "Thanks."

I sighed. First red flag of the night and it was a doozy. Of course, whether a guy I dated liked jazz wasn't all that important, except—it was really, really important! I was from a jazz family. I spoke jazz. Hell, as many exes and wives as Dad had brought home, they all shared a love for jazz—well, everyone except Dahlia, who was an oddball anyway. Even Avery, for all his problems, loved jazz. It was as if we could always fall back on our two private languages—art and jazz. During the heady days of money and fame, we went to see Jason Moran at the Village Vanguard. Moran was lost in every song, and whatever he was feeling he sent through his fingers and onto those piano keys and out to us. Avery and I didn't touch or look at each other for the entire set, we were so transfixed. Once we were home, though, without warning, Avery kissed me hard on the mouth, then pushed me over the couch headfirst, and somehow my pants were off and he was behind me and—*Hell, Avery was a liar and a cheat and a lying cheat, but, oh glory, he was so good in—*

Anyway, enough of Avery. There was a red flag on the table I had to deal with. Samuel didn't like jazz. Not the biggest problem, but it was a problem, and I could feel the doubt creeping in as different parts of me bounced off one another.

My heart: *He wants kids and he's great with his mother and he's so cute. Who cares that he doesn't like jazz?*

My head: *Slow down! You haven't known this guy for two hours. Give him time. It's just the first date. You* can *teach* him *about jazz!*

My gut: *Date's over. I'm out. This is bullshit. I don't want to date anyone who doesn't like jazz. And I don't trust the whole uptight thing you find so charming. Something seems off, like he's too rigid. Check, please!*

I considered my options until he took my hand.

"Hey," he said. "You okay?"

Suddenly nothing else mattered except the feel of his skin on mine. "I'm fine. Except I have one more question: You don't like smooth jazz, do you?"

"No, not really. That's not a problem, is it? Does your father play smooth jazz?"

I almost choked. "Never. Ever." I sighed, relieved. "Well, that's a start. Not all jazz is like what you think. Ever hear Bill Evans play 'All of You' or Miles Davis's version of 'My Funny Valentine'?"

"Can't say that I have."

"Good. I'll have to play a few songs for you sometime. Open up your world."

The waitress appeared with the dessert menu. Bucciolio's was perfectly fine for dinner, but not the best when it came to desserts. I didn't know their pastry chef, but he or she tended to pair odd ingredients for the sake of surprising the patrons and not from any sense of taste.

"I wouldn't mind sharing something," Samuel said, looking over the menu.

"How would you feel about a pear tart served with crème fraîche?"

"Sounds good, but I don't see it listed."

I looked at him from over the top of my menu and smiled. "It's not."

7

In the Middle of a Kiss

I turned on the lights at Scratch, and my bakery was instantly flooded with a soft glow, as if lit by candles. It was after eight, and even though the rooms were empty and silent, I liked to think that the wood tables and floral bouquets in mason jars helped the place emanate warmth and comfort.

Samuel walked around taking everything in—the mahogany bar and exposed brick behind the register, the display cases and the artwork. Scratch was my second home, and it meant a lot that I'd brought him there. "This is nice, Abbey. Very nice. It has an old-timey vibe, but it's hip, too. I like it."

"Thanks." I walked behind the counter, where we kept the stereo, and found the song I wanted. I hit "play" and a melancholy trumpet filled the bakery. I raised my finger in the air as I walked back toward Samuel. "That," I said, "is Miles Davis. To make a horn sound like that? My brother says the trumpet has to have voice." I closed my eyes briefly. "Hear the tenderness? It's like being wrapped in velvet." I took in a breath; then, remembering myself, I opened my eyes and saw Samuel staring. Embarrassed, I went for my apron. "Coffee?"

"Yeah, that would be great."

$\mathcal{T}$he only good thing to come from my breakup with Avery was that it helped me to afford pastry school and the down payment for Scratch. Sales for Avery's original artwork skyrocketed once everyone realized he was never coming back from Mexico, or wherever the hell he was hiding. The story of Avery Brooks Gone Missing added to his notoriety, which added to the value of his *original* work. I owned several of his paintings by then, all gifts and never shown. Can you say *ka-ching*? I took every last piece to his manager and told him I wanted top dollar. Not a month later, what I called my Avery's Artwork Sucks Fund was born. I had enough money to afford a house, or a year of travel around the globe, or both. I chose instead to move out of our loft and rent a studio apartment in a so-so area of Oakland. Thanks to the Fund, I had enough money in the bank to lie on my couch for years, and I was so depressed, I planned to do just that.

One day I happened to watch a cooking show because I was too tired to pick up the remote and change the channel. I watched a woman bake dinner rolls. Seems simple now, but back then I was fascinated. *That's yeast?* What?! Bendrix's mother, who'd passed only a year before, had made everything from scratch, including dinner rolls and buttermilk biscuits and cinnamon buns dripping with icing, but I'd never actually watched her make anything. In her honor, I copied the recipe, got off my butt, and went to the store to purchase ingredients. My rolls came out like rocks, surely hard enough to knock someone unconscious, but I hadn't felt as excited about anything in years. Baking gave me that old feeling I'd had when Bendrix and I were graffiti artists.

How to describe it . . . ? *Joy* might be one word. There was the added bonus that baking was something I'd found for myself and had nothing to do with Avery, or his career or his art. I began teaching myself to bake—*everything.* All too soon I was in charge of baking my family's birthday cakes and all other treats and desserts. A year later, I decided to attend pastry school.

I gave Samuel an edited version of my story. Much edited. When he asked how I became interested in baking, I took a sip of the cappuccino I'd made and told him that I'd discovered I had a talent for it and left it at that.

We headed to the kitchen. I brought out one of the chairs from my office for him to use while I took out the tray of single-serving tart crusts and grabbed a handful of sliced pears. After arranging the pears, I coated the tart with butter, sugar, and cinnamon. As I worked, I told him about Art Tatum, whose song "In the Middle of a Kiss" was now playing.

"You really know a lot about jazz."

"My dad isn't just any old musician; he's kind of a legend." I sounded irritated.

"I think I've heard of him, now that I think about it, but I don't know his music." I could tell he was scrabbling, which irritated me more. I didn't like that he'd lie just to be polite, especially when it really didn't matter.

"Seriously. Don't worry about it." But I could still hear the tightness in my voice.

I shaved cinnamon on top of the tart, my movements less fluid than before. The mood between us grew solemn. I'd been irritated with him for maybe a second, but now I was angry with myself for coming across like I was looking down on him and for basically ruining what had been such a pleasant evening. I could already see myself telling the wives and Bendrix how I'd ruined the date with my mood and how the night took a turn for the worse. I saw myself in the wives' room at Dad's house, clutching a pillow to my chest as I whined, *He was so handsome and interesting. He was just the kind of guy I'm looking for. He wanted kids! And I could tell he was trustworthy and decent and sexy. And I blew it! I came off like some uppity jazz fanatic who looks down on people who don't listen to jazz!* And then Bendrix's reply: *You are an uppity jazz fanatic who looks down on people who don't listen to jazz.*

I knew it was my responsibility to turn the tide, to say something—anything—that would put Samuel and me back on the road to romance, but I couldn't think of anything and continued torturing the tarts. I kept moving, happy for an excuse not to look at him. Art Tatum, sounding like he was banging on the piano now, was the only sound in the bakery.

I was so intent on the tarts, I hadn't noticed that Samuel was on his feet. *Here we go*, I thought. I waited for an excuse about why he had to leave—*Hey, listen, my mother just texted me and I have to bolt. Catch you another time?* Whatever. Fine. I'd finish the tarts and take them to my house and eat them with Carmen. Men were jerks. Men sucked. Just because I sounded a little annoyed, I was suddenly too much to deal with or whatever he thought. He was probably looking for some placid woman who he believed was born to serve him, a woman who had his dinner ready and waiting as soon as he was home from work. Well, that wasn't me. I had a business to run. I had opinions, and, yes, damn it, I had mood swings. *It's called being alive, Mr. Howard. . . .*

He stepped closer. I felt my heart skip when he stood behind me. I stopped all my fluttering about as soon as I felt his hand on top of my hand. I felt like a character in a nineteenth-century novel where handholding was as sexually charged as a full-blown kiss. He brought his face so close to mine, I could feel his breath against my cheek and his chest touch my back ever so lightly. I inhaled the scent of his aftershave. He didn't say a word, just laced his long fingers through mine and held on. "I think this music is working on me. Who did you say this was?"

I snorted, unladylike and loud: the sound of relief. "Art Tatum."

I turned and he touched his nose to mine and we kissed. I kept my hands in the air so I wouldn't get flour all over him— not that he seemed to care. I was soon falling back against the counter. "The tarts." I laughed.

He smiled and pulled away. "I want to tell you something."

"Uh-oh."

"Try not to be so negative, Abbey."

"You're right." I grabbed a towel and wiped my hands. "So?"

"Well." He picked up a ladle and positioned it next to one of the tart pans. He then dug his hands in his pockets. "I just want to tell you what a nice time I'm having tonight. I love what you've done with this bakery and that you own your business. You're smart, bright, and like I said, I feel relaxed around you and you seem like a very together woman."

I decided to help him along: "Buuut . . ."

"But . . . nothing. I was going to say, I'd love to see you again."

I felt the crease in my eyebrows collapse. "Really?"

"Yeah. Would you want to see me again?" I watched his face for some clue that he was joking with me. Then he cut his gaze as if my answer might be anything other than an emphatic yes, and looked down at the ladle and moved it again with his thumb so that it was even with one of the tarts. It was then I remembered the boyish nerd in him. He'd mentioned during dinner that his parents were so strict, so concerned with his doing well and getting into the college of his choice, that he hadn't been allowed to date much. He'd laughed it off when he saw the surprise on my face, and the subject was dropped. I imagined that he'd been forced to wait so long to date that he was a nervous wreck around girls and so unsure of himself that by the time he turned sixteen he hadn't wanted to bother; he was too busy by then with his studies. I saw him neatly dressed every day, always the first to raise his hand in class, always in the front row. While other kids were making out and doing drugs, getting pregnant and going to juvie or zoning out on all the things teenagers zoned out on, Samuel was on the debate team and played chess and kept up with his studies. He had one goal in life: get the hell out of Alameda High and make something of himself. How else did you get into Stanford Law? How else was it that here was this man who seemed to have it all together yet was actually nervous about asking me out on a second date?

I touched the lapel of his jacket and pulled him close. "Of course I'll go out with you again."

We kissed, and I found my hands reaching up to hold either side of his face. I heard Shirley Horn singing "My Heart Stood Still," in her slow, breathy voice. Perfect.

Not thirty minutes later we sat at the counter taking our first bites of the warm pear tart. He wasn't a big fan of jazz, but he had confessed to having a sweet tooth. I fed him another mouthful and he chewed slowly. I felt dazed as I looked into his eyes. Now that we'd kissed, we couldn't stop touching each other. We'd talked enough. We never wanted to talk again. In fact, after a few more bites I was staring at his lips as they moved closer and closer to mine.

I'm not sure how I ended up off the barstool and on my feet, but I no longer cared who heard me moan; I no longer cared that I was grabbing hold of Samuel's back.

"Four years . . ."

"What's that?"

I mumbled a breathless "Nothing," then grabbed him by the collar and forced him to continue kissing me; my body was a wild bucking horse let out of the gate. My leg hooked around his thigh. Samuel took the move for the hint that it was and, after pausing to catch his breath, ran his finger down the length of my throat in a singular journey that ended at the tip of my collarbone.

His expression grew stark.

"What?" I whispered.

He tilted his head slightly, then took both my hands and pulled my arms out wide like a man finally taking control of his assailant. My chest jutted forward as his knee separated my legs and he pressed his body into mine with what felt like everything he had, harder and harder, while his lips kissed me everywhere—my face, my neck, back to my face again.

Four years! Now I wondered what the hell I'd been waiting for and let my body relax. I closed my eyes and rammed my tongue into his mouth. *The dry season ends right now. Tonight. Right here!* I heard him moan loudly as he cupped his hand over my breast. And then . . .

Then . . .

Nothing. Absolutely nothing. No hands pinning me down. No lips pressing against mine. I opened my eyes and stared at the ceiling. I then shot my head from left to right. *"Samuel?"*

I hoisted myself slowly up, only to see Carmen of all people staring back at me. She was breathing heavily and wielding a rolling pin over her shoulder like a batter at home plate.

"Carmen?"

"Are you okay?"

"Am I okay? Wha—?"

Finally, I saw Samuel standing off to the side of the bar, holding his hand to the back of his head while raising the other toward my sister as if to ward her off.

When he stepped forward, Carmen braced herself to take yet another swing. "Get back! You want some more of this, huh? I'm calling the police on yo' ass! You mess with my sister, and you mess with me! You best believe that shit!" If she sounded stilted, it was because her only knowledge of "street life" came from watching episodes of *The Wire*.

Samuel's eyes drooped. "I feel sick."

"Oh my God! Carmen, what did you do?"

She ignored me and moved closer to Samuel with her weapon, and trust me, we used professional pins made from marble, so depending on how you were holding them, they most certainly could be used as weapons.

I rushed over to Samuel. "Are you hurt?"

His head lolled one way, then the other. "I think I need to sit down."

"You know this guy?" Carmen asked.

"Of course I do!"

"But I thought he was trying to attack you!"

Samuel wobbled off to his left as though hoping to find footing on a sinking ship. "Hardly," he said.

"You should sit down." I took him by the elbow and led him to the nearest table. His head circled in a wide arc and he moaned.

"Carmen, look what you've done!"

"I barely hit him! He's exaggerating!"

Samuel looked up from where he sat while rubbing his head. "She hit me more than once. I think I feel something on the back of my head." I stood behind him and began searching for injuries. It wasn't long before I saw a small bruise about the size of a quarter. I immediately brought my hand to my mouth.

"I thought he was attacking you!" Carmen whined.

"Attacking me? Carmen, he's my date!"

She blinked. "Since when do you go on dates? Oh, is he from online?"

"What does it matter? Why are you even here? I thought we were meeting at my house."

"I went there first, but you were taking so long I figured you'd be here."

"Oooooh," Samuel groaned. "I feel sick." We both looked at him.

"Call nine-one-one," I barked.

"Nine-one-one? I didn't hit him that hard!"

"I beg to differ," he said.

"You beg to differ?" Carmen looked at me: *Who is this guy?*

"Let's calm down," I said. "Call Bendrix. Someone should look at him. He might have a concussion for all we know."

Carmen went for her phone. "Uncle Benny? It's Carmen. Can you come to the bakery? We kind of need your help. There was this guy I thought was raping Abbey. No, no! She's fine. Just get here." She hung up. "He's on his way."

"Run and get a bag of frozen—anything."

I leaned over so I could look at Samuel's face. "I'll get you some water. I'm so sorry. How are you feeling?"

"Better. I think it was the shock of it."

Carmen started toward the back but stopped mid-run. "I'm sorry," she said to Samuel. "I thought you were attacking—"

"Attacking your sister." Samuel sighed. "Yes, I know."

*B*endrix kept whatever opinion he had of the bruise to himself as he examined Samuel's head. Next he lifted Samuel's eyelids one at a time and checked his pupils. "Are you feeling nauseous?"

"Not anymore."

"Inhale for me."

Samuel took a deep breath and exhaled when he was told.

Carmen and I stood off to one side, holding hands. "This is kind of your fault, you know," she whispered.

"*My* fault?"

"Yeah. How was I supposed to know you knew him? God, the way he was going at you, it was like watching a vampire movie." She had the nerve to snicker.

I cut my eyes. "Is he going to be okay?" I asked Bendrix.

"He'll be fine." He offered his hand to Samuel. "Bendrix, nice to meet you."

"Samuel," he said, returning a weak handshake. "Thanks for your help, man."

"We're all just glad you're okay." Bendrix glanced at me and raised his brows: *He is good-looking.*

I widened my eyes: *I know!*

I heard Carmen calling my name from somewhere near the kitchen.

"Abbey! I need your help."

I said to Samuel: "I am so sorry this happened. I hope you'll forgive my sister."

He rubbed the back of his head and sat up fully. "Consider it forgotten."

Carmen yelled again: "Abbey. Could you come back here please?"

"No. What are you doing?"

"Just come back here. Now!"

I looked from Bendrix to Samuel. "Excuse me."

I walked back to the kitchen, but no Carmen. "Where are you?"

"In here."

I went to the restroom door, but it was locked. "What do you want, Carmen? What's going on?"

When she didn't respond, I pressed my ear to the door and tried the knob again. I could hear her sobbing. "Carmen? Are you okay?"

"We don't have to go to the clinic tomorrow."

"What? What are you talking about?"

"Why don't you have tampons in your bathroom? This is ridiculous. You should do something about it!"

I played with the doorknob. "Open the door, Carmen."

She began sobbing louder, pausing between words to gasp and take in air. "Abbey, I'm cramping. I don't feel so good."

"I'm getting Bendrix."

"No, don't!"

"What do you mean, no? You need a doctor and we should be grateful he's here." She was quiet. "Carmen?"

"Okay, but don't tell him what's happening."

"Carmen, he needs to know. I'll be right back."

I rushed to the front of the bakery. I was too worried about Carmen to get caught up in the crazy events of the evening: first Samuel with a bruise on the back of his head, and now my sister, sobbing in the bathroom, and from the sound of it, having a miscarriage. I sucked a breath of air in through my teeth. I had no time to agonize. "Bendrix! We need you back here. It's an emergency!"

I sat next to Carmen in her hospital bed. Our legs were stretched out, although she was under the covers and I was on top. We ate pudding from small plastic cups—horrible cafeteria pudding that tasted like glue blended with chocolate syrup. "God, this is terrible," I said.

"Not everyone needs their pudding made from the finest

chocolate in the world." She reached over, a hospital tag on her wrist, and I gave her my mostly untouched pudding.

I thought about years before when she was taking a time-out from her mom and spent the night at the loft where Avery and I lived. We'd been in bed together watching a movie, pretty much like we were now, except we had a bowl of popcorn between us. A man I didn't recognize walked in, and Carmen yelped and covered her mouth. "Oh my God!" Turned out he was an actor on a show she watched, there to buy one of Avery's paintings. Avery made introductions and the actor gave Carmen his autograph.

Now Bendrix sat in the chair near the bed, dozing on and off. He'd been on twenty-four-hour call the night before and working on very little sleep when we'd contacted him from the bakery.

Carmen's doctor had examined her and told us she would be fine, but we had to wait for the release papers. Once Carmen was feeling better, I told her she needed to call her mother (Dad was playing a gig in New York), but she refused. We quarreled about it, and she said she was an adult and she didn't want her mother or Dad to know what had happened, adding: "I definitely don't want Mom showing up here and talking about herself." So we ate pudding. Or rather, she ate pudding.

Bendrix jolted from a snooze, then went into doctor mode and looked at Carmen with keen focus. "How are you doing? Are you feeling okay?"

"I'm fine." She set the pudding on the table and sighed. "I wasn't going to keep it, anyway. I didn't want it. Not even a little. My life would've been ruined. I kept hoping this would happen. Now that it has—do you think I'll be punished?"

"For what?" Bendrix asked.

"I don't know. Maybe I willed this to happen."

"You've done absolutely nothing wrong," I said. "Nothing. This kind of thing happens. Tell her, Bendrix."

"Happens all the time."

"And it doesn't matter what you were going to do or not," I added. "The only thing that matters now is making sure that you're okay and you keep moving forward."

"Punishment has nothing to do with it," said Bendrix.

"Yeah," she said. "It was for the best. Sorry about your date."

I waited for Bendrix to tease her—*Way to ruin a date, slugger*—or I thought of making a joke, but it wasn't the right time.

I doubted I'd see Samuel again, anyway. The lump on his head, my nineteen-year-old sister miscarrying, seemed like too much for him. When we'd said good-bye, in fact, he'd made no mention of our tart or kisses, nor did he offer his hand or say he'd call.

I rested my head on Carmen's shoulder and she fed me a spoonful of nasty pudding. "Blech."

Once we were home, I changed into a pair of sweats and made tea. I also checked once more on Carmen, who was in my bed, then found a blanket and stretched out on the couch with my tea. It had been a long night, and while I was exhausted, I felt wide-awake, too. I supposed that finally being kissed after so many years, having a date with Samuel, and my sister's crisis were responsible. I wanted a moment to process it all. I clicked on the stereo and used the remote to find Charlie Parker. I was back to square one, but that was okay. My sister needed me. Tomorrow I'd spend the early morning with Carmen and go to the bakery at the very late hour of nine a.m. . . . I'd bake cinnamon buns, popovers . . . whatever she wanted. I curled up on my side. Now that I'd had a taste of male energy, I sure wanted more.

I hadn't realized I'd dozed off until I heard my phone. I clicked off the stereo and answered.

"Apologies, Abbey. It's Samuel."

"Hi. Why are you apologizing?"

"The hour. I know it's late, but I wanted to see how your sister was doing."

"She's fine, considering the circumstances. Thanks for checking." I sat up and pressed the phone closer to my ear.

"Are you still at the hospital?"

"No, I'm home. How are you?"

"I'm fine."

"I'm so sorry," I said.

"Now who's apologizing? Don't worry about it. I'm just glad your sister is okay."

"Are you sure you're feeling okay?"

"Yeah. I was also calling because I'd still like to go out again and I was wondering if you're free next weekend."

"Really?"

"You sound surprised."

"My sister hit you over the head with a rolling pin. You seemed standoffish when we were saying good night."

"I was worried about Carmen. I'd also been hit over the head. Abbey?"

"Yeah?"

"Try not to overthink things so much. I like you."

"You do?"

"We've only been on one date, but—damn—what a date."

I laughed.

"If things work out, we'll have a story to tell."

I lowered myself onto the couch and smiled. "Yeah, I guess we will."

"Besides, I never got to finish that tart. I'm hoping you'll make me another one."

"Anytime."

"Are you tired?"

"No, not really."

"You up for talking for a little bit? I like the sound of your voice."

I dug myself deeper into the couch and pulled the blanket up to my chin. "I like the sound of your voice, too."

8

I Fall in Love Too Easily

lmost two months later and I was meeting with Natasha and Kenny and discussing details for their wedding cake. It was an exciting time in my life. Finally, I, Abbey Lincoln Ross, was a wedding cake designer who was actually in a relationship— and, I'd daresay, a fabulous one. For once, I felt as happy as the couples who came to see me. A bonus: My wedding cake designs became . . . *more*—more romantic, more floral, more abstract, more of whatever the couple wanted, because that was exactly what I felt on the inside: *more* of everything. I, Abbey Lincoln Ross, had met a great guy, a gentleman, a grown-up; a guy who held a steady job and who was not interested in the art world and had never heard of the documentary I was in! Yay! He had a 401(k) and owned a house in Yountville. He downplayed it—*"I'd say it's closer to a cottage"*—but it sounded lovely, and we were driving there later that night. The next day, Abbey Lincoln Ross would wake up in Napa Valley's wine country and have a lovely breakfast of coffee and croissants she'd brought from Scratch, and then she and her boyfriend would visit one winery after another, all day long.

I was telling the couple I was meeting most of this—about Samuel and Yountville—when I noticed their rather apprehensive expressions. I supposed I had been rambling. "I'm sorry," I said, catching myself. "This is *your* time, and listen to me going on. I'm usually not like this."

Natasha told me not to worry. "I felt the same way when Kenny and I started dating." She took her fiancé's hand. She and Kenny had met while campaigning for Oakland's recent mayor-elect and were now part of his staff. They were in their early thirties and wore the vibe of a couple that was going places. Natasha wanted nothing to do with traditional wedding décor and had chosen two shades of green as her primary wedding colors. She even planned on wearing a light green wedding gown. Earlier in the consultation she'd said, "I don't care about white. I don't look good in white. So why do I need to wear a color I hate on my most special day? I like green and I want to be surrounded by it. You know what I say? Green represents bling. And that's what me and Kenny are about. Isn't that right, baby?"

Kenny nodded. "Whatever you say."

With her love of green in mind, I sketched a cake that would be made of pale green flowers of every sort with soft pink highlights. Since she wanted a cake that had, as she said, *"Bam!"* I drew tulips shooting from the top of the cake and falling out and over. I explained how I'd make the tulips so that they'd stay in place. If her dress would cause an eye-popping reaction, so would my cake.

Near the end of the meeting, Natasha told me not to worry that I'd rambled on about Samuel. She gave Kenny's hand a squeeze. "Just remember to stay in your man's corner no matter what. Men need to be looked after. Isn't that right, baby?"

Kenny looked up from his phone. "Yeah, baby. Whatever you say." She grabbed him at the jawbone. He had huge walrus-like cheeks and puffy lips. He turned to me and said, "Is the sex any good?"

"Kenny!" she admonished. Natasha's mouth remained wide-open as she groped for words. "Abbey, I don't know what's wrong with him. Kenny, what's wrong with you? Apologize!"

"She's the one yakking about her boyfriend on our dime. I should be able to ask what I want."

"But that's rude. You do realize that?"

"It's okay," I said.

"I wasn't trying to be rude, but . . . whatever you say."

"I shouldn't have to *say* anything."

"It's okay. Really. Let's move on."

"You're being ridiculous, Kenny. I'm so embarrassed right now."

"Whatever you say, Nat."

I felt bad for the guy. I *had* been running my mouth. I wiggled my index finger, indicating he should move closer. "If you really want to know, the sex is fabulous. Beyond great. We can spend hours together getting to know each other's bodies. Samuel's neck is a revelation, his back a newly discovered territory of muscles; his thighs are straits I trace with my fingertips."

Did I say any of this? Of course not! I averted my eyes and mentioned something about the contract. I was too embarrassed to talk about my sex life with a complete stranger—a client, no less—no matter that sex with Samuel was great.

*B*endrix texted soon after Natasha and Kenny were gone:

Still heading to Yountville tonight?

Yes! I'm so excited!!!! ☺

Abbey, I know you're happy and I'm happy
4u but can you cut all the !!!!! and the
☺ when you text?

No! I refuse!!! I'm so excited!!!! I like
him so much!!!

Fine. I'll see you when you get back.

Okay!!!! Yay!☺

Samuel held his hands over my eyes. "No peeking."

"I'm not. I can't see a thing."

I heard the door close. "Okay. One . . . two . . . three . . ."

He removed his hands. The house was much cozier than his apartment, which was so bare I'd assumed he hadn't been there long, and I was surprised when he'd told me he'd lived there for two years. The house in Yountville, on the other hand, felt homey and charming. It was dark outside by then, but at the top of the vaulted ceiling was a row of skylights. There was a fireplace, love seat, and sofa, and accents like deep-pile rugs and brightly colored vases.

Somehow he knew what I was thinking. "My apartment is where I sleep, but I like to think that this is my home. I come here whenever I can." He wrapped his arms around my waist. "Shall I give you a tour?" I felt his lips on my cheek. He held me closer as he took a step forward. The house was small enough that he kept his arms wrapped around me while we explored, our legs pressed together in tight unison. He didn't let go until we finished the tour—two bedrooms, two baths—and reached the kitchen. "Wine?"

"That would be great."

He went to a cabinet that revealed itself to be a wine refrigerator. He took a bottle out and studied the label. "I've been saving this one for a special occasion." I watched him take out glasses and a wine opener that looked like something designed by NASA.

We would have the entire weekend to ourselves. When I'd told my staff I wouldn't be coming in, they'd stared as though something had to be wrong. *Are you sick? Is someone in your family sick? Who died?* That kind of thing. It had been a long time since I'd allowed myself a full two days off.

Samuel and I clinked glasses. Drinking the wine was like drinking in the entire Napa Valley, all the growers and pickers, the leaves dancing under the sunlight, all at once. But I lacked the proper wine lingo and just said, "This tastes really good."

Samuel teased the wine on his tongue before swallowing. "Not bad. Solid concentration. Truffle-like aftertaste." He thought for a moment. "Has fortitude. Reminds me of a pinot I once had in Vienna."

I waited for him to make a joke that would signal he was merely parodying a wine snob. I mean, if any of my brothers had been there, they certainly would have given him shit. I could hear Dizzy raising a pinky: "Reminds me of the Ripple I had in Watts back in 'seventy-two." And then we all would've broken into laughter. But something told me to keep my mouth shut. I could certainly be a snob when it came to jazz, after all.

Samuel joined me at the table. "We'll have to hit a few of my favorite wineries tomorrow." He gazed around the kitchen. "So, what do you think of my place? You like it here?"

"I love it." I'd told him so several times already. I reached over and took his hand and kissed him. "I really love it here, Samuel. Thanks for inviting me."

"It was a dump when I bought it. Needed a new foundation and roof. Everything. I'd come out here and it was like a second job. More like a hobby. And then there was picking out all the finishes. Anyway, I love living in a city, but I want my kids to have a place to run around. I'm not into the country life, but out here is the perfect mix of both. I like to think of them coming here one day." He looked around the kitchen as though the kids were already creating havoc.

I joined him in the fantasy: a boy, a girl, racing into the kitchen and calling out for momma, Samuel telling them not to run in the house.

We grew silent. I listened to the quiet outside, a kind of quiet that a city like Oakland hadn't experienced since the first settler arrived.

"I'm glad you're here. Except for my sisters and parents, you're the first woman I've brought here."

"Really?"

"Yeah. I'm glad it's you and only you."

He ran his finger along the side of my face and kissed me.

He broke away and snapped his fingers. "I have a surprise for you. Stay right there."

About a minute later, I heard "So What" from Miles Davis's *Kind of Blue* playing through the speakers. Samuel stepped back into the kitchen. "Is that okay? I looked up 'best jazz songs' and downloaded a few albums. Do you like it?"

Kind of Blue was the album everyone knew, that and Dave Brubeck's *Take Five*. So yeah, of course I liked it. It was a classic. But it was also—not to sound harsh, or like a jazz snob— overplayed. I appreciated the gesture, though. Besides, I actually hadn't heard it in years.

"You don't like it."

Uh-oh.

"Of course I do. What are you talking about?"

"You sure? I just want you to have a nice time."

"Are you kidding? Just being here with you is perfect. And this album is a classic." I stood and went to him. After two months of dating, I was already learning that he was a perfectionist to a fault. He'd surprised me by buying me a blouse just two weeks before and I'd had to practically convince him that I'd liked it. I would've liked that blouse if it had a pattern of stripes *and* polka dots; it truly was the thought. But for all the money he made, and his handsome face and body, there was something inside Samuel that needed reassurance. We all need reassurance, sure, and I didn't mind giving it to him, but I did wonder where that need in him to be perfect came from, and why he was worried about disappointing me of all people. *Me.* The woman who was happy to hear his voice, grateful that he always called and met me when he said he would. I suppose it just didn't add up. He had everything, but when things didn't go as well as he thought they might, he could become quiet and sullen, like right then.

I wrapped his arms around my neck and began swaying to the music. "Thank you. Thank you. I love your house and I love being here with you."

I'm falling in love with you, I thought of telling him. *I already love you.* But I didn't have the nerve.

After breakfast the next morning, we hit all of Samuel's favorite wineries, then went to a few galleries and stores in town. After a late lunch, we drove to the next town and Samuel surprised me by stopping in front of a place that gave hot-air balloon rides. "Want to?" The reservation had already been made, but if I was afraid of heights or anything, not to worry.

All the guys I'd gone out with before Avery had thought having me over to watch them work on their art was romantic. Then I'd met Avery and we pretty much jumped into bed after the first night. I'd never been wooed before—not like this, with gifts and dinners and now a balloon ride. I leaned over and kissed Samuel. "Thank you."

"We haven't gone yet."

"I don't care," I said. "Thank you."

Later that night I surprised him by taking him to dinner at a four-star restaurant I'd always wanted to go to. When I said I was taking him to dinner, he tried to dissuade me, but I refused.

We took a shower and gussied up. My breath caught in my throat at the sight of Samuel in his suit. Just as we were entering the place, he leaned over and whispered in my ear: "Now I have to thank you. Thank you for taking me to dinner tonight, Abbey. I feel very lucky right now."

J woke the next morning to the smell of bacon and coffee. The clock read nine a.m. I stretched and yawned and found my robe, then followed the sound of sizzling bacon. Samuel was at the sink facing the kitchen window. It was gray outside and the overhead light flooded the kitchen, making Samuel look like an actor on a set, a comedy where the handsome actor makes a total mess of the kitchen while preparing a simple breakfast. I'd trained under Madame Pauline, who was adamant that a baker must keep her workstation clean and tidy. The messy kitchen made me shudder, but that lasted only a second before I walked up behind Samuel and wrapped my arms around his waist.

"Morning, sleepyhead."

"If your goal is to spoil me, you need to try harder," I said. "You're doing a terrible job. I mean, come on, a balloon ride, wine tasting, and now breakfast. You call that an effort?"

He turned and grabbed me all at once. "I need to work harder, huh? I didn't hear you complaining last night." He gave my ass a slap before letting me go. "I'm not a cook, but we have bacon and eggs and muffins from my new favorite bakery in Oakland."

"After last night's dinner, I don't know how much I can eat."

"I'm sure you'll do fine. You had a pretty good workout after our meal, if I remember correctly."

"I guess I could go for a little somethin'."

"Give me about ten more minutes and we'll be ready to eat."

"We could've gone out."

"Nah. I'm not here as much as I'd like to be as it is. Need to make use of the place. Now, go get cleaned up and let me finish this."

After washing up, I wrapped myself in my sweater and went outside and picked a few wildflowers I'd noticed growing near the tree in front of the house. I took a moment to gaze out at the vineyards in the distance and the trees that framed Samuel's half acre. Their orange and red leaves popped against the gray sky. The houses on either side of Samuel's property were far enough away that the property felt secluded. I thought: I want this. I want to be a part of his life. I saw our two older kids, a boy and a girl, running around the front yard while I bounced our latest baby in my arms. No, wait. I was closing in on forty; there would be no time for three kids. We still needed to date and marry, after all. Maybe I should stick with two. Yes. Okay. Start over . . . I saw Samuel chasing our oldest child, a son, running around the tree, while I bounced our baby girl in my arms.

My daydreams were becoming hokier by the minute—and I reveled in every single one. But that's what Samuel did to me; he made me believe it was possible to have a home and family. So when my brain told me to slow down—*You've only been dating for three months!*—I told it to shut up. I knew I was being hokey, but I couldn't help it. If I wanted to fantasize about having his kids, that was my prerogative. And with that, I went back inside for breakfast.

"The thing about working at the firm is that I feel I'm being watched."

"Watched?"

"Yeah, like everyone is expecting me to ruin a case."

We were midway through breakfast. Samuel was explaining the frustrations he was feeling at work. Dave Brubeck's *Take Five* played in the background. I imagined Phin or Theo rolling his eyes. *What is this, Jazz 101? You need to show the brother what's what. Come on, Dave Brubeck?!*

"Have you ever messed up a case?"

"No, I'm one of few in a predominately white firm. I have to prove myself." He pointed with his fork. "Besides, you always have to be ready for the other shoe to drop in life. Always. You always have to plan for the worst. Never be caught off guard."

"Sounds harsh."

"Hey, life is harsh."

I picked up my coffee and let my gaze wander toward the refrigerator, where under a magnet that read FUN IN THE BARBADOS SUN there was a picture of Samuel's parents standing on the beach and waving to the camera. On the fireplace mantel there was another family photo of Samuel, his parents, and his two younger sisters, who were only a few years older than Carmen.

I sipped my coffee. The flowers I'd picked in the yard sat on the table in a small vase.

"Did your parents teach you to plan for the worst?" I asked.

He turned when he saw what I was staring at and regarded the picture a moment. "Yeah. They did. Father raised me to have to prove myself. You were expected to make top grades and behave yourself. Anything less meant punishment."

"Sounds harsh," I repeated.

He dug into his eggs with revived interest. "Not really. It was nothing out of the ordinary—to me anyway."

"How would he punish you?"

"Let's just say he didn't have a problem taking out his belt when he needed to."

I was shocked. I wasn't raised around belts. Belts to me sounded like abuse.

He saw my alarm and shrugged it off. "Hey, he might have been hard on me, but it was for a reason. He's just old-school. Mom, too. She'd lock me in the closet and call it solitary confinement. I'd be in there for hours. Sometimes I'd fall asleep, which helped pass the time. Don't ask me what I did to warrant it. I swear I don't remember being that bad a kid. They just didn't want their son misbehavin'."

"*Samuel.*" I couldn't believe he sounded so cavalier. Belts and closets? He'd been just a boy.

"Hey, I'm not looking for anybody's sympathy. No sirree. Father was preparing me for everything he knew I'd have to go through in life. Black boys are expelled at triple the rate of their peers. If the teacher is going to have her eye on any student, you can bet it will be the little black boy. Dad and Mom weren't going to expect anything less than the best, because they knew we had to prove ourselves. Coming up, you were expected to make top grades on every assignment. You knew exactly what to expect if you brought home anything lower than an A."

"What do you mean?"

"Bringing home a B?" He set his fork down and held up both hands. "And a C?" He held up ten fingers, then raised his hand again and held up five.

"I don't get it."

"Licks of the belt." He grinned slowly as though surprised I hadn't understood. "Ten licks for a B, fifteen for a C. I never found out how many for a D. No way. Father had no problem holding back with his belt. Sometimes he'd whip me just because. That thing was leather, too." He cupped his hand around his mouth and laughed, but there was nothing genuine about the gesture and only betrayed that his story was no laughing matter.

I could feel my stomach turn. I didn't see the handsome man sitting across from me. I saw a boy terrified of bringing home any grade lower than an A. I saw a boy locked inside a closet with his knees pulled to his chest and trying to pass the time by thinking up stories or playing games until he fell asleep. Samuel saw an old-school traditional father. I saw an authoritarian's abuse. "Samuel . . ." My voice was barely above a whisper.

"Don't, Abbey. I'm not looking for sympathy. I was the kid in class who always had his hand raised and always knew the answer. I was obnoxious as hell, but it got me where I am today. Father was tough, but I appreciate him for it. And nothing felt better than to make him proud. Still doesn't." He cut into his bacon, then dug his fork into his eggs.

I pushed my plate away. "It sounds like abuse."

"Stop." He chewed on his food with hard bites and would not look at me.

"I feel bad for you."

"Don't. No one is asking you to feel sorry for me. Look around, Abbey. Whatever my parents did? It worked."

"But—I feel bad just thinking you'd be whipped like that. And locked in a closet? How old were you?"

"Old enough to know better." He leaned back in his seat. He stared at the ceiling as if irritated.

I reached over and wrapped my hands around his wrist. It took a moment before his eyes met mine.

"We were having a nice time. Let's not ruin it."

"Nothing is ruined. You never talk about your family. I want to know."

He picked up his fork and started eating. "Your food is going to get cold."

"Samuel."

"Look, my parents did the best they could. My two sisters

never gave them any trouble, because they might be harsh, but they know how to parent. I mean no offense, but you would never see my sisters getting pregnant before marriage."

I pulled back. "My parents love us."

"My parents love me, too. I really don't want to talk about this. Let's eat."

He continued to eat. *End of discussion.*

Fine. I didn't want to force him. I used my fork to swirl my eggs on my plate. I was too upset to eat. Yeah, maybe my folks were too lenient, but I didn't understand the mistreatment of children. Avery had grown up in foster care, and his stories were heartbreaking. He'd told me about the family that made him serve the meals and do most of the cleaning up before he was allowed to eat whatever little remained. And another set of parents who called him names like stupid and dummy. The stuff that made for bad TV? He'd lived it. Anyway, maybe I was projecting Avery's stories onto Samuel. Maybe I wasn't being fair. Samuel seemed fine.

He touched my arm lightly. "Hey. Where'd you go?"

I looked up from my eggs. I wasn't sure how long Samuel had been watching me.

"What were you thinking?"

I shrugged and reached for my coffee. "Nothing."

He picked one of the flowers from the vase and held it under my nose. "Don't be mad."

"I'm not mad."

"Promise?"

"Samuel, I have nothing to be mad about."

He returned the flower. "You have a good heart. You're sensitive. I didn't mean to spoil your mood."

"You didn't."

He moved his chair next to mine and took both my hands. "You really do have a good heart. You make me feel special."

"You make me feel special, too, Samuel."

He touched his forehead to mine. "Do you love me?"

I cupped his face between my hands and closed my eyes. In all my daydreams and fantasies about Samuel, I never imagined that I'd say it first, but I didn't mind. I wanted him to know. "I do," I whispered. "I love you."

He pulled back and searched my face. "I'm glad. Because I love you, too, Abbey."

"You do?"

"I do. You make me very happy. I love you."

9

Don't Worry About Me

A week later, and Bendrix and I were driving a rented van to the Jamela Graham Center in East Oakland. Bendrix was holding his annual celebration in honor of his mother, Arlene, who'd volunteered at the center before she died. The Graham Center was a place for youths to visit after school and for seniors to play nightly bingo, and a general community center for hosting meetings and small events. Adjacent to the building was the clinic where Bendrix volunteered bimonthly, giving free exams and taking on cases the volunteer nurses needed help with. Once a year, he rented the center and threw a birthday party in honor of his mom that included games, music, and baked treats provided by Scratch. The highlight of the night, though, was the raffle. With donations from community leaders and his colleagues at the hospital, he'd load a van with flat-screen TVs, Game Boys, bikes, electric heaters, iPads—a slew of prizes that were often out of reach for many of the people who came to the center. All the winner had to do was provide a winning raffle ticket; and for kids eighteen and under, if they earned straight

As, they picked the prize of their choice. It was a fun night and the perfect way to honor Arlene's memory.

We took a left on Grand and began to ascend the on-ramp to the freeway. We were in the middle of deconstructing my weekend in Yountville with Samuel for the umpteenth time. Bendrix had already met Samuel again by then—over lunch and a second time at the bakery.

He said, "Type A personalities like Samuel are usually hiding something, even if it's letting the world know how insecure they are."

"You should know," I said dryly.

He gave me a sideways look. "Hysterical."

I said, "He might be type A, but when he kisses me, I can't think straight. I'm so happy."

"I get that, but he sounds like he has issues."

"Don't we all? Besides, when he kisses me I feel like we can solve anything."

"Fabulous. I wish you'd stop sounding like you're in a 1950s romantic comedy, though."

"I can't help it! I'm Doris Day and Samuel is my Rock Hudson."

"Abbey, you do realize Rock Hudson was gay, don't you?"

"He was?"

"Good Lord."

He switched lanes and said, "What you've told me about his childhood explains why he seems rather on guard at times. His parents sound more than overbearing. Frankly, I agree with you. They were abusers."

I made Bendrix promise not to tell a soul about my conversation with Samuel. We were vaults when it came to keeping each other's secrets, but I'd made him promise, nonetheless.

"Do you know if he's ever been to counseling?"

"I doubt it. He barely wanted to talk about it."

He paused. "A certain someone once said the only way we escape the past is to walk through it."

"Oh my God, are you quoting Anthony? You are, aren't you?" As soon as he tensed his jaw, I knew I had him. If Bendrix was willing to quote his ex-lover, it meant he was thinking about his ex-lover and love of his life. And that was a start. "Say his name, Bendrix."

"No."

"Say it."

"I refuse. I was only trying to make a point. Don't start."

"I think you're thinking about Anthony; that's what I think. It's okay, you know. It's only natural that you'd think about him right now." For once I didn't exaggerate. Anthony and Bendrix had first met at the community center. Anthony worked there as a counselor before his position was cut. On the day he and Bendrix were introduced, that was it: Take two abnormally handsome men, introduce them to each other, mix, stir, and voilà! Passion. Romance. Love.

Bendrix turned up the volume when Sammy King's version of "Everything Happens to Me" began playing, no doubt to drown his thoughts and the conversation. It worked.

King's quintet increased the tempo faster and faster until we began nodding our heads at the flurry of notes coming at us. "Miles is so jealous of Sammy's solo here!" I said over the music.

"As he should be," Bendrix shouted in return.

We descended the freeway and drove directly into the bowels of East Oakland. Some argued there were two Oaklands: East Oakland and large sections of West Oakland were infamous for high concentrations of crime and drugs; North Oakland was the antithesis. If Oakland made the news, the broadcast usually had something to do with the latest murder or shooting. North Oakland, especially areas like Rockridge and Temescal, where

Scratch was located, were gentrified bubbles of fine dining and low crime.

Bendrix had grown up in East Oakland and called it Oakland's forgotten child. People moved up and out and either forgot about it or avoided it altogether.

He looked out the window as we passed by the familiar pattern of liquor store, liquor store, church; liquor store, liquor store. . . . Windows were barred, buildings abandoned. He turned on East Twenty-second Street and slowed. Back in high school, when we were Benz and Ross, we'd tagged a few buildings in the area. All the buildings Bendrix and I had painted were long gone, except one factory that had been set for demolition, but year after year it remained. We made it part of our routine to stop by before Arlene's birthday celebration.

The building was covered in mostly shitty graffiti; someone would paint his street name only to have someone else come along, cross it out, then paint a new name over it. And there were the more insightful comments on police brutality—*Fuck da poleeces. Pigs suck.* Holding its own in the center of the building, though, fading and surrounded by tags and profanity, was our version of Chagall's *Lovers in Green,* left unscathed. We'd used as many variations of green spray paint as we could find and a perfect red for the woman's dress. We'd changed things up by putting a large yellow Afro on the female's head and the man in a hoodie. Our painting was pale now but as striking as ever, and that it had been left untouched meant that the other artists and taggers still gave Benz and Ross mad, proper respect.

I turned in the passenger's seat, and Bendrix and I bumped fists. "Word, baby."

"Word."

Once at the center, we went about setting up. We placed a photo of Arlene on the main table with candles and flowers.

Arlene had raised Bendrix as a single mom on her bus driver's income. She took Bendrix to every event that included the word *free* or *educational* and applied for every scholarship out there. She knew early on she was raising a gay son in the hood and taught him to fight, literally, in their garage when he was just a boy. She taught her son how to throw a punch, to kick, to do whatever he had to do. By the time he'd turned fourteen, she'd saved up enough to move into a neighborhood with a better public high school, which was where we'd met.

We'd just finished putting out the desserts and hanging the banner when the gaggles of single women started pouring into the center.

To explain, a brief fairy tale . . .

They came every year, these young maidens, from the heart of East Oakland. Their prince was a handsome doctor who drove a shiny BMW and lived in the North, a land rich in Whole Foods, farmers' markets, and fine dining. The maidens knew their prized prince was *gay (hello)*—many had even met his ex-boyfriend—but that didn't matter! Skanks walked up and flashed cleavage and mothers introduced their daughters, all in hopes of turning the prince's eye. Even the security guard hired for the event secretly gave Prince Bendrix his card. Take my number, man. I like your style. But their actions were all in vain. The prince refused to date because, as his best friend knew, he was brokenhearted over Prince Anthony. The end.

One good thing about having Bendrix's suitors around, with all his groupies banding together, was that the event went off without a hitch and the center was cleaned up and the van packed by nine. Bendrix's aunt Nag found us as we were heading out to empty the last of the trash bags. Aunt Nag was Arlene's oldest sister by sixteen years. She was in her late sixties and as tall as a ten-year-old girl, with the same body weight. Her hair was combed in its usual four plaits, and she wore one of her many oversized T-shirts paired with matching tennis shoes. Her un-derbite was so severe that when she stared up at Bendrix, it looked as if the bottom half of her mouth was swallowing up her nose and upper lip.

She put her hand on her hip and stared at Bendrix as though she was about to scold him—although, frankly, she treated everyone this way.

"He's back," she said. "Mmm-hmm. He's back, all right."

"That's great, Aunt Nag," Bendrix said. After Arlene had died, Aunt Nag had become a second mother to him, which was why they needed no pretense.

She held up a piece of paper. "He's back from Haiti, and I have his number."

"Are you dating someone, Aunt Nag?" I asked, hoping to de-cipher her code.

Her eyes were darts. "Stop being foolish. *Anthony. Anthony is back*. He called me today and he left me his number."

"Where was he?" I asked.

"Haiti. That's what I'm tryin' to say. He was there for a year, helping people after the tornado."

A large question mark materialized above Bendrix's head and mine. "Tornado?" Bendrix said. "You sure you have that right?"

"Whatever went on there last year about this time. He went to counsel those kids after he got money from the government."

"Do you mean a grant?" I asked. "He got a grant to help kids in Haiti?"

"Listen, you two. My *point* is that he *called* me and I have his number." She held the paper in front of Bendrix's face.

I grabbed my friend's hand and jumped up and down. It was all coming to me. "Anthony's back! Anthony's back! I get it! Aunt Nag, we were just talking about Anthony on the way here!"

"Good for you."

"I think it's a sign. Bendrix, he called Aunt Nag because what he really wants is to talk to you. He gave her his number because he wants you to contact him. He wanted you to know he's back! Bendrix, he's making contact. He misses you. He still loves you."

Bendrix stared down at my hand, which was currently clasping his. I let it go.

"Aunt Nag, Abbey: I have no idea why neither of you will listen to me. I obviously have no speech impediment. I use my words clearly and, more often than not, say what I mean and mean what I say. However, since you refuse to listen or believe me, I will say this *one last time*: I don't want to talk about Anthony. What we had is over."

Aunt Nag moved so close, her nose almost touched his shirt. "You don't know what you talkin' about. You don't tell me what to do. Your mother asked me to watch over you. Anthony is the only person I know on this earth who can put up with that attitude of yours, besides this one here"—she chucked her thumb at me—"and why she puts up with you, that's between you two. Now, your mother asked me to look after you, and I know she doesn't want to see you alone like you are. And you and Anthony were good together."

"Oh God," he moaned.

"I agree. I started dating someone recently, Aunt Nag, and we're crazy about each other, and I want Bendrix to be as happy as I am. His name is Samuel and he's—"

"Abbey, this isn't about you. Did you hear me say your name? I'll hear about you in a second. Right now I need to talk some sense into this Harvard-educated fool standing before me."

Bendrix arched a brow.

"That's right. Just because you got brain sense don't mean

you know a thing about your heart. You focus on all that intel-
lectualizing and don't know how to love a person." She kept her
hard glare on Bendrix while taking the paper with Anthony's
number on it and shoving it inside his front pocket. "You act like
you're too good, but your shit stinks just like everybody else's.
Born and raised in East Oakland. That's you. You don't think I
can't put you in your place because you went to a few fancy col-
leges? You need to stop acting like everybody owes you something just because you walk the earth. I don't know what went
on with you two, but you know Arlene wouldn't want to see you
like this."

They didn't call her Aunt Nag for nothin'.

"I'm fine," Bendrix said. "More than fine. You don't need to
worry about me. I've heard everything you have to say." He
picked up the two trash bags. "I'm tired and I have work tomorrow and I think it's time we end the discussion."

Aunt Nag continued to keep her eyes fixed on his, then began wiping at his shoulder.

"What are you doing?"

"Trying to knock that damn chip off your shoulder. It's bug-
gin' the hell out of me."

I stifled a laugh.

"Try to make him call, Abbey," she said, before turning to
leave.

"I'll do my best, Aunt Nag."

After she was gone, Bendrix took the number from his
pocket and tossed it into one of the trash bags.

"Bendrix!" I shoved my hand in the bag and retrieved it. I
opened the paper and stared at the number and Anthony's name.
One reason I was fighting so hard for Bendrix to make up with
Anthony—and I'm sure this went for Aunt Nag as well—was
that we missed him. When I was at my lowest, right after seeing

the documentary, Anthony came to the studio I was renting with takeout from a Vietnamese place and warmed the soup and made sure I ate it. He sat next to me on the couch—where I'd been for days, mind you—and told me I didn't have to talk if I didn't want to and didn't have to do anything except try to eat. He stayed for several hours and we sat and he let me put my head on his shoulder while we watched TV and ate soup. He was my friend.

I looked at Bendrix. It was his life. I needed to let go of the idea that we would all be friends again. I opened the trash bag and put the paper back inside.

I then touched Bendrix's breast pocket. "You are an island, Bendrix. And now that your mom is gone, I'm the only person you let in. I won't mention a certain person ever again except to say that when I was at my lowest he once told me the heart is stronger than we think and it always rebounds. Thing is, you have to try. You told me the same thing. I won't bring him up anymore, but you need to do something besides push people away. You can't be happy closed off the way you are."

I picked up the trash bags and started toward the door. It was a rare occasion when I had the last word.

10

For Heaven's Sake

*I*n early November, I met with Nancy, my last consultation of the day. The bakery smelled of all things pumpkin and orders were already trickling in for the Thanksgiving holiday. By this point, Samuel was spending almost every night at my place and he had his own drawer and key. I was seeing him later that night but had to call and let him know I'd be running very late. I still needed to finish two wedding cakes and, thanks to Nancy's missing fiancé, it looked like our meeting was going to run way over schedule.

I tried to sound enthusiastic and upbeat during the consult, even though it also didn't help matters that Nancy's attitude veered toward noble gentry; that is, she was a bit of a snob. She was in her late twenties and registered her disapproval by raising her nose in the air as if my designs repelled her. Granted, her fiancé was so late we were forced to start without him, but usually choosing a wedding cake and discussing possible designs had the ability to . . . *oh, I don't know* . . . make a person *smile* now and then.

I clicked my laptop to a crowd favorite, hoping a more over-the-top, four-tiered concoction would force her out of her apathy. "Something like this is easy to modify to your taste," I told her. "I could make a different type of flower if you prefer something other than lilies. Almost any flower looks nice on the side or on the top of a cake."

She studied the picture long enough that I thought I'd found something she liked, but then she raised her nose. "I don't think so." She spoke as softly as a lady in King Edward's court and had the countenance of a woman who thought it a given that the world would lean in and listen to her every word.

I moved my lips into what I hoped was a smile. *Okay, so she's not a big fan of extravagance. That's fine.* I clicked through a few pictures until I landed on a cake barren of flowers or sentimentality or, dare I say, *romance.*

She looked from the cake to me as though I had to be kidding. She then glanced down at the face of her phone and rolled her eyes.

"Maybe he's stuck in traffic. Do you want to call him?" I suggested.

"It's not just this time. He's been late for every consultation so far, *if* he shows up at all. I've been planning our entire wedding by myself."

"Some men aren't invested in the wedding—not your man! I mean, he's fine. I just mean you can't equate how he feels about preparing for the wedding to how he feels about you. I've seen it a million times before."

"Are you married?"

"No."

Her ladyship's face soured and she went back to her phone as if anything the naive peasant sitting before her said mattered not a whit.

I showed her another cake, a whimsical one with crooked

layers piled one on top of the other. Pink and white stripes covered each layer, and on top, a little statue of the bride and groom. What can I say? Some people like whimsy.

Her ladyship, though, regarded me as if she might send in the guards to whisk me off to the towers. "Are you kidding?"

Just then, a man looking exasperated rushed inside and began searching the bakery as if in a panic. I prayed under my breath that he was Brett, Nancy's very tardy fiancé. Sure enough, he hurried over and started to give her an apologetic kiss, until she blocked his oncoming puckered lips with her hand. "You're late."

"I apologize." He forced a smile at me. "Hi, I'm Brett. I'm sorry I'm late."

"Don't worry about it. We're just glad you made it." I caught Noel's attention and motioned that he should come over when he had a second.

Brett sat next to Nancy but kept his attention on me and said, "I am sorry. It couldn't be helped."

Nancy turned and shot him a look. "Forty minutes?"

"There was traffic."

"We're a fifteen-minute drive away."

"Not when there's traffic."

They both stared at me now and waited for me to—to what? Decide who was at fault? Save their relationship?

I turned my laptop toward Brett. "I was just showing Nancy possible designs."

He studied the crooked cake and slowly arched his brow as if wondering what the hell he was looking at. I clicked to a new cake. Noel came to the table and Brett ordered an espresso. When Noel was gone, Nancy grumbled under her breath: "Forty minutes, Brett? Really? And you're going to use traffic as an excuse?"

"I said I'm sorry. What more do you want me to do, give blood?"

I noticed that the song "For Heaven's Sake" was playing and for a second I considered going for a joke to lighten the mood, but I let that idea go fast. I said, "Planning a wedding can be stressful, but I'm sure we can find a cake you both agree on." I reached for my sketch pad and pencil. "Maybe you can give me a better idea of what you're looking for?"

"He doesn't care about the wedding or the cake. If he cared he would have shown up on time."

"Nancy expects perfection from everyone; screw up once, and you can forget about it."

"*Once?* You haven't been on time for a single appointment."

"You exaggerate."

"Hardly. It's your wedding, too, you know."

"Do I ever."

"What's that supposed to mean?"

I interjected with the profound . . . "Uh."

Noel arrived with the espresso and we had a moment's reprieve. I said, "I'd be happy to make a more modern or contemporary cake. My goal is always to have the cake reflect the couple's love for each other."

They both stared blankly at me.

Nancy said, "I'm not sure what kind of cake would reflect our relationship."

Brett took a sip of his espresso. "Make anything with darts?"

Nancy continued to look at me. "Past actions predict future actions. . . ."

"Here we go." Brett sighed.

"Based on Brett's previous actions, all I can do is assume that my future husband will be late for the wedding"—she touched the table with the tip of her fingernail—"late for the birth of our first child"—tap—"and late for her high school graduation . . . if he remembers it at all."

Brett: "Based on previous actions, I can expect my future wife to hang on to my every mistake and never give me a fucking break!"

Nancy: "*That* would be impossible. You make far too many mistakes to keep track of."

Brett crossed his arms and muttered, "You are a real bi—"

"Don't say it!" I burst out. I glared as harshly as I could and he looked down at his espresso. "Once something is said, you can't take it back."

He glanced at Nancy, who showed no expression at all except for her lower lip, which twitched ever so slightly. Brett rose from the table and finished off his espresso, then drummed his fingers. "Cheers," he said. And with that, he was off.

Nancy remained immobile while I craned in my seat and watched as he walked directly out the door. I turned back to her, my mouth agape. "Soooo . . ."

"Let's go with the first cake—the design with the stenciled damask. Four tiers. The stencil in antique white set against ivory icing. A spray of rosettes on top in antique white. For the cakes, I'd like two lemon, one white, and one carrot. Brett hates those flavors. For favors let's do sugar cookies with the same pattern but in pale blue."

She was typing in her phone now. "Maybe we shouldn't make any decisions right now," I suggested. "Let things cool off. It's probably best not to make your choice when you're angry."

Her ladyship trained her large green eyes on mine: "How dare you say a word against her ladyship's request. If I say make cookies, you will make cookies! To the towers!" Her ladyship's guards in full armored regalia grabbed me by the arms. "Off with her head," she commanded. "No later than when the cock crows at dawn."

"No!" I screamed. "Please, Your Majesty! I plead for mercy! I am your most humble servant and cake baker!" But her ladyship only turned in disgust, and her two knights pulled me from the table, kicking and screaming. "Noooooo!"

In truth, she continued to stare, her eyelids at half-mast. "If it's no trouble to you, I'll decide if I'm angry or not, and when I should or should not order my own wedding cake. Does that work for you?"

I rubbed my throat, grateful that we lived in a time when I couldn't be beheaded. I smiled politely and began taking notes. "Carrot, lemon, and two white cakes."

It was almost nine by the time I arrived home. Samuel's car was parked in front of the house when I pulled up. After the day I'd had, the thought of a glass of wine and a hot bath sounded so good.

I started to open the door but could hear music coming from inside. Loud music. I stood and tilted my head. Was that . . . electronica? Rap? Samuel still wasn't the biggest fan of jazz, but he hadn't told me he liked rap so much that he'd play it loudly enough for the entire block to hear.

I opened the door, and my first impulse was to cover my ears. The music wasn't only loud; it was dreadful, painfully so.

I stole a peek around the wall separating the short entryway from the living room. A man who looked to be in his early twenties stood in front of my fireplace with his arms outstretched and his palms facing the ceiling. He wore flannel over a sleeveless T-shirt and let the flannel hang loosely off his arms. I would've screamed except that Carmen was on the love seat, one leg thrown over the armrest, watching TV with the volume on mute. Dahlia and Samuel were on the opposite couch—Samuel engrossed in something on his laptop while Dahlia traced her finger around the edge of Samuel's ear and cooed while pressing her cleavage against him. Okay, yes, I exaggerate, but only a little. She did sit close enough so that her right breast touched his arm anytime either of them moved.

The guy in front of the stereo started shouting along with the chorus of the song: *"I found my kitty. She found my kitty. He found my kitty. We found my kitty."* The chorus was on infinite loop and the rapper had a synthesized voice that sounded like a satanic leprechaun. *"I found my kitty. She found my kitty. He found my kitty. . . ."*

The guy was blue eyed with dark blond hair shaved into a crew cut. His flannel shirt fell down his arms, showing off perfectly toned muscles. He had the kind of bravado that made him look like he'd be perfectly cast in a movie about young men sent off to war; hard to tell if he'd be the hero of the film or set to die within the first thirty minutes.

I found the remote on the table behind the sofa and turned the music off, but the silence was lost on Mr. Performer, and he continued to sing at the top of his voice: *"I found my kitty! She found my kitty. I found——!* Yo, what happened to my song?"

I stepped out from hiding.

"Who are you?" he demanded.

"I live here. Who are you?"

Carmen clicked the TV off. "Jake, this is my sister Abbey; Abbey, Jake."

I noticed Dahlia moving her boobs away from Samuel as unobtrusively as she could. "I already saw you, Dahlia. In the future, please sit at a respectable distance from my boyfriend."

Jake covered his mouth with one hand and pointed at Dahlia. "Ahhhhh!" he laughed, kicking up his sneakered foot. "She told you! Sit at a respectable distance! Ahhhhh!"

Samuel rose from the couch and gave me a peck on the cheek. "Hey, babe. Finish everything okay?"

"Yeah, everything went well. What's going on?"

"Can you turn the song back up?" Jake asked. "It's almost over."

I ignored him. "What's going on?"

Samuel went back to his computer. He still had on his office attire, though no jacket. "I got here about an hour ago. I hate to bring work home, but it couldn't be avoided." He began typing again. "I'm almost finished."

"How can you work with all the noise?"

"I don't mind," he said, continuing to type. "Keeps me alert."

Carmen made a show of hefting herself up from the couch. "Jake wanted to play Gnome Death Three, but we don't have anything like that in the dorms, so we went to Dad's. So then we were playing—"

Jake hopped from foot to foot like a jogger waiting for a stop-light to turn green. "Have you ever played Gnome Death? It's crazy. You get all these gnomes lined up and you just start shoot-ing 'em and then they start to do this nasty dance." He jumped forward and ran his hand over his groin area. "It's so funny!"

Carmen slapped his leg. "Don't you know better than to interrupt when someone's talking? So *anyway*, we were playing, but then Louis and Charlie came over with Leslie and I wasn't in the mood—"

"And I wanted pie," Jake said. "Your pie is slammin'."

"I should hope so," I said.

I glanced at Dahlia. "And you have your own house—excuse me, my dad's house, so . . . ?"

"I was at the house," she explained. "And I was bored, so I thought I'd come with them. Now that I'm single again"—she couldn't help but glance at Samuel—"I'm by myself all the time. I don't like going to the main house as much because of Aiko and that wailing baby."

"So you follow your nineteen-year-old daughter around. Makes sense."

"What's wrong with that?" Dahlia asked, turning toward Carmen. "I want to spend time with you. I never see you."

Samuel broke his attention from his work. "It's not my business, Dahlia, but children need to separate from their parents so they can become independent."

"Thank you!" Carmen exclaimed. "It's embarrassing! What parent shows up at their kid's dorm? You're insane."

Samuel looked at Dahlia. "You went to her dorm room? That *would* be embarrassing."

"Thank you!" Carmen said.

"I'm not trying to take sides; it's just something to think about," Samuel said.

Dahlia lowered her eyes as though she were shy and demure. "I'll do that. I guess I see your point."

"I have my kitty, you have my kitty." Jake had earbuds in by now and stood in front of the fireplace bopping to a beat that only he could hear, singing to himself. *"Times are hard. I'm covered in lard. My soul's in shards."*

I thought back to the photo Carmen had shown me months before of the goofball who'd impregnated her with his drunken sperm. Was this the same guy? No. It couldn't be. That guy had black hair and was tall and skinny. I watched this new goofball continue rocking out to the music piping into his ears. "Does he go to school with you?" I asked her. *"Is he high?"*

"I can hear everything you're saying right now, yo," he said. He made a point of taking out his earbuds. "I don't like to listen to my songs all loud because I don't want to damage my hearing. You ask who I am?" he said, widening his muscular arms. "My name is Jake and I ain't no flake. I'm on the make, for heaven's sake." He pointed to his vacant skull. "Carmen and I met in class, but I'm taking time off. What I really want to do in life is create music and, like, head my own company."

I had to stop myself from rolling my eyes. Then again, I thought—*Why?* And rolled them anyway.

"I'm serious! Look at all the heavyweights. Jobs. Zuckerberg. Gates. None of them graduated." He raised his hands in the air as if by listing three geniuses he'd proven his point.

I looked at Carmen. "You're not dating him, I hope."

"Hey, man, I'm right here. Yo, I can *hear* you!"

"He's not as immature as he seems," said Carmen, returning to the couch.

"Apparently he's a math genius," Dahlia added dubiously.

Jake kicked his foot in the air. "My name is Jake and I'm no flake. Skipped two grades and now I'm in a phase. To create a label and show I'm able. I wanna wear sable. Create musical fables—about this girl here." He pointed at Carmen. "She's so fine. She expands my mind. Her body is an equation. A week-long vacation." He moved in front of her and began pulling his shirt up his torso while gyrating down into her lap. A male stripper in heat.

Carmen laughed and pushed him away. "Get off me."

He put his earbuds back in his ears and started dancing again. *"Fuck those bitches!"* He pointed at Carmen. *"You my bitch and tonight all the other bitches gonna see what I'm made of. Fuck the other bitches."*

Samuel looked up from his laptop. "Hey, man, that's not cool." When Jake continued to dance and rap, Samuel rose from the couch. "I said that's not cool!"

Jake turned and pulled his earbuds from his ears. "What's not cool? It's a song."

"I don't care what it is. You don't speak to Carmen or any woman like that. Show some respect."

"But it's a song."

"It's a song that uses foul language against women. It's inappropriate."

Carmen's eyes were wide. "I don't think he meant anything."

"Doesn't matter," Samuel replied. He kept his gaze locked on Jake, waiting. While Jake was lean bulk, Samuel was all height and his clothes and stature gave him the appearance of a father chastising a son. Jake seemed as surprised as Carmen at being reprimanded, but he took a step back. "I didn't mean anything. Like I said, those are the lyrics."

"You need to apologize."

"Hey, man, fine. I apologize. I didn't mean anything."

Samuel shook his head. "Not me."

Jake looked at Carmen. "Sorry, Car." He then said to Dahlia and me, "I apologize, ladies."

Dahlia beamed. "You're so thoughtful, Samuel. It's like we have a real man looking after us. I love it!"

I pursed my lips at her. I wasn't so sure I agreed. Jake was doing what any kid his age did. I certainly didn't need a formal apology, at any rate.

"It's fine, Jake," I said. "It's late and if any of you are as tired as I am, we should call it a night. Let's forget it."

"Can I stay here tonight?" Carmen asked.

"Sure." I realized I'd spoken too soon. Since Samuel was staying, should I have checked in with him first? Before I'd met him, Carmen had stayed over regularly, but she hadn't spent the night since then. Samuel didn't seem to care and started collecting his things.

I asked Carmen if she had pajamas.

"They're in my backpack."

"Why do you want to stay here when you have a perfectly good dorm room of your own?" Dahlia asked.

"I need a break from the dorms."

"Too bad. Why do we pay for you to live there if you're always somewhere else?"

"You don't pay anything; Daddy does."

Jake covered his mouth and kicked his foot. "Ahhhhh!"

"Well, why don't you stay with me at the house? We can keep each other company."

Carmen shifted her gaze. "I haven't seen Abbey in a while."

Dahlia pursed her lips while looking me over. I raised my hands and shrugged in response.

"Fine," she said. She chucked her head toward Jake. "What about him?"

"I have my skateboard."

"It's dark out. I don't want to be responsible for you getting killed on your way home." She looked him over as if he were a dirty rag she'd have to put in her car. "Where do you live?"

"Bezerkeley. Land of the homeless, the potheads, the rich, annoying liberals—like my mom! *Ahhhhh!*"

"Well, at least Berkeley is on my way. Come on."

He went to Carmen and stretched out his arms and they hugged good-bye. He took my hand next. "It's been real. Your chocolate pie sent me to the sky. I won't lie."

He and Samuel shook hands. After they left, Samuel looked at Carmen for a beat. "I think you can do better."

She lowered her gaze. "He's not like what he seems. Seriously. He's super smart. No, *really*," she added, seeing our faces. "He's one of those brainiacs who doesn't know what he wants to do with himself. He's taking a year off from school, but he really is smart."

"Foolish, more like it," Samuel said. He pointed at her. "You. Deserve. Better." He then gave me a kiss on the cheek. "Mind if I steal the shower first? I'll be quick."

"No, go ahead."

Another kiss and he left. "Nighty-night, ladies."

Carmen watched him disappear down the hall. "He's like a grown-up."

I laughed.

"I mean, like, he's not like your other boyfriends at all. He's respectable."

"Yeah," I muttered. "That's the point."

She followed me to the hall closet, where I took down a towel and an extra blanket. "Can I tell you something?" she asked.

I paused, already suspicious. "You're not . . . ?"

"No! God, no! No!"

I sighed in relief. "Thank goodness. What is it?"

"I got a C on my econ test. A C. I've never gotten a C in my life."

To be honest, while I knew I should help support Carmen in her obsession with perfect grades, I never understood her fixation on seeing the letter *A* at every turn. The Ross children were all perfectionist in one way or another—me with baking, my sisters and brothers with art and music—but Carmen beat herself up and tended to stress. Even in junior high and high school, she worried about her grades far more than Dahlia or Dad did.

I gave her the blanket and we went to the guest bedroom. "It's only the beginning of the semester. You'll pick it up," I said.

I turned on the light. Carmen fell on the bed, back first, and hugged the blanket to her chest. "But what if I don't? I can't afford bad grades if I'm trying to get into a good law school. I swear, Abbey, this past year has just been so fucked." She tossed the blanket, then sat up and ran her hands over her face and through her thick, curly hair.

"Maybe you need to talk to someone." I sat beside her. "Is

what happened—the miscarriage—what's making you upset? Do you still think about it?"

"No, not really. Except to be happy I'm not a mother."

"What's going on with Jake?"

"I don't know. He's funny. He's gonna help me with econ."

"There you go; that's a start."

I lifted a stray hair making its way down her cheek and tucked it behind her ear. "Did you ever have any time with Dad?"

"We talked on the phone while he was in Austin. We were going to have breakfast, but then he had to cancel. I just hope to get some time in before he has more kids."

"*Carmen.*"

"It's true. Anyway, I don't need him as much as you think I do. He was never really around for me anyway."

I started to argue with her, but I knew it hurt that Dad had canceled. It pained me to admit it, but maybe he'd reached the point where he was spreading himself too thin. He was sixty-five, after all, with a new wife and two new babies.

I put my arm around her. "You'll be okay. Just try to focus. And see your professor during office hours. Put a face to your name."

"Yeah."

I slapped her thigh lightly and stood up.

"Thanks for letting me stay. It's so weird that you have a boyfriend now."

I wasn't sure how to take that. "It's not that weird."

"Yes, it is. I like him, though."

"I'm glad. He likes you, too."

We said good night and I took a quick shower while Samuel sat in bed with his laptop. He was in the same position minutes later. I stood in the doorway and took a moment to completely objectify him, strip him down to his bare sexual appeal.

I moved from the doorway. "You know what I'm thinking? You should go to work on Monday without a shirt. It would make everyone very happy."

He looked up and smiled. "Stop being silly."

"I'm serious. You'll win every case."

"No," he said, keeping his gaze on the screen, "I'll get fired." He continued with whatever was on his laptop while I climbed in next to him. I saw that he was on three different Web sites at once, comparing prices on winter coats.

I heard the water running in the guest bathroom. "I hope it was okay that I let Carmen spend the night."

"It's your house. I'm a guest here myself."

I kissed his naked shoulder and inhaled his soapy smell. "You're more than a guest; you know that."

I told him about how stressed Carmen was feeling about her grades.

"I get that," he said. "If she wants, I can help her get an internship at my firm, or I know a few people I can call in the East Bay. An internship will help when it comes to applications."

"Can you?"

"Of course. She needs to watch who she hangs out with, though. If she wants to get ahead in life, she needs to surround herself with people who are going places. That Jake person is going *nowhere*. She needs to cut him off—like, yesterday."

"He was all right. Carmen says he's some kind of genius."

Samuel huffed and clicked out of the clothing sites, then went to a political blogger he liked and began scrolling through articles. I watched him bounce from Web site to Web site while telling him about the couple I'd met earlier that afternoon—his lordship and her ladyship. "Let's never be like that," I said. "There was so much animosity between them. It was unreal. Why get married if you hate the person you're with?"

"At least you made a sale," he replied, his attention on the article he was reading. "That's all that matters."

"I guess. But I also want my clients to be happy."

"Some people like drama. If they choose to be miserable, that's on them. You're there to make a profit, not play counselor."

"Yeah," I said. But, I thought, I was also there to make cupcakes and pies and cookies and to make people smile. I left it alone, though.

He set his laptop on the nightstand and raised his arm so that I could snuggle against him. "I have a surprise for you."

I peered up from under the crook of his arm. "Yeah?"

He hopped off the bed and took his duffel bag from the closet. He took out three boxes of different sizes and piled them in front of me, one on top of the other. "Open this one first."

"It's like Christmas," I said, pulling at the purple ribbon. "You're so sweet. Thank you."

I opened the first box and pulled the tissue paper away. Inside was a pair of strappy black shoes with eight-inch heels, clear and shiny. They were shoes made for a woman who knew how to do a wide split while sliding down a pole. Stripper shoes. I glanced down at the lid on the box to check the brand name; maybe they were designer shoes and I just didn't know the trend. I read the label: *(s)HOES.*

I balanced a shoe on the palm of my hand and studied it as though I'd found it on an archaeological dig. *A fine object we have here, created by the Wasubi tribe on the northern coasts of Papua New Gunner. Probably used as a torture device.*

Samuel nibbled my shoulder. "They're for you. Not for work, of course." He laughed.

I returned the shoe to the box.

"I stole a peek and found out your shoe size." He handed me the next box, but I was afraid to open it. *What next?*

I pulled out a see-through negligée made from cheap lace the color of bing cherries. Granted, I liked to look sexy in bed now and then, but cheap lace and stripper shoes weren't my style. I was more of a silk camisole and matching panties and bra kind of woman.

"Baby, you're going to look *hot* in that. I can feel myself getting excited already." He took my hand and placed it directly on his—well, I doubt that I need to explain. "Last but not least."

He handed me the largest box. I didn't want to open it but told myself maybe it was all a joke and the last box would be a silk lavender slip and matching robe.

Nope. I pulled the tissue away and stared down at four strands of white rope, coiled like snakes. "Ha-ha," I laughed, hoping he'd join in and we'd laugh and laugh at his prank. "*Stripper shoes and rope!* Ha-ha-ha!"

He pressed his mouth next to my ear. "You've been a bad girl and it's time Daddy taught you a lesson."

What the—?

"I'm going to tie you up and give you the spanking you deserve."

All these months and our lovemaking had been exactly that—lovemaking, passionate yet sweet. He'd never once said anything about *rope*. Not that I was a prude. I just didn't want to be tied up. What if there was a fire or a burglar? And my sister was in the other room!

He whispered, "Say something dirty to me and then you'll get punished."

"I . . . I . . ." I could feel myself blushing. Who was this person? *What have you done with my respectful, courteous boyfriend? I want him back!*

"I'm gonna teach you a few lessons tonight. You've been a bad girl and Daddy's gonna have to give you a spanking." He waited

for my response. "Now you say something. Say something *nasty*.
Come on, baby, I want to hear it." He pulled back, his eyes ex-
pectant.

"I—I hate it when people don't wash the dishes before they
go to bed?"

He stared at me, waiting.

"Dirty sheets. I hate dirty sheets. They're *naaasty*."

He grinned. "Okay. You'll get the hang of it. Go put your
outfit on. I'll wait for you." So he wouldn't see me recoil after
seeing him lick his lips, I grabbed the tacky shoes and negligee
and scurried to the bathroom.

I looked like a fool. The negligee sagged where my small
boobs weren't big enough to fill it. The shoes fit, but my feet
looked like trapped rodents. I didn't want to go back out there. I
felt like a clown, an imposter. I leaned against the sink. I knew
other women loved this kind of stuff; of course they did. And I
honestly wasn't judgmental when it came to sex. Do whatever
you want! Masks, whips, sex games, or toys. I knew what was out
there, and it was all good. Hell, I saw the Marina Abramović
retrospective at the Met—twice. Bendrix and I had gone through
Mapplethorpe's sex books in high school. *I did not judge.* It's only
that cheap lace and ugly shoes were not me. I understood that
relationships always came with problems, but I didn't want to
play the part of a stripper or a character from *Fifty Shades of Grey*
or *Story of O*.

Samuel called from the bedroom just then. "Put some lipstick on, baby. I wanna see you work it."

I closed my eyes and pressed my forehead against the mirror.
Compromise. *Everyone has to compromise in a relationship*, I told
myself. *You have a good man and you have to do your part.* I found
my lipstick. I assumed he wanted red instead of my usual neutral
color.

The stripper shoes felt more like stilts, and I had to stretch out my arms to keep my balance as I tottered back into the bedroom.

Samuel leaned back against the bed and clasped his hands behind his head. "Baby, you look hot."

"I feel like a clown, Samuel. I can't believe women dance in these things."

He took a piece of rope and let it dangle on the hook of his finger. "Come here."

I remained dead still.

"What's wrong?"

"I feel like a goof."

"But you look so sexy."

I wanted to be the woman who could easily dance around a pole, who'd take lessons on how to move like a stripper and walk in eight-inch heels, but I also hoped he'd understand. "I don't think this is me, Samuel. I've never felt so un-sexy or so un–turned on in my life." I felt ashamed even having to say it, but there it was. The truth.

"But you haven't tried it. You can at least try it for me, can't you?"

"I feel stupid. I don't feel sexy at all."

Samuel sighed. "I don't know about you, but our lovemaking has been becoming stale lately. Don't you want to mix things up? I'm not saying we have to do this every time, but, you know, sometimes there has to be a trade-off in a relationship; it's not as if we're going to like *everything* we do together."

"Stale? We haven't been together a year."

"Why are you making such a big deal out of it? I want to have some fun and you're making it out like I'm asking you to do something most women wouldn't enjoy."

We're not talking about most women, I thought. *We're talking about me.* I didn't say it, though. A part of me felt ashamed that I wasn't like other women, who'd love to have a man as handsome as Samuel do whatever he wished. I knew I was being the boring girlfriend.

"What if I tie you up?" I offered.

"No. Nooooo." He chuckled. "I'm the man."

"So?"

"I'm dominant. It's the natural order of things."

"That's crazy. What if we were two men? Then what would you say?"

"We're not two men." Irritated, he sucked in his breath and shook his head. "Forget it. Let's just go to sleep." Before I could respond, he turned on his side and pulled the blanket up under his chin. When I walked to the edge of the bed and sat down, he clicked the light off, leaving me in the dark. I took off the (s)hoes and climbed into bed.

I lay on my back with my hands folded on top of the covers. I waited for him to say something, but he remained silent. "I just feel uncomfortable knowing Carmen is in the house," I said.

"It's fine."

"And, you know, maybe we can figure out something we both feel comfortable with."

Silence.

I closed my eyes, but there was no way I was going to be able to sleep.

Years ago, my dad was once asked by a mega pop star to be a part of a band she was putting together. She was transforming her sound for the umpteenth time and for her latest recording she wanted to do a jazz-pop album. Dad could have made serious money, especially going on the planned world tour, but after hearing her ideas and a demo she had put together, he turned her down. When Phineas asked why—*Pops, you could make serious bank*—he'd said, "That shit ain't me. You be you and do what you want to do and I'll be me. And that shit ain't me."

I listened to Samuel breathing. Could I lose him over something like this? Would I be betraying myself if I had sex the way my boyfriend wanted? My heart chimed in: *You'll hurt his feelings if you say no.* My brain: *Don't be so uptight. Lighten up.* And my gut: *This shit ain't me.*

"Samuel? Are you asleep?" My whispery voice penetrated the dark silence.

I pressed my body into his back and rested my chin on his arm. "Okay," I whispered.

"Okay what?"

"I'll try it."

He rolled over. "You sure?"

"Yeah. Let me put the shoes back on."

11

My Mother Would Like You

*T*wo months later, I'd invited Samuel to Sunday dinner to meet my family for the first time. Rita and I were watching him play with my nieces and nephews in the backyard. He was pretending to be a monster with his arms straight out and his legs assuming a Frankenstein gait. Without warning, he broke into a run and chased them around, and they squealed and laughed.

It was a beautiful and sexy sight. And I thought, *There is nothing sexier than a man who loves children.*

"Have we discussed an engagement or marriage?" Rita asked.

"No. *We've* only been together nine months. It's too early for that."

"Please. It's never too early. Doug and I were engaged within three months. Your father and I married within a year."

"Yeah, and look how that turned out."

"Yes, we divorced, but we were together a long time and produced our lovely Dinah. My point: When you know, you know."

"*Rita.*"

"I'm only trying to give a little motherly advice." She turned and looked at me. Her Greek-inspired hairdo was piled on her head, with small pearl-like beads showing here and there. "You can't tell me you haven't thought about it."

Oh, I'd thought about it, all right. By then, I'd convinced myself that our sex life might be awkward some nights, but you couldn't get everything in one person. I'd even gone online to find dirty sayings so I could better play my part. I considered it my foray into acting. And it wasn't always "Tie me up, tie me down"; we continued to have romantic, sweet sex as well. And besides . . . *look at him. Just look at him.* He was utterly adorable running around with my nieces and nephews. And yes, I did think about our wedding. I pictured myself in my gown (something simple and elegant), standing in front of him at the altar and gazing into that handsome face. I imagined him sliding on my wedding band and our kiss. . . .

As if reading my thoughts, Samuel turned and smiled. I smiled back and waved.

My nephew Riley had his arms wrapped around Samuel's thigh, and when Samuel raised his leg, he lifted Riley into the air along with it. Riley squealed while Samuel brought his hand to his lips and blew me a kiss. Before I could respond, Rita puckered her lips and blew him a kiss in return.

I smirked.

"What?" she said, bringing her hand to her pearls. "I thought the kiss was for me."

Sunday dinner was, as usual, loud and chaotic, with the typical assortment of exes, siblings, and anyone who could make it. Since I was introducing Samuel, the wives had made sure to show up. We ate Sunday dinners and larger family meals in the second dining room, which had so many French windows it was almost like eating outside or in a greenhouse. There was a long wooden table with candles placed down the center. Artwork by family and friends decorated the walls, and directly overhead was a light fixture made from candles and trellis lights. Rain was falling outside by the time we sat down, but the all-gray light outside and the sound of raindrops against the window-panes contrasted with the warmth of the candles made the room more intimate and cozy.

Dad asked everyone to close their eyes so he could bless the food. He waited for us to settle down before clearing his throat. "I'm grateful this evening for loved ones near and far. But now that I have my seat, I gotta say I wanna eat. I know grubbing on this food will be a feat, but I look forward to this treat. Bailey's gumbo sure can't be beat. Now I gave y'all my rhyme, so let's eat."

With that, everyone broke into laughter and chatter. I noticed Samuel looking at Dad as if he wasn't sure what he'd just heard, so I leaned in next to his ear. "He always says a rhyme for grace; that's just our thing," I whispered. He forced a smile and went about eating.

"Corporate attorney, huh?" Dizzy addressed Samuel from the end of the table. Next to him, his wife Sharon held their daughter Hope in her lap. "That's some serious bank."

"You like it?" asked Phin.

"Yeah, I do," Samuel answered. "Some cases can be interesting. It can be a lot of work, though."

I said, "You have no idea. He works all the time."

"I don't work any harder than this one here," he said, smiling at me.

Dahlia made a point of flipping her hair and sitting up in her seat. "Samuel helped Carmen get an internship at a firm downtown. Wasn't that nice of him? And Carmen says she really likes it there. Everyone is very nice."

"I can speak for myself, Mom."

"Couldn't be prouder of you, baby," Dad said. Even though Samuel said it was nothing, Dad had thanked him more than once for helping Carmen get the internship. He pointed the tip of his knife her way now and winked. "I'm going to let you handle all my legal affairs soon as you graduate. Matter of fact, you'll be the family's lawyer. Carmen McRae Ross, Esquire. Gotta nice ring to it, don't y'all think?"

Carmen beamed. I hoped their newly found connection would stick. After hearing how crushed she was when he'd canceled breakfast, I'd called Dad the next day and told him to reschedule with her. When he procrastinated or forgot, I went straight to Aiko and asked her to talk to him. Sure enough, Dad and Carmen were meeting for breakfast within days. Like all of Dad's wives, Aiko didn't put up with Dad slacking on his responsibilities, and she was smart and direct; I think you'd have to be, coming into a family like ours.

She bounced baby Ornette in her arms now while trying to soothe him. Ornette was ten months old by then. Bud, who sat between Aiko and Dad in his high chair, was twenty-eight months.

Aiko's once jet-black hair had turned silver-gray, thanks, she liked to say, to having two babies while in her forties. Before marrying Dad, she'd worked as a journalist and had interviewed Dad for a long piece she was writing for an anthology on jazz masters.

Ornette let out a wail, and I asked if I could try to calm him.

"Cheers," Aiko said, handing him over.

I held him against my chest and inhaled his baby smell. "There, there, sweetie," I cooed in his ear. "It's going to be okay. These hard times will be over soon, and one day you will learn to walk and ride a bike. You just wait."

Daddy motioned toward Bud. "Watch this, everybody. Say *truck*, Bud."

Bud clanged his spoon against his high chair.

Aiko, still chewing, said halfheartedly, "Babe, don't. It's embarrassing."

Daddy said, "It's cute and you know it. Bud, say *truck* for Daddy."

"*Fuck.*"

"That's my boy. Say it again: *Trrruuuck.*"

"Fuuuuck!"

We all laughed. I began patting Ornette's back.

"You look good holding a baby," Bailey said.

"Momma," Theo warned. "Don't embarrass Abbey like that."

"What did I do?" Bailey cut into her turkey. Her hair was dyed the same deep blue as her blouse and short skirt. "She does look good holding that baby. Should I lie?"

I could feel my face growing hot but managed to avoid everyone's gaze, especially Samuel's, by reaching for a spoonful of sweet potatoes.

Daddy said, "You listen to much jazz, Samuel?"

Samuel set his fork aside and rubbed his hands up and down his thighs as if he'd been anticipating the question but hadn't figured out how to respond. "Abbey's teaching me a lot. I'm learning to like it."

Theo's eyes widened. "Learning to like it? *Learning to like it?* That's like having to learn to like iced tea on a hot day; that's like having to learn to like sex!" He laughed. "That's like—"

"We get it," Dizzy interjected.

Doug leaned out from Rita's side. "Don't mind Theo. If you look around the table, you'll understand that this family is on the weird side of things."

"Doug!" Rita admonished. "We are not weird."

"Well, now, honey, if the shoe fits. Don't you worry, Samuel, I'll look after you. Takes some getting used to, exes and wives sitting at the same table and the obsession with jazz music, but they're actually an okay bunch." He shoved gumbo into his mouth. "You stick with me and I'll show you how it all works."

"They're the only family I've ever had," Dahlia said to Samuel. "Before this family took me in, I grew up being shuttled around, you see."

"Here we go," Bailey said, reaching for her wine.

"Well, it's true!"

"I like having my children around," Dad explained. He glared at Doug with a playful spark in his eye. "And if that means welcoming people like that into the fold, so be it."

Joan sat at the far end of the table. "It's true," she said. "We are an odd lot. And thank God for it." She raised her glass and a few of us joined in.

Ornette had calmed enough that I started to return him to Aiko.

"You sure you don't want to keep him?" she asked.

Bailey looked from me to Samuel. "So, when's the wedding?"

We all moaned and shouted at once: "Bailey!" "Momma!" "Leave them alone, Bailey!"

Amid all the commotion, Samuel gave me a peck on the cheek. *Love you*, he mouthed.

I wasn't to meet Samuel's parents for another two months. Judging by Samuel's nervousness, you would've thought we'd been invited to a state dinner. He wasn't sweating-bullets nervous, but he was tense around the edges. The night before we were to drive to his parents', he started watching baseball highlights on YouTube and studying stats of players. The odd thing was, he didn't like baseball and never watched it. When I asked what he was doing, he said that his dad was a baseball fanatic and liked to discuss the games.

The next day while waiting for me to dress, he'd spent more time catching up on baseball. He'd already taken his shower and was sitting on the couch with his shirtsleeves rolled up.

I walked in wearing my robe. "I still don't get why you're doing this. Why don't you just tell him you don't like it?"

"It's not a big deal. It makes him happy."

"Yeah, but there's no reason to put yourself through this. You should tell him the truth and find another way to make him happy."

He shook his head as if there was no sense explaining; I'd never understand. I waited for him to respond, but he kept his eyes on his laptop. "The dessert's okay?" he asked.

"Since you asked an hour ago?"

"Why don't you get dressed? We don't want to be late."

He was still at the computer when I came back out.

"You're wearing that?"

Not what you want to hear when you're about to meet your boyfriend's parents. Mmm . . . actually, not what you want to hear *ever.*

I looked down at my vintage-style dress with cap sleeves and a floral print. I liked it because it was just tight enough to give me the appearance of at least pretending to have curves. "What's wrong with it? I thought you liked this dress."

"I do, but it's too much for the family."

"Are they Amish?"

He made his face go slack. "Please, baby? Something else?"

"There's nothing wrong with this dress."

He turned from his laptop. "Sweetie, I know I'm probably acting crazy. But it would mean a lot to me if you changed. They're conservative; I've told you that."

"Yeah, but it's not like I'm wearing a miniskirt. Should I go find my burka? Would that help?"

He rose from the couch and walked over. He raised my chin with the tip of his finger. "I want them to fall in love with you. And I know they will. When they do, wear whatever you want, but trust me, you want to go with something less flashy today. For me? Please?" He kissed me then. Long and deep, and as the seconds passed and his hands ran up and down my thighs, it came to me that I could just as easily change into something else. He gave my ass a pat as I headed back toward the bedroom. "You do look good in that dress," he called after me.

I gave a shake. "Your loss."

On the drive to his parents' house in El Cerrito, I thought it would be funny to listen to Heather Rigdon's "My Mother Would Like You." Rigdon wrote witty, sarcastic standards for her three-piece trio. After hearing a few bars, Samuel asked me to turn off the stereo. "You should know that my parents follow a prophet and you're going to see his picture up in the house, but it's nothing."

I wasn't sure if I was more surprised to hear about this prophet or that Samuel would mention something so important just minutes before we were to arrive. *"It's not a big deal."* He was always repeating this refrain in this tone, and I'd long ago gathered that he thought I turned everything into a big deal.

He explained that his parents had converted when he was a baby. The family even flew to Trinidad, where his father was born and where the prophet lived, for the ceremony of "commitment and transformation." He assured me his parents were strictly Christian; believers in the prophet simply had a more intellectualized view of the Bible. "They believe in evolution, that women can be as successful as men, all of that," he said. "The prophet teaches that the followers of Christ should become engaged in intellectual rigor. I mean, that's one reason Father was so hard on me. He believes we should be the best we can be."

"Do you believe in—Hadah—Hadah . . . How do you say his name again?"

"Hadad . . . Rimmon . . . Jaha-leel Hach-a-liah."

Whoa.

I attempted to repeat the name but became exhausted somewhere around Rimmon.

Samuel's parents still lived in El Cerrito, only a fifteen- or twenty-minute drive from Oakland. I asked him to tell me more—quick.

"Look. I'm not trying to scare you. I just wanted to give the heads-up. I don't want you to freak out or have you thinking they're in a cult or anything crazy."

I tried not to freak out or start to think they were in a cult or anything crazy, but it sounded crazy—*and like they were in a cult.* Samuel exited the freeway. I felt my body tensing as we passed the El Cerrito BART station. I wanted to give Samuel's family the benefit of the doubt, but I'd already lined up too many points against them.

After that night in Yountville, we'd never discussed the beatings he'd received as a child, but I'd sometimes trace the keloid scar on his lower back and think about the strap of a belt. I didn't ask about it, though, because I didn't want to pressure him into talking about something that would make him uncomfortable. He'd made it so clear, after all, that he didn't want to discuss his childhood. I leaned against the window, wishing I could talk to Bendrix. I could already hear the blow by blow I'd give later. "They worship some prophet I've never heard of! And Samuel didn't want me to wear the dress I chose! I wore a gray skirt and a white blouse. I looked like I was going to a business meeting."

"Where are you?" I heard Samuel ask. He reached over and took my hand. "What are you thinking?"

"Nothing."

He gave my hand a squeeze and returned it to my lap. "They're going to love you, Abbey. Try not to be nervous."

Samuel's father greeted us at the door. He was much as I expected—dignified and hardened, a man who would look at home striking a pose in a colonial uniform with his rifle while standing next to his kill. I doubted I would have had the same impression if I hadn't known anything about him. He was actually tall and handsome. Fairer in complexion than Samuel but with the same cleft chin.

When we shook hands he stood so far away he looked as though he were bowing. "Nice to meet you, Abbey."

"You, too, Joseph."

"Mr. Howard, if you don't mind."

I cringed slightly. "Yes, of course. Apologies."

Samuel introduced his mother, who sang a hello and fidgeted her hands in the air and kissed my cheek. "You can call me Phyllis. Don't mind my husband." Her voice dipped and twirled and did a pirouette. She made me think of fairy godmothers and sugarplum fairies and all things nice. Her face was round and she had small bright eyes with a mole near the right eye and another on her cheek. "We're so happy you're here, Abbey. Ruth? Esther? Say hello to Samuel's friend."

Samuel's sisters stepped forward. They were both nurses in their mid-twenties, just a year apart in age. Like me, and their mother, too, they wore skirts and blouses. I extended my hand but they remained stiff and frozen. Esther, the oldest, glued her eyes on me as though she were casting a spell, and Ruth kept glancing at Esther as if seeking guidance on how to treat me and what she should do next. I said hello and they mumbled hello in return.

Phyllis clasped her hands to her chest. "I see pink boxes!" She started to reach for the cake boxes Samuel was holding but then stopped herself. "I'm very temped to see what you brought, Abbey, but I think I want to be surprised instead."

"My wife has a real sweet tooth," Mr. Howard said.

"I aim to please," I said, not recognizing my voice.

There was a moment of silence. The sisters—Evil One and Evil Two—glowered.

Okay, I thought, *this is going great.*

Mr. Howard gestured toward the dining room. "Well," he said, "let's not stand here all day."

After a few minutes of chitchat, we moved into the dining room, where Mrs. Howard told us to help ourselves to the meal she'd prepared. There was a platter of roast beef and bowls of asparagus and mashed potatoes. After we had helped ourselves, Mr. Howard explained to me that the family believed in eating in silence as a way of showing appreciation for God's bounty. Once he said grace, we would concentrate on the meal without talking as a way of showing our gratitude. He added that we would eat this way for fifteen minutes.

I guess I did a poor job of hiding the surprise on my face. Seeing my reaction, Mrs. Howard reached up and touched the cameo at her neck. "I know it must seem strange. But, you see, if you eat silently, you focus on the food, and that's how you appreciate the food and God. Did Samuel tell you about Prophet Hadadrimmon Jahaleel Hachaliah?" She pointed to a photo on the wall in a gold frame with plastic flowers strewn on top. Hada

Hada What's His Name sat in a chair with a young woman, whom I assumed to be his wife, standing at his side.

"Phyllis—," Mr. Howard interjected. "There's no need to explain. Abbey is a guest and she knows a guest has to put up with the hosts—whether she wants to or not."

He chuckled gaily, but only Samuel joined in. "Abbey understands," Samuel said. "I've told her all about the prophet. She's probably sick of hearing me talk about him."

He reached over and took my hand while I stared blankly. I remembered to move my lips upward. "Yes," I said.

"Very well," said Mr. Howard. "Shall we bow our heads?

"Dear Lord, we thank you for this meal and for our blessings. We thank you for your son and for his prophet, Hadadrimmon Jahaleel Hachaliah. We thank you for guiding our lives in heart, mind, and soul. For these things we are grateful. Lead us to do thy will, Father, and keep us and protect us. In thy son's heavenly name, we all say amen."

We all said amen and silence fell over the table and over the entire house. Mr. Howard picked up his knife and positioned his wrists in the air for optimal meat cutting. When he moved, so did the evil sisters and Phyllis and Samuel. After he took his first bite, everyone began eating.

The room was so quiet I could hear my every bite. The ticktock of the grandfather clock in the next room sounded as though it were directly next to my ear.

I stole a peek at Phyllis, who chewed with her lips locked, as if counting every bite before swallowing. As if her life depended on grinding whatever she ate to nothing before she consumed it.

I let my gaze wander to the picture of the prophet. He wore a beige military uniform and hat. Otherwise, he was what you'd expect—a fat round stomach and fat round face that said life as a prophet was darn good. Not much to do except collect money and give a sermon now and then. No surprise, either, that the "woman" at his side appeared to be just out of high school.

On one side of the portrait was a photo of a grinning Barack Obama and on the other was a Howard family portrait taken many years ago. An unsmiling Mr. Howard stood next to Samuel, who looked to be about ten, and adorable. Phyllis sat in a chair looking exactly as she did that night, same hair and basic blouse and skirt. Esther and Ruth stood next to her, grinning wildly, as they basked in the five minutes of fame granted by a one-man paparazzi.

I took a bite of my asparagus and listened to myself chew. The grandfather clock ticked and tocked, ticked and tocked. Funny how time slowed when you ate in silence.

I looked up from my plate when I felt the evil sisters staring at me from across the table. They bore their eyes into mine. In moments their eyes went completely red and their faces an odd green. I widened my eyes and raised my hands from the table in surrender. *What? Why are you guys so weird? What have I done? You don't even know me!*

In response, Ruth lifted the corner of her lip ever so slightly.

I glanced at Samuel, hoping he caught what was going on and would tell his sisters to back off—albeit silently—but he was concentrating on his food. If I'd felt bad for him before, I felt for him even more now. I didn't mean to pass judgment, but there was no warmth in the room at all. I reached over and let my hand rest on his knee. He let it stay there for a moment, then gave his leg a shake that indicated there was no touching at the dinner table, even in secret.

Tick. Tock.

Tick. Tock.

I thought about sending Bendrix a clandestine text: *Heeeeeelp!* Could our families be any more different? I imagined a split-screen version of dinner with the Howards versus dinner with the Ross clan. My own split screen would look something like:

My Family	Samuel's Family
"Did you hear about that senator and that video they found?"	Tick
"When are these fools gonna learn that everything's recorded these days?"	Tock
"Dad, I think I got that gig up in Saratoga. Five nights out in the open-air theater."	Tick
"Somebody take Ornette so Aiko can eat in peace!"	Tock
"I love me some gumbo, but it gives me gas."	[Cough]

"Uncle Walt!"

I picked up my wineglass. Thank goodness Hada Hada What's His Name approved of alcohol.

"The roast beef is very good, Phyllis." I practically jumped at the sound of Mr. Howard's voice breaking through the silence.

We all complimented Phyllis on the food. Time regained its normal pace once we were allowed to talk, and I started to relax. Phyllis began telling stories about Samuel and how cute he was and every award he'd earned. She added a couple of stories about Esther and Ruth.

Mr. Howard smiled now and then. At one point he added, "Nowadays people would say Phyllis and I were too strict, but I'll tell you one thing: You never saw my kids out there in the streets, and they never brought home any trouble."

That's because you beat them.

Mr. Howard cut into his meat. "Samuel mentioned that your business is going pretty well. You plan on expanding?"

"I'm not sure. Not now."

"You should think about it. If you've made a business that gets people giving out their dollars, you have to take advantage when things are hot. You should go into a neighborhood that needs a bakery. Simple as that. If you have a good product, and it sounds like you do, people will come to you."

He said more, but I began to drown him out. Before retiring he'd worked as a manager for an electrical company, and I wasn't sure how much he knew about business and how much he liked to give advice, whether he knew what he was talking about or not.

Samuel said, "That's a great idea, Pops." He turned. "You should think about expanding. It's a good idea."

I was exhausted running Scratch. No way was I taking on more. "Yeah, I'll have to think about it." There was my mystery voice again. I would've sworn everyone could tell I was lying.

"Don't just think about it," Mr. Howard said, as if he knew me and I'd asked for advice in the first place. "You have to act. What do I always say, Samuel? Tell her."

Samuel looked at me with a tinge of apology in his eye. "Never think too much. Thinking only gives you time to build up fear."

"That's right."

Esther twirled her fork near her ear. "I mean no offense, but all these fancy bakeries and gourmet this and gourmet that have gotten out of hand. Why can't people just bake a cake? The bakery where I go near the hospital has all this stuff on the menu that makes no sense. Why do I need a fig tart? Who likes figs? And how crazy is a chai cupcake? Why not just make a cupcake?"

Ruth added: "And the prices! A slice of cake can cost as much as a meal!"

"So why do you go there?" I asked.

They both paused. Esther said, "Because it's nearby. I just get a cup of coffee because her coffee is pretty good. I leave the rest alone."

"Me, too. I like the cinnamon rolls, but that's about it."

Phyllis sang, "Oh, the suspense is killing me. What did you bring, Abbey?"

I looked at the sisters. "A golden génoise and a rosewater pear tart."

Esther said, "You brought a golden gee-no—what was it?"

"It sounds very exciting," chirped Phyllis.

"Abbey is an incredible baker," Samuel said, surprising me with a kiss on the cheek. We held eye contact for a couple of seconds, and without thinking I leaned over and kissed him on the lips. I pulled away when I heard Mr. Howard clear his throat. Phyllis moved her chair back from the table, looking anywhere except at Samuel or me. "Oh, yes," she said, fumbling for words. "I should stop eating so I can save room for the dessert. Everyone finished?"

Esther and Ruth began collecting plates along with her.

"I should help, too," I said.

"Yes, Abbey," said Phyllis. "Samuel and Joseph can make themselves comfortable and we'll put on the coffee." I picked up empty plates and silverware, feeling as if I'd fallen back in time. My brothers were expected to clean and cook as much as my sisters; there were too many of us to expect the wives or exes to wait on us hand and foot.

Phyllis hummed to herself as she moved about the kitchen. She told Ruth and Esther to join their father. "You sure?" Esther asked.

"Abbey and I will handle it. Isn't that right, Abbey?"

"I'd be happy to."

"You two go ahead and get off your feet."

Esther told her she would at least turn on the coffeemaker. Ruth took out a tray of cups and saucers. Esther stared at me as she and Ruth left the kitchen. I was tempted to stick out my tongue.

Phyllis pointed out the drawer for knives and forks, then continued to hum as she took down a cake platter. Here was a woman who allowed her husband to beat her child, and she herself locked him in the closet, but otherwise she had a sweet way about her. I wondered if the weird sisters had suffered any abuse; something had to explain their evil.

I put the génoise on the cake tray and took out the pear tart.

"Those look amazing," Phyllis exclaimed. "I tried to bake when Joseph and I were first married, but everything I made ended in disaster."

"Baking's a science as much as anything else. Follow the directions to a T, and things usually turn out all right. I find it relaxing." I waved the cake knife over the tart. "Plus, there are the final results."

"I can't wait to try them." She hummed a merry tune, then paused in a way that said something was on her mind. She smiled, head tilted. "I'm sure we must seem peculiar to you with our beliefs, Abbey, but this is a special family for a reason. The girls graduated from their nursing program top of their class. And we are all so very proud of Samuel." She stepped closer and her voice dropped. "I wanted to tell you that we know about your family. Samuel told us you come from a broken home and your father lives a musician's lifestyle, and I just wanted you to know that that's okay. I know Samuel thinks highly of you. He doesn't bring female friends home to meet the family, so you must be very important to him. But I want you to understand that we have strong beliefs about marriage and commitment. If you two continue on this journey, you'll have to accept that." She stopped short. "Nothing against your family. I only mean . . . you see . . . the prophet wants us to raise kids in a two-parent household. And to be respectful and urge them to be the best they can be. In our church, all the children are in the top of their classes. Isn't that amazing? Every one. This is what we would want for you and Samuel—if I don't speak out of turn. But I can see how much he cares for you."

Once her speech was over, her face brightened and I could see her shifting back to fairy-godmother mode. She picked up the plates and began humming.

I considered telling her that my family was anything but "broken." I thought of telling her that the prophet could kiss my relatively flat ass. But I was tongue-tied and unsure of what to do, and Phyllis was already walking away. "Dessert is ready!"

12

You Don't Know Me

I told Bendrix about dinner with the Howards the next morning. I told him all about the silent eating and that after dessert we sat in the living room watching TV sitcoms without much conversation, except for Samuel and Mr. Howard, who briefly talked baseball, another story in itself.

We were in the kitchen at Scratch. Bendrix had stopped by before going in to the hospital. He sat in a chair I'd brought from my office, eating a brioche and drinking espresso while I regaled him with stories.

Rows of cupcakes lined several large baking sheets. I squeezed the pastry bag I was using and crowned each cupcake with a thick layer of ganache. The twist with these particular cupcakes was that I'd made a well in the center when baking them, then used a variety of pastry tips to make the ganache look as if it were rising from the middle in several swirls of rich chocolate. We called the cupcakes the Cannonball Adderleys, and they were heaven to any and all chocolate lovers.

I squeezed the pastry bag just so and watched the ganache ooze from the tip. "And his mom was going on about how if we have children, they have to be successful. It's part of their religion or something. She comes across like this perfect mother— except she locks her kids in the closet. Do they expect me to stay at home like she did? I want to stay home, but I want to be here at the bakery, too. I can do both; I'll just cut down on my hours."

Bendrix took his time with his espresso. "Jumping ahead, aren't you?"

"She brought up children, not me."

"Did you talk to Samuel about any of this?"

"Not really. He was happy with how things went."

"You still have to let him know how you feel and"—Bendrix shook his head as though flabbergasted—"share your thoughts. I think that's how relationships work. I think I read it somewhere."

"I didn't even tell you the worst of it. Mr. Howard said my génoise was too rich! Can you believe that? My génoise is *not* too rich. It's supposed to be rich and moist and chocolaty. It's a génoise, for goodness' sake." I stopped what I was doing and pointed my finger into the table. "And you know what that man had the nerve to do? He brought out a plate of boxed cookies and ate cookies instead of my génoise. Right in front of me! And of course the evil sisters wanted cookies after they saw him. Mind you, I was trained at the École Nationale Supérieure de Pâtisserie in France—"

"That's a mouthful."

"—by none other than Madame Pauline, and my génoise is not too rich. My génoise is perfection."

"I'd have to agree with you there. It's incredible."

"Of course it is!"

"So what happened when you went home? What did Samuel think?"

I quieted when Beth walked in and took down a tray of muffins. She was getting the front of the bakery ready, and I didn't dare speak until she was gone. I waited until I could hear her footsteps fade.

"He was in a *mood*."

"What kind of mood?"

"You know."

Bendrix laughed. "You mean he brought out the rope?"

"It's not funny."

He laughed some more.

"*Bendrix*." I glowered, then went back to making swirls.

"I'm sorry." He caught his breath and waited before speaking. "Abbey, you need to start talking to him. You do. You tell me everything, but you're in the relationship with him. Talk to him."

"I can't."

"Why not?"

"I don't know. It's just easier to leave things alone. He's happy. And I'm happy, too. I just need to let off steam."

His phone vibrated. He grinned when he saw the message. "Speaking of letting off steam. Check it out."

I set my pastry bag aside and stood behind him.

On the screen a man flexed his muscles in front of a mirror. His nipples stood erect underneath an extra-tight mesh shirt. His hair was dyed blond even though he looked of an ethnicity where he should have left the color alone. His jawline was scary sharp. "Who's that?"

"*That* is Manuel. He's a personal trainer and we have a date later tonight."

"He looks like a dum-dum."

"He's not that bad. I'm thinking about bringing him to the ballet next month." Rita and Doug had given tickets to any

family member who wanted to attend the annual fund-raiser and
benefit for the Oakland Ballet.

I looked at Manuel. "Now you're the dum-dum."

"Why shouldn't I invite him?" Bendrix asked. "I want to see
what he looks like all dressed up."

"What do you have in common with him?"

He raised a brow. "Do I need to have something in common?"

I went back to my cupcakes.

Beth walked in and Bendrix held up the picture. "Take a
look."

"New boyfriend?" she asked.

"Maybe."

She headed to the rack of muffins and traded the empty trays
for a tray of fruit Danishes and almond croissants. "I'm pretty
sure I saw your ex the other day," she said to Bendrix. "He was
walking down Piedmont." She started back to the front of the
bakery. "What was his name again?" she asked over her shoulder.

"Anthony," I said. I reveled in an excuse to say the name I
was never to speak again. "His name is Anthony Wilson!" I
called out. "He was in Haiti doing volunteer work. But now he's
back."

I returned my gaze to Bendrix, and he glared, mouth tight.

"She asked." I shrugged.

At home that night, I wanted nothing more than to order
pizza, open a beer, and watch a movie. Samuel was spending all his time with me, and he was already at the house by the
time I made it home that evening. I'd been thinking off and on
throughout the day about Bendrix's suggestion that Samuel and
I talk. We'd been dating for almost a year, but when I thought
about it, we never really *talked* talked. He told me about his cases
and we discussed my customers and we watched TV together,

but serious talks were growing few and far between. Why, for instance, was Samuel wasting his money paying rent on an apartment he never used? Why hadn't he told me about the prophet before yesterday? And now that I thought about it, he was on his laptop too often. And why were his sisters so evil? I could go on. Not that I wanted to point fingers, but that was the purpose of talking, right? He could let loose on whatever bothered him about me, too.

By the time I made it home, I wasn't so sure why I'd been so reluctant to talk in the first place. Samuel was on the couch with his laptop by his side and didn't look up when he greeted me. I cut him some slack. How was he to know the laptop bugged me if I never brought it up?

Carmen was watching TV. "Hey," she said.

Jake popped up from the couch. "Hey, Abbey, don't look so crabby. Your cakes? They ain't shabby. Ahhhhh!"

"Hi, Jake."

Samuel started to get up, but I told him not to bother and went to him instead. I moved his laptop to the end table and plopped down next to him. When I asked Carmen and Jake to what we owed the pleasure of their visit, Carmen explained that they were coming from seeing friends and thought they'd stop by. She had a few ideas to run by Samuel. Spring semester had started, but she was concerned that her grades from her previous semester—two As and two Bs—would hurt her in the long run, and they were discussing her signing up for extracurricular activities like joining the campus newspaper or running for an office.

Considering her miscarriage and all the stress of last semester, I thought two As and a couple of Bs sounded great, but I left it alone. I did wonder aloud, though, if writing for the school paper or running for student government, plus classes and her internship, would be too much. That's when Samuel said, "Everyone has a solid GPA these days. Carmen has to show she's well rounded. Besides, the girl is smart and going places. Right, Car?"

"That's right." Carmen smiled.

Samuel's influence was definitely rubbing off, and I had to admit that I liked seeing her growing more confident.

Jake leaned over and kissed her. "My girl is smart and she looks good whether she's in jeans or a suit. Proud of you, babe."

"Thanks, Jakey."

I noticed Samuel stiffening. Jake had long since charmed me, but not so much Samuel. It didn't help matters when Jake said, "You guys got anything to eat?"

"Got any money?" Samuel retorted.

"Ahhhhh!"

"I'm in the mood for pizza," I said.

"Sounds fine with me," said Samuel.

"Me, too," said Jake. "Pizza has all the nutrients I need."

Carmen poked him with her elbow. "We were actually about to leave."

Samuel said, "Stay if you want. May as well—pizza for all."

"And beer," I added. "And a movie. I just want to chill."

"How did it go meeting the family?" Carmen asked.

Samuel put his arm around me. "Abbey wowed them, of course. My mom already called me to say how much she liked her."

"She did?"

"She called today at the office. Said she thinks you're *amazing*, and she loved your desserts."

"I'm glad someone did," I muttered.

Samuel pulled me closer. "Don't be like that. Dad just likes the basics."

He planted a kiss on my cheek, but I kept my arms firmly at my sides. I was resolved to have that talk.

*L*ater in bed that night, I couldn't quite figure out how to start the Talk, which was what it had become in my head. My position on the bed, however, far enough away from Samuel that I threatened to fall off, surely signaled that something was on my mind, and eventually he did notice that I wasn't in my usual spot, right by his side.

"You all right?"

"I'm fine."

"You don't sound fine. Why are you so far away?" He closed his laptop and set it aside. I did the same with the book I'd been pretending to read. It was now or never, I thought, and started by telling him that I'd felt uncomfortable during dinner and that he should have told me about the prophet sooner. I told him that his sisters had been rude and mentioned a few of the things his mom had brought up in the kitchen. It seemed the more I talked, the more Samuel withdrew. I couldn't blame him. Listening to myself ramble, I realized the problem with holding off on having a talk: If you didn't discuss real issues often enough, you risked unleashing a disaster, unleashing your inner Aunt Nag.

Poor Samuel sat next to me looking stunned. After what felt like several minutes he said, "I was afraid to tell you about the prophet sooner because I knew it would scare you."

"But that's actually my point, Samuel. I want us to be able to talk about anything."

He folded his arms and fell silent, then said, "The prophet means a lot to my parents. You're only hearing bits and pieces of his teachings, so try not to judge. I don't agree with every- thing the man says, but I do agree with what my mother told you. I want my kids to be successful and I'll be ready to do anything to help them achieve that success. Any parent would want that."

Angry and irritated, he rolled onto his side.

I didn't want to give up, though. "If we're going to be close, you have to talk to me. And I have to talk to you."

I let my gaze fall to the scar on his back, shaped like a half square. I touched it now and felt him wince. If we loved each other, we needed to talk. I said, "Does the prophet teach that it's okay to hit children?"

Silence.

"The scar, Samuel, is that from your dad?"

He rolled onto his back. "It is, Abbey. And you know, I'm starting to regret ever telling you about any of that."

"Have you ever talked to anyone about what happened? Like a professional?"

He sat up with a loud sigh. "Why are you always putting this in my face?"

"What do you mean? We talked about it in Yountville and that's about it. I just met your parents, so it's kind of on my mind."

"If I ever feel the need to talk to someone, I will. Until then, you need to drop this. My parents were nice to you." He started to turn on his side but changed his mind. "Maybe they took the teachings too far, but you have to look at the results: I didn't end up on drugs, in jail, or on the streets. No, I'm the opposite of all that. If anything, I owe them. And you see how proud they are of me."

"You guys hardly talked. You hardly have a relationship."

"That's just the way it is."

"Samuel, you have to trust me. I just want us to be able to talk."

"I *knew* you wouldn't like them."

"I never said that."

"You're implying it. My parents are good people. Hardworking. Still married, and they raised me the best they knew how. I know you're used to loud and crazy, and people telling jokes over dinner and people coming and going, but everyone wasn't raised the same way as you. Hell, no one was raised like you were. And your family is far from perfect. At least Father takes responsibility for the children he brought into the world."

"That's not fair. My dad takes responsibility and you know it." Now it was my turn to roll onto my side in a huff.

So much for talking. Jerk. I never wanted to talk to him again. If he wanted to stay closed off and shut down and live behind his stupid computer—fine with me. Asshole.

After a few moments of seething, I felt him give me a shake. "Abbey." Getting no response, he shook me again. *"Aaabbeeey,"* he sang. *"Abbey Lincoln."* I'd never heard him sing like this before and felt myself give a little.

"What?"

"Sit up so I can see you. Please?"

I sat up. I refused to look at him, though.

"The point of meeting each other's families is to move forward. I wanted you to meet my parents to see what they're like because I wanted you to get a sense of why I am the way I am. One of the teachings from the prophet I do appreciate is that cohabitation breeds problems. If you love someone, you love them enough to marry without any need to practice beforehand. I like that teaching. You love someone and you're in it for life, or you don't. I didn't mean to start coming over so much. I have to admit I don't feel comfortable living together."

"What?" I honestly had no idea what he was talking about. "Who says we're living together? What are we talking about? I thought we were talking about dinner last night."

"We were, but now we're not. I'm always here, Abbey. Most of my things are here. By definition we're living together."

"You're not by definition helping me with my bills."

"You want to know about me? Well, you should know I don't like doing things halfway. I'm either fully committed or not. And all of this"—he flung his hands around the room—"makes me uncomfortable."

"Fine. I'm glad you're telling me. This is what I mean. We need to talk."

"I'm trying to talk. I'm trying to tell you how I feel."

"No one is forcing you to stay here every night."

"I know that."

"Then what the hell are you complaining about?"

"I'm not complaining. I'm trying to tell you—" He shook his head and shot out of bed. "Fuck it."

"What's with you?"

I watched him go to the closet, where he knelt over his duffel bag. "I wasn't going to do this tonight. But whatever. If you want to know how I feel, I'm ready to show you how I feel." He shoved his arm out as though handing me a wad of trash. "Here."

"Here what?"

He opened his hand to reveal a small velvet box.

Uh.

"Take it."

"No."

"Abbey, take it."

I was suddenly embarrassed, not to mention shocked. I wanted to rewind, reboot. Start over. "I don't want it."

"Why not?"

"Because if that's what I think it is, I don't want it to be like this."

"Abbey, I love you and you drive me crazy and I want to make a commitment to you. A proper commitment. You're the kind of woman a man marries."

My eyes instantaneously filled with tears. But they weren't all joyful. My engagement wasn't supposed to be like this. My engagement was supposed to be YouTube-worthy, videoed with the sun setting while my fiancé sang an original song he'd composed just for me. Or there was supposed to be a funny surprise like when Pete, who couldn't sing at all, took the mike from my sister Dinah and sang for her before getting down on one knee. Or, hell, I'd take simple: a proposal at a romantic restaurant with everyone breaking into applause. *Anything but this.* We were practically fighting. Hell, we *were* fighting!

Samuel sat next to me on the bed.

"Don't cry, Abbey. I'm sorry. I love you."

"But this isn't romantic."

He laughed. "It can be. Open the box. Come on." He gave me a nudge. "You know you want to." He wiggled the box in front of my nose. "Open me," he said, making his voice like a cartoon frog. "Open me. Peek inside."

I reached for the box, but he pulled it away before I could take it.

"Sucker."

When I smiled, he climbed off the bed and dropped to his knee. "Abbey Lincoln Ross, I love you and I want to spend the rest of my life with you. Will you marry me?" He slowly opened the box.

Rays shot out from the diamond and the room lit up. I stared down at that gorgeous ring and all my fears and doubts flew out the window. *Bye-bye!* I loved Samuel. I heard myself say, "Yes," then repeated it. "Yes, I'll marry you."

As he slipped the ring on my finger, I forgot all about our

discussion, his family, and Prophet Hada Hada What's His Name. I forgot it all.

I was engaged! And this time I'd stay engaged until I was married. Finally!

I saw the magic pixie dust and then Ella swooped down singing "Our Love Is Here to Stay." She pressed her cheek to mine. *Look at that diamond! It's huge!*

13

Out of Nowhere

Two weeks later, and I was watching men in tights leap and twirl across the stage at the Paramount Theatre. Bendrix had indeed brought Manuel as his date, but the guy kept dozing throughout the performance. Samuel wasn't much better; he leaned over and whispered that he was having a hard time keeping his eyes open, but he did his best. Besides, who cared? He'd given me an amazing engagement ring and I was ready to forgive him anything. Every now and then his head would dip, but then he'd clear his throat and sit up straight. Bailey and Joan were with us as well. As platinum supporters of the Oakland ballet, Rita and Doug received a bottle of champagne to enjoy during the performance, and we all sipped and reveled in our box seats.

The only problem of the evening, really, was that by intermission Manuel had fallen flat-out asleep and was snoring so loudly people were beginning to stare. Bendrix, embarrassed and livid, gave the mound of muscle sitting next to him a hard shake. After he'd whispered what appeared to be heated words in

Manuel's ear, they both stood up and we all rubbernecked until
they disappeared.

Bendrix returned moments before the second half of the performance was to start, without Manuel. He sat down in a huff,
straightening his suit while staring directly at the stage. When
Bailey asked what had happened to his friend, he said, eyes still
on the stage below, "He won't be returning."

"Told you," I whispered.

Bailey and I exchanged looks while trying not to laugh.

After the performance, Rita and Doug suggested dinner at a
restaurant nearby. Slowly we made our way out of our seats. The
wives led the way while Samuel, who was already busy on his
phone, kept up the rear. I was teasing Bendrix about his muscle-
man when he stopped short, and I bumped into him from behind.
"Hey—"

"He's here," he said.

"Who's here?"

He kept his gaze on the vacating audience down below. I
searched and searched the crowd until I saw him. I grabbed Bendrix by the arm. "Anthony!" I said. "It's Anthony!"

"Lower your voice, would you?"

"He can't hear me. Unless I shout."

"Don't you dare."

We both stood staring as we continued to inch our way to
the aisle. Anthony, no surprise, was still gorgeous. When he
laughed at something the woman he was talking to said, his
smile shone up to the balcony, as beautiful as ever.

"What do you think he's doing here?" Bendrix whispered.

"The same thing you are," I whispered in return. I noticed,
then, dots of perspiration on his forehead. "Benny, are you're
sweating?"

"It's hot," he snapped.

I took a tissue from my purse and dabbed at his face.

"We need to get out of here before he sees us," Bendrix said.

Bailey looked past Rita so she could catch his attention. "Bendrix! I think I see your Anthony!"

"He's not *my* anything," Bendrix replied. "And, yes, I know. Thank you."

"Anthony's here?" asked Rita. "Where is he?"

Joan peered over the balcony. "Near the exit. See? Right there."

"Don't draw attention," Bendrix muttered. "I don't want him to know I'm here."

"That's funny," Bailey said. "You deal with life and death on a daily basis, but you can't face your ex. He looks good, too. *Damn.*"

"He does," said Rita.

Doug looked up from his phone. "What's that?"

"Nothing, sweetheart. It's Bendrix's ex. He's here."

"Terrific." He went back to his phone.

Samuel, also lost in his phone, said, "Who are we talking about exactly?"

"Bendrix's ex is here," I said.

"Ah," he said, half-distracted. I'd told him enough about Anthony that he knew the story, but he didn't understand how excited I felt. Just seeing Anthony briefly made me realize how much I missed him. I wanted to catch his attention, but how? Yell down to him? Push through the crowd and meet him at the entrance? In the end, I knew my ideas were silly and I'd only embarrass myself, not to mention Bendrix. So I remained frozen, only to watch as Anthony exited the theater.

Over dinner, everyone toasted Samuel and me on our engagement. Rita went on about wedding plans until Doug told her she should let me eat in peace. Bendrix relaxed enough that he no longer appeared ready to faint or bolt, even though I was certain he was still thinking about Anthony.

We left the restaurant sometime around eleven thirty. After Doug and Rita had walked off to their car, I heard a familiar laugh coming from somewhere behind me: part hyena, part machine gun, the kind of laugh that made you laugh yourself because it was so odd. I turned, knowing exactly whom I'd see.

Anthony rounded the corner with his head thrown back, while laughing into his phone. As soon as he saw me, his eyes widened and his smile grew, but then Bendrix turned and Anthony's steps faltered and he abruptly closed his mouth. He said to whoever was on the other end, "I've gotta go."

Seeing him, Bendrix stared down at his feet, then watched a bicyclist pass as if he wished he could take the guy's bike and speed off.

Joan saved us from our descent into complete awkwardness by walking over and giving Anthony a hug. "Anthony, what a lovely surprise." She peered up into his eyes while giving his chest a few firm pats. "You are just as handsome as ever, I see. Bailey, look at this. Look who's here."

Anthony smiled, making sure to avoid eye contact with Bendrix and me. Bailey walked over. She wore a strappy top, a sequined skirt, and heels that made me wonder if they'd been designed by (s)hoes. "You do look good. Life treating you well?"

"Yes, Bailey. It's good to see you."

"You, too. Really good. I won't lie, though. I saw you at the ballet."

"You did?"

"Yeah, we all saw you. That one there didn't want us to say anything."

She pointed at Bendrix, who quickly turned his head toward the street. She smiled up at Anthony. "Why you standing there like that? Stop acting like you're not happy to see me and give me a hug." They laughed and hugged.

I tapped her shoulder after giving them a moment. *My turn.* Anthony's face softened when our eyes met. He pulled me into his arms and we hugged for what felt like a good long time. "I've missed you," he said.

"Me, too."

He took a step back so he could look at me. "How have you been?"

That's when I shoved my left hand into his face. *Pow!* "I'm engaged, baby!"

"What?"

Joan said, "She's been telling so many people I'm surprised you haven't heard. I thought the entire city of Oakland knew by now."

I turned and smirked.

"Miracles will never cease," Anthony said. "Congratulations." We hugged again.

Samuel was still preoccupied with his phone, but I dragged him over. "Samuel, this is Anthony."

"Congratulations," Anthony said, shaking his hand. "You've got yourself a very special woman."

"Thanks, man. Don't I know it. Nice to meet you."

Bendrix stood far enough away to imply he wanted nothing to do with the meet and greet we were enjoying. Anthony did the same and refused to look his way. He explained that he was having dinner with a friend just up the street, then told us a little about his Haiti trip. Bendrix had to be dealt with in one way or another, though, and since it looked like he definitely planned on playing the pouty child, Anthony finally broke from the group and stuck out his hand. "Bendrix."

Bendrix's face remained impenetrable, but I knew under his

hard eyes that catching a whiff of Anthony's scent was rattling him to the core.

"How have you been?" Anthony asked.

"As if you care."

Anthony withdrew his hand. "Really? You're going to play it like that?"

Bendrix cut his eyes.

"Bitterness only hurts the person who's bitter," Anthony said.

"That's profound."

Anthony clenched his jaw. "It was a mistake, Bendrix. Get over it. And you weren't perfect, either. You get a kick out of playing the victim."

I heard Bailey go, *"Ooooh."* I shot her a look over my shoulder and she closed her mouth.

The word *victim* hung in front of Bendrix's face. Anthony knew what using that word would mean. "Victim? Hardly. *You* chose to take things outside of our relationship. You chose to ruin what we had."

Samuel stepped close to my ear. "Abbey, stop being nosy. We should let them have some privacy."

"Yeah. You're right." But I stayed put.

Bailey said, "Those two are in their own world, anyway. We may as well be invisible. They're just pickin' up as if no time has passed at all."

True. It was unbelievable how they'd started right in. I'd wanted this to happen, but I hadn't expected them to exchange words right in the middle of downtown Oakland. I thought of stepping in and telling them they should go somewhere private— but I didn't. I was too shocked that all of it was happening in the first place. It was surreal.

Anthony pointed his finger toward the sidewalk. "I left the country feeling guilty, but I realized you were just as much at fault for the breakup as I was."

"Oh, really? So I went behind your back and made out with another man."

"No, but you stopped trying. You weren't involved in the relationship. You checked out."

"Call it what you will, but I didn't cheat."

"It was a kiss, Bendrix. I could've done a lot more."

"Spare me."

Samuel was suddenly standing in front of them, doing what we probably should've done minutes earlier. "Fellas, what do you say we cool down, take this discussion somewhere else?"

"Yes," Joan said. "We've all eavesdropped long enough."

Just as Bendrix and Anthony broke eye contact long enough to remember where they were, a police car swooped up alongside the restaurant and lights flashed. The officer on the passenger side rolled down his window. "Everything all right here?"

"Of course everything is all right!" Bailey shouted. "Don't we look all right to you? You blind or something?"

Have I mentioned yet how much Bailey disliked cops? Well, she tended to get a little angry around them. Every one of her sons—each of my older brothers—had been pulled over, ticketed, or somehow harassed at one time or another by a cop, and when Bailey was a teen, her father had spent time in jail after he'd been falsely accused of robbery.

Bendrix and I both went into action. Bendrix cautioned, "Bailey, let's calm down."

"Yeah, Bailey, there's no need to shout," I added.

Joan said under her breath, "This is turning into quite the evening." She laughed lightly, as if she were having high tea with the queen. If Rita disliked Bailey's rather bold personality, Joan loved it.

Bailey marched over to the car in her skirt. Mind you, the cop in the passenger seat looked like Dizzy when he was a boy and didn't appear threatening in the least. The cop in the driver's seat, on the other hand, was much older, with a world-weary expression that said he'd been on the job one too many years.

"Why did you need to stop? Tell me, Officer. Is it because you saw all these fine men out here talking with each other? What, you think they're in a *gang?*"

The young cop stared up at her as if not knowing what was going on. The older cop leaned over and said, "We're going to need you to step away from the car, ma'am."

"I'm trying to make a point. Why did you need to stop?"

The cop in the passenger seat seemed dubious. "Someone called and said there was a disturbance."

Bailey tried to make eye contact with the few people passing by, as if to catch the snitch in action. "Disturbance? How are three men talking on the street a disturbance?"

Samuel intervened by trying to pull her away. "Everything is fine, Officer."

"Don't kowtow to the likes of them, Samuel. I'll have you both know that this man here is a lawyer and that one is a counselor and that young man is a doctor. There is no need for you all to be pulling over and checking in or whatever it is you're doing." She shouted, "Racial profiling! Racial profiling in progress!"

Samuel tried to pull her away. "Bailey, you're going to get us arrested. *Calm down.*"

Anthony added, "Bailey, we're fine."

"You're the problem right now," said Bendrix.

Bailey looked at us all. "None of you see what's going on?"

"Bailey, it's late," I said. "Let it be."

By now a handful of people had stopped. One guy had out his phone and was filming. The older cop let his gaze land on Samuel. "She's all yours, man. Good luck."

The cops drove off. Once they were gone, we all let out a collective sigh.

"Bailey, are you nuts?" I asked.

"They had no right!"

"You only helped to escalate the situation, Bailey," said Anthony.

I noticed Bendrix staring at him. He swallowed and said, "Now that Bailey isn't going to jail, I should leave."

"What about a drink?" I suggested. Bendrix and Anthony had been arguing, yes, but at least they'd been talking, and while it was clear that they were still angry, wasn't that a sign that they cared about each other? I took Anthony's arm, then Bendrix's. "Let's all get a drink! Calm our nerves."

Bendrix removed my hand. "No. I'll talk to you later." He said good-bye to Bailey and Joan and Samuel. He then turned, jaw clenched, and started up the street.

"Bendrix!" I called. "Don't leave."

Anthony shook his head. "Let him go." He then offered a brusque good-bye of his own. "Hope to see you again, Abbey." He said good-bye to Samuel. "Nice meeting you." He hugged Bailey and Joan, then headed in the opposite direction.

"Guess the show is over." Bailey sighed.

I cut my eyes at her. *"You think?"*

Joan took Bailey's arm. "You certainly told them, didn't you?"

"Don't you start," Bailey said. They decided to walk back to Bailey's car together.

That left Samuel and me. I took out my phone.

"What are you doing?" he asked.

"Calling Bendrix."

"Abbey, he's a grown man. Leave him alone."

"I know, but I don't remember the last time I've seen him so upset. He's never wanted to hear Anthony's side of things."

"Bendrix is smart, is what he is. Some things, like cheating, shouldn't be forgiven."

"It was a kiss!"

I listened to Bendrix's phone ring. When he didn't pick up, I sent him a text asking that he call me.

Samuel and I headed to his car in silence. Samuel didn't speak until we were driving out of the parking garage. "What the hell was going on with Bailey? She was acting nuts."

"She has issues with cops."

"Who doesn't? Her behavior was beyond embarrassing. Not to mention she could have had us all arrested. Me in particular. I've been pulled over for no reason more than once," he said soberly. "It only takes one moment of poor conduct or mistaken identity for a person's life to change."

"I know. That's just Bailey. You handled it well, though." I reached over and touched his hand, and he seemed to relax.

"We'll have to think about all these types of issues when we raise our sons, you know—if we have any. That's another thing about the prophet's teachings. He's all about keeping humble and low-key. Keeping your feelings in check. Never too out of hand, never too upset." He added after a beat: "My mother would never in a million years behave like Bailey."

I gazed out the window. The beauty supply stores, the Korean grocers. I wasn't in the mood for one of his lectures on how people needed to behave.

"Hey, I'm not judging. I believe respect is earned. No one is ever going to respect a woman who acts and dresses like Bailey."

"I disagree," I blurted. "Bailey has helped keep our family together. She's the number one wife."

Samuel chuckled. "I wish you knew how you sounded right now. Anyway, you can disagree all you want, but I know I'm right. Father says if you want people to follow you, you have to behave accordingly. You see how Carmen is coming around already, don't you? That's a direct response to her watching my behavior. I want our kids to be something in the world, and we have to lead the way by setting a good example. I guess I'm trying to make my point because I'm excited about becoming a father. You excited about having kids, baby?"

"Of course."

He smiled. "We're going to have to start right away, you know. I'm getting older, and you're one year older than me."

"And you won't let me forget it." He sometimes liked to tease me about our "age difference." I smiled and gave his chin a pinch. I liked thinking about making a baby right away.

We came to a stoplight. "How old were you the first time you went steady?" he asked.

"*Went steady?* I don't know. Fifteen. His name was Miguel Perez. His family was originally from Guadalajara, although he was born here. He was into graffiti."

"And your first time?"

"What's with the questions?"

"I'm marrying you. I should know these things."

"I was sixteen. His name was Rashid Washington."

"Miguel . . . Rashid . . . You're like the United Nations, you know that?"

"That's me. How about you?"

He turned on Fortieth and we waited behind a bus while people exited. "The prophet teaches that the young should wait to have sex. That's what's interesting about the man. He's not against premarital sex, but he advocates having sex at an appropriate, mature age."

I held my tongue. I was hearing more and more about the prophet now that we were engaged. The prophet, the prophet, the prophet. *Ugh.*

"He teaches that men should wait until they're twenty; twenty-one for girls."

"Great." My sarcastic tone was not lost on him. "Makes sense to me."

"*Anyway,*" he said, giving me a look, "I played the good boy until the end and I waited."

"Until you were twenty?"

"Twenty-one."

"Wow. You really were a good boy."

"What can I say? The prophet's teachings were ingrained."

We continued up Fortieth, but then, without any warning, he veered the car over to the side. My body fell against the door as I let out a gasp. "What the hell?"

He pulled up to the curb and cut the engine. We were on a residential street by now, not far from my house. "What's going on?"

"Calm down. Everything is fine." He unfastened his seat belt, then turned and rested his arm on the steering wheel. He wore a mischievous look on his face that gave me pause.

"You're making me nervous."

He continued wearing the odd grin, but I soon noticed a bashful glint in his eye.

"Are you okay?"

"I never had a chance to really kiss a girl in high school."

"And?"

"Wanna make out with me?"

I stole a quick glance around the quiet residential streets. "Make out with you? *Now?*"

"Just for a couple of minutes. Let's pretend we're fifteen and we're dating. I can't take you home yet because I want to kiss you; I want to ask you to be my girlfriend."

Hearing this, the moment shifted from odd to entirely sweet and innocent. I laughed when he started creeping toward me. "You're serious, aren't you?"

"Come on, be my high school sweetheart." He moved closer, then reached across my waist and unfastened my seat belt. "What do you say? Would you be my girl?"

J woke to the sound of my ringing doorbell. I sat up in bed. Samuel was still sound asleep beside me. I found my phone to check the time—seven fifty. I noticed Bendrix had called, poor guy. Whoever was at the door began knocking again. I returned the phone and grabbed my robe.

Through the peephole I saw my brother Dizzy's globe-shaped head. I opened the door and he stepped in, taking up most of the space with his height and girth. He held Hope against his hip; Duncan and Bessie stood on either side of him.

"Hey-hey," he boomed.

"Hi."

"Can I have a cookie?" Duncan asked.

"Me, too!" said Bessie.

Hope sucked her thumb and continued resting her head on her father's shoulder. I bit down on my lower lip. My brother showing up like this with his kids was odd. I had a strong feeling I'd somehow goofed. Sure enough . . .

"You forgot, didn't you?"

"No?"

"You said you'd babysit today."

I thought back to dinner at Dad's a few weeks before. Dizzy and his wife had been talking about their lack of alone time, and, yep, I'd offered to take the kids for a day. But I never wrote it down on my calendar, and if it wasn't on the calendar, it didn't get done. *Oops.*

Dizzy frowned. "I'll warn you: If you make me take these kids back, you'll have to deal with Sharon. She's been looking forward to this for days."

Luckily, it was Sunday and Beth was running the bakery. Samuel and I had no plans. "Nope. I've got you covered." I wiggled my fingers at Hope and she skydived toward me. I kissed her and hoisted her farther up my hip. I thought about the night before—specifically Bailey and the cops. "Have you talked to your mom, by chance?"

He paused and tilted his head forward. "Now what did she do?"

"Almost got us arrested." I heard Samuel's footsteps. "But I'll tell you about it later. It's no big deal. Just Momma Bailey being herself."

"Can she be anything but?"

We were smiling when Samuel joined us. He pulled at the belt of his robe. Sleep dug in the corners of his eyes. "Mornin'."

Dizzy walked over and stuck out his hand. "Hey, congrats on the engagement."

"Thank you. Good to see you."

Dizzy told the kids to say hello and I explained that I was on babysitting duty.

"Sounds good to me," said Samuel. "We'll look after them." He held up his hand and Duncan gave him a high five.

If I'd made an imaginary chart of Samuel's pluses and minuses, all of my concerns were trumped by his love for kids and his desire to start a family. And he was a good man, handsome and kind and trustworthy. You couldn't get everything you wanted from one person, and I guessed the pluses still outweighed the negatives.

Bessie took my hand. "Can I have a cookie?"

I looked at Dizzy. "You have time for breakfast?"

"I could eat. Sharon is out cold. I wouldn't be surprised if she sleeps most of the day. The kids had cereal, but—hey, if you're offering."

"Of course." I took Bessie's hand. "You guys can have a cookie later. Let's see what we can make for breakfast."

I kept a basket of toys in the spare bedroom and a small shelf of children's books for when any of my nieces or nephews were visiting. The kids played while Samuel, Dizzy, and I headed to the kitchen. I put on music and started coffee. When Dizzy heard Ray Brown playing "Out of Nowhere," he pointed and said, "I haven't heard this version in years."

"I like Ahmad Jamal's version more, I think."

"I think you're nuts."

"Jamal plays it with feeling."

"Feeling?" Dizzy said. "Hardly."

"You dare criticize the one and only Ahmad Jamal? Who do you think you are?"

"A man with an opinion."

"And a huge ego."

"I call it like I hear it, my little sister who does not play the piano nor any instrument and does not know what she's talking about."

"Watch it," I said halfheartedly.

He started to continue, but then the doorbell rang and we all looked at one another.

From the living room, Bessie yelled: "I'll get it!"

"You stay put," Dizzy called back.

I went to the door and asked who it was.

"Why haven't you answered my texts?"

Bendrix.

I swung open the door. He stood tall in a leather jacket and aviator shades. His hair was coiffed and he was clean-shaven. "You look terrible," I teased.

He lowered his shades so I could see his eyes, then pushed them back into place. Keeping his gaze glued on me, he raised his left hand and wiggled his finger.

A man peeked out from the side of the house. "Good morning!"

My mouth fell open. "Anthony? *What?* Oh my God! *Anthony!*"

I brought him in for a hug. I pulled back so that I could see it was really him. I had to swipe at a tear that was trying to escape.

Anthony said, "Aww, don't cry, honey."

"Who says I'm crying? I'm just shocked. What happened? You guys made up? You're back together? Oh my gosh! When did this happen? How did it happen? You guys were so pissed last night—"

"Whoa, whoa," Bendrix said. "Calm down."

"We're just talking," Anthony replied. "But it's a start." He smiled at Bendrix.

"I tried to call," Bendrix said.

"I know. It's been hectic here." I waved for them to come inside.

Samuel and Dizzy were already in the living room; they walked over and everyone shook hands.

I hooked my arm in Anthony's while smiling at Bendrix. "I was just about to start breakfast. Do you guys want quiche? I can make cinnamon rolls, too. I have prepared dough in the fridge."

"Calm down," Bendrix said.

I smiled up at him and in a burst of giddiness waved my fist in the air. "Yay!"

Bendrix rolled his eyes.

14

Hesitating Blues

*A*fter spending that morning with my house filled with people I loved, I assumed things would only get better. And they did. Except for a few glitches. For starters, now that Samuel and I were engaged, he and I started going to dinner at the Howards' at least once a month, and this meant more of the same—silent eating and evil sisters and listening to his dad give lectures on subjects he knew little about. *Okay, fine.* I knew Samuel wasn't brimming with love for my family, either. He thought we were too loud, and he still didn't understand our "cuckoo" familiarity with one another—ex-wives hanging out together and all that.

And then there was the wedding itself. I knew planning a wedding could cause strife between couples—I was a wedding cake designer; I got it—but Samuel wanted a wedding that was completely different from what I wanted.

We'd been engaged since May. He wanted to get married that August, which was not the problem. The problem was that he wanted a "small and simple" wedding. His idea of a wedding: exchange vows at the courthouse and invite a few friends and family afterward. Prophet Guess Who taught his followers that weddings and ceremonies should remain "humble." While I knew only a handful of the Prophet Whodawho's teachings, so far Samuel seemed to agree with every lesson I hated. In particular, screw small and humble! I wanted a lavish wedding. I was closing in on forty and I wanted to celebrate the fact that I'd met the man of my dreams. I wasn't a bridezilla, but I was the daughter of Lincoln T. Ross, and this meant: (a) my family was huge, and (b) we needed space to dance and play music. Samuel argued that he'd been raised on the notion that big weddings were only a display of self-congratulation and importance, and an act of vanity. He wanted small and intimate because he hated the idea of standing in front of a bunch of people he hardly knew and "celebrating with a bunch of lookie-loos." He added that spending so much money on a single day was a waste, and we could take the thousands and thousands of dollars we would spend to rent a space and hire a caterer and a limo and all else a big wedding entailed and use it for our kids' schooling and college education instead. Or we could use it for a down payment on the house we were going to have to move into once the kids started coming.

Granted, everything he said made perfect sense. But I didn't want to make sense. Sense had no place in my wedding. I wanted quixotic romance at its best.

We went back and forth for days. With no plan, we couldn't set a date. I was so frustrated with the situation, I even called my mom for advice. And then I remembered why I never called my mom for advice. Once I explained the situation, she sighed and said, "You're a grown woman, Abbey. You'll have to figure it out. I don't know what to tell you."

And then there were the wives.

Rita: "Abbey, no! You can't possibly go small. It's your wedding! What are you telling the world about the love you share with Samuel by marrying him in a courthouse? You may as well exchange vows in a bathroom!"

Bailey: "I don't give a damn what y'all do as long as the music is good."

Joan: "Except to give you business for your cakes, I'm not sure why people marry at all anymore."

I was thinking about the wedding nightmare one Thursday afternoon at the bakery while working on a five-tier color-wash cake that made me envy the bride and groom and the money they were spending to celebrate their nuptials. A mother and daughter had shown up to discuss the cake, and they knew exactly what they wanted. The color of the cake was going to match the bridesmaids' dresses, and the design would match the intricate embroidery on the bride's wedding dress. I had already covered the four tiers in fondant and made the color wash with gel and food coloring. After that I would use a paintbrush to "paint" the cakes the requested soft pink with lavender highlights. I was prepping for the embroidery when Noel walked back. It was five o'clock and we'd be closing within an hour.

"How many left?" I asked him.

"Under ten. Say, there's a woman here. She says she needs to talk to you."

"A client?"

"Nope. I asked, and she said it's a"—air quotes—"'personal matter.'"

I grabbed a towel and followed him out front. Phyllis stood near one of the booths in the front, staring up at the Shelton Lynn painting. She wore her usual skirt-and-blouse combo and a pair of flats. She carried a shopping bag from which protruded a white box made for a suit or dress. She turned when I said her name. "Hello, sweetheart."

"This is a surprise." *Truly.*

"I wanted to see where you work and thought I'd surprise you."

Noel asked if she wanted anything.

She stared briefly at the tattoos lining his arms. "Just a coffee. Decaf."

She returned her gaze to the painting. We always showcased various local artists, but I'd bought Shelton Lynn's mixed-media piece outright. The canvas was a spattering of oils with a provocative gash of spray paint down the center. It was one of the first paintings I'd bought for the bakery.

Phyllis continued to stare. "I've never understood art. What is this called exactly?"

"*Untitled.*"

"He should have called it ugly. Because that's what it is!" When she broke into laughter, I instantly saw the bitchy side of her personality that she'd passed down to Ruth and Esther.

I kept my voice as even as possible. "Sometimes the artist doesn't want to feed the viewers' interpretations of the piece, and the fewer clues or hints, the better. By not giving a title, the artist is saying, take whatever you want from the work."

"Sounds like you know something about art."

"I have a master's degree in art history."

"Oh, really? Samuel didn't tell us that. I don't know, Abbey. I never understood the point of art." She walked past the next two paintings, puzzled by it all.

"Humans have been creating art since the beginning of time, Phyllis. It's what makes us human. It's a form of expression."

"Well, I know that, but that doesn't help me understand it.

What I do get," she said, turning on her heels and walking toward the display case, "are those beauties over there. Everything looks so good," she said, peering inside. "What would you suggest?"

"What about a slice of coconut cake?"

"Sounds delicious."

I asked Noel to bring everything to my office, and Phyllis followed me to the back, stopping short when she saw the cake I was working on. I told her a little about the process.

"These brides today. Spending so much money. You know, Joseph and I had a small wedding." She raised both hands. "No fanfare."

Ah . . . so that's why you're here. Samuel ratted me out. Okay.

I forced what I hoped was a pleasant enough smile, then led her into my office.

Noel brought the cake and coffee. When he was gone, she leaned in and whispered, "My children would *never.* They learned what was allowed and not early on."

I assumed she was referring to Noel's tattoos. Frankly, half of my family, including Bailey, had one tattoo or another, but I didn't feel like defending body art on top of everything else.

Phyllis leaned in close and touched my arm with her fingertip. "I tell you, we wonder why the youth are as lost as they are. Parents don't raise their children."

I bit down on my lip to keep from saying anything. I wondered if I should tell her off, but I didn't feel it was the time or place. She was my future mother-in-law. What I needed, I thought, was some innocuous NPR host to do the dirty work. Where was Terry Gross when you needed her?

Terry: Phyllis Howard, welcome to Fresh Air. Can you tell us, Phyllis, what made you decide to lock your child in a closet for hours at a time?

Phyllis: Is locking a disrespectful child in the closet abuse? I don't think so. Samuel needed to learn that when I told him to do something, I meant business. I don't care what they say about all this time-out madness they teach these days, Terry. Look where our leniency with our children has put us as a country and as a people.

An hour too late, I said, "I was given time-outs, never spanked, and I turned out fine."

"You're an exception." She switched to her fairy godmother voice. "Now, let me taste this cake." Subject changed, she sliced into the cake. "Absolutely delicious. I've always had a sweet tooth. I'm so lucky you're going to be my daughter."

She noticed the photo of Samuel and me on my desk, taken on our last trip to Yountville. Samuel stood behind me with his arms around my waist.

"May I?" she said, already reaching for it. She stared at the photo for a moment. "My son loves you, Abbey. And the more time I spend with you, the more I understand why. Abbey, I wanted to talk about the wedding. Samuel mentioned you two are having trouble deciding what to do about the ceremony. I just hope you can at least try to see things from his side."

"I wish he hadn't said anything in the first place. We'll figure it out."

"You're going to be a wife soon. I know you've been alone for many, many years, but now that you're getting married, you'll have to learn to share your life and to compromise. A marriage can never work without the two Cs." She beamed and gave my arm a knowing push. "You want to know what the two Cs are, don't you?"

Let me guess, Phyllis. Coitus and cunnilingus?

"Cooperation and conciliation. And your future husband, my

one and only son, my oldest and beloved—all he wants is to make sure his new family is financially secure. He's a corporate lawyer, Abbey. I would think you'd trust his financial know-how. And I'm sure he's told you that he wasn't raised to make a show of things. He was raised to save his pennies and spend wisely."

I looked down at her hand currently resting on my wrist.

"Don't be upset."

"I'm not upset."

"You look upset."

"I'm not upset." *I'm pissed off.*

"Please take that look off your face. You probably don't realize it, but Samuel can be very shy."

"Shy?"

"Yes. He didn't have a lot of friends growing up and he doesn't do well with crowds. And all these people you want to invite are disconcerting. Do you want him to feel anxious at his own wedding? Because that's what will happen."

I assumed my role as future daughter-in-law was to respect my future mother-in-law and not argue, but I'd had enough. A person can only hold her tongue for so long. "Phyllis, I appreciate you coming by, but this is between Samuel and me."

She made a point of picking up her fork and taking a bite of cake. She chewed with her eyes closed. "Absolutely delicious." I watched while she dabbed at the corner of her mouth with her napkin, then took a sip of coffee. "He says he's been doing his best to talk to you. I'm only here to help, not meddle." She waved her hands in the air. "I have something for you!" She reached into the bag at her feet and handed me the white box. "Here. It's something special from me to you."

I opened the box and pulled back the tissue and saw the ugliest wedding dress I'd seen in my life. Bright white. Fringe at the collar. "Oh my God."

"It's my wedding dress!" she sang. "I want you to have it. I know it's probably a little big for you, but we can have it taken in."

"Phyllis, I couldn't."

"But I want you to take it."

"Really. I couldn't."

"My girls won't be marrying for a while, and I want to show you how much you mean to me. I insist. Stand up and let's see."

The shape reminded me of something Laura Ingalls Wilder would wear skipping down the prairie. I thought, *If I wear it over my head, I could go to my wedding as Casper the Friendly Ghost.*

Phyllis stood in front of me and held the dress at my shoulders. "You are going to look so beautiful. We can get a seamstress to take it in where it's sagging." She tilted her head to the side and smiled. "You know what I'm thinking, Abbey? Simple, pretty dress for a simple, romantic wedding."

I had to finish the cake I'd been working on before leaving the bakery and didn't get home until after seven. Samuel had already texted to say he'd be home around eight. He and his staff were working on an IPO for a pharmaceutical company, and he'd been getting home later than usual over the past week. Since I had the house to myself, I took a shower and ate cold pizza and drank beer for my dinner. I sat on the couch with Phyllis's wedding dress spread out next to me. I listened to *Nina Simone Sings the Blues* with the volume turned up louder than I normally played the stereo.

I thought about a couple I'd met a few months before: older couple, second marriage for both of them. The woman was going on about how much she liked her fiancé's family, and at one point after noticing my ring, she said, *"Make sure you like his family. You're not just marrying the man; you're marrying his family, especially his mother."* She was originally from New York and spoke with one of those heavy accents; *mother* sounded like *motha*. I took her advice lightly then, but now I was starting to get what she meant. I draped my arm over my eyes. Sad thing was, I could already feel a tinge of regret. I already knew I was going to give in and have the small wedding and wear the dress. I didn't want to believe it, but while my mind wanted me to hold the fight— *This is your wedding! Your life! Do what you want!*—my heart was making the case that Phyllis had a point. I needed to learn to compromise. She was giving me her wedding dress; how could I turn her down? My heart told me not to be selfish or mean. *Don't start off your marriage being selfish! Don't be so mean as to turn down your future mother-in-law's wedding dress! Show everyone that you can be flexible and that you're not a bridezilla. Make Samuel happy and you'll be happy.* When Nina began singing "In the Dark" I shot up from the couch and shoved the dress back inside the box and closed the lid.

I was still on the couch when Samuel opened the door. He gave me a kiss, then went to the stereo to turn down the music. He went on about his day and told me what was going on with the IPO. Still talking, he sat next to me and helped himself to the second bottle of beer I'd started. He began unbuttoning his shirt after taking off his shoes and stretching out his legs. Finally he seemed to notice the box on the coffee table. "What's that?"

I explained, adding that I didn't appreciate him telling our business to his mother.

He sighed and leaned back into the couch as though he couldn't believe that on top of everything else, he had to come home to a nagging girlfriend.

"You tell your family our business all the time—and you tell Bendrix everything. So what? I had a talk with my mom."

"I might tell my family things, but they don't butt in the way your mother did today."

"She was only trying to help, Abbey." He looked over at me after a moment. "She gave you her wedding dress?"

I nodded. *And it's ugly as hell,* I considered saying.

He took my hand. "That she gave you her dress to wear means a lot. You can't turn her down. I've been feeling frustrated and I needed to talk to someone. I never thought she'd go to the bakery, okay?"

He leaned forward while letting out a long, exasperated breath. He closed his eyes and ran his hands over his head. "I'm under so much pressure," he murmured. He picked up one of the bottle caps on the table and played with it between his fingers. He leaned back and spoke into the ceiling. "I go to work and I have to prove myself. I'm here with you, and now you're upset. Everything is so damn stressful right now. Even the wedding." He shook his head and fell forward again. "All I know is pressure. It's constant."

I felt my heart tugging. *See there? He needs you. Don't add more stress to this man's life. He needs to know how much you love him. It's just a wedding, Abbey. It's just one day. Let it go.*

I studied his face and saw the puffy bags under his eyes and his unkempt hair. He needed me. I traced my finger around the curve of his ear and he fell into me like a child in need of a hug. I held him through the remaining bars of "Day and Night." Then I kissed him on top of his head.

"Small wedding," I said. "We'll keep it simple and stress free."

He looked up. "You sure?"

"Yeah, it's fine. It's just a day."

He sat up and kissed me, his lips opening and closing with mine.

My gut, though, not trusting what had just transpired, whispered from somewhere deep, deep inside—*Suuckeeer.*

.   .   .

$\mathcal{S}$amuel and I were married at city hall in late September by Sandeep Thapar, a bored officiant who conducted the ceremony as if handling a business transaction, going so far as to read our vows directly from a handbook hidden behind a blue binder. The reception was held at Dad's. With only sixty guests in attendance, it felt like one of his parties. Samuel had invited a few friends from work. His family sat through most of the reception balancing plates of food on their laps while sitting stiff and guarded and talking mostly to one another. My family did their usual thing—dancing, singing, and making merry. Dad danced with me while Bailey and Dinah sang "Love Is Here to Stay" with my sister Billie on guitar and Dizzy on piano.

Mom had flown in from Connecticut and helped me dress before we went to city hall. For a wedding present she gave me a necklace made by an elder from the Masai tribe in Kenya. She said the necklace was very old, but since it was new to me, it covered both "something old" and "something new."

Rita cried. But only because she didn't get to help me plan the wedding she'd wanted for me and thought I deserved. Joan spent an inordinate amount of time talking to Joseph and Phyllis, for which I thanked her. When I saw the wives later at their table laughing, I knew that Joan was laughing at my new in-laws and not with them. At one point she caught me in passing and said, "Dull has an entirely new meaning. God bless you, dear."

Bailey also caught me in passing. She looked at me, then slowly gazed over at the Howards, who sat motionless in their chairs while everyone danced. She then looked back to me. "Who comes to a wedding and sits like that?"

"That's just how they are. They don't mean any harm."

She scowled. "What the fuck?"

My wedding cake was three tiers, with a blooming hydrangea

on top and smaller hydrangeas on the bottom two tiers. It took more than twelve hours of work for Beth and me to make the sugar petals for the hydrangeas, but I was proud of our work: From a distance, the flowers looked handpicked from a garden.

I wore Phyllis's dress, extensively altered to where it looked . . . decent enough.

My sister Sarah, in from Austin, took photos. In one of my favorites, I sat in Samuel's lap while we watched the sunset with our backs to the camera. My head rests on his just so, and my shoes dangle off my feet.

Later that night after the Howards and more guests had already gone, I stood off to the side and watched my brothers and a few friends play "Get Me to the Church on Time." Carmen danced with Samuel; Jake danced with Bailey; Anthony danced with Rita; and Bendrix danced with Aiko. Everyone was having what looked like a great time.

I felt my mom watching me. "You okay?"

"I'm great."

She had one of those smiles that turned downward in a sly, knowing manner. She was skinny, with thin bone structure and a small nose and mouth. Luckily, I had her metabolism, which allowed me to run a bakery without becoming as large as the bakery itself.

She kept her gaze on the crowd. Mom wasn't a talker. She wasn't the kind of mother who tried to get me to open up and share every little thing. When I'd visited every summer and during winter break while growing up, she'd kept to her own routine, leaving me to fit myself into her life. So I was surprised when she bumped my shoulder. "You sure you're okay?"

I watched Samuel switch from dancing with Carmen to dancing with Rita. He twirled her with one finger and she did a low back kick, resurrecting a move from her years as a dancer.

"I'm fine."

"It's a fun wedding, Abbey. Look at everyone. And your cake was stunning. No one wanted to touch it."

"I could make you one, if you ever remarry."

"That will never happen. I'm too headstrong."

We watched everyone dancing and whooping it up. Samuel—my husband—clapped to the music with his hands in the air. I said, "I thought I'd feel different."

"Different how?"

"I don't know." I sipped from my flute of champagne. But I did know. I had expected to feel happier. I had expected to feel more alive, and oddly enough, more me; but in truth, my wedding reception felt like any other of Dad's parties—a *fabulous* party, to be sure, but not a wedding reception, not *my* wedding reception. I knew I was going to look back on my one and only wedding and think—*eh*.

Mom said, "Abbey, trust me on this: It's the marriage, not the wedding. Your father and all those jazz standards have ruined you for reality."

"Don't say that."

We smiled at each other. Mom was shorter than I. The edges around her barely there Afro were graying. Her eyes were small and intense enough that I felt I could spy in them all her years of travel and work.

I thought: *I have such odd parents, don't I?* A musical genius for a parent was enough to make for an interesting childhood, but toss the wives and exes in, and then there was Mom, who'd call from Bora-Bora after studying some tribe's music or wherever to wish me a happy birthday. It took years before I understood that she genuinely loved me and I needed to let go of my resentment of her work and travel.

Anyway, Mom was right. I didn't get my dream wedding,

but I should focus on the marriage. My kids would have two parents who would never divorce and never miss a birthday. I would be part Phyllis and make sure they knew how devoted I was to them, and part Mom: I'd keep the bakery and continue to work, but only while they were in school. They would have the kind of stability I didn't have, and they'd have all the love. Because although my family could be wacky, at least I'd always known I was loved.

Mom eyed me closely. "What is it, Abbey?"

"It's nothing. I'm okay. Better than okay." I finished off my champagne and took her hand. "Come on, you. Let's dance."

15
You're Driving Me Crazy

We went to Yountville after the wedding, having decided to use Samuel's annual bonus money for a real honeymoon . . . Italy or Argentina. We celebrated my birthday while we were in Yountville by dining at the French Laundry. I have to say, eating that exquisite food with my husband was a great way to welcome in my thirty-ninth year.

I stopped taking the pill on my wedding night. I would've stopped before, but Samuel made it clear he wanted nothing to do with having a kid out of wedlock.

And then we waited to become pregnant.

And waited.

And waited.

Month after month after month.

By the time our one-year wedding anniversary came around, I began suggesting adoption, but Samuel said he wanted his own kids. I argued that he'd love any kid we adopted as his own, but he wasn't amenable to the idea. We were both tested for any fertility problems and came out in the clear, except I was closing in on my forties, and the doctor told me in her own professional manner that I was foolish for thinking I'd get pregnant right away. Of course it was going to take time, she cautioned, if I was lucky enough to get pregnant at all.

Time did its thing. Days and weeks continued to pass. I mean to say, no baby.

In early spring, about a year and half after the wedding, I was featured in *Brides* magazine. I stood next to my van Gogh cake, named for its electric colors and sunflower design. Requests skyrocketed after the issue came out, and I began working longer hours to keep up. Samuel was busy at the office, too. Looking back, I think our work gave us an excuse to avoid each other and to "connect" only when we were too exhausted to do much more than watch a movie. We had sex whenever I was ovulating, but less frequently when it wasn't crucial.

I had no idea a man's biological clock could tick as loudly as a woman's, but Samuel wanted kids even more than I'd realized, or maybe even more than he realized, and it was heartbreaking to have to break the news to him, month after month, that my period had arrived.

"So why don't you just adopt already?" This was Anthony's advice.

About a month after the doctor's exam, when Samuel and I were told everything was "fine," we were invited to Bendrix's for dinner. Samuel had to work late, so I took advantage of his absence and allowed myself to eat too much of Anthony's paella and vent about my marriage. Aunt Nag was there. Bendrix and Anthony had been vacationing in Santa Barbara during her birthday and were making it up to her with dinner. She loved my cream puffs, so I'd brought several. We ate them in the living room with a dessert wine Bendrix had opened.

Anthony didn't bother hiding his frustration. "I've worked with many kids who were dumped into the foster care system and destroyed by it. Kids who need *homes*."

Bendrix's house sat on a hill overlooking Lake Merritt. It was beautiful, with vaulted ceilings and dark wood beams that worked well with his modern aesthetic. The chair Aunt Nag chose was by a contemporary designer, bright orange with a high arching back that swallowed her whole. She looked so tiny she brought to mind Alice in Wonderland, except old and eating a cream puff.

Anthony continued. "You could at least start the adoption process while you wait to conceive."

I said, "Samuel won't even think about it. He wants his own kids."

"That's some bull, right there," Aunt Nag said. "They'll be his own kids just as soon as he sees them. They'll really be his when he pays for their college."

"I know, Aunt Nag, but I can't force him."

"Sure you can. Adopt 'em on the sly and bring some home one day and tell him, Hey, here are your kids, shut up."

We all laughed, although Aunt Nag remained perfectly serious, as her face disappeared behind her giant cream puff.

Anthony cozied up next to Bendrix and wrapped his arms around him. Bendrix bristled, then appeared to remember that human contact from the man you loved was a good thing. I watched as he eased his shoulders back into a relaxed position and smiled at Anthony. Anthony, though, pressed his luck when he tried to play with Bendrix's ear. "Okay," he said, pulling his head away. "Let's not get carried away." Anthony shook his head at Bendrix: *I love you despite your curmudgeonly ways.* Bendrix scrunched up his nose: *I love you, but you're right: I'll never change.*

I could feel a sense of envy rising. From the way they looked at each other, I knew they had something (*but what?*) that Samuel and I didn't have. They turned from each other when they felt me watching. Feeling like I'd been caught, I bit into my cream puff and pulled my socked foot up onto the couch, a moss-colored thing that was anything but comfortable and should have been left at the high-end boutique where Bendrix had found it. I said, "I can't believe I'm talking like this, about wanting to adopt and my fertility issues. Whoever thought?"

"Maybe you and Samuel should consider getting marriage counseling," Anthony ventured. "Never hurts to check in."

I tuned up my nose. "Samuel would never."

"Have you asked him?" Bendrix said.

"No, but I'd be willing to bet this god-awful couch I'm sitting on that he'd say no."

"That particular couch is highly sought after by those who appreciate fine furniture. And if you don't like it, the floor is beneath your feet and you're welcome to sit on it."

We simultaneously exchanged half smirks, half smiles.

Anthony said, "I'm not saying this because I'm a therapist— hell, yes I am: You two could use a check-in. With in-law issues, no-baby issues, and technology-addiction issues"—I'd complained how Samuel was always on his laptop or phone—"it would not hurt."

"We'll be okay," I said. I was feeling guilty about being so negative. "I wouldn't say he is addicted to his laptop."

"Sounds to me like he uses it to zone out."

Bendrix raised his wineglass. "No laptops in the bedroom," he intoned. "The bedroom should be a techno-free zone; so says *our* couples counselor."

I explained that things weren't as bad as I made them out to be. I told them about Carmen doing so well in school and how Samuel never complained about my work schedule. I added, "And he always makes sure the oil is changed in my car."

"Sounds romantic," said Aunt Nag. She licked cream from her fingers with tiny smacks.

Bendrix said, "You know, Abbey, instead of talking to us, you would probably benefit from speaking to a well-trained, impartial professional who can help you express any subconscious fears in the safety of his or her office." He grinned. "I must say I, personally, *love* therapy."

Anthony said, "Don't mind him. He really does love it. Admit it." He gave Bendrix a nudge. "Go on." Another nudge.

Bendrix gave in. "It's true. It's helped us. A lot."

"Maybe you can talk to Samuel for me," I ventured. Right off, though, I heard how needy and immature I sounded. "You could play it off like the idea came from you."

Aunt Nag said, "You don't need no therapist, child. Sounds to me like what you need is a damn backbone. Why you thinking about having a kid when you can't even talk to your damn husband like a grown woman? Ain't you and Bendrix the same age? But you trying to get Benny to do your dirty work. Don't you bring my nephew in this mess when what you need to do is talk to your husband on your own. Hell, you married him. Use your damn voice. That's what God gave it to you for." Her cream puff long gone, she went about dabbing at her plate with the tip of her finger.

When I looked over at Bendrix and Anthony, they stared back with wide-eyed grins. *She told you*, their faces said. *Mmmm-hmm.*

I went home with Aunt Nag's words stinging my ears. I told myself that I had to talk to Samuel. It might take another year before I became pregnant, and we couldn't let our happiness depend on whether we had a kid or not. Counseling wouldn't hurt, either.

I opened the door and noticed a pair of tapping sneakers poking out from one end of the sofa. Carmen and Samuel sat at the dining room table. A pizza box was opened and books were everywhere.

"Hey."

"Hey," they called.

I assumed the tapping feet belonged to Jake.

I kissed Samuel hello. He was on his laptop and raised his arms and yawned. He asked if I'd had a nice time at Bendrix's and I told him yes. "What time did you get home?" I asked.

"We finished earlier than expected. I didn't feel like socializing. Hope you don't mind."

"That's okay," I said, rubbing his back.

He glanced at Carmen. "This one here thinks she's ready for the LSAT, so I was running her through her paces."

Carmen looked at him and smirked. "I'll be ready. Just watch me."

Dad, no surprise, thought Carmen should take a year off to travel before she entered law school, but she was anxious to start right away.

Jake, from the couch: "Hi, Abbey!" He sat up and I saw the massive speakers on his head. He'd gone from wanting to be a music producer to working as a landscape designer. He'd been out of school for almost two years and was as devoted to Carmen as ever. I was surprised they were still together after all this time, except Carmen, to my surprise, was still gaga over Jake. She'd once told me, "He's my best friend. I love him."

Carmen yawned. "I should get going. Jakey-Jake? Come on. Let's get."

She gave me a hug. She was growing more confident and more beautiful. She'd lost a few pounds, but I think the main difference was that she no longer tried to hide her body behind sweats or dumpy outfits.

Jake came over and took us both in his arms. "Group hug! Ahhhhh!"

Carmen and I laughed.

Samuel drank from a half-empty bottle of beer. "Car, if you stick with this guy, you'll probably have to be the bread-winner."

"Hello! I'm standing right here, man."

"Hey." Samuel shrugged. "I call 'em like I see 'em. Who's prepping for law school and who's—what *are* you doing, anyhow?"

"I'm still working on my music and doing landscape design. Abbey, have you heard Monk's 'Evidence'? Carmen played it for me. Imagine Monk over some electronic with some rap thrown in." He started moving his shoulders in torturous poses.

Samuel pursed his lips at Carmen. "You really plan on taking him to law school with you?"

"Like I said, man, I'm standing right here."

I pressed my nose between Samuel's shoulders. "Ease up on him, babe."

"You don't have to defend me, Abbey."

"You don't," said Carmen. She held her books and purse in her arm. "Jake'll go back to school."

"How do you know?"

She rolled her eyes. "You want me to help clean up?"

"I got it," said Samuel.

"Cool." She gave Jake a shove, then grabbed at his shirt-sleeve. "Let's go."

"It's hard out here for an idiot savant," he said, letting Carmen drag him off.

"Use protection!" I called.

"Abbey!" Carmen cried. "Damn!" She added solemnly, "No one has to worry about that. Ever. Like never, ever."

Jake clapped his hands and stuck each foot out from side to side like a cowboy doing a jig. "Ain't got time for babies. Only the ladies. I don't act shady or crazy. The girl's gotta use the pill if she wants her fill—"

"All right, all right," I said, frowning. "There's absolutely no way you're smart."

"Ahhhhh!"

"Bye!" Carmen called, pushing Jake out the door. "Love you guys!"

When I turned, Samuel was already leaving the room, carrying the empty pizza box and as many plates as he could hold.

*I*n remembrance of my single days, I climbed into bed a few minutes after Samuel in a pair of sweats and a T-shirt. I wanted nothing to do with lingerie or anything sexy. I wanted comfort. Good, old-fashioned sweats-and-a-T-shirt comfort.

As soon as Samuel saw me, he gave me a sideways glance. "The wife in sweats," he murmured. "We haven't even hit the two-year mark."

"I want to be comfortable. Sue me."

"You forget who you're talking to," he deadpanned.

He opened his laptop.

"Hey." I was becoming a real master at talking with Samuel, all right. I nudged him. "Hey."

He sighed. "Now what?"

"Bendrix and Anthony are in couples counseling. Anthony says it's like getting a checkup."

Samuel started typing.

"Are you listening?" I asked.

"Bendrix and Anthony are in couples counseling," he repeated flatly.

"They call it getting a checkup. Maybe that's something we could do."

"A checkup for what?"

"I don't know, Samuel. I mean, look at us. Sometimes I feel I can't talk to you."

"You've been saying that since we met. Trust me, we talk all the time."

"I still think it would be a good idea if we went to see someone."

"Why? We haven't been married two years."

"Time shouldn't matter. It couldn't hurt. We could talk about—"

"First of all, we have no issues. Nothing that we can't handle ourselves. And second, you need to think about the word itself. The. Rapist. Get it? Therapists exist like everyone else—to make money and get what they can out of innocent people willing to pay a stranger to listen to them whine."

"Bendrix and Anthony aren't like that, and they say it helps."

"Good for them. We're not them. You need to stop comparing, Abbey." He leaned over and kissed my shoulder. "Sweetie, we're fine. Think about it. We're just busy; nothing more. Everything can't be love and romance twenty-four/seven. You love me, right?"

"Of course."

"See there? We're fine. If you look for problems, you'll find them. You have to stay positive." He started typing again. "You know what would really help our relationship?"

"What?"

"For you to take off those sweats." He laughed lightly. "They remind me of gym class."

*P*aul stretched Jenny's head and kissed her fully on the lips. When he felt Jenny's body relax, his tongue parted her lips as though they were the doors to a great party circa 1979. Given the era, his tongue wore a white disco suit and just enough gold chains to keep things classy. Upon entering his fiancée's mouth, his tongue sought out Jenny's tongue and they began dancing to a catchy disco hit by the Bee Gees.

From my perspective, across the table from where they sat, Paul looked as though he were giving Jenny pornographic CPR.

I cleared my throat loudly.

Paul turned, his face red and marked by splotchy white imprints at his jaw where Jenny had held him. She was flushed as well. Their chests rose and fell.

"So"—*now that the porn show is over*—"shall we finish discussing your wedding cake?"

"Yes, yes. What were you saying?" Paul asked. He waved to Noel, who walked over. "Hey, man, can I get another espresso and another latte for my girlfriend?"

"Fiancée."

"Yes, my fi-an-cée." He started kissing her again.

Noel and I raised our brows at each other. "Sure thing," he said. "Be right back."

I waited patiently while they made out. I'm sure they kissed for only a few seconds, but PDAs can feel like a lifetime when you don't know the couple—and sometimes even when you do.

Paul was a good thirty years older than Jenny, give or take a decade or two. A spry five-eight or five-nine, with spiky hair and a graying soul patch, he wore yellow-tinted glasses and a thick silver bracelet on each wrist. Jenny was a pixie of a woman with a close-cropped hairdo that brought out her big, luminous blue eyes. She looked like she belonged in a land of fairies and hobbits, riding a white horse and speaking Hobgoblin.

Coming up for air, Paul tapped his finger on the table and stared at me. "I'm sorry. What was that? What were you saying?"

"We were choosing the last cake."

"Yes, that's right."

I didn't mind that Paul and Jenny were taking forever to finalize their order—it was their money—but I did have concerns. There was the age difference, not helped by the fact that Paul treated her like a child, going so far as to make all the decisions about the cake in his own manipulative way: *"Are you sure you want chocolate, honey? Not everybody likes chocolate. Are you sure you want caramel filling? What about something more traditional, like, say, vanilla?"* Added to that, after Noel returned with their drinks, they proudly announced that they'd been dating for only three months.

I knew it wasn't my place to offer advice—I was there to make cakes and wish them well—but I was feeling sensitive since my conversation about couples counseling with Samuel a few weeks before—if you could call it a conversation. I had tried to talk to him about it again, but after a certain point, I knew I was wasting my breath. What did it mean, though, that he wouldn't even consider it? I was worried and I knew I had a reason to be: It was not the best situation when you wanted to try counseling and your partner refused. And once I really thought about it, we weren't all that happy. I wasn't happy. Samuel wasn't happy. Anthony had called it: Samuel was zoning out, and I was, too. I was actually looking for excuses to go in to work early and leave late. And I didn't have to look very hard, since there was always something to do.

Anyway, if Samuel and I were having problems so early in our marriage, what of Jenny and Paul? I normally didn't give advice, but now that I was on the other side, so to speak, I felt I should warn them that marriage was about a hell of a lot more than sexual attraction, something Paul should've known, given his age, but he was obviously thinking with an organ other than his brain—or heart—if you get my drift.

I looked at them both. "Three months? That's not very long."

"Three months, eight days," Paul said, turning to Jenny for a kiss.

"Still," I said, "why the rush?" I tried to smile, even as Paul began to glower as if catching on to what I was up to. "Why not get to know each other more? Take it from me," I said, fanning my wedding ring. "Marriage comes with its ups and downs."

"We know each other," Paul said defensively.

"Do you?"

"Yeah." He started tapping his finger. "We know each other well enough that we're here for a wedding cake. Isn't that right, love?"

Jenny tucked herself under his arm and stared at me with her big dopey eyes. "I don't think you understand. Paul and I are *soul mates*. We knew instantly."

Paul kissed her forehead. "Yes, soul mates. She is the light of my life." He looked at me and snorted. "And even if we aren't soul mates, this little cutie here is only twenty-three, with the body of a . . . *twenty-three-year-old*! And I'm going to marry her and keep shagging her until she matures enough to realize I'm an egotistical old prick. *Yippee!*"

Okay. So no, he didn't say that—per se. But that was the gist. He added, "So as you see, we are very much in love and we're getting married and we're here to order a cake from someone who's getting paid to make us a cake."

Point taken. I returned his chilly smile and picked up my pen.

He was right, after all. It was a good reminder that by the point the couple was at the cake-buying stage, it was time for me to wish them my absolute best and make the cake of their dreams.

I made myself a cappuccino after the couple left and sat and watched people coming and going and sitting at tables enjoying their cakes and pies, cupcakes and tarts. Several regulars smiled. It was Saturday, and since Mr. and Miss Delusional were my last appointment of the day, I didn't have any reason to stay at the bakery. There was always plenty to do, but nothing pressing, and we'd be closing in a couple of hours. I told Beth I'd be leaving and asked her to close. I then went to my office to get my things. Samuel was at his office working. Even though I'd have the house to myself, I didn't want to go home. I was getting my purse when I saw he'd left a text:

```
Mother & Father coming to visit tonight.
7:00pm. See you then.
```

Crap. Now I definitely wanted time to myself. I checked my watch: a little after three.

The great thing about having so many stepmoms was that I could pick and choose among them depending on my mood. Shopping? Rita. A drink and live music? Bailey. Joan, though— Joan was for lazing around. Comfort, I'd guess you'd say. I called to see if she was home.

*J*oan lived near the border of the Berkeley Hills, a few curvy miles down from Dad's house. I found her in her studio, a rectangular building separated from her house by a grove of evergreens. She spent as much time in her studio as in her home, and she'd set up a comfy corner at one end with a Persian carpet, two couches, a desk, and a small fridge and electric teapot. While lying on my back on one of the couches, I watched her work on a new piece. She was creating a series of eight statues, each about twenty inches tall and made from clay and beeswax. The statues were of little girls in various poses, all perfectly sweet except for the horns coming from their heads, the pointy devilish tails sticking out from their skirts, and the sword each girl aimed at the doll or flower she held. I could already hear the critics describing the pieces as Joan's commentary on gender inequity, but I knew Joan and guessed she simply felt like putting horns on little girls.

She walked around the table, taking time to study each

figure. She paused now and then to futz with a skirt or foot. She wore her smock and clogs; her bifocals teetered on the tip of her nose. After several moments she looked at me and allowed her gaze to linger before walking over and plopping down. "Scoot," she ordered. I moved my legs over to give her room. She kicked off her clogs, then stretched out with her head on the opposite armrest from mine. I moved my hand over my eyes to block out the light coming through one of the large skylights. We listened quietly to the whir of the ceiling fans. The great thing about Joan—if you didn't want to talk, she wasn't going to press you.

The couches may have changed over the years, but our facing position stayed the same. I thought back to when Joan's lover Katherine was alive. She was always coming and going and chattering away. After she died, Joan spent weeks working through her grief in her studio. I tapped my foot against her shoulder. "Do you miss Katherine?"

"Now, there's a silly question."

"You're right. Sorry about that." I sat up. "Do you ever date?"

"Those days are over. I had two great loves. I'm not one to be greedy."

"Why didn't you ever have children?"

"You're full of questions today." She pulled herself up onto her elbows so she could meet my gaze. "Never wanted any. Not every woman wants children. Some of us are meant to be aunties or stepmums. I make a terrific stepmum."

"Don't hold back, Joan."

"I don't intend to."

I snorted. "You are a good stepmother."

"I know it. I was petrified when Lincoln said he had three boys, but we got along famously, mostly because they liked coming here and making a mess of things and having me boss them around like they were my little helpers. Phineas could've been a sculptor if he'd wanted to—had a real eye, that boy." She leaned back against the couch. After a minute or so, she said, "You'll have kids, Abbey. You mustn't worry."

"I'm not sure that I am worried anymore." As soon as the words drifted from my mouth, I knew it was true: I didn't care if we had a baby together or not. I didn't like what trying to have a baby was doing to our relationship. I then wondered if it was right to blame a non-baby on our problems. Wouldn't they exist whether we had a kid or not? I still wanted to try, but if it didn't happen, I honestly didn't mind adopting.

Joan sat up again and began searching my face. Satisfied that I was telling the truth, she gave a nod. "Good. It's really not the end of the world if you don't conceive. Your father has certainly made sure that the Ross clan will go on." She gave my thigh a slap. "What do you say we hit the rink? I wanted to go earlier but talked myself out of it. Now that you're here, I'm sure it's a sign."

Besides her walks and hikes, Joan loved to go ice-skating. She'd been skating since she was a kid. "Can I see if Bendrix wants to come? He's off today."

"Bendrix?"

I didn't blame her for the reaction. Over the years, Bendrix had always refused to join us for ice-skating. But since getting back together with Anthony, he was doing his best to try new things. So far he and Anthony had gone rock climbing, which didn't go over all that well; tried bowling, which Bendrix said he'd be willing to try again, if not for the hideous shoes; and tried Vietnamese cooking—too much work for the result. He'd already made a point of telling Anthony he was never going to attend gay square-dancing night. Like, never.

An hour later, Anthony and I stood on either side of Bendrix, carefully holding him at the elbows like two nursing aides assisting a patient. He wobbled across the ice, threatening to fall every few seconds.

Bendrix said, "This is the last time I'm trying anything new; I'll tell you both that much. I can't believe I'm out here trying to be a part of the damn Ice Capades."

"If you'd stop complaining and focus, you might enjoy yourself," Anthony quipped.

"That's impossible. I don't see what's fun about falling on my ass."

Joan, skating backward, tried her own brand of encouragement. "I'm sure your ass can take it, Bendrix."

His upper body began to collapse like a wilting flower. "Look up," I told him. "You're falling over."

"Stop pulling me and I will."

"We're not pulling," Anthony countered.

"We're trying to help." I gave him a hard tug forward and giggled.

"Stop it!"

Skaters whizzed by, laughing and holding hands. Two boys raced each other. A young girl of about eleven skated past executing a perfect arabesque; once she saw she had enough room, she twirled in the air and landed in a tight spin.

"Show-off," Bendrix muttered.

Joan slowed after her second or third loop. "Let go of him, you two. It's the best way to learn. You need to learn to stand on your own, Bendrix."

Anthony and I did as we were told and Bendrix began rocking back and forth, as unsteady as a drunk. "Oh . . . my . . . God." His arms jutting out one way and his butt the other, he looked like an umpire calling a play.

"You can do it, Benny!" I called.

But just then—he kicked a foot. "Whoa!" He kicked again. "Whoa!" And again. Three more speedy kicks and—"No!"— down he went.

Anthony knelt over him, doing his best not to laugh. "Are you okay?"

Bendrix gazed up at his circle of onlookers and gritted his teeth. "I'm fine."

Anthony and I burst into laughter.

"Would you two stop laughing and help me up?"

"No!" Anthony laughed some more.

Joan extended her hand. "Don't mind them, Bendrix. Anthony, come on and help me." They pulled him to his feet and he began dusting ice from his pants.

After making sure Bendrix was okay, Joan skated off. I joined her after Anthony said he'd look after "our charge."

The arena played songs only from the sixties to early nineties. At that moment, Michael Jackson's "Thriller" was playing and a couple began imitating zombies.

Joan picked up her speed, forcing me to keep up. We skated past Bendrix and Anthony. Bendrix was trying to make his way back to the railing and safety, but they hadn't moved very far.

I let out a yelp and raised a fist into the air as Joan and I skated around the rink faster and faster. Joan's face remained serious, but at one point, she turned backward and forward in a split second, while pulling wisps of hair from her face. She smiled a little—her own way, I was sure, of letting out a yelp. Around and around we went. I called out to Bendrix, who was already sitting in the viewing area: "Hey, Dr. Henderson, how's your ass?"

Joan and I continued to skate. I had to admit that I didn't miss having Samuel with us. I didn't want to hear him complain or watch him occupy himself on his phone. The thought saddened me, though. It seemed plain old sad that I wouldn't want my husband around when I was having so much fun.

Noticing that my pace had slowed, Joan skated alongside me. She took my hand and we slowed to half our speed. A sixties girl group sang. You never knew what they were going to play at the rink, which was part of the fun. "Never talk yourself out of what you're feeling, Abbey," Joan said after we'd circled together. "We have our feelings for a reason and mustn't be afraid of them."

I wasn't sure what she was getting at.

"That's something Katherine taught me. And your father. We feel things for a reason and there's no need to fear what we feel. Just some unasked-for advice."

I nodded. "Thanks, Joan. I'm fine." To prove it, I moved in front of her and gave her a wink before speeding off.

J joined Bendrix and Anthony in the sitting area at the side of the rink after a few more rounds. When I heard "Hey Jude" start to play, I went to the railing and sought out Joan. She loved the Beatles. "Come here. You guys have to see this."

I looked through the crowd until I found her. Joan, eyes closed, raised her leg behind her while lifting her arms up and down along with the music. Her arabesque was low to the ground and slightly bent, but she was all grace and elegance. People began to make way as the music swelled and her movements became larger. Some of her movements were stiff, but it didn't matter. She was in her own world.

"She's amazing," I heard Anthony say.

"Yep."

"Are they allowed to play the Beatles?" Bendrix asked. "Isn't that some kind of copyright infringement?"

"Bendrix," Anthony said shortly. "Who cares? Are you watching this?"

Joan quickened her pace as the music began to crescendo. Faster and faster. As the song went into its popular chorus, several skaters sang along—"*Na-na-na, Na-na-na-na! Na-na-na-na! Hey Jude!*" Joan turned to the side and began to skate sideways, preparing for a jump. She kicked up her leg and leaped, and the momentum of her landing sent her into a tighter spin. A guy began to skate alongside her, but he had to make room when she went up again, flying through the air. They were the jumps and twirls of a sixty-year-old woman, awkward and imperfect, yet pure gold.

*J*t turned out that my in-laws weren't just paying a visit that evening; Phyllis had decided to make dinner. I came home from ice-skating happy and excited, only to find her in the kitchen wearing one of *my* aprons and standing at the stove stirring a large pot.

"We discussed going out to eat when you got here," Phyllis explained, "but Samuel mentioned you two have been eating out a lot." She lowered her voice. "I think it was his way of saying he wanted a home-cooked meal."

"But you didn't have to do it. I could've put something together."

"I wanted to. I like to make myself feel useful."

She began dancing about the kitchen singing a cheerful song about the joys of cooking and cleaning. Her faithful birdie friends landed on each shoulder and joined her in the chorus. *The best place for a woman is the kitchen, tra-la-la!*

Not that there was anything wrong with cooking for your husband. God no. It irked me that Phyllis bought into the belief that *every* woman should love to cook and clean as much as she did, especially if that woman was her daughter-in-law.

Samuel walked in and poured himself a glass of water. "It's our lucky night, babe. Mom's making her special chili." He kissed me, then his mom. "Father wants to know how long before we eat."

Phyllis popped open the stove and told him the bread would be ready in a minute or two.

When he was gone, Phyllis gave her chili a taste, then reached for the salt. "Just a pinch more. We have to watch Joseph's high blood pressure. It's down to a good number."

"I'll set the table." I started taking down plates and silverware.

"You know, Abbey, you should think about passing on responsibility at the bakery."

I kept my back turned so I could properly roll my eyes.

"You show your man you love him by cooking a good meal for him. That old adage about the way to a man's heart is through his stomach is very true."

"The way to a woman's heart is through her stomach, too," I quipped. "We love food just as much as men do." She turned, looking both surprised and piqued by my remark. Remembering to smile, she said, "Samuel grew up in a home where he knew he was looked after. He didn't expect to have to fend for himself once he was married." She glanced inside the stove. "Hurry and set the table if you're going to do it. I'll bring out the chili."

Phyllis was already out the door with glasses in hand, while I was still trying to think of what to say. I hated that I was so slow to speak when caught off guard. Why couldn't I be like Bailey when it came to the art of rapid-fire comebacks?

I sat eating chili in silence. At least I was finally used to the fifteen minutes of no-talk eating. Another positive was that Esther and Ruth weren't there.

As usual, Mr. Howard broke the silence by complimenting Phyllis's cooking. (After Samuel and I were married, Mr. Howard had told me I could call him Joseph, but in my mind he was and would always be Mr. Howard.) He then continued the dinner ritual by holding court on some subject. That night he told us in detail about a news program he'd seen on PBS dealing with genetically modified foods. Samuel apparently knew enough about the subject to keep up with his father, or at least try to.

I took a nap with my eyes open.

The topic of GMOs exhausted, Samuel asked me how Joan was doing. Before I had a chance to respond, Phyllis said, "Now, which one is Joan? There are so many of them, I get them mixed up."

I didn't bother trying to hide my impatience. "Joan is from England. As a matter of fact, we went ice-skating together."

"Today?"

I gave a nod.

"Well, I'll say!" Phyllis said, gazing around the table. "Must be nice to go off and ice-skate while your husband is working hard at his job."

Mr. Howard wiped his mouth with his napkin. "What Abbey does with her time isn't our concern, Phyllis. Would someone pass the garlic bread?" Samuel gave him the bread, then jumped in with news about his job and how well he was doing.

"Glad to hear it, son," Mr. Howard said. "Now, if we could just get some grandbabies around here, you'll really make your mother and me happy."

Samuel and I exchanged looks.

"We're doing our best, Father. Might have to try IVF. Whatever it takes. Right, Abbey?"

I smiled while widening my eyes at him: *Do we really have to discuss this over dinner—in front of your parents?*

He ignored me and dug into his chili. "I'd like to give it a few more months, and then we'll move to the next step."

"I'd like to adopt," I said. I touched my glass with the tips of my fingers.

"Abbey," Samuel started. He placed his hand on mine. "We're not giving up. Adoption isn't even on the table right now."

Mr. Howard said, "You don't know what you get when you adopt. Those kids come with all kinds of problems."

I could feel anger rising in me. Joan had told me not to be afraid of what I was feeling. Well, I was feeling pissed. I hated this family. And I hated the way Samuel was looking at me like I was a little pet to be quieted.

I looked at Mr. Howard. "Whether we adopt or not, you better not lay a hand on my kids."

If Mr. Howard was surprised by my comment, he didn't show it. He didn't falter for a second. He picked up his glass. "Samuel, I suspect you need to control your wife."

"You see . . . Abbey's been . . . ," Samuel started to explain, to at least try to stand up to his father, but he couldn't do it and he turned to me. "Abbey, you need to apologize."

"That's not gonna happen."

Phyllis's eyes darted about the table. "I think we all need to calm down."

"Have you seen the mark you left on his back?"

"Abbey!" Phyllis yelled. "Samuel?"

"Abbey." Samuel tossed down his napkin and shot up from the table. He held me by the arm. "Come on, you're upset."

"Of course I'm upset!"

Samuel started to drag me from the table. He leaned in. "Abbey, please?" I could see the alarm and hurt in his eyes.

I stared down at my arm and he let go. I went to the bedroom and shut the door.

I lay flat on my back and closed my eyes. I caught snippets of the conversation. Samuel, mostly, explaining that I was upset that we weren't pregnant.

After growing tired of eavesdropping, I turned on my side and closed my eyes. I'm not sure how long I stayed there, except I heard water running and then the house finally grew quiet.

I kept my eyes closed when I felt Samuel crawling into bed. I waited for the lecture about how I'd embarrassed him and how his parents deserved respect and blah-blah. But he surprised me by putting his arms around me and not saying a word.

He inhaled with his nose pressing into the back of my neck. "You don't have to worry, okay? They know that you're upset about not being pregnant. Father even wanted to tell you that he's sorry. He didn't mean to push your buttons." Samuel gave me a shake. "Abbey, are you listening? They mean well. They do." He waited, then said, "Babe, you have to stop taking everything so personally. It's just upsetting you."

He gave me another shake.

I rolled over just to get him to shut up. I stared into the ceiling, thinking about the sensation of rushing past the other skaters earlier with Joan. I thought about how elegant she'd looked twirling to music by the Beatles. In the meantime, my husband went on and on and on. I listened. Sort of. I didn't want to talk. I was sick of talking. We were so stuck. I didn't know why he didn't see it, but we were. I listened to him breathing next to me. I thought about the advice Joan had given me earlier, about allowing myself to feel what I felt. I knew I was angry, but as I lay there following the in and out of my breath, the rise and fall of Samuel's head on my stomach, my eyes started to glisten. *Lonely*, I thought. *I feel really lonely.*

16

But Not for Me

$\mathcal{A}$lmost two weeks later, I met with Gina Kendrick, a prospective bride who worked for a dot-com in the city that had recently been bought out by another dot-com behemoth and was now worth triple its original price. She'd seen the article in *Brides* and liked that I could work with ideas inspired by fine art. After an initial meeting, she'd e-mailed links to several works by Matisse and asked that I come up with a few ideas based on the paintings. She'd also sent a list of the cakes she wanted to try at the tasting. She was never bridezilla demanding and always polite, but she was an executive at a multimillion-dollar company and a woman who knew precisely what she wanted. Women like Gina were actually as exciting to work with as women who wanted more of my input: I enjoyed proving myself and giving them more than they expected.

She was talking rapidly as I approached the table. A man who I assumed was her fiancé sat next to her. It wasn't until I was sitting in front of them that I realized Gina had a phone clipped to her ear and was talking to someone on the other end. A gifted multitasker, she began typing into her tablet while managing a silent hello and shake of my hand. Her fiancé smiled politely and tossed his head toward Gina in a way that said, *She'll just be a second.* He bobbed his head to the music on the stereo, Art Tatum playing "Give Him the Ooh-La-La."

After another minute or so, Gina told whoever was on the line that she needed to call them back. I guessed her age to be thirty-two or thirty-three. She had a liveliness about her that made me think she was a former cheerleader, or leader of her high school's debating team, or probably both. She was gymnast petite and solid, with a whistle of a nose and huge white teeth that made up for their largeness whenever she smiled. Because when she did, you went, *Whoa, wow, what a smile.*

She placed her phone down. "I am so sorry about that. Abbey, this is my fiancé, Jason. Jason, Abbey."

Jason reached across the table and we shook hands. Where Gina had the plucky spirit of a morning talk-show host, he gave off the impression that he wasn't one for agendas and as of now was happy to enjoy the music and the company of his future bride.

We went through the drawings I'd come up with. On one cake, I'd copied Matisse's *The Dance* all around the side of the cake; on another, I suggested using his *Landscape at Collioure.* After a few exchanges of ideas, we finalized the details and moved on to the tasting. Jason, who'd been mostly silent until then, widened his eyes and rubbed his hands together. "Now we're talkin'," he exclaimed.

I pointed out the five cakes Gina had requested, adding that I'd played around with her instructions a tad on the first three. If she didn't like them, we could always go back to her specific requests.

They tasted the caramel cake first—Jason's bite four times the size of Gina's. Gina nodded and raised her brows in pleasure. Jason barely swallowed before he took another mouthful. "Holy Mother of God. *That* is f'ing amazing." He threw his hands in the air as if someone had scored a goal.

Gina looked at me. "He's from Canada," she said, as if this explained everything.

"That I am," Jason said, rubbing his hands together. "And what's that one right there?" he said, pointing to a cake. "It's speaking to me."

"That's a very light orange blossom with crème filling."

He looked at Gina. "Shall we try the orange blossom with the light crème filling?"

I was never one hundred percent sure how often my assumptions about couples matched reality, but it was clear from the way Gina's eyes lit up when she looked at Jason that she was crazy about him. My guess was that he brought out the playful yin to her workaholic yang. And Jason, who was bored with all the young women he had dated, who were gorgeous but lacked drive and chutzpah, wanted a woman like Gina, a powerhouse who inspired him. He was twice Gina's height, his brown-blond hair was thick and wavy, and he had large green eyes and a nose that looked like it had been broken and never reset properly. But he was good-looking, a perfect match for Gina's more delicate features. They were going to have some seriously beautiful kids.

He picked up his fork and bumped her shoulder. "Ready, chief? And none of that girly stuff. Take a nice big bite with me. Okay?"

She smiled and her huge white teeth shone.

"Okay. Here we go. One. Two. Three."

They both took extra-large bites of the blossom cake. Gina laughed and covered her mouth in fear of crumbs falling out.

They chewed, their cheeks as big as squirrels'. Jason, seeing a bit of cream in the corner of her mouth, found his napkin and dabbed at her lip, then kissed her as though he couldn't help but kiss the adorable woman sitting next to him. They both nodded like kids.

"So good!" he said.

"Right?" she said. They finished chewing while I smiled. I loved my job. I really did.

Jason began bobbing his head to the music; Cannonball Adderley was fading out. "What else do you have for us, Abbey? So far we are on a roll."

Gina saw she had a message and apologized before starting a text.

Jason pointed toward the ceiling. Chet Baker could now be heard piping through the sound system. "I think I must be in heaven: all the cake I could want plus Art Tatum, Cannonball Adderley, and now Chet Baker. Very nice. You guys always play music like this here?"

"Ninety-nine percent of the time."

"You ever hear Chet play 'Chabootie'?"

"Oh yeah."

"It's nuts, isn't it?" He paused and looked at me. "You listen to jazz?"

I smiled to myself. "A little." I had a strong feeling Jason had "big ears." He not only listened to jazz; he got it and loved it.

Gina apologized again and set down her phone. "These are all delicious, Abbey. Let's try that one." She pointed to the chocolate mocha and they continued their trip around the table.

Once all the cakes were tasted, Gina gave her stomach a pat. "We'll probably go with a four-tier. Don't you think, honey?"

"No, five-tier. With that last cake over there"—he pointed to the second chocolate cake—"as a little side dish for the groom. I want it all to myself."

Gina shook her head at me: *See what I have to put up with?*
"Honey."

"Seriously. I want them all. For this wedding, the groom
wants the cakes he wants. The bride gets everything else."

She shrugged and looked at me. "Fine with me. Maybe we
can come up with an idea to help the fifth *appetizer* cake fit in.
What I don't want is so many cakes on top of each other they're
as tall as I am. That's tacky."

"That should be easy enough," I said. "There's nothing like a
man who likes his sweets. What about two cakes on the side,
three-tier in the middle?"

"That should work just fine. Honey?"

Jason bit into the chocolate and nodded his head a few times.
"Sounds good. You've got talent, Abbey. You should go into baking."

Gina and I looked at each other. "Thanks," I said.

He pointed with his fork. "And she listens to jazz, babe. Proof
that there's one more person under fifty who likes the stuff."

Gina rolled her eyes and picked up her phone. "I'm so sorry,"
she said, typing furiously. "Bad times on the job. Everything—I
mean, everything—hit the fan this morning, but I wasn't going
to cancel this. There was just no way. Hold on, please."

While she sent her text, I asked Jason what he did for work.
Gina, thumbs still whirling across her phone, responded for him:
"He started his own Web site. He covers what's hip and writes
reviews of different gadgets or interesting companies. There."
Text sent, she set the phone down. "His site also has personal
essays. It's a style and culture magazine geared toward men, but
women love it, too. It's very fun and smart—*and* it's a total hit in
Canada."

Jason kept his eyes on me while pointing to Gina. "What she
said. This one here is my number one fan." He leaned over and
gave her a kiss.

"I am," she said. "I can't help it."

"What's it called?" I asked.

"Cooper. My full name is Jason Ethan Cooper. Highly original title—I know."

"But you should see the font," Gina said. *"Perfection."*

"She's not proud of me at all."

"I can tell." I grinned.

Jason kept his head down in embarrassment as she told me more. Every month there was a centerfold, but the centerfold was a brilliant woman, or man, posing—*clothed*—on her or his desk; or the centerfold was the latest gadget Jason thought his readers would like.

"Okay, sweetie," he said, resting his arm on the back of the booth. "Abbey can look it up if she wants."

"I can't help it, baby. It's a great site." Gina looked at me and lowered her voice. "Advertisements are pouring in. He's just being humble."

"I'm Canadian," he said, employing the same matter-of-fact tone Gina had used earlier. "We prefer prideful humility or to be humbly prideful, either one."

"He's going to do a feature on Oakland in an upcoming issue. He's never been here."

"No?" I asked.

"Just moved here. I've been getting to know San Francisco, and from the little I've seen, I like it. I plan to hang out while Gina goes back to work."

"Good. It's a great city. It has its problems, but I love it here."

Gina's phone buzzed. "Christ!"

Jason leaned in and began running his hand up and down her arm. "We probably shouldn't have come today, babe."

"No, don't say that. I needed this." She kissed him on the forehead and made a pouty face, then picked up the phone and began directing the person on the other end about the file that was giving everyone trouble.

Jason lifted a finger in the air and closed his eyes. "Damn, I *love* this version. He gets it just right." He moved his fingers on the table as if playing the piano.

It was Dad on the stereo now, playing "Our Love Is Here to Stay." Some mornings I added so many albums and songs to the playlist, I didn't know who would come up during any given hour. I normally didn't add Dad to the mix. I usually saved listening to his music for when I was in a particular mood—whether happy or sad or just needing to hear him—but I guess I'd plugged him in. I didn't say anything to Jason, though. A part of me wanted to tease him, or skip telling him at all. I wasn't sure.

I hummed along. "Lincoln T. Ross. Stockholm, 'eighty-six."

He went for the remains of the orange blossom cake. "You're close. 'Eighty-eight."

He was wrong, but I smiled anyway.

"If you listen—*here*, he goes out just far enough with the melody—ah!" He bowed his head and clutched at his heart. "Then he comes back to the standard—right . . . *here*—so that you get back into the regular rhythm of the tune and you hear it in an entirely new way, thanks to how far he goes in the previous measure. It's just so f'ing perfect."

Jason definitely had big ears.

Gina was off the phone by now and stared apologetically. "Sorry. He gets like this. We all have our thing."

Jason said, "This is Lincoln T. Ross. The guy I was telling you about."

She shook her head indifferently, then looked my way. "Jazz: kind of all sounds the same to me."

Jason looked at me now. "I still love her."

"Abbey's last name is Ross," Gina said absently. She reached for her phone. "Coincidence," she muttered. "Honey, Abbey: I'm sorry, but I have to step outside. It appears everyone at the office needs their fucking hands held today."

Jason stood so she could move out of the booth. She barely reached his chest, even in her high heels. She started giving orders into her phone as she marched away from the table.

I asked how they'd met and he explained that Gina's best friend from college had moved to Ontario a few years before. Gina was visiting and they'd connected at a mutual friend's birthday party. "And there you have it. Now I'm here in the mighty U.S. of A. about to be married. We were long-distance for two years, but it was time to make that little powerhouse all mine." He looked out at the street with a grin. I turned and saw Gina pacing back and forth while speaking intently into the sky. I loved couples like Gina and Jason; they reminded me that marriage and love were possible and cynics be damned.

Jason was staring at me when I turned back around. He motioned toward the ceiling—at my dad's playing—then to me. A glimmer appeared in his eye.

"You're not related to Lincoln T. Ross, are you?"

"I'm his daughter."

"No!"

"Yes."

"No!"

"Yes!"

"Get. Outta here. You're kidding me, right?"

I shook my head. "No, I'm not. And it was Stockholm, 'eighty-six, just so you know."

He ran his hands through his thick hair, his face covered in shock. "I'm so . . . I can't believe it . . . I'm sorry!"

I laughed. "Why are you apologizing?"

"Because I'm an idiot; that's why. I was going on about

music—your *dad's* music—and here you are his daughter, the daughter of Lincoln T. Ross." He looked around the restaurant like he might make an announcement; then he bowed slightly. "You're like royalty, girl."

"Hardly."

"I can't believe this." He turned in his seat like Dad might pop out at any moment. "No wonder you're playing such good music. So. So what is he like? I'm sorry. Do you mind me asking that?"

"Not at all. He's kind of like you'd expect."

"Cool?" he said, after a thoughtful pause.

"Yeah. Very. How do you know so much about jazz? Do you play?"

"Naw. I played hockey as a kid. My parents listened to jazz, though. Growing up, I thought it was the worst music ever—I liked Led Zeppelin and rap and anything but. Until I was about fourteen and they forced me into seeing Keith Jarrett's trio. I was obsessed after that. It was like the lights went on and I saw and heard music for the first time." He paused and looked at me. "I can't believe your dad is Lincoln T. Ross. Wait until I tell my folks."

Gina returned and Jason stood up so she could sit. "Guess what. You'll never guess, but try."

"What?"

"Abbey's father is Lincoln T. Ross."

Gina stared at me blankly.

"The musician we were just talking about? That's her father!"

"Nice," Gina said as politely as she could. "Must be fun to have a father who's a musician." She smiled again, then turned to Jason. "I need to get back. It's going to be a late night, but I think we can finish by ten if I keep everyone focused. Abbey, can we get to whatever we need to sign?"

I went to the office and found the necessary contracts. On my way back, I stopped at the stereo and changed the track from Sarah Vaughan, who'd just started singing, to Sonny Clark playing "It Could Happen to You." Sure enough, Jason looked up and searched the bakery until he saw me at the counter. When he caught my eye he gave me a thumbs-up.

He put his arm around Gina as I returned to my seat. "Sonny Clark on *Dial 'S'*? *Are you kidding me?*"

"What about his version of 'Gee Baby, Ain't I Good to You'?"

"What about Bird's version of 'I Remember You'?"

"Nineteen sixty-eight . . . ," I said. "Ella Fitzgerald. 'April in Paris.' Live at Newport."

"If you're mentioning Ella, you gotta bring up Germany. 'Mack the Knife.'"

We said, at exact same time: *"She forgot the words!"*

"And then that scat!" he said.

We eyed each other until we felt Gina staring. She wore a concerned expression that caused a crease at the top of her nose. "You two need to start listening to music by people who are *alive.*"

Jason feigned offense. "Hey, watch it. Jason Moran is a genius. And Joshua Redman."

"Brad Mehldau," I offered.

"Mehldau's solo version of 'My Favorite Things'?" He slammed his hands on the table. "Amazing."

"Or *Live in Tokyo*—"

"Totally," he said. "'Exit Music for a Film.'"

We looked at each other. "'River Man'!" we cried at the exact same time.

Gina reached for her purse. "All right. All right. Abbey, it has been a pleasure. Are you staying, babe?"

"Yeah. I think I'll do some exploring. I'm sure I can get an article out of this."

I remembered the art crawl was that night and told him not to miss it. "Galleries and shops stay open late. Live music. It's a pretty big thing. You're lucky it's the first Friday of the month."

"Excellent." He said to Gina, "Walk you to BART first?"

She made her way out of the booth, but then Jason stopped her and asked that we pose for a picture. "I can use it for Cooper."

"He's keeping a groom's diary; it's pretty funny," she explained.

"Yeah," Jason said, taking out his phone. "It's mostly about how to keep the bride happy by agreeing with everything she says."

"Jason."

He ran his fingers through her hair and kissed the top of her head. "Tonight I'll write about jazz and cake. You two stand next to each other."

I put my arm around Gina. She was such a teeny-tiny thing, but it was easy to feel how physically strong she was.

"Say Canada!"

"Canada!"

I asked Noel to take another picture with the three of us. There were only a few patrons in the café by now, and Nico was busy wiping down the inside of the display case. We'd be closing within the hour.

Jason started putting his phone away. "Say, Abbey, can you spare a couple of minutes? I'd love to ask a few questions about your dad. It'll be for Cooper."

"Jason," Gina admonished.

"Gina, it's not every day that you—"

"It's okay," I interrupted. "Sure. I'd be happy to."

"Great. I'll walk Gina to BART and come back."

"This is how they do things in Canada," Gina said. "They're very friendly. Next thing you know, you'll be showing him around Oakland but thinking it was your idea. Don't be afraid to tell him no." She looked up at him and again there was that exchange of love mingled with flirtatious fun. I thought of Samuel as I circled my wedding ring around and around my finger. Why was it so easy to see what worked or didn't with other couples, but my own feelings could get so convoluted at times?

After Jason and Gina left, I made a call to Horizon Grains, our flour supplier. When I returned to the front, Jason was at the counter with a notepad and pen. He wore a pair of rimless glasses and I noticed he also wore oxfords with his jeans. I'd had an inkling earlier that he was like those men who didn't want to grow up—a man-child—but the glasses and shoes brought out his other side. No surprise. A woman like Gina wouldn't marry a man she couldn't lean on when need be.

I asked if he wanted anything to drink and made an espresso for him and tea for me.

I sat next to him at the bar and noted the pen in his hand, heavy and expensive.

He regarded it a moment. "Yeah, my father gives me a nice pen for my birthday every year along with a Moleskine notebook. I think it's his way of saying he's proud I became I journalist. But knowing Dad, if I switched careers to auto mechanic, he'd be just as happy to give me a wrench every year. So, you ready?"

"Ask away."

"What is it like to be the daughter of a living legend?"

"Jumping right in, I see. Well, okay . . ."

I told Jason about life with Dad. Told him how from a young age, I had learned to share him with his fans and our big family. One follow-up question led to another and soon we were talking about our families, travel, movies. And jazz. We talked a lot about jazz. We talked for so long I noticed Beth walking to the door and turning the handmade *ouvert* sign to *fermé*.

Jason stared down into his espresso cup before draining the remains. The silence that fell between us hinted that we should part ways, but I wanted to keep talking. I liked him, and I couldn't ignore how hungry I was for conversation. Now that Bendrix was with Anthony, it was my turn to get used to not having him around as much, just as he had had to get used to not having me around when Samuel and I first got together. Anyway, I was also just plain ol' hungry. I looked at Jason. "You want to grab a quick bite to eat?"

"You read my mind."

"Let me call my husband."

"Sure." He took out his phone. "I'm going to see how Power Smurf is doing. I have a feeling they're going to need her until midnight, poor girl."

I went back to the office. Samuel picked up on the second ring. "Hey, babe."

"Hey. I have to stay late tonight. I'm working on a cake and need a couple more hours. I was helping Beth and she messed it up enough that I'm going to have to redo it." I hated to throw Beth under the bus. I hated lying. But I didn't want to tell him I was having dinner with a client and have to explain why. It was too much work, although I did wish I'd stop talking. "Luckily the cake isn't for a wedding. Just a birthday, but they need it by tomorrow."

I brought my forehead down and touched it to the wall. *Shut up.*

"Take your time. Carmen and what's-his-name are here and we're watching a movie. I ordered pizza. It's a night of chill."

"Thanks, babe. Love you."

"Love you, too."

I redid my ponytail twice and applied lipstick. One last check in the mirror and I went to meet Jason out front.

. . .

We ate dinner at Chop Shop and continued to talk and laugh and talk some more. A few beers later, we were laughing at almost everything. At one point, he nodded toward a man walking inside the restaurant. "Hey, look—Salman Rushdie!" It took me a second to catch his joke. The man had a comb-over and his eyebrows bore down into a bit of a scowl. I looked around the restaurant and gave him a nudge when I saw a short man with bulging eyes.

"James Baldwin to your left."

He found the man I was referring to and clinked his beer bottle to mine. "Very good."

Our game of find-the-celebrity continued as we started walking through the outer edges of Art Crawl. It was still early, but the crowds were starting to build; by eight or nine o'clock the streets would be jammed. I was never sure how or when Art Crawl started, but a few years ago on the first Friday of every month, it became the thing to head to downtown Oakland and hit the art galleries. It built from there to include street vendors, bands, and some retail stores and bars allowing people to dance inside. I explained all of this to Jason and he asked if I'd like to join him while he walked around. Hell, I didn't want to go home at all by then.

He took out his pen and notebook and asked a few vendors questions. He also took pictures as we walked. We went into galleries and spoke to artists. We walked the entire length of the crawl, enough to work off most of our dinner, which gave us the excuse to eat tacos and later join a mile-long line in front of a specialty ice cream truck. We found a bench to sit on under a tree. We were feeling comfortable enough that we used our spoons to taste each other's ice cream—strawberry for me, toffee for him. It was dark by now, the sky overcast. A bandstand had been set up at the end of the block and on one side of a building they'd be showing movies later.

We ate in silence until Jason asked, "Got any marital advice for me?"

The answer came in an instant. "Marry your best friend."

"Did you?"

"My best friend is gay."

"So would you say your husband has become your best friend?"

"Yes." *This lying thing was coming in handy.*

"Gina's my best friend, so I guess I'm doing okay in that respect." He grinned and let his head fall back while gazing at the sky. I stared at his long neck, wondering if he felt attracted to me. But then I thought, it didn't matter. *The problem here, the big problem, Abbey, is that you're attracted to him.* No. Erase that. I was bound to feel attracted to other men at least once or twice before I died, so I couldn't blame myself for being attracted to a handsome, smart, funny, and fun man—*who loved jazz.* No, the problem was that I knew I wasn't nearly as happy as Jason and Gina were. Samuel and I had been two people dating who'd moved straight into marriage based on a mutual attraction. But I couldn't remember the last time we'd had an intimate conversation about anything that didn't involve baby making. And we hardly ever laughed.

Jason moved his gaze from the sky to the ever-growing crowd. "What a great night." He stretched out his arms. "I love you, Oakland!"

Someone passing by replied with: "Oakland loves you back, bro."

We smiled at each other and I tried not to stare into his eyes.

I finished my ice cream. He startled me out of my thoughts by taking my hand in his, his eyes bright and hopeful. "I think I love you."

I felt a bolt of fear. Had he had feelings for me all along? I
opened my mouth and waited for my thoughts to form into something that made sense. I knew there was a vibe between us, a
connection or something, and I knew that in a different life I
would so want to explore whatever was going on, but I did love
Samuel despite our problems and he obviously loved Gina. I
started to tell him he was probably experiencing premarital jit-
ters. And then I found myself leaning in. . . . Hey, a kiss never
hurt anyone, right?

He let go of my hand and looked out toward the small bandstand. "They're an indie band. I Think I Love You! The lead
singer is from Canada. I can't believe this! We have to hear a
couple of songs. Okay?"

"Yeah, sure." Finally I saw the sign next to the stage: I Think
I Love You was listed with three other acts.

Jason took out his phone and started toward the small bandstand. "Honey! I Think I Love You is playing! I know! I can't
believe it. I'm going to hang a little longer, okay? Yeah, she's still
here. She's being a real trouper showing me around." He smiled
at me as we continued to make our way closer to the stage. "You
get a full massage tonight for all your hard work. Yeah, yeah. I
will. Okay, babe. I'll see you in a bit. Love you, too." He returned
the phone to his pocket. "She said to tell you hello and to remember you don't have to put up with me unless you want to." A
smile stretched across his face. "So. Are you sick of me yet?"

Not at all. I could spend the entire night looking at you smile. "I'm
still here, aren't I?"

A crowd of people gathered as the band warmed up on their
instruments. Jason cupped his hands around his mouth. *"Caanadaa!"*

The lead singer shaded his eyes. "Who said that?"

Jason whooped.

The lead singer grabbed his mike. *"Caaanadaa!"* He was a

skinny thing in extra-tight pants, his hair slicked into a fifties fishtail. He pulled the mike in and said, "I have something very important to say, everybody. Quiet down for me, please. I need some silence for a very important announcement."

The crowed quieted as best it could. Some people looked worried. He put his mouth close to the mike. When he had our attention he shouted, "San Francisco *sucks*! San Francisco can *kiss my white ass*!"

Everybody whooped and yelled at once.

He then screamed at the top of his voice: *"Oaklaaaaaaand!"*

And with that, he banged his guitar and he and his band-mates kicked into a fast-paced rock song that had us all pogo-sticking up and down and thrusting our heads and arms like mad people.

Jason and I shouted in each other's faces every now and then, laughed and jumped. This went on for two more songs until we were out of breath. By the fourth song, we were hunched over and gasping.

"Fuckin' hell, I'm old," Jason said, clutching his stomach.

"All the beer and food we ate didn't help."

We made our way back to the bench and plopped down like two people no longer in their twenties.

"They're a fun band, though, no?"

"They are."

"They aren't jazz . . ."

". . . but they're fun."

Then it hit me. *Why hadn't I thought of it sooner?*

"You okay there?"

"Yeah." I stood up. "Jason?"

"Abbey?"

"You wanna meet my dad?"

"Don't kid a guy, Abbey."

"I'm serious."

His mouth fell open as he stared up at me and pressed his hand to his heart. "It would mean the world."

J called Aiko before we left Art Crawl to be sure he was home. (That Dad never answered his cell or the phone at the house was a running joke in our family.) She told me to come on over.

Jason's luck continued to rise. Dad was giving a private concert to a few out-of-town jazz students. He'd be finished playing soon, so she told me to get there quickly.

Jason called Gina and explained what was going on while we rushed back to my car. I called Samuel and was glad to find him too distracted to ask any questions.

*W*e could hear Dad as soon as we walked through the door. I led Jason to the practice room, where a crowd of twenty or so people sat listening. The only person I recognized other than Dad was Aiko, who gave a small wave when she saw me.

Jason and I found seats in the back. I thought it was pretty funny when I recognized that the song Dad was playing was "Lady Be Good." We were able to hear only a few bars before he finished. He took a sip of water and announced his next song, "Stairway to the Stars." He played slowly at first, with the focus on the melody. As the song started to build, however, so did his speed, and four minutes in, his fingers were a scrambled blur as they moved up and down the keyboard. His body arched back when he reached a crescendo, then fell in on itself when he moved into an unexpected pianissimo. As Theo would say, Pops was on fire.

I looked over at Jason, whose eyes were glistening. When he felt me staring, he turned. *Thank you*, he mouthed.

I reached over and gave his hand a firm squeeze, then let go.

. . .

$\mathcal{T}$he room burst into applause when Dad finished. When he saw me, he pointed and clutched at his heart. "Looks like my daughter is here. Everyone, the one and only Abbey Lincoln Ross."

The small group turned and I gave a shy wave.

"Baby, I'm about to do my last encore. What can I play you?"

I fanned my hands toward Jason. He looked at me curiously. "Go ahead," I told him. "Pick a song."

"I—" He choked and cleared his throat. Everyone stared. I nudged him with my elbow. "How—" His voice broke like a teen's going through puberty. A few people, including myself, laughed lightly. He cleared his throat again. "'How Deep Is the Ocean.' Please. Sir."

Dad paused but then grinned as if charmed. "You got it."

The room fell quiet. Dad played in a straightforward manner but then began to coax the melody as if trying to wake the song from a deep sleep, each note pulled and tugged into something altogether new, each measure adding a more soulful layer. He leaned back with his eyes closed. The intensity with which he played blurred the lines between music and musician: He was the song and it poured out of him.

When the song ended, we all rose to our feet and applauded wildly. I glanced at Jason, who wiped tears from his cheeks and sniffled. When he felt me staring, he reached over and gave me a quick sideways hug, pressing his cheek on top of my head. He then let go and stuck his fingers between his lips and whistled.

We took pictures with Dad before leaving, and Dad chatted with Jason briefly and autographed his Moleskine notebook. Jason had to catch his train, however, so we didn't stay much longer.

He stared out the car window as we drove back down the hill. I guessed he was reliving his night with the one and only Lincoln T. Ross. Once we reached BART, he leaned over and gave me a long, hard hug, hard enough that I could feel his fingers gripping into my back and the warmth of his body against mine.

I saw pixie dust momentarily and Billie Holiday floating down from jazz heaven. *It had to be you*, she started to warble, but I closed my eyes and willed her away. I was too sad for jazz heaven. Plus, Billie was wrong to try to play matchmaker. Jason was for Gina.

After we separated, I kept my eyes locked on his. I wanted to tell him things that were entirely inappropriate: *I think it's beautiful that you cry. Thanks for reminding me what it's like to have fun. You have beautiful eyes. I don't want to go home.* I was surprised when my eyes began tearing up.

"Hey," he whispered. *"Hey . . ."*

I looked up again and I was suddenly crying full on—tears bursting, snot, all of it.

"Hey . . . hey . . . Abbey, what's wrong?" He took me in his arms, and that made it worse. I cried for what felt like hours.

I didn't want to go home to my husband. I didn't want to make a baby with him. I shook the thoughts away. I'd never cheat, unlike some people I knew (Avery Brooks), but my tears spoke volumes. I was miserable.

Jason was kind enough to let me cry on his shoulder. He then gave me time to pull myself together.

"You want to tell me what's going on? I've been told I'm a good listener."

"I'm sure you are, but it's just life stuff. I'll be okay."

"You sure?"

I nodded.

The speaker system announced his train, but he didn't budge.

"You should leave," I said.

"I'll catch the next one," he said. We sat together, not talking, just watching people pass.

He looked out toward the BART station. "You're going to be okay. You're Lincoln T. Ross's daughter."

I smiled.

We fell silent again. To be honest, I just wanted to sit there and be with him. After a moment he said, "You know, under different circumstances—say, we met a hundred years from now in the future, I'd ask to see you again. If you were a guy, I'd ask right now. But you're not a guy. You're clearly not a guy."

We grinned at each other. "Thanks for saying that, Jason. I understand."

He stared out at the street again as if he wanted to say more but then let out a breath. "I should go."

I nodded.

He climbed out and closed the door but then slapped his hand against the window to get my attention. I rolled it down.

"Thanks for tonight. You'll be okay, Abbey. You're too special not to get what you want."

"Thanks."

He hit the roof of the car as his good-bye. I watched him walk away. When he was near the entrance, he turned and gave a wave.

I didn't turn on my stereo until I reached the first stoplight. I searched for the song I wanted and the singer—Ella, "But Not for Me."

I told myself I'd listen and let myself think of the what-ifs until I reached my home; but afterward, no more. I hit "play" and continued to drive. I drove slowly and took the longest possible way back.

17

A Simple Matter
of Conviction

That very next day I told Samuel I wanted to see a marriage counselor. He guffawed and went through his usual spiel about how we didn't need a therapist and that we were fine, but I held my ground. I didn't know how to save us on my own, and we were in sore need of a rescue. Anthony gave me a few referrals. In the end I chose Pamela Watson, based on her reviews and a brief talk over the phone.

During our first two meetings we sat on the couch with the distance of the Atlantic Ocean between us, and we remained that way through the third session, even though by that time Samuel's body language indicated he was finally willing to open up. He sat on the far end of the couch and clasped his hands like a man deep in thought.

Pamela watched him closely. She had the long limbs of a dancer and wore her hair like Mom's, except her Afro lacked any gray; and where Mom rarely wore jewelry, Pamela wore bracelets and necklaces with chunky beads and long earrings. She crossed her long legs and rested her hand under her chin. "Samuel, you have something on your mind?"

He gestured a thumb my way. "She complains how unhappy she is, but she has no idea what I go through in life."

"If you can, please speak from a place of *I*. I feel . . . Give it a try. *I feel . . .*"

He started to roll his eyes but stopped himself. *"I feeeel . . . ,"* he repeated. "I feel resentful that Abbey says she's unhappy when she has nothing to be unhappy about. I'm going to work and having to prove myself every single day; meanwhile, all she does all day is make cookies."

My eyes shot open at hearing this. *Make cookies all day? Was he serious?* I started to respond, but Pamela held up her hand. "So you're saying you feel pressured. How does that affect your relationship with Abbey?"

"A man needs to feel he's appreciated. He wants to come home to a clean house and have a meal waiting; not all the time, I'm not that needy, but at least most of the time."

I turned. "You put pressure on yourself, Samuel. You're doing fine at work; you just got a huge bonus. You're competitive; that's the problem. If the next person is billing one hundred hours a week, you have to bill a thousand."

"That's not humanly possible."

"You get my point."

"He's allowed to feel what he feels," said Pamela.

He looked at her. "If I'm competitive, Abbey gives up too easily. She wants everything to be easy."

"Are you nuts? You think Scratch made itself?"

"Yeah, you work hard with your bakery, but not with this marriage. I don't think you know what it means to be a normal wife. She practically grew up in a commune. With all her father's women coming and going."

"I—"

"Let him speak, Abbey."

Samuel chuckled to himself as he glanced over to my side of the couch. "I feeeeel she could do better. She grew up with no responsibilities—breaking the law painting graffiti and hanging out. Her family thinks life is about playtime." He paused and looked at me. "It's no wonder Carmen thanks me all the time for helping her with school. She says it's the first time she's ever felt any sense of normalcy. I don't blame her." He turned back to Pamela. "Her sister was pregnant and unmarried when we met. I guess that's what happens," he added, as if the idea had just come to him. "You have all these kids with different mothers. . . . No parental guidance."

I said coolly, "So why don't you tell Pamela about the parental guidance you grew up with?"

"My parents were strict. Very strict."

"His father beat him and his mom had no problem locking him in the closet."

Pamela didn't bother trying to hide her concern. "You want to tell me more, Samuel?"

"No, I don't, Pamela. My parents did the best they could. Abbey won't let it go, but I'm fine with it."

Pamela's voice dropped. "It sounds like you were ill-treated. This could have serious ramifications. We—"

Samuel was already intently shaking his head. "I'm not going there. It's in the past. I see no need to discuss something that happened years ago."

Pamela turned to me, but I only shrugged. *Now maybe you see what I have to put up with.*

She said, *"Blah blah blah."*

Samuel said, *"Blah blah blah blah."*

My way of saying, I checked out. If therapy was helping me

learn anything, it was that I loved Samuel—I did—but I didn't like him all that much. And the sad fact was that deep down, I wasn't sure Samuel liked me much either.

Pamela gave us a homework assignment: a list of exercises intended to help us take baby steps toward each other instead of pushing each other away.

We drove home in silence and spent the night being polite but not really talking. After dinner and a long, hot shower, I sat at the dining room table with tea and Bill Evans playing in the background. It was some time before my temper cooled and I began talking myself down from the ledge of giving up.

Brain: *Do you want to be the divorced woman who makes wedding cakes? How's that going to look?*

Heart: *Don't give up! You have a handsome, successful man who women would kill to marry! You don't want to be alone again, do you? Please! Let's not be alone again!*

Gut: *I'd rather be alone than miserable.*

I went around in circles a few more times. Eventually Samuel came out and joined me. He began massaging my shoulders. I tensed at his touch but didn't pull away.

"I'm sorry about earlier. I want to keep trying, Abbey. I know I was an ass in therapy today, but I was upset." He knelt down next to my chair and peered up at me. "Don't give up. Listen, I'll even consider adoption. Not right away—I want to keep trying, but I won't rule it out."

I could feel my heart swell. That pull. We were two people stuck in a dance, and we knew the choreography inside and out. Push, pull. Push, pull. Backward. Forward.

He sat next to me. He was going to fight hard enough for both of us. He loved me. But did he? Sometimes it felt we were focused on the marriage more than on each other. He stared at me and then I saw his eyes well. I touched his cheek.

"Please don't give up."

I wiped near his eye. I couldn't stand seeing him like this and leaned over and kissed him. "I won't," I said.

He smiled and dropped his head.

"You want to try one of Pamela's exercises?"

"Sure."

18

Yes, I Know
When I've Had It

Over the next few weeks, I have to say that Samuel tried to be more present. He stopped bringing the laptop into the bedroom and had flowers delivered to the bakery. I tried, too. I met him at work one day and took him to lunch. I started cooking more. I hated every minute of it, but I tried. I never knew how much I hated cooking until I convinced myself to do it more often. There was magic in baking—things like yeast and rising dough, the design of a perfect rose on top of a wedding cake— but with cooking, *eh*. Why bother when you could order in or eat out? But I tried.

About a month after we regrouped and started working harder on our marriage, I stopped by Dad's before going home. Samuel said I'd been cooking so much, he thought I deserved a break and was planning the meal for the night. We'd had spice cake on the menu that day and Aiko's favorite, green tea cupcakes, so I thought I'd surprise them before heading home.

I found Aiko in the kitchen standing at the stove. Bud was

seated at the table and Ornette in his high chair. I could hear Dad in his practice room; otherwise, the house was surprisingly quiet.

"Where is everyone?" I asked.

She looked over her shoulder. "You know the silence won't last long."

I gave her the desserts and we hugged hello.

I went to Ornette and kissed his cheek. He was big enough now to do things like sit up on his own and drink from a sippy cup and hold a spoon. He ignored me when I buried my nose in his head of black curls, and continued to reach for the dry cereal on his high chair, his chubby arm and hand working like a crane on a construction site. I kissed him again, wondering if it was possible for me to finally get pregnant now that I was trying so hard to be a good wife. The idea seemed immediately ridiculous, but I was ready to hold on to anything by that point. I sat next to Bud at the table. He dangled string cheese high above his head before chomping down. "If I eat everything, I can watch cartoons." He brought a piece of broccoli to his eye and studied it as if it were a tree that he could never harm, then tossed it and stuck out his tongue.

As if she had eyes behind her head, Aiko caught him in action. "Bud, don't throw your food like that. And stop sticking out your tongue; it's rude."

I picked up a piece of broccoli and took a bite. "It doesn't taste very good, but I hear it makes you strong."

"You want tea, Abbey? Something to drink?"

"I'm fine."

She grabbed a box of macaroni from the counter and dumped the contents into boiling water. She then took a sip of beer from the bottle on the counter. Now that the boys were older and she was getting sleep, she was back to her old self—slim-fitting jeans, T-shirt—and her hair was cut in a pixie and shaved in the back. She was forty-eight but looked easily ten years younger.

"I'm glad you're here." She spun around and brought the bottle to her lips again, her eyes bright. "So . . . guess who has an interview with Midori Takase next month?"

"No way! Congratulations!"

I stood and gave her a hug. A musical pioneer, Midori Takase had helped prove to the industry that a female keyboardist could attack and shape sound with the best of them. She was one of the early musicians to use silence and dissonant chords back when people didn't know what to make of her more modern aesthetic. She'd moved to Berlin several years ago and was now a recluse in her seventies. Since Takase never granted interviews, Aiko's news was indeed a very big deal.

"How did you get her to agree to talk to you?"

"I basically stalked her. I kept sending e-mails, and I sent several of the articles I've written on other musicians. And speaking the little Japanese I know helped, too." She rested her elbows on the center island while sipping her beer. "And I did it all without dropping your dad's name a single time. The magazine that wants the story is pretty big in Europe. They're already talking about sending out a photographer. When I finally told Midori whom I was married to, she said she'd love to meet him, so your dad and the boys are coming with me. I'm pretty excited."

"You should be. Now I wish I'd brought champagne with the desserts. This is great, Aiko."

She remembered the pasta and turned off the burner. She took out a white packet and emptied orange powder into the pot. "I swore when I had kids I'd never resort to string cheese and boxed macaroni and cheese: I was going to have my kids learn to eat whatever I ate. Now look at me."

She held up an eggplant from a stack of vegetables piled on the counter. "Your dad went crazy over the eggplant at the

farmers' market today. He's in charge of the grown-up dinner."
She sliced into her apple with a paring knife. "You staying? Phineas is stopping by with Laticia. And Megumi and Curt are coming over." Laticia was Phineas's girlfriend. Megumi was Aiko's
younger sister and Curt her husband.

"No. I can't stay, actually." I ran my hand through Bud's hair
until he pulled away.

"Stop it!"

I watched Aiko move about. "Did the age difference between
you and Dad ever worry you?" I asked.

"Not really. Seems so long ago now. I *think* I remember dating." She smiled. "To be honest, I knew right away I was going
to spend the rest of my life with him."

"How?" From the way she stopped to stare at me, I must
have sounded borderline desperate for an answer. She grabbed a
small handful of cereal and tossed it onto Ornette's high-chair
tray.

"Your father got me. I knew he really got me. And I got him.
I'm Aiko with him, and he's who he is, and he's not just the musician; he's Lincoln. Why?"

"Just curious."

"You and Samuel okay?"

"Yeah. We're fine."

She sliced into an apple, keeping a wedge for herself and giving one each to the boys. "Look, if you guys are getting stressed
about babies, take it from me, everybody is lying about how great
it is. It *is* great. I love my boys, but it's hard work. Enjoy your
honeymoon phase and try not to sweat it. Seriously."

I leaned over and rested my head on top of Bud's before he
had time to push me off. "I should say hi to Dad before I take off."

I left as she muttered something about a misplaced fork she'd
been holding only a second ago.

Daddy sat at the piano, jotting down notes. I paused in the doorway. The last time I'd been in Dad's practice room, I'd been with Jason, and the memory of sitting with him while Dad played, the look he gave me, his eyes glistening with tears as Dad performed—well, it almost knocked me over with sadness. I'd been managing just fine not to think about him. It wasn't as though I missed him. I hardly knew him, so how could I miss him? But I'd felt something with Jason, and talking with Aiko, I now realized, had helped me to see what that something was. I'd been myself. There'd been no sense of making an effort. We'd been together for only a few hours, but I knew, I just knew it . . . He got me.

"Hey! Look who's here!" Dad startled me from my thoughts. I went over and gave him a big hug and sat next to him on the piano bench.

"That husband of yours with you?"

"No, I'm just stopping by. I brought you some spice cake."

"That's my baby. Aiko tell you her news?"

"Yeah, it's pretty exciting. I'm happy for her."

"It's Aiko's show. I'll be there to watch the boys. But it'll be nice to pop in and say hello to the legendary Midori Takase. Can you stay for dinner? I don't know what I'm making, but I promise it'll have eggplant and it'll be *gooood*."

"I'm sure it will. But I can't." In truth I didn't want to go home. I wanted to stay and have dinner with Aiko and her sister and my brother.

When I felt Dad staring, I blurted, "I'm fine."

He pulled back, puzzled. "I didn't ask how you were doing. But since you're acting so strange, you wanna tell me?"

"Not really. I think I have a tendency to overthink things."

He kept his eyes locked with mine as he played a few bars of "Down with Love" and afterward the chorus of "Trouble Is a

Man." Two songs and he proved he knew exactly what was on my mind. He grinned.

"Funny, Daddy."

He gave me a nudge. "You know why I named you after Abbey Lincoln?"

From time to time, he liked to tell me why he'd named me after the quirky, idiosyncratic singer. He did the same with my other siblings. The thing is, he always knew the right moment to remind me. He played with a few keys, a disjointed melody that came together in the last chord. "You were my first girl and I wanted you to be like her. Her voice was off-key just enough and she was sometimes a note or two behind, a beat or two in front. In the early days she'd wear the tight gowns and all that, but one day she took a match to one of her dresses, tossed it in the trash, and never wore a gown again. Started wearin' suits and hats. Wore her glasses with pride." He chuckled to himself. "Yeah, Ms. Lincoln was a true original. You know what I'm sayin'?"

I nodded.

We could hear Aiko's sister's voice coming from the kitchen, followed by Phineas coming through the front door. *"Lucy, I'm home!"*

Dad hit the opening chords to Beethoven's Fifth: the iconic *da da da daaaaa!*

I rolled my eyes but smiled. I so wanted to stay.

"I guess I better figure out what to do with all those eggplants I bought or Aiko is going to get on me something fierce. She told me not to buy so many. You sure you don't want to stay, baby? Call that husband of yours and tell him to come over."

I didn't have time to respond beyond, "No, thank you." Phineas and his girlfriend walked in and soon we were hugging one another, and I was saying my good-byes. I needed to get home.

. . .

J had to wonder if my resistance to going home had been a premonition, because as soon as I opened the door, I saw Esther and Ruth sitting on the couch. If that wasn't bad enough, they were watching—to my horror!—*Avery B: His Rise and Fall.*

They hadn't heard the door open, and I found myself standing frozen in the entryway, watching along with them. I hadn't seen the documentary since Bendrix and I had watched it a few months after its release on DVD. We'd watched it in its entirety, safe and snug at his house while drinking straight from a bottle of tequila.

On the screen, Avery was painting a seven-foot-high canvas in jeans and no shirt. Believe it or not, he wasn't playing it up for the camera. I remembered how hot it had been that day, especially with the added lights in the studio.

After so many years, I guess I'd forgotten how beautiful he was. And I do mean beautiful, by the way. Not handsome. Not hot or fine. Beautiful. He was a man you wanted to stare at and study as if *he* was the piece of art. He moved his arms up, and his muscles glistened under a thin veneer of sweat.

Avery, I thought. *Avery.* He had done me in, all right. Took my heart and bounced it around like it was nothing more than a toy.

The camera zoomed in on his painting and I remembered it wasn't just his beauty; he'd been blessed twice—his looks and his artwork. The camera panned over the painting, an acrylic-and-oil paint stick in blues of every shade, all vying for the audience's attention.

Cut to: A shot of Avery and me at the Met. Avery taking my hand as we study Jacques-Louis David's *Death of Socrates*. I point to the top of the painting and Avery laughs.

Larsen (offscreen): Why do you think you and Avery hit it off so well?

Me (on-screen): We both love art, for one thing. We can both spend hours in a museum and we like to discuss things about design and architecture. We live in the same world that way.

Cut to: **Larsen** (leaning in as he looks at me): But other women can talk art, as you say. Why you?

Me (on-screen): I get Avery. I'm his confidante. We're soul mates.

Remaining dead still, I stared at my gullible younger self. How could I have missed so many other women? Why hadn't I known he was cheating?

Cut to: Avery and me at a café having coffee. Cut to: Avery and me leaving the café, holding hands.

I noticed how gaga I looked as I stared at him. Maybe I was wrong for putting myself down so much for not knowing about the women. I didn't know much about myself back then either. I'd been a so-so art critic at a small magazine, and from there, I'd fallen into another man's life. I'd been young and ready to shape myself into anyone else's life, any *man's* life, rather than my own. Why should I blame that young woman on camera for missing the signs? She was too busy losing herself in another person's life to begin with. She didn't want to see any signs.

I shook away my thoughts and must have made a noise, because Esther and Ruth turned and said hello, then went right back to watching.

"I can't believe you didn't know he was cheating!" Esther said.

Ruth laughed. "She was blinded by his beauty." Esther stared at her briefly.

I found the remote and clicked off the TV.

"We were watching that," Esther complained.

"Not anymore."

They both called out for Samuel as though they were still kids in need of their big brother.

Samuel walked in, feverishly whisking the contents of the bowl he was holding. He gave me a perfunctory kiss. "How ya doin'?"

"She turned off the documentary," Esther complained.

"And we haven't finished watching it," said Ruth.

"I told you this would happen."

"Why does it bother you?" Esther asked me. "It shouldn't. It happened a long time ago." She nudged Ruth, who actually had the nerve to pick up the remote and turn the TV back on.

I gave Samuel a look: *Would you do something about your sisters, please?*

He resumed whisking. "Don't worry about it. I don't see the harm." He'd watched the documentary after we'd started dating. He'd called Avery a loser and we'd left it at that. "Check it out," he said, showing me the contents of the bowl he held. I stared into a yellow and red concoction. "I found a recipe online I'm pretty excited about." He started toward the kitchen.

I turned on my heel and followed.

"I wish you'd tell them to turn that documentary off. Do they have to watch it in our home?"

"You tell them." He sprinkled chopped basil into a small bowl, then reached for olive oil. "You come home to your husband making you dinner, I would think you'd let some things go. Most women would be ecstatic."

"You don't care that they're watching my ex-boyfriend?"

"That guy is an idiot. And a cheat. I have no respect for him. He's so off my radar they may as well be watching a cartoon. Besides, they asked, and I thought it would be good for them to see it. I want them to know how some men are." He walked over and kissed me on the lips. "You need to calm down, Mrs. Howard."

"Why are they even here?"

He raised a brow. "Because they're family."

I muttered an apology.

"Speaking of, I told Carmen she could come by. She was at her mother's, so Dahlia is coming, too."

I made a face. "You're kidding, right?"

"Wow, you are in a mood. Carmen hasn't been seeing much of her mother. Since my folks couldn't make it, I thought it would be nice. Hey, it's going to be an excellent dinner—if I don't screw up this sauce!" He went to the stove and gave the bubbling sauce a stir, then went for the wineglass on the table. "Oh, and guess what. There's also been a turn of events. Carmen finally broke up with what's-his-name."

"She did?"

"Don't look so sad. Carmen is going places. That dude?" He rolled his eyes while taking a sip of wine. "Let's just say their breakup is *long* overdue."

I felt my heart sink a little. I was sorry to hear about Jake, and surprised. I really liked him; plus, he was good for Carmen. He loved her. I didn't care what Samuel said.

I grimaced when I heard Avery's voice from the living room: *"Art takes you out of your head, man. That's what it's for. It's to pull you out of the ordinariness of life."* I covered my ears and yelled, "Could you two at least turn it down in there?"

Samuel took down a wineglass and poured from the open bottle. "Here," he said, handing me the glass. "Why don't you take this, climb into the tub, and by the time you're dressed, your dinner will be waiting for you. Shouldn't be more than forty minutes." He found his glass and tinged it against mine before drinking. "Go relax. You're tense. You're always in a mood when you're tense."

"*I*sn't it gorgeous?" Dahlia held out her wrist so she could show off her bracelet, a gift from her new boyfriend, Ted Stein. Ted, she was all too happy to tell us, was a dentist in the dental office where she worked as a receptionist. He was old for Dahlia's taste, close to her own age, that is; but from the way she kept calling him *Dr.* Stein, it was easy to tell that his being a dentist made up for his advanced age and balding head.

"I could hardly contain myself. Every time I reached for the phone today, there it was, shining back at me." She kissed Ted. "You're so good to me."

Carmen said, "Are you going to have to pay him for it?"

Dahlia narrowed her eyes but then remembered to laugh. "Of course not! It's a gift!"

Ted put his arm around her while lapping up her cleavage with his eyes. "Something lovely for my lovely."

I tried not to puke.

Esther complimented her. "I love the stone."

"Thank you! It is beautiful, isn't it?"

Carmen moaned from the end of the table.

Ruth, oblivious to the undercurrents, and possibly buzzed on red wine, stared into the ceiling and murmured, "Avery Brooks is like a man dipped in caramel. He's a jewel."

Esther studied her sister as if she no longer recognized her. Samuel chuckled lightly.

"He is gorgeous, isn't he?" Dahlia said. "There's that one scene where he's painting without his shirt on?" She sucked her breath; then, remembering Ted, she reached under the table and presumably squeezed his knee. "Abbey was in a documentary. She dated a famous artist."

"Oh, really?" Ted said. "That's interesting."

Now *I* moaned.

"It was up for an Academy Award!" Ruth added.

I dug into my chicken, hoping to squelch the subject. "It was years ago. A lifetime ago."

Ruth asked, "Do you ever see him?"

"No. Never. Last I heard he was living in Amsterdam. Honey, this chicken is amazing."

"Thank you, babe. I found the recipe for the chicken and the risotto online. I'm starting to enjoy cooking; saves money and it's healthier than eating out."

"It is," I said, hoping my diversion would stick.

It didn't.

"Did you know he was forging paintings?" Ruth asked.

"Of course not."

"She knew," Esther said. "How could she not have known? They were so *in love* and together all the time. She had to have known."

"I didn't know, Esther."

"You did."

"I didn't. Why would I lie?"

I didn't bother explaining that it was impossible to know Avery's every move, nor did I watch him make every single painting. I was as dumbfounded as everyone else when he confessed. He was basically self-taught, and the pressure to create more and more work had caught up with him. I assumed Esther was being ornery, anyway. What did she know?

Carmen came to my defense. "Hey, she didn't know. She wouldn't lie about something like that."

Ted snapped his fingers. "I remember that guy! I saw him on

60 Minutes. He was a hotshot. I saw him in the *Times*, too. I didn't read the article, but if I remember correctly, he's making a comeback." He nodded slowly, happy to have remembered.

Samuel regarded the look on my face and rested his hand on mine. "Let's give my wife a break, everyone. It was a long time ago. And now we're here. And to Abbey's credit, she made it through and is happily married. At least I hope she is."

He leaned over and we kissed. "I am," I said. "Thank you."

Dahlia stared at us over her wineglass. "Samuel, I have to thank you for all that you've done with my daughter."

"I'm not a pet, Mom."

"I know that, Car. I just mean, all the weight you've lost and your internship. You're really coming around."

Carmen rolled her eyes.

"Well," said Samuel. "I'm pretty lucky that I have a wonderful niece, and two wonderful sisters, and a wonderful wife." He raised his wineglass.

I caught myself staring at him. The documentary and my visit with Aiko and Dad had left me in a mood. I watched him. He was as content and happy as he could be. *I am married to that man,* I thought, *and he is the complete opposite of Avery.* Something about the notion unnerved me.

J thought I'd check in with Carmen about Jake after everyone left and she was walking to her car. When I asked what had happened and if they'd had a fight, she responded with: "I don't want to talk about it. We weren't going to make it," she added. "Besides that, I deserve better. I'm working hard and I'm going places. I need a boyfriend who'll support me in staying focused."

"Seems Samuel finally convinced you to break up. You sound just like him."

"I don't get you. You should be happy I'm not getting serious with anyone."

"Yeah, you guys are young, but you were good together. You reminded me of Bendrix and me."

She leaned against the car. "Samuel says you guys are doing better. I'm glad."

"What are you talking about?"

"The couples counselor and everything. He says it's going well."

"Oh, he did, did he? What's he doing telling you about our personal business?"

"Don't be mad, Abbey. He didn't go into detail or anything. I just hope you stay together."

I felt a throbbing pressure between my eyes as I ran through the various ways I was going to curse out my husband.

"Don't be mad. Please. And don't tell him I said anything."

"Carmen, what goes on between Samuel and me should stay between the two of us."

She glanced down at her phone. A smile started at the corner of her lips but disappeared. She held up her phone and showed me what looked like a mathematical equation. "See. It's from Jake. We're still friends."

"What does it mean?"

"Who knows? He just keeps sending these math formulas." She looked at his message again and put her phone away.

After saying good-bye to Carmen, I went back into the house and directly into the kitchen. Samuel was filling plastic containers with leftovers for Esther and Ruth.

I went straight up to him. "If you ever need to talk about our marriage? Talk to me, not my sister."

He stared blankly at me, then gave me the look of a parent when he's completely fed up with his child. *Now what?* He narrowed his eyes: *You're going to call me out in front of my sisters?* But I was too far gone to care about him or his manliness.

He set down the container he was holding. "What are you talking about, Abbey?"

"I'm talking about Carmen. Apparently you've been talking to her about our marriage. Like she needs to know."

Esther and Ruth stood with their arms folded and their heads moving back and forth between us.

"Hey, you talk to people all the time. Bendrix, I'm sure, knows *everything* and then some."

"That's different. He's my closest friend and a grown man. Carmen is barely twenty-two. You have no business telling her anything."

Samuel seemed to remember his sisters watching us and grabbed my arm. "Let's talk in private. Esther, Ruth, go ahead and finish up. I'll be right back."

I stared down at his hand gripping into my arm and looked slowly up at him. I snatched my arm away and stormed toward the bedroom.

He closed the door and pointed at me. "We were having a nice night, and now you have to ruin it. Embarrassing me in front of my sisters. I fucking cooked for you. What's your problem?"

"Just don't talk about me with my sister."

He took a step closer, still pointing. "This is something we are going to discuss with Pamela. You are sabotaging everything, Abbey. And don't ever embarrass me in front of my sisters or my family again."

"Fine. Just don't talk to Carmen about our marriage."

I sighed and went to the door. When I reached for the doorknob, I heard four distinct footsteps running down the hall. I hated my in-laws. I wasn't all that keen on my husband at the moment either.

Jake and Bendrix sat in the back booth. Bendrix didn't have to go into work until nine and had stopped by for coffee. I'd helped at the counter off and on until Noel arrived and then joined them. Jake wore a hoodie pulled low over his head. He'd already had two slices of pie and was working on his third. Bendrix sat across from him, comforting the poor lad by reading the paper and drinking an espresso.

I sat scooched in next to Bendrix and touched Jake's hand. "It's going to be okay, Jake. Tell him, Bendrix."

Bendrix took a sip of espresso and continued to read the paper. "Yeah, it happens."

Jake took a disinterested bite of pie and dug his hand into his pocket. He held an envelope in the air and gave it a little shake.

"What's that?"

When he shook it again, Bendrix looked up from his tablet and snatched it.

He began to read: " 'Dear Jake Thomas Allen, we are pleased to inform you that you have been reinstated to the Mathematics Department at University of California, Berkeley.' "

"Jake, this is great!" I exclaimed.

"Congratulations," said Bendrix.

I went around to Jake's side of the booth and gave him a hug. He hung his head over his cup.

"Jake! Why are you so sad? This is great news."

"She doesn't care. I texted her. I called. I know we broke up and everything, but I thought she'd at least talk to me."

"I'm sure she'll get back to you, Jake." I took the letter from Bendrix and reread it. "You really are smart," I said.

"Tried to tell you."

"What was up with all the—" I waved my arms like a rapper with no rhythm.

"That was a phase. I'm like Michael Jackson: I never had a childhood."

"Did she know you'd applied?"

"Naaaah. I wanted to surprise her. I wanted to know she liked me for my body and not my brains." He grinned. "Ahhhhh."

I caught Bendrix's eye and we smiled at each other.

Jake pulled back his hoodie. "People, I have to tell you, it's too late for me and Car. She's been brainwashed against me. Someone doesn't think I'm good enough, and so it's bye-bye, Jake. I'm not going back to school for her, I'm not saying that, but I won't lie either. This hurts. You guys remember what it's like to be in love, don't you?"

Bendrix cocked an eyebrow.

"Who do you think is brainwashing her?" I asked.

Jake stared back at me, deadpan.

"Samuel means well, you know," I said. "Regardless, if Carmen loves you, she'll come around."

"I agree," Bendrix said. "If it's meant to be, it'll happen."

"I doubt it," Jake said. "What hurts, though . . . The thing about it is . . . she was my bestie. So I miss her as my girl, but I what I really miss is my best friend." He raised his fingers toward the ceiling. "Phineas Newborn, Roy Haynes, Paul Chambers. Album: *We Three*. Song: 'Sneakin' Around.'"

"Very good, Jake," I said. "I'm impressed."

"I'm OCD. Once I'm hooked on something, I'm hooked. Like your sister. *Ahhhhh!* But seriously, folks, listening to jazz helps me study. I think it has something to do with the rhythms. It helps me see all the equations and formulas. It relaxes my brain, so I don't go insane and don't become a pain . . . *Ahhhhh!*" He finished the remaining pie in four bites and gave a drum roll with his fingers. "Well, I'm outta here. You make good pie, Abbey."

"Thanks, Jake." He tossed his messenger bag over his shoulder and pulled his wallet from his back pocket. "It's on me, Jake—don't worry about it. Congratulations."

"Thanks, Abbey. See you around, Doc." And he left with an "Ahhhhh."

Bendrix went back to reading.

"He was right about Samuel brainwashing Carmen," I said.

"Samuel never liked Jake, and if he'd kept his mouth closed, Jake and Carmen might still be together."

"Try not to worry, Abbey. He'll be fine. I've learned from Anthony, if it's meant to be, it'll be."

I gazed at him with a sinking feeling. Jake was right; it was one thing to lose a girlfriend or romantic partner, but another thing entirely to lose your best friend. The thought came that I had lost Avery and survived, and I could lose Samuel, but if I lost Bendrix?

Without looking up, he said, "Stop staring at me like you're falling in love. I'm taken."

"I'm glad you're my bestie, Bendrix."

He studied me for a beat, comebacks and quips darting through that sharp brain of his. But he only returned his gaze to his tablet. "Me, too, grasshopper."

19
Cool, Cool Daddy

*A*fter our argument about Carmen, Samuel and I both re-
treated for a while. Samuel began staying at the office for
longer stretches and working on weekends. I'm sure he was relieved to have a merger to work on—a legitimate excuse to stay
out of the house. Due to our schedules and general lack of moti-
vation, our meetings with Pamela became more haphazard. But
I will say this: We kept trying to make our baby. We'd go for
weeks without having sex. When I was ovulating, though, we'd
make love like athletes, focusing all our concentration on the
yellow ribbon at the finish line. Afterward, I'd position myself so
that my head was upside down and my torso in the air. I willed
Samuel's sperm—*just one of you squirmy bastards. All we need is
one!*—to swim through the vast darkness of my uterus and find
its way to my moon-sized ovum and penetrate. *Penetrate, damn it.*
We agreed again that if we didn't get pregnant within the next
three months, we'd start IVF and the adoption process. We even
shook on it. We needed a third to save us. We needed a baby to

love so much that we'd remember we'd been in love once, too. In the meantime, we went about our lives as though waiting for the marriage fairy to float into our home, wave her magic wand, and make things better between us.

Sometime in early February, a few days after Dad and Aiko left for Germany, Bendrix held a party in honor of Anthony's thirty-seventh birthday. Anthony loved sixties soul music and asked that everyone dress as a singer from the time period. Karaoke, he warned, would be involved.

Bendrix dressed as a member of the Temptations and wore a suit with a sequined collar and an Afro wig. Anthony came as Ray Charles, sporting sunglasses and a harness that held a harmonica near his mouth, along with a cardboard piano strapped to his midsection. I went as Diana Ross, which gave me the excuse to wear a sequined gown and high bouffant wig, along with a pair of long Audrey Hepburn gloves that went up to the elbow. Samuel had passed on joining us. He'd been in the office all day and wanted to relax with takeout and TV. *Fine.*

Anthony was like my dad when it came to the number of people he knew, and every inch of Bendrix's house was filled with guests, some from as far as the distant lands of Davis and Sacramento.

It was a fun night. We danced and sang and pigged out on catered Cuban food. Aunt Nag bragged that she had a beautiful singing voice but sang "Respect" off-key and searching in vain for the beat. I made it to the karaoke machine myself after several hours of dancing. To be honest, I hadn't had so much fun since I'd spent time with Jason back in May, almost eight months ago. I sang "Ain't No Mountain High Enough." I am not being humble when I say I cannot sing, but I did my best, helped by Anthony, who backed me as a Supreme. Bendrix absolutely refused to go anywhere near the karaoke machine, no matter how much we begged. As he so drolly put it: "Last I checked, hell had not frozen over."

Sometime near eleven, while I was watching one of Anthony's friends dressed as John Lennon sing "Help!," Bendrix grabbed my hand and said he needed to talk. Bendrix never took my hand and said things like *we need to talk*, and from the ashen look on his face, I gathered I was about to hear terrible news.

He led me outside to the backyard, where fewer guests mingled and we had some privacy. After leading me to the edge of the fence, he looked out at the fairy lights surrounding Lake Merritt and turned to me. "It's nice seeing you have so much fun, Abbey."

"But that's not why I'm out here," I said when he wouldn't look me in the eye. "What is it? You're making me nervous."

He swallowed and tensed his jaw. "I'm thinking of asking Anthony to marry me."

"No!" I cried. "I mean, yes! Yes, yes, yes!" I jumped up and down. I felt my bouffant wig topple and snatched it off. "I'm so happy for you!"

"Hold on, now. Hold on. I haven't asked him yet."

"But you will! I mean, I hope you will."

He stuck his hands deep inside his tuxedo pockets and dug his foot into the ground: his way of blushing. "I do love him," he said.

"I know you do. Oh God, Benny, I'm going to make the most beautiful, the most elegant, most outstanding wedding cake for you guys. We could do something in chocolate. Maybe something with ribbons. Do you have a favorite flower? You don't, do you . . ."

"Abbey—"

"Oh, I know. We could go with boutonnieres! Wait, what am I thinking? I'll make a tuxedo cake!"

"Abbey—"

"Oh God, that's so cliché. What the hell am I thinking? Sorry. Just give me moment. I think I'm caught off guard."

"Abbey." He grabbed me at the shoulders. "Abbey, would you shut up for a second?"

I closed my mouth.

"So you think I'm making the right decision, right?"

"Ha! You're asking me? Ha-ha-ha!" I laughed. "I don't know what the fuck about marriage."

I saw how he studied my face, and I calmed down. "You are absolutely making the right decision. I'm not the poster kid for how to have a happy marriage, but you and Anthony make each other better. I'm really happy for you."

We hugged.

"Dance with me?" I asked.

He stared down at me in his arms. "Let's not get carried away."

"Fine. I'll dance for both of us."

Since he refused to dance, I partied with Janis Joplin and later Sammy Davis Jr. I was still dancing when I heard yelling over the din of music and talk. "Is there an Abbey Ross here? Abbey Ross? She has a call." Mick Jagger stood at the edge of the living room holding the landline. "They say it's important."

I gazed around the room and sought out Bendrix. He was already walking toward me, looking concerned.

I took the phone. Dizzy was on the other end. "Abbey? I've been calling your cell. Samuel told me where you were. It's Dad, Abbey . . ." He choked then. I could hear his voice catching in his windpipe. "It's Dad—"

"*Dizzy?*"

"Abbey?" Bailey's voice.

"Yeah. I'm here."

"I'm so sorry, honey. I'm so sorry to have to tell you this, but your daddy's gone."

I knew perfectly well what she meant, but I tried anyway. "You mean he's in Germany. He's in Germany."

"No, honey. I mean he's gone. Aiko called from Germany and said he was suffering from chest pains. He had a heart attack. I'm sorry, baby."

The floor shook. *You have to be kidding me. An earthquake? Now?* I looked around when I heard screaming. When I saw Ike and Tina Turner and the Shirelles all staring back, I knew the screaming was coming from me. I wailed again. I heard Anthony in the distance trying to calm me but saw that he was standing right next to me. Bendrix tried to pull my hands by my sides, then grabbed me with full force. I collapsed in his arms and wept.

*D*ad's funeral (still hurts to put those words together: *Dad's funeral*) was held at First Baptist, one of the largest churches in Oakland.

The immediate family, including the wives and exes and their spouses, all my siblings, Uncle Dex, and Uncle Walter took up the front of the church; friends and extended family, some media, filled the rest of the sanctuary all the way up to the balcony. The family had decided to wear pastels in Dad's honor to symbolize that he would not want us to focus on his passing as much as on the incredible life he'd lived. Aiko and the boys wore white. It was heartbreaking to see Bud and Ornette in their suits.

Bailey and Dinah sang a rendition of "You Taught My Heart to Sing." Theo played Bud Powell's "Elegy" on his trumpet. Uncle Dex and Uncle Walt, each looking like he'd aged ten years, joined Miles, who played piano, in a version of "Going Home." One of the saddest and strangest sights was seeing my uncles up there without Dad. I think the entire church broke down.

There were lighter moments, too, however. Dad would've wanted it that way. Several people told funny stories. Rita had two performers from the Oakland Ballet perform to a medley of Dad's songs. Finally, all of my siblings who played or sang joined together and performed a song Phineas had written titled "Cool, Cool Daddy." I wasn't sure when they'd had time to practice, but they sang and danced and played their instruments like they'd been rehearsing for weeks. I felt Dad's presence off and on. I knew he was proud of us, at any rate.

I stayed at Dad's with my brothers and sisters for a couple of nights. It helped to have them and to reminisce together. I went to bed once I returned home and pretty much stayed there for five days straight. Samuel tried to coax me out by telling me I needed to get back to work, but I couldn't. I didn't want to think about wedding cakes or cream puffs. I'd already spoken to Beth and asked her to close the shop for three days. I then asked if she'd run the place while I was out sick. I had cakes to get to, but they'd have to wait. I needed to get used to the idea that my father was gone.

Mom had flown out for the funeral and stayed at the house to look after me. In an uncharacteristic fashion, she crawled in bed with me one evening and told me stories about the early days of her courtship with Dad. She played with my hair and held my hand and basically was an odd touchy-feely mother I'd never known before. At one point I told her she was making me nervous, and we laughed.

By day seven, after Mom flew back to Connecticut, I started going to Dad's house, where the family was congregating every night. We all wanted to be there for Aiko and the boys and for one another. It helped that all of my brothers and sisters stayed in town for a while. Night after night, we banded together at the house and swapped stories, ate, argued, and of course played and listened to music. Rita came up with the idea to set up a fund in Dad's name, something that would raise money to help bring music back to Oakland's public schools. Joan and I went ice-skating. Carmen and I watched a couple of movies—comedies, of all things.

Three weeks after Dad's passing, I woke up at my old baker's hours and left a note telling Samuel that I'd gone to check on Scratch and not to eat because I'd return with breakfast.

I drove through the dark, empty streets, one of only a hand-ful of people out and about at three a.m. I let myself in and turned on the lights. I went to the stereo and programmed a mix that included Nina, Billie, and Otis. I went to the kitchen next and scooped flour and cracked eggs. I took my time mixing and shap-ing dough.

While currant scones and banana nut muffins baked in the oven, I went to my office to check the mail. There were several sympathy cards mixed with the usual. I sat in my chair and looked at the names and decided which ones to open and which I'd save for later. I froze when I came to an envelope with the surname Cooper in the upper left corner. I used my thumb to tear open the back flap. There was a homemade card inside. On the front, glued to stock paper, was a black-and-white photo of Jason, Dad, and me, taken the night he'd met Dad. I opened it and read the note inside.

Dear Abbey,

I was deeply sorry to hear about your father's passing. I count hearing him play that night as one of the best nights of my entire life, and I will never forget it as long as I live. He was a genius at the piano and he will be sorely missed. I don't know if you believe in heaven, but I like to believe your dad is in a better place, somewhere up there playing with all the greats—Bird, Miles, Coltrane, Basie . . .

Please know that you and your family are in my thoughts and prayers. Gina sends her condolences as well.

Sincerely,
Jason

I pulled a photo from inside the envelope: Jason and Gina posing next to their wedding cake, their hands joined over a knife as they prepared to cut. They looked as happy as I would've expected. I drew the picture closer and stared at Jason while thinking about our night together and the fun we'd had. I felt my heart rise into my throat and my breath constrict. Tears came hot and fast. I'd known him only that one night, and I felt silly for thinking it, but I longed for him to hold me.

I went home with a bag of warm muffins and scones. Samuel was already awake and sitting at the dining room table reading on his laptop. He kissed me hello and offered coffee. Since Dad's death, he'd been treating me as if I might break or was ill. I stood at the edge of the dining room while he went to the kitchen to pour mugs full and grab plates and napkins.

He said, "I'm glad you're feeling better. Mom called while you were at the bakery to see how you were doing and I was glad that I could tell her you're ready to go back to work. She wanted to know if you wanted anything." I was still standing in the same spot when he returned with my coffee. "You okay? Why don't you sit down?"

I let my bag drop and walked up to him. I took the mug of coffee from his hands while I stared into his eyes. Then I reached up and clasped my hands behind his neck. I didn't want to feel or think, and I especially didn't want to talk. Just for a few minutes, I wanted . . . I wanted . . .

"Let's have sex."

"What?"

"Sex."

"*Now?*"

"Yeah, now." I pulled his mouth toward mine and kissed him on the lips. Funny, I couldn't remember the last time we'd kissed just for the sake of kissing. When I heard his breathing deepen, I started to pull him toward the floor.

He laughed nervously. "What are you doing?"

"Let's do it here."

"Are you kidding?"

I pulled off my T-shirt and started to unfasten my pants. "No, I'm not. Let's do it on the floor."

He shrugged doubtfully. "Okay. If you say so."

Coffee and muffins forgotten, we moved to the floor. He looked at me briefly as though I might change my mind, but he was wrong. When he pressed his body into mine and I felt my body tense, I tried to relax. I tried to remember all the things I liked about Samuel, his eyes and smile, how responsible he was. His intelligence. I tried to remember those early days when I was crazy about him. I squeezed my eyes shut until it hurt and kissed his neck, then bit his ear. I did my best to try to relax and remember. When the note Jason had written came to mind, I told myself not to think. But then I gave up and imagined that Samuel's lips were Jason's, Samuel's hands on my hips were Jason's. Feeling guilty, though, I forced him out of my mind and focused instead on moving in ways I knew that Samuel liked.

I rested my head on his chest afterward and thought briefly of Dad. He once told an interviewer that the difference between a real musician and someone toying with the idea was that a real musician followed his or her gut. A real musician wasn't afraid to go there, to feel the music and leave all the rest behind. A real musician followed his or her gut, which was real quiet-like. Pianissimo. The gut doesn't have to go on with a lot of nonsense because the gut knows it's right. It's just waiting for the player to have the courage to listen.

Samuel helped me up and we dressed. He picked up a scone and took a bite. "We should go somewhere today. A drive or something." He took a sip of my coffee. "This is cold." He went to the kitchen and I heard him dump the coffee down the sink and pour more. "What do you say to a drive?" He came back out with jam and butter. "We could go to Santa Cruz. It's kind of tacky, but why not?"

I was on my feet now and zipping my sweater. "Samuel?"

He went back to the kitchen and returned with my coffee and set it on the table.

"Samuel."

"Yeah?"

"I want a divorce."

20

Sneakin' Around

"We want one cake shaped like Beauty and the second like the Beast."

"It's our favorite movie, you see. Jane is my Beauty."

"And Burt is my Beast turned into a handsome prince."

Burt and Jane were in their mid- to late fifties and hailed from the moneyed land of Danville. Burt was a computer software engineer who had worked for HP in the early days. Now he enjoyed fishing and his mineral collection. After thirty years of searching, he had met the love of his life, his Belle, Jane. They told me about all the songs they knew from the movie and all the Disney resorts they'd been to.

"We're going to the Disney Polynesian resort for our honeymoon," said Jane. "For our wedding we're going to sing a medley from *Beauty and the Beast*."

Rita stole a peek my way: *Are they serious?* She had stopped by to pick up surprise treats for Aiko and the boys, but in her own Rita-like way, she'd managed to join the consult after explaining

to Burt and Jane who she was, and—"I would love to know what
you two are planning. Mind if I sit for a moment?"

Burt explained that they'd met on a Disney cruise last year
while they were both watching the live musical version of (drum-
roll, please) *Beauty and the Beast.* Burt said they wanted a gazebo
on top of the cake with little Beauty and the Beast figures kissing underneath.

"The Beast should have on a blue tux," said Burt.

"And Belle has to wear white with a blue ribbon," said Jane.

I pulled up images of the cartoon characters on my tablet,
then took out my sketch pad. Rita placed her hand on mine before I could start drawing and looked at Burt and Jane. "I
cannot—I absolutely refuse to let you do this. You don't want to
look back on your wedding day and see Beauty and the Beast."

"Yes, we do," said Jane.

"We do," said Burt.

I kept a strained smile on Burt and Jane while muttering:
"Rita, Burt and Jane can have whatever they want. It's their
money."

"I don't care whose money it is," said Rita. "I can't let them
do this. No. Draw them something else, Abbey. Anything."

I turned, keeping my smile in place. "You can't tell people
what cake to order. It's their wedding." Granted, I agreed with
her fully, but every so often I had to deal with a couple with bad
taste. Tacky happened.

"But, Abbey, they're trusting you to help make their special
day beautiful. You can't possibly let them have a Beauty and the
Beast cake. It's beyond ridiculous."

Smile still plastered, I asked if I could speak to Rita alone,
then promptly dragged her off.

"They are allowed to do whatever they want. If they're paying me for Beauty and the Beast, that's what they'll get." I

glanced back at them, happy-go-lucky in their matching khaki shorts and tennis shoes. "They're obviously in love. Who are we to judge? Isn't that what Dad would say?"

She frowned. "It shouldn't be allowed."

"Everyone heard you."

She studied me while fussing with the collar of my chef's coat. "How are you? Samuel all moved out?"

"Yep."

"Poor thing. First your father and now a separation."

"Divorce. There will be no trial separation. It's over."

"Are you sure you want to make such a big decision so soon after your father's passing?"

"I think losing Dad helped me to come to my senses."

She nodded and pressed her hand against my chest. Rita was the only wife who seemed upset about the breakup. When Joan and I had had tea, she'd shrugged: "Life goes on, dear. Keep your chin up and do things you love." Bailey was also rather indifferent: "He was fine, I'll give him that, but he had a way about him. Kind of stiff, you know? And at least you won't have to put up with that weird-ass family of his." *Amen to that.* When I told Mom about the divorce, she asked if I needed anything. Marriage and divorce were social constructs, in her opinion, irrelevant labels, when you got down to it. You were either happy and getting on with life or not. She supported me in moving on.

Samuel stayed at the house for a few weeks until he found an apartment, a loft, actually, in a hip pocket of West Oakland. At first he was heartbroken that I wanted to end the marriage. He told me his parents were disappointed in him and he was disappointed in himself. He was the first in generations of Howards to get a divorce and he felt disgraced. *We didn't even make it to the four-year mark. We don't have a child. Why did you marry me if you weren't going to keep your vows?* Social construct or not, I felt guilty as hell, and there were moments when I was crazy with doubt. But my gut, that quiet pianissimo, told me I was doing the right thing.

By April, after Samuel had settled into his place, he called one night to "check in on me." He told me he was feeling much better and he was "getting his life back on track." He was also rather proud to announce that he was dating again. No one serious, he added, but he wanted to move on. (My internal response to that: *I feel for the woman dating a man who separated from his wife two months ago.*) Near the end of the call, he said he felt sorry for me because I didn't know the meaning of commitment, and I would end up alone.

Dad liked to say you know who a person really is when things fall apart and you see how they behave when they're hurt and upset. I managed to listen to Samuel's rant without lashing back, only because he was letting me see how mean and petty he could be.

Even so, I had to hand it to him. He swore that once we started divorce proceedings, he wouldn't go after the bakery. "I know what that place means to you," he started. After a pause he added, "I know the bakery means more to you than I ever did."

I gave Rita the edited version of my talk with Samuel while walking her to the door. Before leaving she told me Aiko and the boys were hanging in there. It had been three months since Dad's passing, but no matter how Aiko tried to explain to the boys that their father wouldn't be coming back, they still thought Dad was on tour and they were waiting for him to come through the door.

Rita and I said good-bye and I returned to my couple.

"Your stepmother is very beautiful," said Jane.

"And nice," said Burt. "It was nice of her to be concerned about our cake. We know what we want, though. We don't care what other people think."

"Yes," I said. "It's nice that you know what makes you happy." These two, I thought, were going to go the distance, and I was going to make the most beautiful Beauty and the Beast wedding cake ever. "Now, where were we?"

There was some good news during the lousy months of Death and Divorce. For starters, when Phyllis called I felt no sense of obligation and hence had no problem hanging up on her.

Phyllis: "Abbey, I have to say I'm extremely disappointed in—"

Me: *Click!*

When she called again and later again, I didn't bother answering. It felt so good.

On an even happier note, Carmen found out she'd been accepted to Berkeley's school of law. She was struggling with Dad's death, though, and admitted she was upset about my divorce from Samuel. We met for dinner at a popular Burmese restaurant not far from Scratch a week or so after my consultation with Burt and Jane. Carmen was especially despondent and mostly played with the vegetarian dish she'd ordered. I did my best to console her, but my heart was broken, too, and I could only hope we'd all feel better over time.

She scooped up rice and goo on her fork, but then returned it to her plate. "The thing that hurts most," she said, "is that I feel like I was just beginning to know Dad as one adult to another. He really stepped up and I felt like I wasn't just one of the bunch, but he was really getting to know me."

"Try to focus on that, Carmen. Dad stepped up and you had a better relationship. He loved you."

"Yeah. I just—I feel like crap lately. I'm going to start law school in a couple of months and everything feels out of whack."

"Your father just died. Of course things feel out of whack."

I watched her drag her fork around her plate. She usually had a hearty appetite, but it was clear she was losing weight, and from the dark circles under her eyes, I gathered she wasn't sleeping either. "You know, there's never any shame in talking to a professional. If you're having such a hard time, you might consider seeing a counselor, someone you can talk to about Dad and whatever else you're going through."

She snorted. "That's what you'd tell Samuel. You think everyone needs a therapist—except you."

"Excuse me?"

"I just don't think I need therapy."

"Fine." I took a sip of my water. I already knew her answer but asked anyway. "So . . . you still talk to him?"

"Of course. And he needed *you*, not a therapist."

"What has he told you?"

"He mentioned he had a tough upbringing, and that's all you wanted to focus on. It's like you wanted to be unhappy."

Thank goodness the waiter showed up just then. While he cleared the plates, I took a moment to remind myself that my sister was upset about losing Dad. *Okay. Do not slap Carmen. Stay cool.*

After the waiter left our table, I picked up my water. "I wasn't happy, Carmen."

"You can't be happy in a marriage all the time. Samuel was trying to keep you happy, but you kept pushing him away."

"You know," I said, in a kind of exaggerated thoughtfulness, "I'm not sure I'm comfortable with you two being friends right now."

"Too bad. You chose to divorce him. That doesn't mean he and I can't be friends. What did he do that was so horrible, anyway?"

"I'm not going to talk about this with you. Look at you and Jake. You broke up with him, but I have to respect your decision."

"I wasn't *married* to Jake. You made a commitment."

I took in a deep breath. *Do not slap your sister. Do not slap your sister.* I stabbed at my rice while envisioning life as an only child. I said finally, "I know you're upset about Dad, and my divorce, but that's no excuse for being rude."

"I'm just expressing my feelings."

"I wish you wouldn't."

She let her fork fall against her plate and leaned far back in her chair. "Anyway," she said. She picked up the napkin from her lap and placed it on the table. "You know what Mom told me last week? She's tired of my moping and thinks I should get laid. What kind of mother says that when her child has lost her father?" She shook her head bitterly, then rested her elbows on the table and ran her hands over her ponytail. "Anyway, I'm going away for a few days."

I took her changing the subject as a truce and was all too happy to move on. "That's good. Where are you going?"

"My friend Jasmine's parents have a place in Monterrey."

"Time away will help, I'm sure. When do you leave?"

"Next week."

"Try to enjoy yourself with Jasmine. It's good you're getting away. See? Everything will be okay." When she lowered her head into her chest, I reached over and took her hand. "You'll be okay, Car. Just give it time."

A week later, I spent my entire morning working on a cake with strawberries and white chocolate. With everything going on, I was reminded yet again how much I still loved to bake; it was my constant—mix, stir, bake, decorate. Enjoy. It was also hard to be too down when I was surrounded all day by people who were smiling and happily eating the pies and tarts and everything else we made.

When I took the cake I'd been working on out to the front, I saw Jake sitting at a table covered with his math books. He'd enrolled in three summer classes so he could begin making up for lost time and would sometimes study at the bakery. He'd been showing his more serious side since the breakup, but Jake was Jake, and that morning he wore huge yellow sunglasses like a celebrity hiding out from the paparazzi. I went to say hello after putting the cake on a stand and setting it next to the cash register. That baby would sell in no time.

Jake raised his finger toward the music playing. "Betty Carter. 'Mean to Me.'"

"You really catch on fast, Jake. How are the classes?"

"Making all As gets old, but I have to do what I have to do. I admit, I enjoy running circles around the other students; it's good for my self-esteem."

"Don't forget the little people."

I stood behind him and glanced at the formulas he was working on. I whistled. "That looks extremely difficult."

He responded in a professorial tone: "'Mathematics rightly viewed possesses not only truth, but supreme beauty.' Bertrand Russell—*baby.*"

I shook my head at the numbers and figures. *Blech.* I was about to start toward the kitchen when he asked, "Hey, is Carmen back from Yootville? Not that I think about her every second of the day or that I'm a stalker or anything."

"Back from where?"

"Yootville."

"I think you're mixed-up. I just saw her last week and she said she was going away with her friend Jasmine to Monterrey."

"Who?"

"Jasmine."

"Never heard of her. I asked her if she wanted to see a movie this weekend—not that I'm stalking her—but she said she was going somewhere called Yootville."

I mouthed the word silently: *Yootville*. I felt light-headed, as if I'd been holding my breath for hours. I pulled out the chair next to Jake and sat. I said, stunned, "I think you mean Yountville."

He picked up his phone and scrolled. "Yeah, you're right. *Yount*ville." He showed me Carmen's message:

```
Can't make the movie. Going to Yountville
with a friend. C U when I return.
```

My stomach churned and spun. I lowered my head into my arms and closed my eyes. As sure as the shiver running up and down my arms, I was not going to bother trying to talk myself out of what I knew: Carmen was in Yountville with Samuel, and there was no reason for them to go to Yountville unless something romantic was going on between them. I felt sick. I felt ready to throw up.

"Abbey? You okay? Hey, Abbey . . . Noel, can we get some water over here? *Abbey*."

I heard Noel setting a glass next to me. "Abbey, you okay?"

My hands were shaking as I lifted my head and stared at Jake. "I can't drive right now, but I need a ride to Yountville. Can you take me?"

"You look horrible. I don't think you should be going anywhere."

"Can you take me or not?"

He slammed his math book closed. "Sure."

We drove to Yountville in Jake's . . . actually, I had to ask him. "What kind of car is this?"

"Nineteen seventy-eight Gremlin, *ba*-by! You don't see these

beauties on the road much anymore. She's my precious jewel." He
rubbed the dashboard. "You don't have to worry; I rebuilt the
engine myself. She can go the distance and then some."

The Gremlin had a fresh coat of orange paint with a white
stripe running along its side. It was triangular in shape and
small enough that I felt like I was riding inside a large shoe. An
Einstein bobblehead in the center of the dashboard bounced
and wiggled on every bump. Papers with Jake's scrawled notes
covered the floor. I leaned back and closed my eyes. If I'd been
thinking straight I would have given him my car keys.

I heard: "You going to tell me what's going on?"

"Let's get there first."

The drive from Oakland to Yountville usually took an hour and
fifteen minutes, but in the Gremlin it took an hour and
thirty. The difference wasn't much, except that for the entire
drive I felt nauseous and short of breath. I knew what was coming and what I'd find, but I didn't want to face it.

Samuel's car was parked in the driveway when we pulled up.

"Whose house is that?" Jake asked. He was wearing the yellow sunglasses again.

"Wait here."

"You're gonna do me like that? After I drove you here?"

I stepped out of the car and slammed the door. I walked to
the edge of the lawn, thinking about my dreams of one day having kids with Samuel and bringing them here. A part of me
didn't want to believe it, but even seeing his car in the driveway,
I knew. I started up the path. When I stumbled, Jake gave a light
honk of the horn, but I turned and gestured for him to stay put;
I was fine.

Once at the door, I gave my T-shirt a tug and realized it was
covered in flour. My clogs looked no better. I took a breath—
Who cared that I looked like shit?—and knocked.

Carmen answered the door. As soon as she saw me, she clasped her hands over her mouth and inhaled so strongly she hiccupped.

I glared, unblinking, while she began walking backward into the house. Except for the terror in her eyes, she looked perfectly at home. Her hair was out of its ponytail and falling to her shoulders. She wore a tank top and jeans and flip-flops; her toes were painted blue.

"We didn't do anything," she muttered.

Samuel came from the kitchen. "Who's—" He was wiping his hands on a towel and stopped short. If he was surprised to see me, he wasn't going to let it show. He narrowed his eyes and took a long breath. "Nothing happened, Abbey, so I need you to stay calm."

"What is she doing here?"

"We didn't do anything," Carmen cried. "I swear we didn't do anything."

Samuel raised his hands in the air while walking toward me. He continued to speak to me in a calm and even manner like someone trying to convince a person not to jump off a bridge or shoot a gun. "We were spending time together; that's all. We're friends."

Carmen was crying by this point. "We didn't do anything but kiss. I swear!"

I glared at Samuel: *You fucking kissed her?*

"Okay. Yes. But nothing beyond kissing. I've been in a state. We've all been through a lot these past months."

"He's right," said Carmen. "We've been through a lot. But I swear we didn't do anything more than make out."

"She doesn't need details, Carmen," said Samuel.

I looked at my sister. I heard myself say, *I thought we were friends. I thought we were close.* But, no, I hadn't said a word. I returned my gaze to Samuel—and that towel in his hand. He was cooking. I could smell the aroma of bacon and toast coming from the kitchen. His shirt was open. He wore a T-shirt underneath, but the sight of him . . . so relaxed . . . so at home . . . *with my sister* . . . I felt my stomach threaten to heave up and out the croissant I'd had earlier. It wasn't until my foot caught on one of the rugs that I realized I was backing away from them.

Carmen reached out her hand. She'd stopped crying, but her face was splotchy. "Wait. I can explain. I didn't mean for this to happen."

Jake was by my side as if from nowhere. *"What the . . . ?"*

Carmen cried, "Oh my God. Not you, too! *Please.* Jake, what are you doing here?"

Jake looked from Carmen to Samuel. "What are *you* doing here?"

"Let's everybody calm down," said Samuel. "It's been an intense past few months and we need to talk this out. Carmen and I can explain."

"It's been an intense past few months," Jake mocked. "Jesus. Listen to him, Car. He's such a pretentious prick."

"Hey now, watch it," Carmen warned.

I heard a loud crash and realized I'd backed into a lamp.

Samuel started toward me. "Abbey, why don't you sit down?"

"Don't you say a word to me." I was not going to let him have the satisfaction of watching me lose it. I turned to Jake. "Come on, Jake. Let's go."

He remained still until I pulled him along. I heard Carmen call out, "Let me come, too. I can explain!"

We didn't give her a chance to follow. Once we were in the car, Jake sped off, giving us no time to rethink or look back. "Fuck," he said, hitting the steering wheel with his fist. "Fuck! Did you know?"

"Not until you mentioned Yountville." My phone started to ring and I turned it off.

"Fuck," he mumbled. After a long pause: "Fuck."

"Okay, Jake. I know."

His voice low, he said, "Abbey, we've been cuckolded. We've been betrayed. Cheated. Lied to. That fucker is old enough to be her father."

"Just drive, Jake. Let's get out of here."

21

This Night Has Opened My Eyes

Carmen and Samuel continued to call and send texts, but I ignored them. When Carmen showed up at my house that afternoon, I refused to open the door. The only person I talked to after Jake dropped me off was Bendrix. He came over and listened to me rant and held me when I finally broke down and cried.

Carmen must have told the wives her side of the story, because they began calling, too, and telling me that I needed to talk to her. And then my sister Dinah called from wherever she was on tour. They all left messages saying I needed to forgive Carmen; she was my sister.

You never would've known a thing was wrong, except a few days later, after making a perfectly delicate two-tier wedding cake, I had a flash of my sister's blue toenails, and within seconds, I poked my finger into as much icing as I could hold and shoved it in my mouth. Beth stared at me, wide-eyed. When I couldn't taste the icing on my tongue, I dug my finger in again. I stared at that cake with its stupid painted flowers and stupid damask while licking icing from my finger. I used my arm to move the cake across the long worktable and straight into the trash bin. Beth shouted—"Oh my God, Abbey!" I finished licking the icing. It felt good to destroy something.

I went home early. Around seven, I heard someone knock. I saw through the peephole that it was Samuel and refused to open the door. "I know you're there, Abbey. Your car's out front." He waited, then started speaking through the door. He said he hadn't been thinking straight. He and Carmen had always been close, but he hadn't meant for things to get out of hand. He said, *"Blah blah blah."* And *"Wa wa wa wa."* He then cried, *"Wacka doodle! Wacka dack!"*

Just so I wouldn't have to listen, I went to my bedroom, grabbed two pillows, and pressed them over my ears. He stood outside my door for a good fifteen minutes, but I was so finished, so over him, so disgusted, I never wanted to see him again.

I'm not sure how long I stayed in my bedroom, but when I finally went back out, I saw that he'd slipped a note through the mail slot.

Abbey,

<u>I'm very sorry.</u> I will admit that I crossed a line. But we only kissed. You also have to understand that my actions were a result of cracking under the pressure of our divorce. <u>Can we please talk about this?</u>

Samuel

I called Bendrix and read him the note. He was at the hospital and on his way to the OR but laughed and said, "Read it again. That's brilliant. He's nuts." He then said he had time to wait while I burned it. I held the phone close to the flame so that he could hear the crackling of the paper. "Good girl," he said.

*T*he wives showed up two days later. I threatened to call the cops if they didn't get off my porch. I did not want to discuss what had happened. I did not want to talk to Carmen, let alone forgive her.

I sat on my couch and listened.

"Open this goddamn door right now, Abbey." Bailey, of course. "You need to talk to your damn sister. She needs you, and you need to forgive her! Hello? Abbey Lincoln Ross! I know you're in there! Open the goddamn door!"

Rita next: "Sweetheart, we have flowers for you and a bottle of pinot. It's from Doug's collection and very rare. Open up and we'll have a drink."

A few seconds later, I heard Bailey again: "I told you a bottle of wine wouldn't work."

"Well, it's certainly better than cursing and scaring the entire neighborhood."

Joan: "Abbey, why don't you open up? You won't have to say a word; just let us in. We're all here to see that you are all right."

Not until I heard Aiko's voice did my defenses begin to crack. *Aiko was with them?* "Abbey? I have your brothers with me. You're going to leave us out here? They're hungry. Bud, tell your sister how hungry you are."

After a moment I heard Bud say, "I'm hungry."

I straightened up from the couch and swung open the door. "Really, Aiko? Using two innocent children?"

"A woman has to do what a woman has to do," she said.

I stared at them all, huddled on my porch. "You guys look like a witches' coven."

Joan raised her fingers in the air and pulled back her lips. " 'Fair is foul, and foul is fair: / Hover through the fog and filthy air.' "

Bailey gave her a look.

"It's Shakespeare," she said. When Bailey continued to stare, she added, "He was once known as a great playwright?"

Bailey rolled her eyes.

I picked up Ornette and brought him close to my hip. "Come on in."

I made the boys peanut butter and jelly sandwiches and opened the bottle of wine Rita had brought. We sat in the living room.

Bailey said, "I knew that man couldn't be trusted. There was something in his eyes."

Rita huffed. "You thought he was handsome."

"So did you," Bailey snapped.

I brought my feet up on the couch and sipped my wine. "I do not want to talk about *him*. If you mention *him* again, I'm going to ask every one of you to leave."

Rita said, "Carmen swears nothing happened beyond some kissing, and I believe her."

Joan said, "She made a good point. She wanted to be found out; otherwise, she wouldn't have told Jake where she was going."

Bailey looked at me and said, "Y'all two fighting right now is just not good for the family."

"Family," I mocked. "Why are you getting on me about family? Look what she did."

"She's young," said Rita. "Her mother is a mess; let's not forget that."

"True," said Bailey. "That asshole is the culprit here, though. Carmen is only, what? Twenty-two? He manipulated her."

Joan stared at me for a long moment. "She's your sister," she said. "Like it or not, family is family."

I looked at them all: *Fuck family.*

Aiko pulled Ornette into her lap. He was still eating his

sandwich. "Joan's right, Abbey. Family is family." When she kissed the top of Ornette's head, I felt the weight of her words. "I know that what they did was painful and wrong, but life is too short to hold a grudge. We are a family and we can't have you two not speaking to each other. Your father would not put up with this. And we're not going to allow it either." She gazed around the living room at the wives. When Ornette held up his sandwich, she took a bite and smiled. "Lincoln showed me what it was like to have a real family. We're not perfect by any means, but if anything ever happened to Carmen, and you guys still weren't speaking? You'd hate yourself." She gazed over at Bud. We all watched him briefly as he took a bite of his sandwich and played with a toy car. "Your father told me every single night that he loved me and I was beautiful. No matter if he was on the road or not."

"He did?" said Bailey. "He never told me that—not every night."

"Me either," said Rita, dismissively.

Joan stared at the ceiling. "He made us all feel special, didn't he? It takes an extraordinary man to make a family like ours." She let her voice drop and looked over at me again. When I met her gaze she arched her brow: *Do not blow it, Abbey. Do not ruin your father's legacy.*

Aiko said, "You never know when the last time you'll see someone will be. You should at least talk to her."

I wanted to stay angry, I did, but with the boys in the room— knowing that they wouldn't know Dad like we had, knowing that my dad would hate to know Carmen and I weren't speaking . . . I threw up my hands. "Okay, okay, I give up! I'll talk to her! You guys are too much, you know. You're gonna make me start crying."

Bailey clapped her hands and shot up from the couch. "Great! I'll go get her."

I sat up. *"What?"*

Rita tossed her wine back. "She's in the car."

I watched dumbfounded as Bailey went to the front door. "Car! Get your ass in here. She's finally ready to talk."

Carmen walked inside and began crying right away. Seeing her cry like that brought back memories of my littler sister at five, six, seven years old, running to me in tears and seeking comfort. I instinctively opened my arms.

Aiko was right. They were all right.

J forgave Carmen, but as the days progressed I fell into a funky malaise where I couldn't seem to gain any sense of momentum or purpose. After all, I was officially a two-time loser. As Jake put it, I'd been cuckolded, and not once, but twice. What was wrong with me? And to top it off, I had no baby! My eggs were just as old and shriveled and untouched as they were the day before I met He Who Shall Not Be Mentioned. I didn't understand what was going on with my life. And I missed Dad. I missed him so much.

I was telling all of this—okay, I was *whining*—to Bendrix and Anthony over breakfast. This would be our third meal together within two weeks. Bendrix was trying to cheer me up by keeping me company. But I felt much like I had after Avery and I had split: I didn't want to do much more than sleep and think of ways to sell the bakery so I could disappear.

"What's wrong with me? Why do I have such horrible luck with men?" I asked.

Bendrix sighed loudly. He was tired of my melodrama. "I don't know, but you certainly have a knack for self-pity." He started clearing the breakfast plates from the table.

Anthony stayed seated. Trained counselor extraordinaire, he was used to people's whining. "Life is trying to tell you something, Abbey, and now is the time to listen."

"But what is life trying to tell me? Listen to what?"

Bendrix walked in and picked up the pitcher of orange juice. "Listen to yourself whine and complain like you're the only person in the world with a problem. If you want to see a problem, come to the hospital with me."

Anthony quipped, "Your job at the hospital has nothing to do with the hurt Abbey is experiencing."

"Yeah!" I said over my shoulder.

Bendrix rolled his eyes and left.

"You've been blaming men for your problems, but *you* chose both Samuel and Avery. That's the point I'm trying to get you to see."

His comment gave me pause. I was saved from answering when Bendrix returned with his laptop. "Look at this." He'd pulled up an old photo of Benz and Ross standing in front of one of our graffiti pieces. "Big deal, your soon-to-be ex-husband was an ass. It happens. That girl there, however, would move on."

I took in the picture and our artwork. We'd been hired to paint the sidewall of a surfboard shop and had made a school of fish with a surfer holding a paintbrush and painting the wall while riding on top of a whale. We were posed in front of the camera in our "hip" clothes—a flannel shirt and acid-washed jeans for me and overalls for Bendrix. Anthony laughed. "Baby, how did you get your hair to flop over your eye like that?!"

"We were the height of cool," I said defensively.

"It didn't get any cooler than Benz and Ross," Bendrix added.

We bumped our fists together. *"Word."*

It was the first time I'd smiled in days.

With a start, I sat up in bed later that night. Someone was ringing the doorbell. I checked the time. Two a.m. I reached for my phone, ready to call the police, but then I heard someone calling my name from under my bedroom window.

"Bendrix?"

"Yes, open the door."

"It's two in the morning."

"I know that. Open the door and I'll explain."

He walked inside carrying two paper bags.

"What's going on?"

"I've come up with a plan."

"Fabulous."

I sat on my couch and rested my head against my hand.

"Don't you want to know more?"

"Not really. I'd rather sleep."

"Well, that's not going to happen. We have to leave soon."

"Great."

He put the two bags on the coffee table. Finally I noticed the old pair of jeans and worn T-shirt he had on. He wasn't his usual dapper self at all; in fact, he looked ready for the streets.

"What the hell is going on?"

He started taking things from the bag one at a time—cans of spray paint, surgical masks, gloves—all the paraphernalia we used back in the day.

After emptying the bag, he clapped his hands. "Let's make some graffiti. Benz and Ross, what do you say?"

"I say—*have you lost your mind?*"

He walked over and held me by the shoulders. "Abbey, listen to me. You might never have a kid."

"Wow, thanks, I like where this is headed."

"I'm trying to say, I'm glad you tried with Samuel, and I'm sorry it didn't work out, but there's no sense in going backward. So what if it ended badly? Things end badly. So what if you never have a kid? That might not happen. But you can't give up again."

"But my life sucks!"

"I am so tired of listening to you whine," he moaned. "Listen,

I put all this together to help you remember who the hell you are. You're not a woman who's afraid of life. This is your wake-up call." He donned a 1980s rapper's pose. "Bee-atch."

"Are you high?"

He threw up his hands. "I'm here to help, Abbey. When I tried to convince you to start dating again, I was trying to push you out of your shell. I'm not going to watch you go back because of one ass."

"Two. There've been two."

"Two. Three. Whatever. Like I said earlier today, that girl in the picture wouldn't have given a shit. She was ready to live. Man or no man."

I sulked. "You've been hanging around Anthony too long."

"It's the magic hour. I think it'll be fun. Get up."

The magic hour: two or three a.m. Find an abandoned building, make sure no one is around, and by the next morning your artwork is there for any passerby and all other graffiti artists to see.

"Dr. Henderson, I'm shocked."

"Don't be. I've already found our location. I've taken care of everything we need. What do you say?"

"What are we going to make? You know we can't wing it."

"I've thought of that, too. Here." He reached into one of the bags and took out a drawing of my dad.

"It's perfect." I hugged him with everything I had. After a moment I said, "I miss him. I miss him so much."

"I know," he said, holding me tighter. "I know."

Bendrix and I were obsessed with three bands back in high school: the Smiths, the Cure, and De La Soul, and we listened to them whenever we made our graffiti art. Thanks to Bendrix, that night was no different. He'd put together a playlist of several of our favorite tracks, and we drove to our destination while listening to songs like "This Night Has Opened My Eyes" and "Hand in Glove" by the Smiths, and "Fascination Street" and "A Forest" by the Cure, and De La Soul's "Me, Myself and I" and "Stakes Is High." We sang along and tried to remember words and laughed and reminisced.

The building he'd chosen was near Mandela Parkway, an old factory or abandoned loft, hard to say in the pitch dark. After walking through an empty parking lot, we tromped through trash and weeds to reach our destination. There was a drip tag made by an amateur who didn't know how to properly hold the can, but other than that, the entire wall was ours. We organized the cans, then put on our masks and shared a lucky fist bump. Bendrix started to outline Dad's face and body, while I worked on the color fill. When the basic image was completed, we began making the design come more to life by adding second and third shades of color, sharpening lines and shading in edges to give a 3-D effect. We moved like synchronized dancers, sweeping out our arms one way and then the other, standing on tiptoe then bending low to the ground. We worked fast and hard, as if no time between high school and the present moment had passed at all.

When we were finished, we removed our masks and inhaled the fresh, cool air. We remained silent as we took in our work. Dad stood next to his piano in his shades and hat. His legs were crossed near the ankle while he held up the palm of his hand, where music notes shot up and out in every direction. I was teary-eyed when I raised my fist toward Bendrix and we bumped. "Thanks, Benny."

We were picking up the last of the spray cans and tossing our surgical masks into the bag Bendrix had brought along when we heard what taggers call the *woop-woop*, the sound of a police car siren—two exact *woop*s followed by flashing lights.

I shouted, "Run!" but it was too late; the cop had already blared a spotlight on us, and there I stood still holding a can of spray paint. The cop used his microphone, and a voice blared as if from on high. "Okay, you two, drop down to your knees. Hands behind your heads."

I looked over at Bendrix as we fell to the ground. "Told you my life sucks."

22

I'm Beginning to See the Light

endrix and I met with Judge Lewis in her private chambers. She had a long, narrow head and small eyes that never seemed to blink. She stared at us as though we were the last straw on her road to retirement. Thanks to Bendrix and me, she had officially seen it all.

She granted time to speak and I took the opportunity to go on about Avery and tell her all about Samuel. She listened as I told her about my father's passing and how depressed I'd been.

When I finished, she sighed and looked at Bendrix. "And what's your excuse?"

"I was trying to make her happy."

"By convincing her to break the law?"

He shrugged. "We consider graffiti a form of art." When she glowered, he added a quick "Your Honor."

She went back to staring. Even after everything we'd told

her, it was easy to see that she still had no idea why we were in her chambers or why we had chosen to act like common juvenile delinquents. "In all my natural-born days . . . ," she muttered. She then folded her hands on her desk and handed down the verdict. Dr. Henderson was given sixteen hours of community service at the clinic where he already volunteered. She turned to me next and made it clear she had absolutely no patience for an Oakland business owner who'd defile public property. She then threw the book at me: four weekends, Saturday and Sunday, eight a.m. until noon with SWAP.

"What's SWAP?" I asked, already terrified at the sound of it.

"Guess you'll have to find out, won't you?"

I looked over at Bendrix, who couldn't hide his amusement.

"Do you know what SWAP is?" I asked him.

"I don't, but it sounds funny, doesn't it?"

"No, it doesn't," I snapped.

He lowered his gaze.

I returned my attention to Judge Lewis. "Would you please tell me what it is?"

"Trash picking, Ms. Ross. You will be helping to beautify the streets of Oakland."

Bendrix coughed.

"What? Trash picking?" I cried. "Why do I have to pick trash when he gets to do what he's been doing for years? Bendrix already volunteers at that clinic! How is this fair?"

"Dr. Henderson saves lives. We need him out on the front lines. You, on the other hand, bake cookies. People are already too fat as it is."

"No! Please, Judge. I demand a retrial!"

She narrowed her eyes. "Another word out of you, Ms. Ross, and I'll make it ten weekends."

When I looked over at Bendrix, he snickered.

.   .   .

One week later I found myself riding in a nondescript white van along with fifteen other convicts. We the convicted were angry with the Man and we wanted justice, but that morning we weren't getting it; we were going to clean the streets of Oakland, like it or not. The two men in charge, Dwayne Hicks and Alvin White, chatted and made jokes up front. Dwayne was a short wad of muscle topped by a mass of Jheri curls. Al, his assistant, was Dwayne's tall, skinny opposite.

I was in hell not so much because of the trash picking I was about to do, but rather the horrible, nightmarish smooth jazz Dwayne and Al played inside the van. Growing up, I was taught two things about smooth jazz: Smooth jazz was crap Muzak, and smooth jazz was diarrhea.

When Dwayne turned, I realized I'd spoken out loud. "What did you say?"

"Nothing. I was wondering if you could turn that off? It sucks."

My fellow inmates giggled.

"Who are you?"

"Abbey."

He took out his roster and looked through the names. He gave a nod after reading my report. "So you're an *artiste*, huh? Like to draw, *Mizz* Ross?" He caught Al's attention. "Our friend here got busted for spray-painting walls."

Everyone in the van turned to stare at me.

"You're a little *old* for spray-painting graffiti, aren't you, Mizz Ross?" He locked his eyes on mine, then reached toward the radio. The diarrhea music grew louder and louder. A no-talent horn player piddled spineless notes while a female singer, more suited for pop music, sang about bullshit.

So far, SWAP was just great.

. . .

"We all know perfectly well why you are here today. Those who can, do; those who can't, get caught, and you, my feebleminded friends, got caught. I'm here to make sure you don't come back after your sentence is up. How am I going to do that? I'm gonna have fun. I'm gonna sit in my comfortable van with my assistant here, and come lunchtime, I'm gonna eat the nice meal my wife prepared for me. Meanwhile, you all will be out in the hot sun regretting your actions. Understand?"

Silence.

"I said, *Do you understand?*"

"Yes, sir!"

Dwayne walked up and down the line we'd formed. Over time, I'd learn that Dwayne would give this same exact speech every Saturday and Sunday. My fellow SWAP mates would come and go, depending on their sentence, but Dwayne and that speech stayed the same, as did the style of khaki pants he wore, with the severe crease running down the center.

During my first weekend, I, along with the rest of the condemned, cleaned several streets along the Emeryville-Oakland border, an alleyway off San Pablo, and so many gutters I lost track of who I was or why I existed. When we passed apartment complexes, it was as though the inhabitants didn't own trash cans and merely tossed items they no longer wanted in the front of the building. *SWAP is here! Throw everything out the window! Yay!*

Our tools were extra-large trash bags and the Nabber!, a forty-inch pickup tool with an aluminum handle and nifty magnetic grip(!). We wore fluorescent orange vests with the letters *SWAP* on the back. We spent hours picking up everything from empty beer cans to used condoms, from candy wrappers to items of clothing. We, the condemned, were graffiti artists, taggers, gangbangers, and petty shoplifters. We either took our punishment and never returned or went on to greater offenses. I worked alongside young men with tattooed necks and women with dark makeup and pierced eyebrows and chins.

After only one weekend, I felt broken and demoralized. I went home and showered until my skin felt ready to melt under the hot water. I then headed straight to the bakery to catch up on work. For once, baking did nothing for my spirits. Judge Lewis had been right: All I did in life was make people fat.

By my second Saturday, I'd learned to wear a big hat and sunglasses to protect myself from the sun and keep my identity hidden. There were only six of us that Saturday. After giving his speech ("Y'all cronies got caught and I'm here today to make your lives miserable!," etc.), Dwayne told us it was a very special day. "Today, you people will be improving the city of Oakland by painting trash cans and bicycle racks. Lucky y'all. If you look to my left, you will notice buckets of paint. Al, show 'em."

Al waved his hand over the buckets of paint.

"You will hold your brush like so. Show 'em, Al."

Al held a brush with his arm straight out like he was about to start a fencing match.

Dwayne continued. "The point, here, is that you want a nice wrist-like action—see? *Al?*"

Al moved the brush up and down, making sure to emphasize a taut flicking action in his wrist. Dwayne then sought me out in the crowd. "This is your lucky day, *Mizz* Ross. You get to paint to your heart's content." He and Al laughed. "Now, you cronies, make sure you don't use more paint than what you need; otherwise, you'll make more of a mess and I will be required to add on to your hours. Understand?"

I heard a slow, silky voice coming from my left. "Those two . . . are, like . . . so . . . stupid."

I turned and saw a young woman, no more than thirty,

chewing her gum as slowly as she talked. She was tall and feline, with dark skin and jet-black hair that glimmered beneath the hot sun. She wore a midriff top that showed off a pierced navel and a pair of shorts that revealed mile-long legs. She made the mandatory orange vest we wore look like couture. While we listened to Dwayne give his speech, she entertained herself by cracking her gum and staring at her nails.

I asked her name after we were assigned to work together and she looked at me steely eyed. "Vel. Vet." And a second later— *pop!* went her gum.

"Gum isn't allowed," I whispered.

She glanced at her nails. "Ask me . . . if I care."

Velvet and I were assigned to paint two rows of bicycle racks blocks away from the van where Dwayne and Al played games on their phones. Velvet decided she didn't want to walk and appointed a group of men to carry her on her Egyptian-styled chaise to the area we were to paint. Once we reached our spot, one man held an umbrella above her head while another fed her grapes one at a time.

In short, I worked while Velvet leaned against a tree, watching.

I tried to convince her to help me, but she said I looked like I was doing fine.

"You don't feel guilty watching me sweat in the hot sun?" I asked.

She considered me, then tilted her head as if realizing I might be useful after all. "When is lunch?"

I rolled my eyes and went back to painting. A guy from SWAP took a risk by leaving his partner behind and sneaking over so he could chat Velvet up. She cut him off by ordering him to get her a soda and chips. He ran to the liquor store at the corner and returned with her requests. When he was gone, she popped her gum. "Men . . . are idiots. You ever notice that?"

I smiled for the first time all day. In truth, I no longer cared that I was doing all the work. I liked Velvet. I liked her aloof confidence and bored attitude.

Most of all, I liked that she had the nerve to ask the guy who bought her the chips to help us—*me*—finish the bicycle racks. After he took over, I joined her under the shade of a tree. We stood quietly for a while, and then I asked, "So what did you do, anyway?"

She took her time turning her attention away from the street. She then bit down on a chip and considered my presence. "None . . . of your damn . . . business."

She watched me laugh.

During my third weekend, Alvin drove us to a run-down park in West Oakland. There were about twenty grumpy, irritable SWAP members that morning. We half listened to Dwayne give his speech, then went to work; everyone except for Velvet, that is. She was back, as feline as ever. While the rest of us went to work, she managed to saunter over to Alvin and pull him into a conversation. I had to hand it to her: She kept him talking the entire time we were cleaning the park.

Next we drove to the warehouses near the 80 freeway. We were then told we'd be working in threes. "For those of you who don't know how to count," Dwayne said, "that's this many." He held up three fingers, and he and Alvin had a laugh.

I picked up my bag and my Nabber! I was surprised when Velvet walked over and stood next to me; a woman who introduced herself as Myrna asked if she could be our third. Myrna was squat, with pudgy arms, but she walked to our assigned area as though she meant business. In fact, when she saw that Velvet planned on leaning against a tree and watching us, she marched over and looked her up and down. "Oh, no you don't, Miss Think You're All That. You gonna work like everybody else." She stood in place and stared Velvet down. The expression on her face said, *You wanna mess with me?* She took another step forward: *Do you?*

Velvet broke Myrna's gaze by staring down at a single fingernail and popping her gum. She rolled her eyes for all they were
worth and picked up her trash bag. One. . . . leisurely . . . catlike . . .
step . . . in front of the other . . . and she actually walked to an
empty soda can and picked it up!

Myrna crossed her arms and raised her brow at me: *This is
the way you have to do these young girls these days.*

Things went smoothly after that. Myrna was as industrious as
they came and moved about as if being paid top dollar for every
trash bag she filled. Thanks to her help, we gained an extra five
minutes on our fifteen-minute break. We found a seat under a tree.
Myrna ate from a bag of chips and Velvet ate candy. They both
stared when I took out a sliced bagel and bag of figs. "What?" I
asked.

"Where are you from?" Myrna asked.

"*Here.* Oakland."

She and Velvet looked at each other and laughed. *"Nuh-uh!"*

"I am!"

"Rockridge . . . ain't Oakland," said Velvet, still laughing.

"I'm *not* from Rockridge," I snapped.

Myrna leaned back on the bench. "So what did you do, anyway?"

"You two first," I said. "Velvet, what did *you* do?"

She clicked her tongue and folded her arms. "Got caught."

Myrna said, "I don't mind telling you what I did. I was smoking weed at the park with my friend. Now, I don't smoke weed all
too often. I only smoke on special occasions. I just lost my job,
and I figured I needed an antidepressant. But Mr. Policeman was
in a mood and arrested me anyway. I told him I'd lost my job, but
he didn't care. My friend got off but the judge said since I'm a
mother I needed to learn a lesson. I think that judge was high.
I'm out of work and here today instead of with my kids." She
shook her head and went for more chips. "So what's your story,
Abbey? Because for the life of me I can't figure you out."

I started with Avery and by the time I moved to Samuel, we were cleaning near the freeway entrance. I talked and talked. I think I used that day as my own therapy session and was hoping to figure out how I got from point A to point SWAP. Myrna was surprised by it all and kept asking questions like: "So you're saying your best friend is a doctor? Like a doctor doctor?" And, "You own a *bakery*? Like a real bakery? Where people go and buy stuff?" And, "You were married to a lawyer?" That's when Velvet said, "Can he come . . . and get us out of here?"

After another hour of work, we walked back to the Dumpster with the last of our trash bags. I was telling them how depressed I'd been, how I still didn't understand how I could've chosen two lousy men.

Velvet threw the first of her two trash bags into the Dumpster. A man ran up and asked if she needed help with the second. She pointed to Myrna and me. "Yes . . . and dump their bags, too." The guy did as he was told and Velvet waved him away. She then stepped closer to me. "I don't understand . . . what your problem is. You depressed? Depressed about what? Seems to me . . . you giving yourself problems just to give yourself something to talk about."

"What do you mean? I'm back at square one. No, it's worse. I'm getting a divorce and I'm here picking trash—and I'm childless."

"You can have my kids," Myrna laughed. "They drive me crazy."

Velvet looked at me. "You seem okay, but you whine too much."

I raised my Nabber! into the air. "I do not whine!"

She blinked slowly. "I should give you a crown, because you're a drama queen."

Myrna laughed and said, "I think what Miss All That is trying to say is: Who cares that you were in a documentary? You got to be in a movie and that's more than what most people can say. And you don't have any kids with your ex-husband so that means you won't ever have to see him again; I call that a celebration. And you own your own bakery. You don't just have a job; you give jobs."

Velvet said, "Mmmm-hmm."

Myrna rested her hand on the Dumpster and gave me the same steely-eyed look she'd given Velvet earlier. "SWAP will be over for you next weekend, and then you go back to your boohoo life with your boohoo, I'm-getting-a-divorce problems, and boohoo, I don't have any kids. *Adopt a kid.* So many kids in foster care who need homes—am I right?"

Velvet pursed her lips and gave a nod.

"And I'm sorry about your father, but at least you knew him."

Dwayne appeared, pushing his shirtsleeves up his arms. "Having a tea party, ladies? I didn't give you enough to do that you can stand around and gossip?"

I did my best Velvet impression and spoke to him as though I had all the time in the world. "We're . . . finished, *Dwayne.*"

He stared at me as though I might have heatstroke, then took out his whistle and blew it in my face. "Let's close our mouths and line up! Time, people! Let's get outta here!"

We sighed at the sight of him.

Once inside the van, Velvet and Myrna grabbed the seat behind me. Velvet entertained herself on her phone and Myrna rested against the window and closed her eyes. I sat next to a man who took up most of the seat and looked like he could crush a small car with his fist. He pulled out his phone and I joined him in gazing at pictures of a baby only a few days old. "You're looking at my heart," he murmured. "After I'm done with SWAP, I'm through. You won't see me in no kinda trouble."

I wondered what offense the guy had committed but thought

it best not to ask. Instead, I took in a few of my other SWAP mates and thought about the possible stories they had to tell. I'd already learned that Myrna was a single mother of two and out of work. Velvet, who still refused to tell us why she was there, had mentioned that her younger brother *and* her father were both in prison.

I thought about what Myrna had said earlier. Yes, I'd felt hurt and confused by what had happened with Samuel, but sitting in that van I was starting to see that Myrna and Velvet had been right: I'd been looking at life through a big, whiny prism of *boohoo*. Okay, my life took a few unexpected lousy turns, but what was I going to do about it? Was I going to keep telling and retelling the story about Avery only to now add Samuel to the mix? Who was I without my boohoo stories and drama crown? I'm not trying to say I needed to forget what happened; I mean, my soon-to-be ex-husband made a play for my little sister— *eww!*—but just because things were tough didn't mean, as Bendrix had told me, I needed to retreat from life.

Yes, I sat in that funky van smelling my own stench (not to mention my neighbor's), but that didn't mean my life was falling apart; as Myrna and Velvet had pointed out, things were actually the opposite. Because, seriously, even at my lowest, picking trash with SWAP, I still had it pretty good. I had a wonderful family, an amazing best friend, and a job I loved.

I smiled to myself while taking out my phone. Bendrix had gone back to the piece we'd made of Dad during daylight hours and had taken a picture. The resemblance to Dad was exact enough that anyone who knew him would know they were staring at Lincoln T. Ross.

I eased into my seat, feeling my smile grow. The Ross of Benz and Ross would be proud of me. She'd believe that every minute in SWAP, including my aching back and stinking armpits, was worth that night with Bendrix. She would've laughed at getting caught and laughed her way through hours of trash picking.

Al started the engine. Dwayne turned in his seat, and after making eye contact with me he reached for the radio and turned up the volume. Smooth jazz filled the interior of the van, a sax over a synthesizer—a synthesizer! I couldn't take it, not for another second. I banged my hands against the seat in front of me. "Turn it off! Turn it off!" The guy next to me grinned and raised a fist. "Turn it off!" he shouted. Soon, Myrna and Velvet joined in, and a few others as well. I doubted that they knew the specifics of our protest, but the excuse to yell made it worth it. *"Turn it off! Turn it off!"*

Dwayne stood and began making his way down the row of seats. "Y'all need to shut up! Either shut up or expect more hours. You hear me?"

We closed our mouths.

When he turned his back, I whispered, "Turn it off!" Myrna and Velvet giggled.

Dwayne gave the thumbs-up to Al and he proceeded to drive us back to our meeting point at the police station. He returned to his seat, but not before raising the corner of his lip and turning the volume up even louder.

That's when I saw the magic pixie dust. It was Dad and Louis Armstrong visiting from jazz heaven. Dad wore his hat and shades like in the painting Bendrix and I had made. He pointed to me and told Louis that I was his oldest daughter. *Oh yeah*, said Louis in his sweet, gravelly voice, *I see the resemblance.* Dad took off his shades then and said, *Real proud of you, baby.* He grinned and gave a wink. Louis wiggled his fingers at me, and then they were gone.

I leaned back in my seat and closed my eyes. I no longer heard the terrible diarrhea Muzak. No, I heard Dad's piano. He played a lovely medley for me, communicating as he liked to do with each song: "Lady Be Cool," "I've Got the World on a String," "Our Love Is Here to Stay," "I'm Beginning to See the Light." I smiled the entire way back.

On my final day with SWAP, I invited Velvet and Myrna to come back to the bakery later that evening and celebrate. Velvet mentioned she'd never had a cream puff before and asked if they were like Twinkies or Ding Dongs. I shook my head and said, "Whatever you do, come by the bakery. I'm going to make you a very happy woman."

When Bendrix texted and asked where I was working that day, I didn't take the time to wonder why he needed to know and texted back that we were near Market Street near Fortieth. I then went back to picking up tossed fast-food bags and empty cups in front of a car repair shop.

About twenty minutes later, I heard honking from up the street. I saw what looked like Bailey's Mercedes coming toward me. (I guessed it was hers because it was brown and from the 1990s.) Myrna and Velvet stopped what they were doing, as did a few other SWAP mates. The Mercedes slowed and Bendrix leaned out the side window with a sign that read FREE ABBEY! Joan and Rita sat in the back. Joan waved and Rita leaned over in her seat and yelled, "We love you!" Bailey continued to honk the horn. "Make sure you take a shower once you get home!" She laughed. Bendrix held the sign higher. "Benz and Ross forever!" he yelled.

When they were gone, Myrna said, "Who was that?"

I stood watching the car make its way down the road. "That was my best friend Bendrix and three of my mothers."

Velvet blinked. "Damn . . . girl. How many mothers do you have?"

"Five." I smiled. "But who's counting?"

23

What's New?

A year after my release from SWAP, I thought it would be fun to commemorate the date by giving out cupcakes at Scratch. What I called SWAP cakes were made with chocolate buttercream, coffee, and fine Dutch cocoa, and I gave them out for free until noon. Myrna was working at the counter by then. She was bossy and in everyone's business and perfect for the job. Velvet was taking cosmetology classes but stopped by to say hello. I'd hired more workers because I was starting the adoption process and knew once the baby came I would have to cut back on my hours, at least for the first few months.

Around New Year's, Carmen and Jake announced their engagement. They were going to have a party with the family later in the month, but I wanted to do something with just the three of us and took them to hear the Mark Rollins Trio at Yoshi's. It was after they played "I Remember You" that I heard someone whooping and whistling from behind. When I turned, I saw none other than Jason Ethan Cooper sitting alone at a table and clapping loudly while grinning up at the stage. I smiled and kept my eyes trained on him until he finally looked my way. His face brightened when he saw me. *"Abbey?"*

He gestured at the empty seat next to mine and I waved him over.

"How have you been?" I asked.

"How have *you* been?" He smiled.

Memories of our night together came rushing back. I couldn't take my eyes off him. After a moment I heard Jake say, "Hell-loooo? You going to introduce us?" Since the musicians had started the next song, I had to speak quietly. After everyone shook hands and said hello, Jason moved closer so we could talk.

We were being rude, whispering to each other while the musicians played—a big no-no, especially if you were a Ross, but I couldn't help it. Jason leaned next to my ear and told me how sorry he was about Dad. At one point I asked about Gina: Where was she? How was she doing?

That's when he told me they'd divorced.

I giggled.

He looked at me, confused.

"I mean, I am so sorry to hear that." I tried to feel sad. I did.

"And you?" he whispered. "How's your husband?"

I held up my ringless wedding finger.

"Can't blame us for trying." He grinned.

The drummer from the trio hit his cymbal and the bass player took his cue and slowed the beat. Jason closed his eyes and leaned back in his seat, but then just as quickly looked over and smiled. "It's good to see you, Abbey Lincoln Ross."

I laughed. "It's good to see you, too, Jason."

After a moment, I glanced at Carmen and Jake, who were both staring wide-eyed. Jake pointed. *"Ahhhh!"*

Todd Foster

Renee Swindle is the author of *Shake Down the Stars* and *Please Please Please*, a Blackboard bestseller. She earned her BA from UC Irvine and MFA in creative writing from San Diego State University. She lives in Oakland, California.

A Pinch of of Ooh La La

Renee Swindle

A CONVERSATION WITH
RENEE SWINDLE

Spoiler Alert: "A Conversation with Renee Swindle" and "Questions for Discussion" tell more about what happens in the book than you might want to know before you read it.

Q. An earlier version of this novel began with Abbey doing community service in an orange jumpsuit. What was your first inspiration for the novel, and how did it take shape as you wrote it?

A. I first saw an image of a woman in prison, actually, and that led to several oddball ideas as to how she got there. The writing became so much easier after I dumped the prison idea and went with community service. I see people in my neighborhood picking up trash and wearing these SWAP vests, and I just loved the idea of writing about a woman who has to do that. Once I realized she had a passion for graffiti art, I knew exactly how Abbey would end up wearing orange; thankfully, it didn't involve murder or any of my initial prison story lines!

Q. I love your description of Abbey's bakery, Scratch—the place itself, the food she makes there, and that it becomes a community hangout by the novel's end. Can you comment on the research you did? I'll bet it was loads of fun!

A. I made Abbey a baker because I like to bake myself. If I liked working on cars, she would probably be a mechanic. Writing *Shake Down the Stars*, for instance, gave me the excuse to write about astronomy.

I can't remember how Abbey's specialty became wedding cakes, but I loved the idea that she was a wedding cake designer who'd never been married. I already owned several books on baking, and I now own three in-depth books on how to design wedding cakes. If writing doesn't work out, I officially have a plan B!

Abbey's bakery is a composite of a couple of cafés I like to visit, plus details I imagined. "Designing" my own café and writing about a woman who had such a great talent in baking was fun. I hate research with a passion, so if I'm going to open a book or look anything up on the Web, it has to be something I'm personally interested in.

Q. You've said you want to write stories about imperfect characters who make mistakes. Does that mean you think Abbey is partly responsible for her romantic failures, and that you have a lot of sympathy for Avery and Samuel?

A. Great question. I do have sympathy for Avery and Samuel. Avery was looking for someone to ground him and help him grow as an artist, so he jumped right into a relationship with Abbey. Abbey was caught up in Avery's looks and the "wow" factor. I think Avery and Abbey really fell in love and had a close relationship, but Abbey became swept up in Avery's life and Avery lost sight of himself. After the Avery fiasco, Abbey chooses Samuel because he is safe and a "catch" by society's standards. Samuel, I think, is ready for kids; Abbey also brings more fun into his life. But do those two really get to know each other on a truly intimate level? No. Abbey is dazzled by Samuel's looks, his career, and her engagement ring as much as anything else. Poor girl.

Q. In an effort to maintain her relationship with Samuel, Abbey makes allowances for his beliefs, even when she disagrees with them, and for his behavior, even when it makes her uncomfortable. It's a dilemma many women face—when should you accept differing values and adjust your expectations to build a relationship, and when does doing so mean you are being untrue to yourself? Can you comment on what interests you about this question, and why you wanted to explore it?

A. I sometimes start novels by asking a question or putting the character into a situation I'll have to write myself out of. With Piper in *Shake Down the Stars*, I wanted to know if she could ever find happiness again after experiencing tragedy. With Abbey I was curious about why women ignore red flags.

From what I'm learning—and since I'm no therapist, I'll speak only for myself—my body will actually react when I know I'm being untrue to myself. Sometimes I'll feel my stomach shrink or an ache of some sort. This sensation might last for only a moment, but I know it's there. Making adjustments and compromises, on the other hand, feels just like that—a way to keep things fair and the relationship happy and balanced. I think the problem is that we often talk ourselves out of what we're feeling. That tendency to rationalize can be a sign that we're not honoring our true feelings. If I have to explain away or analyze whatever I'm feeling, then usually something's not right.

I'm sure other women can relate to this issue. But, you know, I don't think men are all that great at paying attention to their true feelings either. It takes courage to learn to follow your gut; but once you start to honor your true self and desires, no matter how big or small, there's no turning back.

Q. *Your knowledge of jazz is broad and deep, and you use jazz in many ways to enrich the novel. Would you tell us something about your personal relationship with jazz?*

A. I don't know as much about jazz as I'd like to, but, yes, I listen to it all the time. I love the improvisation. I love that a single song can have a thousand interpretations. I love the incredible skill and talent of the musicians. You know . . . I pretty much love *everything* about jazz. And the lyrics to many of the standards are absolutely beautiful. I used so many song titles throughout the novel because you can tell from the titles alone that there's a story inside every song. It's hard for me to express how much I love jazz—which is why I let Abbey speak for me!

Q. *Abbey's wild, creative, rambunctious family, with all the ex-wives and ex-girlfriends, siblings and half siblings, is one of my favorite aspects of the novel. I'd love to be invited to one of the warm, raucous, jiving parties at Abbey's dad's house! Yet you also make clear that however fabulous a musician, and however loving a father, Lincoln isn't able to "be there" for everyone who needs him. What do you most hope readers will take away from your description of Abbey's family, and what originally inspired it?*

A. I'm an only child and have always been curious about the ways families, especially siblings, interact. My father comes from a family of thirteen, mostly made up of half brothers and sisters. Whenever there was a family reunion, you wouldn't know who was a "full" sibling and who wasn't. My mother comes from a family of eight—and they are crazy funny. I didn't base Abbey's family on my parents' families in any obvious way, but I did like the idea of writing about a big family, and I'm sure my parents' families played a part in the writing.

In my first draft, everyone in Abbey's family was getting along too perfectly. I have to thank a few early readers who called me on my tendency to avoid conflict. In an earlier version Abbey mentioned that her dad was on the road a lot, so I went back to the story and highlighted the problems that can come when a parent is overextended. In a sense, Abbey's sister Carmen represents the downside to having such a large family.

My intention was to explore the idea that family is whatever we want it to be. Bendrix is family to Abbey as much as any of her brothers are. And while others may judge Abbey's father for remaining close to his ex-wives, it works for them and I like that he wants to stay in his children's lives. I hope readers can see that while these characters aren't traditional, they definitely love one another. Samuel's family, on the other hand, maintains strict ideas about what constitutes family, yet they aren't very close at all.

Q. As in Shake Down the Stars, *Oakland, California, is a lively setting for this novel. Is there anything in particular about Oakland that you wanted to convey in this novel that you didn't in the previous one?*

A. I wanted to focus on the Temescal neighborhood. I changed the names of the restaurants, but Abbey's bakery and almost every restaurant mentioned in the novel are located in the Temescal area of Oakland. I also wanted to get in the First Friday art walk, which takes place downtown.

I added the dig the bandleader makes about San Francisco because that rivalry does exist for some of us. I like visiting San Francisco, but I wouldn't want to live there, as the saying goes. There's more diversity here in Oakland, and it's mellower and has a fun, eclectic vibe. Some areas have serious problems that need addressing, and I hope to write about the crime and other issues in future books, but I get tired of people who don't live in Oakland putting it down. So there!

Q. Many years elapsed between the publication of your first novel, Please Please Please, *published in 1999, and your second,* Shake Down the Stars, *published in August 2013. In that time, many changes took place in publishing, the rise of e-books being a major one. What differences about the two publishing experiences struck you in particular? What remained the same?*

A. I remember the first time I learned about e-books. I thought, *That will never work.* Boy, was I wrong. Then again, when *Please Please Please* came out, people were still using beepers. Of course now we have Twitter and Facebook and everything else. I guess social media is the biggest change in publishing. Thanks to social media, writers can get the word out about their novels and have a direct dialogue with readers. All the e-mail, posts, and tweets have helped make writing feel less solitary.

What's remained the same for me since my first novel was published is that I wake up early to write before starting the rest of my day. The publishing industry is going to do what it will; my job is to stay focused and keep writing.

Q. Do you have a method for keeping your creative ideas flowing, and for remembering them once you feel the "zing" of inspiration? We've all had the experience of getting a terrific idea in the shower, or while dozing at five a.m., only to forget it later!

A. I daydream a lot. I figure out scenes in my head while I'm walking my dogs or during my commute to work. I sometimes replay scenes over and over until I get the kinks out or resolve an issue. By the time I'm ready to sit and type, it's as if I've written out a draft. I'll occasionally jot down a note or two, but for the most part, if I can't remember the idea, it's not worth remembering.

Q. Where do you keep your to-be-read pile, and what's in it?

A. I'm usually reading two books at any one time. I have to keep them on a bookshelf in my room or I'll forget where I put them. I still haven't tried to read from an e-reader and have books everywhere. Right now I'm reading Gillian Flynn's *Gone Girl* and David Benioff's *City of Thieves.* I just finished

Twelve Years a Slave by Solomon Northup and *Me Before You* by Jojo Moyes. These are all great books. I've been on a reading high lately. Talking to you gives me the idea that I should post my latest favorites on my Web site. Thanks!

QUESTIONS FOR DISCUSSION

1. What did you most enjoy about the novel? What will you remember about it long after you've finished reading it?

2. In the beginning, Samuel seems so perfect that Abbey won-
ders why he hasn't already been snatched up. Are you willing to
share your own experience of a seemingly perfect man who
turned out to be not so perfect after all?

3. What do you think of Abbey's untraditional extended family?
Discuss the advantages and disadvantages of living in such a
family. Discuss in particular what Abbey gets from her family,
and why she was willing to give up living with her mother on
the East Coast in order to return to her father's family.

4. Early on, Abbey gets one "red flag" about Samuel, but she
convinces herself that his good points outweigh the negative.
By the time she realizes there are significant ways in which
they are incompatible, he is practically living with her. Does
she jump into the relationship too fast? Or must every woman
struggle with the question of how much of herself she should
give up for a man?

5. Abbey sees Samuel's father as an authoritarian figure who maintains control of his children through intimidation and abuse, yet Samuel defends him and credits his own success with his parents' insistence on discipline and achievement. How do you see Samuel's father? What do we learn about how Bendrix achieved success, compared to Samuel?

6. Bendrix is Abbey's best friend, and she comes close to saying that if he were straight, he'd be a perfect romantic partner for her. Do you agree? What do you think Bendrix and Abbey have together that she doesn't have with Avery and then Samuel?

7. Discuss the various couples who come to Abbey to discuss wedding cakes. It might be fun to imagine which ones will stay married and which will crash and burn.

8. After each failed romantic relationship, Abbey reassesses her life. Talk about what she learns, how she changes, and what about her life she comes to appreciate more fully.

9. For Abbey and Bendrix, tagging buildings (i.e., spraying graffiti art on them) is an act of joyous creativity as much as civil disobedience. Is some of their creativity inspired by the awareness that they're breaking the law? Does their punishment fit the crime? Did you find Abbey's arrest and community service at all funny, or were you disappointed in her?

10. The death of an important character spurs Abbey to take action. Discuss these events, and especially what motivates her.

11. At the end of the novel, Abbey seems to be headed for happiness, but the author doesn't take her all the way there. Did you find that approach satisfying?

4